NOTHING MAGICAL ABOUT MIDNIGHT

MICHELLE HELLIWELL

COPYRIGHT

Cover Design: Selena Blake

Editor: Donna Alward

For all the princesses who took themselves to the ball.

ACKNOWLEDGMENTS

Some stories come faster than others. Some characters pop into a writer's head fully formed, and others take a little while longer reveal themselves. Such was the case with Colin and Kitty. Kitty came to me first, much in the way I suspect she once saw herself...as an afterthought. Kitty Boxford came alive in a single line of description in *No Prince Charming*; a line that almost made it into the delete bin more times than I care to admit. But even as those words stumbled onto the page...*"Five thousand pounds too poor and a stone too heavy to make anyone a good marriage"*, she stumbled into my heart, and I knew she had to have her own story, and her own hero. So for those of you who have waited patiently, who've sent along comments and notes asking me when this next book was coming, I want to say thank you for your encouragement. Those well wishes are as much fuel for the writer as coffee and food.

I also want to send out a few particular thanks to those who've helped along the way; Donna Alward, my editor and friend, for her steadfast encouragement, patience and cheerleading; The Rose Teaspoon Society – Taryn Blackthorne and Julia Smith Phillips for plot troubleshooting and creative orgasms ; Kelly Boyce, for egging me on to make the conflict more 'conflicted'; Selena Blake, for giving my stories such beautiful covers; Cathryn Fox, for her sharing her wealth of knowledge and her gentle pushes to get me out of my shell; and most especially to my husband Rob and the rest of the family for their support on the days I need it most.

I'd also like to say thanks to some local spaces and places that have been so important to me on my author journey; The Coles/Indigo Store in New Minas, for putting my books on their shelves; TAN coffee in Windsor NS, the Novel Tea Bookstore Café in Truro and Uncommon Grounds in Halifax for being nice little places to tuck away in and write; the Metro Transit #85 Express; Prescott House in Port Williams and Scott Manor House in Bedford for hosting me for workshops and talks…those small museums are so valuable and there is so much to learn from them. And for the lovely grounds at Uniacke Estate Park for just for being there and feeding my creative soul whenever I come. And lastly, I want to give yet another shout out to my amazing fellow authors and writers of the Romance Writers of Atlantic Canada for being there when I had questions, doubts and overall support.

CHAPTER 1

"*D*avis, send for the physician at once. The duke is ill."

Colin Middleton, Lord Ellsworth, gently lowered his father onto a settee in his study as the servant tore from the room. The duke, absolutely pale, grasped his son's shoulders, his eyes wide, sweat beading at his brow.

"Your Grace," Colin said, swallowing deeply to dampen the fear starting to take hold. He'd only arrived at Stormount a few hours ago, eager to escape the incessant society gossip in London. He'd greeted his parents, who both seemed well if not for their rather insistent hovering about his decidedly bachelor state, and fussing over his freshly sprained wrist. All was, in effect, as it always had been.

Until now.

"My boy." His father's words came out as little more than a strained whisper as he grasped Colin's hand.

"The doctor is on his way," Colin said, wishing the man here at once. Of course, even with the fastest horses, it would still take nearly an hour for the physician to arrive, and only if he wasn't out on his regular afternoon visits. In a vain attempt at usefulness, Colin pulled out his handkerchief, gently wiped away the beads of perspiration from his father's brow, and plastered what he hoped was a smile of encouragement on his face. As the only son and heir of the Duke of Weymouth, he'd prepared his entire life to assume the duties that would become his. But he was not ready to lose his father.

His mother's gasp tore his attention to the door, where she paused, her eyes wide with her own fear, before she ran toward them. Mrs. Cooper, Stormount's housekeeper, followed close behind with a small bottle in her hand.

"George," his mother called in a soothing voice reserved for both men in her life in moments of fear. The normally bright and occasionally overbearing demeanor of the Duchess of Weymouth had transformed into something softer, though still with a hint of steel. She knelt beside the settee and cast a look of thinly disguised worry at her son. "How long has he been like this?"

"But a few moments. We were speaking about London and of Lord and Lady Grafton's son. It was not heated in any way," Colin said. Indeed, he'd expected some grief for attending the baptism of his ex-fiancé's son, but he'd been bloody well invited and he'd wanted to see the thing done and over with. "Indeed, his Grace seemed more preoccupied with my wrist and if it was going to interfere with this afternoon's excursion on Long Pond."

They were going to go fishing, Colin and his father. It was the duke's lifelong passion, and Stormount was an estate blessed with a small river that ran through it and a pond which his father had made larger and stocked with fish.

His mother nodded solemnly, then gestured with an outstretched hand to Mrs. Cooper, who pulled the stopper from the small brown bottle and gave it to the duchess. Mother, in turn, put the vessel to her husband's lips. She allowed him only a small sip of the contents before giving the bottle back to the housekeeper.

In a moment his father's terror seemed to subside, and his color returned. He was not himself, but not as excitable as when the fit first took him.

"Jane, my darling," his father said in little more than a whisper as his gaze rested on his wife.

She nodded, and Colin caught the brightness in her eyes from tears she no doubt feared to shed. His mother was a force, and even this hairline crack in her normally robust armor did nothing to alleviate Colin's sensation of the gravity of his father's condition.

"Thank you, Mrs. Cooper," she said, her gaze never leaving her husband's. "Have Davis bring the duke some tea and his favorite biscuits."

The housekeeper nodded and left to his mother's bidding while his mother looked over to Colin, her mouth in a grim, if resolute line, her normally composed countenance strained by the duke's condition.

"Help me up, Colin." She held out her arm. "It is easier to get down on my knees than to get back on my feet, I'm afraid."

Colin went to his mother's side, helped her up, and brought a chair so she could sit next to the duke. She smiled lovingly at her son and husband, never letting go of her husband's hand.

"How are you, Father?" Colin asked, crouched down, his hand on his father's shoulder.

"A little better," he replied, his breathing more measured. "In another hour I am certain I shall be quite recovered, and we can continue with our excursion. I shall have Davis send word to Mr. Campbell that our plans are merely delayed."

Colin looked to his mother, who held a decidedly neutral countenance.

"With respect, perhaps you should retire to your bed until the physician can pronounce your health," Colin said. "I am not especially keen to assume the title just yet."

"There is no need for the physician," his father said, still holding on to Colin's handkerchief. He cast a glance at the duchess, and Colin had the distinct feeling an entire conversation had occurred between them without either of them uttering a word. "Not today, at least."

"Father, this is exactly the sort of episode that requires the physician's expertise."

"Your father will not listen to me," her mother said, her voice in her more usual huff, which somehow brought Colin a certain level of relief.

"He has provided me with some tonic," the duke protested with a bit more vigor, the terror that had gripped him clearly subsiding. He patted his chest, and Colin could not help but be struck by how fragile his father seemed just a moment ago. His father had passed five and sixty only two years ago, and was by all accounts a hearty and hale sort who enjoyed the outdoor pursuits of fishing and overseeing work in Stormount's formidable gardens. His reddish-blond hair had faded to mostly gray, but his back was still straight and his health troubles few—until now.

"Tonic?" Colin frowned, his gaze darting to his mother. "How long have these episodes been happening?"

"Not long after Yuletide," his mother offered. "While you were in Yorkshire, chasing after whatever it was you were chasing after."

Colin adjusted his spectacles on his nose, and pressed his lips together. "A meteorite, Mother. A bit of rock that fell from the heavens and fell into Mr. Shipley's garden." He'd gone to take extensive notes and drawings of this bit of wonder that had fallen in the village of Wold. He'd also gone to make a last and futile visit to Lady Amelia, who was visiting with relations nearby. He'd heard the rumors that the gentleman Amelia had thrown Colin over for was miraculously out of her life. Tossing common sense and all the rules of society aside, Colin had stood at the door of the great house, preparing to throw himself at her feet and beg her to be his once again.

Her husband, Lord Grafton, greeted Colin. So much for rumor. Two days later she returned a small stack of letters that he'd sent since she'd left him. All were unopened. With them was a note she'd penned, clearly stating that whatever affection had existed between them had come from one direction, and it had never been hers.

It was the first of two brushes with misguided passion that winter. Only a few days after, he and several of his companions were nearly killed by a long-lost kin, who'd blamed Colin and the entire aristocracy for the circumstances that had robbed him of what he felt was his rightful place as Duke of Weymouth. Before the night was over, the man was dead after a struggle with Colin in the bitter cold, in which physics—and a bit of luck, Colin conceded—spared his life.

After that, Colin had decided he'd had quite enough of passion. It was much easier on everyone if misguided passion was kept in the pages of tawdry novels, while real life—his life—was dictated by rules. By order.

A light snore coming from his father broke through Colin's reverie. He rose and positioned his father more comfortably, all the while breathing a sigh of relief. For the moment his father appeared to be resting as if nothing had happened.

"Are they getting worse, these episodes?" Colin asked his mother, whose haunted gaze twisted his gut.

She shook her head. "They come and go, with no apparent pattern," she said at last. "The tonic helps to calm his heart and there seems to be few ill effects from it. But one day, I fear he will not recover."

Colin reached out and took his mother's hand. She was as vulnerable as he could ever recall seeing her.

"I pray that day is still far in the future," he replied. "And you know when that day comes I will be here for you."

They sat in contented silence for some time, and soon Dr. Plover arrived. He checked the duke's pulse and listened to his chest. There was little that could be done, he told them, but to ensure that the duke was not given to intense excitement that might strain his heart. But there was nothing more he could offer. He left, giving Colin no more reassurance than he had before he arrived.

"You must marry, Colin." His mother's voice broke through the silence that had settled on the room after the physician's departure. It was not a plea, nor an order, but rather a simple statement of fact. "Your cousin, Lord Mumford, has just had his third son in as many years. He is a dissolute man who looks eagerly to Weymouth to replenish his misspent coffers. Your father will be settled, at least, knowing the estate and the title is in order," she said, not taking her eyes from her husband. "And the sooner, the better."

Order. The word settled on Colin's shoulders like a balm in this moment of fear and uncertainty. He'd been avoiding the very subject of marriage since Lady Amelia threw him off on the eve of their wedding and dashed off with a Scottish lord who was now her husband. Colin had gone between shutting himself off from the idea to foolishly attempting to win back her affection. When he'd attended the baptism of her child, he finally realized how much energy he'd wasted—how much of his heart he'd wasted—devoted to someone who would never ever love him in return. But it was not until this moment that he appreciated how much uncertainly he'd left in his parents' lives.

He stood, casting a glance at his father, still resting, and then his mother. An unmarried heir, particularly at his age, was stretching the rules.

And Colin knew the rules.

He would find a wife. Someone who would never tempt him with passion, or send his world into chaos. He would fulfill his duty, make his parents happy, and get married. Provide an heir. And when that business was done, he could go back to the one part of his life that demanded nothing of him. Lofton Tower and his telescope.

"Very well. What is the quickest way to find a wife?"

CHAPTER 2

Five thousand pounds.

Once upon a time, the very idea of Kitty Boxford desiring such an absurd sum of money seemed laughable. She was not rich by the standards of people who measured wealth by the thousands of pounds, but she had loving parents, good friends, and an excellent position with a kind employer. What more could a girl like Kitty want?

Nothing, perhaps, until this morning. Then, quite suddenly, the idea of five thousand pounds, or even five hundred pounds, seemed terribly relevant.

It would be enough to buy her a bit of freedom.

Kitty gripped the stem of a weed happily growing amongst her beans and pulled. It never failed to amaze her just how easily those unwanted seeds found purchase in the soil, and how effortlessly they grew without all the fuss of more desired plants. If she stretched her imagination just far enough, she could almost feel sorry for them.

After all, once upon a time, she'd been unceremoniously tossed out for being in the wrong place at the wrong time. A mistake that cost her family its livelihood and their home when she was little more than a child. To the cruel Countess Snowdon, the mistress of Gorland Park and her best friend's wicked mother, Kitty Boxford had been little better than a weed. A girl of no consequence, the countess once said, who was "five thousand pounds too poor and a stone too heavy to make anyone a good wife."

Kitty tossed the plant into a nearby basket of garden waste and shook off her moment of indulgent self-pity. Kitty and her parents had twice since found excellent situations, first in the Lakes, and now here in Cheshire working at the home of Mrs. Evelyn Pembroke. She'd provided Kitty with this lovely little garden to grow her lumpers and pumpkins, beans and peas, and some time to work in it. Her strawberry patch already yielded a treasure trove of berries, and she'd picked some as a special treat for today's tea. Indeed, the entire garden was showing signs of promise. Maybe this year would be her best harvest yet.

The thought had barely entered Kitty's head when a second, less pleasant realization struck her. She wouldn't see her harvest here at Kennington Grove.

The weed was being plucked again.

"Stop that silly nonsense, Kitty," she told herself under her breath as she gripped the hoe and gingerly moved it in the soil. She and her parents were moving to Silver Cross, which was barely a half-mile down the road. It was the home of her very best friends in the world, Edmund and Lady Gwyneth Pembroke. Now that they were settled with a growing family, it hardly made any sense at all to maintain two households when there was more than enough room at Silver Cross. Soon Edmund's mother, to whom Kitty was a nurse and a companion, would move and the Boxfords were invited to go with them. And then, her friend Gwynnie reminded her as she broke the news only this morning, they would be together all the time. Just the way they used to be, when they were children.

Except it would never be the same. Not really.

Kitty was certain that when she'd been informed of the plans that she'd managed to smile. She had no skill for hiding her feelings, but truthfully she was uncertain of them. Moving from her home brought a rush of emotions. Much had changed, of course, since she and

Gwynnie were children. Gwynnie was the daughter of an earl. Kitty was the daughter of the earl's gamekeeper. And Gwynnie, as much as Kitty loved her, sometimes forgot that their choices in life were very different indeed.

She *had* felt panic when she'd been told. Panic, followed by a whiff of despair, which had dissolved into plain old discontent. And before she could face another living soul and pretend to be happy about her life being upended, about having to spend it daily with two people she adored, which should have been perfect and yet would never be alone. A short time digging in her garden was not the perfect antidote to the dread and guilt that had assaulted her the moment she'd found out she'd be soon spending every day in close quarters with Edmund, but she'd hoped that by the time she'd collected the strawberries and weeded her bean patch, she might not be quite so miserable about it all.

Kitty pulled the straw hat she'd been wearing off her head, wiped the sweat from her brow with the back of her hand, and started to fan herself. The floppy straw brim created a welcome little bit of breeze that tempered the sun's mid-afternoon heat. She would absolutely need a quick splash of water to refresh herself before tea, which as a special treat, was happening in the little conservatory to one side of the house. As she examined her apron and the hem of her skirts, Kitty realized she might need a change of dress completely.

Plopping her hat back on her head, she dumped the basket of weeds on a pile at the back of the garden, put away her hoe, then retrieved the strawberries she'd collected. She allowed herself one berry as a reward for her labor and she wiped her hands with the edges of her apron. Once upon a time, a very long time ago, a Romani woman had looked at her hands and told her future laid in the lines that ran across her palm. Those hands had grasped onto her future, and then let them go. It was up to her to find them again. *Look aloft*, the woman had said, *and you will find what you seek*. Whatever that had meant. She'd once lost something very precious to her when it tumbled to the ground. And she *had* found it, she wanted to tell that old woman now. Found it years later, a broken piece of jewelry that she never should have taken. And she'd found it by looking down.

Kitty stared down at her hands, seeing nothing now but little ridges of dirt that only a bit of soap, water, and a healthy bit of scrubbing could remove.

"Good afternoon."

Kitty started at the formality and unfamiliarity of the very proper voice greeting her. Her gaze shot to the road, where a gentleman stood wearing quite possibly the shiniest boots she'd ever encountered. The excellent cut of his clothes spoke to his wealth, and he wore one of his arms in a sling, which was no doubt made of a finer cloth than her frock.

Glasses. Red-blond hair. Ramrod straight back. And, as she'd heard described, the sun itself shining down upon him. She could not yet attest to the quality of his teeth, as he wasn't smiling, but she would have bet an entire crown they were absolutely perfect. Lord Ellsworth, heir of the Duke of Weymouth, and, far more importantly, the very apple of his parent's eye.

Oh dear. *Lord Ellsworth.*

They'd met once, awkwardly, not a year ago, and only for the briefest of moments. She didn't know it was he at the time. She'd been on her hands and knees in the grass at Gorland Park, remnants of her mother's long-lost brooch in her hands, her eyes red and puffy from crying. Hopefully he did not recognize her, Indeed, she'd barely had a good look at him at the time. She'd run off, desperate to be alone with her dignity and the shattered pieces of her heart.

Kitty should have immediately lowered her head, but instead found herself uncommonly mesmerized. His eyes were an unusual shade of green that even the lenses of his gold-rimmed spectacles could not hide. Not that she should have noticed. Neither should she have noticed that his legs, long as they were, were perfectly formed and did a credit to the buckskin breeches he wore. Or that his expression was a curious mix of confidence and uncertainty.

"Good afternoon," he repeated, a little louder this time. Good heavens, he must have thought she couldn't hear him.

She hastily wiped her hands on her apron and tried to tuck several of her more persistent curls behind her ears, then dipped into a low curtsey and held herself there.

"Good afternoon, my lord," she replied.

He acknowledged her with the very briefest of taps to the brim of his hat.

"My apologies for disrupting you. I am looking for a bit of direction," he said after what felt like a long and somewhat painful pause. He shuffled his feet a moment, pushed his spectacles up on his nose, then gestured in her direction. "Have you considered gloves?"

Kitty straightened and breathed a sigh of relief. Just as she'd hoped, he had no recollection of her. Not that she would have expected it. Indeed, she wondered if he was speaking to her at all. She cast a glance over her shoulder, just to be sure.

"Gloves?"

He nodded. "You appeared to be considering your hand just now. I thought you might have a splinter, or a blister. Gloves would protect you from both afflictions, I would think."

"It was neither." She shrugged her shoulders, mystified by the topic of conversation. "I was merely examining the lines on my hand."

"I see," he said, though he wore a perplexed expression. His manner was somewhat awkward, which seemed curious for someone who must be a gentleman of the world, but she found herself charmed by it. His lips teased at a smile. "Actually, I do not."

"These lines on your hands." She held up palm of her right hand. "A woman once told me things about myself based solely on looking at my hands." Things she had never told another living soul. Like how she'd lost her mother's treasured brooch and with it, her chance at happiness.

"Mere conjecture," he said, the rather dismissive shake of his head stealing some of the more charitable thoughts Kitty had about him only a moment ago. "The only traits one might deduce from such an examination would be in the broadest of observances. One's rank in society, or perhaps a hint at a profession, and all that is required is a keen eye. For example, I might be able to deduce by the dirt under your fingernails, the rather red state of your cheeks, or the soil on your hem, that you have been working the land. There is nothing particularly magical about observation, except that few people actually do it."

Kitty blinked. Swallowed. And then she dropped her hands out of sight. Pressing her lips into a tight smile and casting a glance down at her feet, any thoughts she'd had about him being charming evaporated.

Are the spectacles merely to make you appear more haughty? Because clearly there is nothing wrong with your eyesight.

"Excuse me?"

Kitty's head snapped up to meet Lord Ellsworth's intent stare. Heavens, had she spoken those words out loud? It happened, sometimes. That little voice inside her head occasionally escaped. It was one of the reasons why she had such a difficult time finding a position in service, her mother had said to her once. But this could not be one of those times, could it?

"My eyesight is not what it should be."

It could.

"My hearing, however, is excellent."

She *had.*

Oh dear. Oh, oh, oh dear. Kitty forced herself not to bury her face in her hands.

She closed her eyes, wishing the earth would swallow her whole. "My lord, I am so sorry. I did not—"

He smiled, her discomfort apparently a source of amusement for one of them, then held up his uninjured hand. It was gloved, of course. Everything about him was impeccable...which was making her feel less impeccable by the second.

"I was not commenting on your appearance," he replied. "Merely observing it. I am not certain how one would yield food without a little dirt on one's apron. And the redness in your cheeks..." He swallowed, contrition in his looks. Heavens, was he nervous? Of her? "It is to be expected in this sun."

What a bewildering gentleman, Kitty thought, entirely uncertain what to make of him.

"Can I help you, my lord?" She had strawberries to deliver, washing up to do, and chores that awaited her before tea.

"Yes, of course," he replied, though he appeared immensely preoccupied. She could not help but wonder what else he was observing about her at the moment—the curls flattened to the sides of her face, or the frayed edge of her straw hat, perhaps?

"I have been invited for tea by Mrs. Pembroke and I am being thwarted by rather poor direction as to the location. I fear I am quite tardy."

His declaration took Kitty off guard. She wasn't aware that Mrs. Pembroke had invited anyone for tea this afternoon. But then again, she hadn't been aware she was moving to Silver Cross until sometime after breakfast this morning.

"I was just on my way back to the house, so I can direct you," she replied. "But I fear you are quite early. Tea is not until four o'clock."

He stiffened even further, if such a thing were possible.

"I pride myself on my punctuality." He pulled a very fine silver watch out of his pocket, which, like the rest of him, gleamed. She leaned forward to take a look at the time, and her stomach dropped a second time.

It wasn't four o'clock. It was five minutes past it.

She picked up the edges of her skirt and started to bound out of the garden when she realized she'd nearly forgotten her strawberries. She scooped up the basket, wrapped it in her apron to protect the fruit, then dashed toward the house, all the while calling out direction to the gentleman in the lane.

"I am afraid I must go," she called over his protests. She pointed down a path that led to the party. "Follow this until you see a cherry tree, then go left. Around the corner of the house, you will see a small courtyard. They will be there."

"But—"

Mrs. Pembroke. Gwynnie. Edmund. Her parents. They would have been needing her for one thing or another, and here she was in a dirty frock, late for a tea, and now had a member of the aristocracy as a guest.

Maybe one day, if she didn't speak it aloud, the heavens would leave her alone and let her be happy. Let her have a garden that stayed in one place, because she could stay in one place. And, just maybe someone who loved—*no.* She couldn't even think that. It was too dangerous to ask for such things. Maybe one day, she would be the director of her own time. Her own life.

But not today.

"Here he is!"

Colin dragged his attention away from the remarkable red-cheeked miss to his friend Edmund Pembroke, who was sauntering down the road toward him. The two had been friends since childhood, though their lives had taken them in very different directions for a time. Edmund had chosen to disappear from society completely for a time, going so far as to change his name, work as a sometimes-agent for the Home Office, and live as a gamekeeper on a large estate in the Lakes. As he approached, Edmund looked for all the world the most contented of men. Of course he did. He'd been converted by love, and wearing the look of a man with that zeal Colin had seen on missionaries.

"My apologies, Edmund. I got a little turned around. One of the servants pointed me in your direction," he said, thinking of the girl and the absolute look of panic on her face when she'd realized she'd spoken aloud. Her candor, unwilling though it may have been, was refreshing. And there was something about her lips, when they parted, that had been...tempting. What an illogical thought.

"Both Gwyneth and mother will be pleased to see you," Edmund said as they walked along the gently curved path. "But I warn you, they will have at least a dozen questions about this bride hunt of yours."

"I am honored by your mother's invitation, and I am very pleased to be able to deliver one of my own," he replied. He'd been answering hundreds of questions daily from his mother about one detail or another. "As long as they do not test me on flavors of ices or styles of dresses, I will do my very best to answer them all."

"In that case, what in the blazes did you do to your arm? Fall off your stool in the middle of the night dozing by your telescope?"

"Hardly," Colin said. "It happened in London, after the baptism of Lord and Lady Grafton's child. I may have over indulged somewhat."

It had been a test, going to St. Paul's for a milestone that he'd imagined he and Amelia would have shared. Instead, she was with her husband, Lord Grafton, looking as beautiful as ever, and happier than he could ever remember. The latter of his observations had been the most difficult to bear, but he'd been civil. He might have even feigned a reasonable smile or two. Then he promptly returned to his Mayfair residence and congratulated himself on his success by drinking far too much brandy. Gravity punished him for his night of self-indulgence.

Edmund let out another laugh. "You were foxed. If only I could have witnessed that."

Colin fought the urge to roll his eyes. "I'm paying the price for my folly. I can barely write my own name, nor record my observations in any sort of legible fashion. And since I lost my last assistant in February, I've had a deuce of a time finding a new one."

"Are you as enthusiastic about finding a wife?" Edmund asked, growing serious. "I am surprised at your sudden enthusiasm to entertain such a public display of courtship. You have never liked crowds."

Colin smiled stiffly, the memory of his father's pallid face and the fear in his own chest still fresh.

"Everything I have done is generally on public display. But recent events have made it clear to me that I can no longer shirk my duties in this regard." This past winter his life, and the lives of those around him, was nearly taken by a distant cousin who'd decided to take his revenge on the aristocracy he'd been forced out of because of an illegitimate marriage. "The title deserves to continue. Finding a match is simply a matter of suitability based on some generally accepted characteristics. Family connections and income being the two most relevant."

"That seems terribly clinical, even for you," Edmund replied. "What if you are not suited?"

"Amelia and I were joined while she was still in the cradle." Colin inwardly congratulated himself on being able to utter her name without emotion. "We seemed to suit well enough, based on those simple calculations."

"And yet she married another," Edmund replied. "So, my friend, perhaps there is a bit more to it."

Colin stilled, struck by the notion that he wanted to throttle his friend for poking holes in his logic. Edmund slowed his gait, his countenance growing serious.

"Are you certain, Colin, this is what you want? Despite your parent's opinion on the matter, there are other ways to find a wife."

"What do you suggest?" His shoulders tightened at Edmund's well-intentioned prodding. "A knock on the door of every lady of consequence in the kingdom, until the right one miraculously appears? Or should I merely kidnap one, like you did?"

"Kidnap" was perhaps overstating the case, Colin admitted to himself. Edmund had interrupted Gwyneth's elopement to a man who had planned to steal Gwyneth's fortune. But the point remained that Edmund hardly had to submit himself to the public spectacle that would consume Colin in only a few days' time. Days filled with socializing and picnics, nights filled with card parties and dancing. It was a bloody nightmare. If only he could hide away in Lofton Tower, change his name, and have the perfect woman land on his doorstep, life would be charmed indeed. But he'd had the perfect woman. And she hadn't wanted him.

Edmund laughed aloud. "A wife and duchess, or someone to scribble notes for you? I can see why your attentions would be so torn between them."

They strolled along to a small courtyard nestled alongside the back of the house. There, under the shade of a small tree, sat Mrs. Evelyn Pembroke, Edmund's mother, and Lady Gwyneth Pembroke, his wife, who was clearly increasing. The irony of meeting Lady Gwyneth—as he once knew her—was not lost on him. At one time, she had been quite set on marrying him based on the very calculation he'd outlined to Edmund just a moment ago. That such an equation would have, no doubt, produced three very unhappy people, he'd decided to ignore. Edmund and Lady Gwyneth were entirely well suited to each other.

"Have either of you seen Kitty?" Lady Gwyneth asked Edmund, concern in her brow. "I do hope she is not in the house packing. Edmund, perhaps you should look for her."

"We dropped a bit of a surprise on poor Miss Boxford this morning I'm afraid," Edmund's mother said, before turning a shrewd eye to Colin. "But nothing like the news we received of your upcoming nuptials to an as yet unnamed lady, my lord. A house party lasting a fortnight, ending in a ball that will see you choose your bride. Her Grace must be in her glory. And you must be wishing it concluded."

Colin could not help but smile at Mrs. Pembroke's keen and pointed summation of the entire affair. Mrs. Pembroke had suffered an accident when Edmund was but a boy that had robbed her of much of her mobility along one side of her body. It had kept her out of society but had done nothing to lessen the sharpness of her mind. And that mind was now turned to Colin.

"I cannot say that I am enamored of the idea, but it is for the best in the end. And, I believe it will be a far more enjoyable time if you all would be so good to come as guests to Stormount for at least some of the festivities."

"That is very good of you, Lord Ellsworth," Mrs. Pembroke said, and Colin could see the hesitation in her eyes. "I am very honored by the invitation. But are you certain you wish me there given—"

Colin knew at once her concerns, reached into his jacket, and presented Mrs. Pembroke with an invitation.

"Mrs. Pembroke, your friendship with my parents has been of a long duration. Indeed, I have a letter from her Grace, begging you to come as your abilities allow. Both she and the duke, and myself, would be incredibly honored by your attendance."

Mrs. Pembroke pressed her lips together and nodded, clearly moved by the invitation.

"Please extend our sincerest gratitude for this acknowledgement," she said at last.

Edmund nodded at his friend. "And my personal thanks, as it spares me endless questions about muslins that I fear I could not answer."

"This will be very exciting!" Lady Gwyneth piped up. "Where is Kitty? She will be—"

"Mrs. Pembroke, ma'am, I am so sorry."

The rushed apologies of a female voice drew the attention of all. She held a tray laden with a bowl of strawberries and a large pitcher of lemonade, which Edmund took from her and placed on a nearby table already brimming with tea and biscuits.

"You are here at last!" Lady Gwyneth exclaimed, her face lighting up at the sight of the girl. "We'd wondered what had happened to you. But no matter. Kitty Boxford, this is Colin Middleton, Marquess of Ellsworth, and one of Edmund's oldest friends. Lord Ellsworth, Katherine Boxford is my oldest and dearest friend. Her father, as you probably know from Edmund, was a gamekeeper at Gorland Park for a time."

Colin lifted his gaze to the woman standing between Lady Gwyneth and Mrs. Pembroke, recognizing her instantly as the servant girl in the garden. The straw hat and soiled apron were gone, along with the dress that had been marked by her labors. An unruly set of brown curls framed her face, which was still flushed. Her eyes were warm, like the color of a fine whiskey, and she possessed the most remarkable set of eyelashes he'd ever seen. Even by the standards of average females, she was short, and he guessed that if he stood close to her, the top of her head might just reach his shoulder. And he found himself suddenly very interested in standing close to her.

"I say, Kitty, do not mind Ellsworth. He was probably up too late last night chasing a patch of clear sky."

Edmund's words snapped Colin out of his reverie. He rose to his feet and nodded.

"My apologies," he said. What was it about her eyes that were so bloody mesmerizing? There was something familiar about those eyes. "My studies do occasionally keep sleep at bay. It has caught up to me today, it seems."

"I was merely saying that it is an honor to make your acquaintance," she replied, seemingly relieved he'd made no mention of their first encounter in the garden.

"Let's take some refreshment, shall we?" Lady Gwyneth suggested, ever the gracious hostess. "A little lemonade and strawberries might revive us. I am eating for two now, and Kitty grows the best strawberries to be found in the county."

Miss Boxford smiled at Lady Gwyneth's praise as she set down the berries and poured several glasses of lemonade, moving quietly in that way servants often did as not to be noticed. And yet, they had made a point of introducing her. Who was this girl?

And, quite pointedly, why did he care?

"We have more news, Kitty, which I hope will be a little less taxing for you," Lady Gwyneth said, practically bouncing in her chair. "We have been invited to Stormount for Lord Ellsworth's house party."

"Oh," she said, and Colin was immediately struck by the idea that, despite her smile, she was as eager for the idea as he was. "That is quite the honor, my lord."

"This is going to be quite the occasion if you are going to entice half of the *ton* out of London in the middle of June," Mrs. Pembroke said.

Colin pushed his spectacles up on his nose, knowing full well the crass truth of the matter—all of society would turn convention on their ear to earn their daughters the chance to marry him. It wasn't ego. He was rich and titled. It was the simplest of maths.

"Parliament is already in recess, and my mother will ensure it is the occasion, I am certain. The house is already buzzing with so much activity that I have taken to spending many of my days, as well as my nights, at the tower. Though," he gestured to his bandaged wrist, "I am even scuppered in my midnight viewing. If I had fallen and sprained my ankle, it would have been far more preferable."

"How so?" Lady Gwyneth asked. "Walking would be a chore, and dancing impossible."

"Just so," Colin replied with a nod. "Just so."

"You do not like to dance, my lord?" Miss Boxford asked, her eyes widening as if she'd surprised herself with the question.

He cast a glance at her, bemused, knowing once again she'd probably not meant to speak the question aloud.

"I am not partial to the exercise."

"You will have to excuse Kitty, Lord Ellsworth," Lady Gwyneth said, looking at her friend with clear affection. "You see, she loves to dance. When we were children, we would spend hours pretending to do a minuet. We shall have to find her at least one partner at Stormount."

"Gwynnie!" The girl's cheeks flushed the deepest shade of red, and she looked away while she composed herself.

Lady Gwyneth merely shrugged. "There is nothing at all the matter with a woman knowing what she wants. Wouldn't you agree, Lord Ellsworth? That is how I found Edmund, after all."

Colin shifted his weight, measuring his reaction to Lady Gwyneth's declaration. While she meant it as a jest, the remark had hit uncomfortably close. Though there were nearly thirty females who were invited to Stormount in a few days' time, there was one woman in particular who'd known exactly what she'd wanted. And it hadn't been Colin.

"May I ask," Miss Boxford interjected, apparently just as eager to move away from the subject of matchmaking and dancing as Colin, "you said something about a tower. Is it a watch tower?"

"Of a sort," Colin replied. "Lofton Tower, an observatory."

Miss Boxford looked at him anew, her eyes threatening to bewitch him again. "*Lofton* Tower?"

Colin smiled, inordinately pleased with the girl's wonder. "It was a watchtower. I have renovated it to a new purpose. Instead of using it to look down over the landscape, it is for looking up at the sky."

The girl froze, clearly lost in her own thoughts. And none of it had to do, as far as he could tell, with minuets or muslins.

"And the telescope," she asked, remarkably single-minded, "you use it to study the sky? Like Mr. Herschel, and that gentleman in Paris?"

"Messier," Colin replied, struck by her use of two astronomers in casual conversation. "I do. My telescope allows me to see much more of the sky than can be seen without it."

"You can see…what is unseen," the girl said, her voice a little more than a whisper.

"I record my observations, and compare them with existing catalogues. I had an assistant for a great many years, but alas, he had other opportunities and has since moved on with his studies. Finding a suitable replacement has proven a challenge."

She nodded slowly, as if caught in her own thought. "What sort of skills would be required for an assistant?"

"Heavens, Mother," Edmund interjected. "Perhaps you will have to replace Kitty."

Colin could not help but notice the sharp look Miss Boxford gave Edmund, as if he was interrupting her thoughts. They were obviously on very familiar terms.

"A general knowledge of the constellations and the planets," Colin began, ignoring Edmund. "Meticulous attention to detail. Excellent penmanship of course. The ability to sit quietly and listen. And I suppose," he stifled a yawn, fatigue from a poor night's sleep catching up with him, "someone who doesn't mind being up at all hours."

Miss Boxford nodded, but she seemed still preoccupied. She reached for a strawberry, holding it to her lips in a most distracting way.

"Sounds perfectly dreadful," Edmund piped up. "No wonder you are having a deuce of a time finding the right candidate. Maybe finding a wife will be easier."

"Indeed." Colin took a sip of his lemonade, allowing his answer to settle. A title and connections. It was, in the end, all that was required. Even when he'd been paired with Amelia, he had not expected to lose his heart in the process. That was no longer in the equation.

"Have you posted for the position, Lord Ellsworth?" Mrs. Pembroke asked.

"Several times, without success," he replied. "But I have decided on one last attempt."

As with the wife hunting.

The conversation carried on merrily for a while longer, blessedly turning away from brides and weddings to more mundane subjects. Miss Boxford was seated next to Mrs. Pembroke, seeing to her every need, watching the conversation, but perhaps distracted by her duties as she said nothing. At least with her mouth. It was clear she was watching everyone. Including, in stolen moments, him. It gave rise to a peculiar sensation that put his entire body on alert in the most pleasurable way.

The bells from a nearby church rang the hour and soon it was time for Colin to leave the Pembrokes and Miss Boxford and return to the onslaught of questions and preparations. The only amiable thing about this entire affair was at least the look of happiness on Mrs. Pembroke's face when he'd invited her to Stormount. And, perhaps, the knowledge that Miss Boxford would accompany her.

He couldn't marry *her*, of course. There were rules about who could marry into the aristocracy, and who couldn't. That he was entertaining even the most cursory thoughts about a gamekeeper's daughter perplexed him, regardless of how pleasurable those thoughts were. Pleasure of that sort could lead most dangerously to passion, and he'd had quite enough of that in his life to no good end. He needed a return to order. To the rules.

And Colin knew the rules.

CHAPTER 3

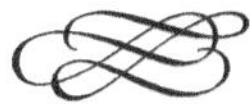

anted:

One gamekeeper, currently employed.

Aged 20-40.

Applicants with children acceptable.

Kitty Boxford drummed her fingers on the corner of the tiny table of her bedchamber at Kennington Grove. It was early afternoon, and a gentle rain was greening the already lush Cheshire landscape.

Gentle nature, not taken to excessive drink.

Humorous disposition.

Was that too much?

Her pen hovered over the paper, when the next item formed in her mind:

Fondness for dancing appreciated. Warm smile that makes your toes curl.

Brown hair. Blue eyes. First name begins with E—

NO. Kitty shook her head. That was *far* too much.

A light knock on the door broke Kitty's day dreaming. Mrs. Pembroke would not be up from her nap for at least another thirty minutes. She set down the paper and went to the door, where a friendly face greeted her.

"Gwynnie!" she exclaimed, happy to see her good friend standing before her.

Gwynnie stood in the door, her hand resting lightly on her middle. She was with child, and far enough along she'd taken to loosening her stays to allow for her growing babe.

"Come and sit," Kitty said, leading her into the room and offering her a chair. "I think motherhood suits you."

"Thank you. Now that the worst of the sickness is over, I am much more settled." Her friend breezed in, her cheeks slightly flushed from the exertion, and took Kitty by the hands. "Are you excited for Lord Ellsworth's party? I made Edmund promise he would dance with you, though it didn't take much arm twisting of course. We shall have to find you some new dresses."

At the sound of Edmund's name, Kitty's face pulled into a tight smile before she allowed herself to brush away an unwanted pang of envy that made her feel like the most horrible, disingenuous of creatures.

"Edmund doesn't need to dance with me," she said. "Besides, I will be there to tend to Mrs. Pembroke, which I am employed to do."

"You know perfectly well that neither Edmund nor his mother would see you without a dance," Gwynnie said. "Edmund would be well pleased to stand up with you."

Kitty nodded, knowing Gwynnie was right. And yet…

"And just think!" Gwynnie continued. "So soon we shall all be together, every day. I never dreamed our situation would end up so perfect."

"Perfect!" Kitty said, forcing the smile on her face to match Gwynnie's, who was utterly genuine in her joy. Joy that Kitty could not quite make herself feel, and she was quickly coming to hate herself for it.

As children, Kitty and Gwynnie once sat under the trees in Gorland Park's orchard, dreaming of their futures. Gwynnie, lady that she was, was going to marry a prince, or at least a duke. And Kitty was going to marry a gamekeeper, like her father.

Except Gwynnie had married Kitty's gamekeeper. Edmund, hiding his true identity behind a gamekeeper's duties, had become her ideal. The affection between Gwynnie and Edmund was impossible to miss, and of course Kitty was happy for them. Still, it was difficult not to be a little sad for herself. Perhaps it might have been easier if Kitty was still not unmarried, still a few pounds too heavy, and most decidedly without five thousand pounds. Or, that she had never quite managed to fall out of love with him.

She loathed herself for it.

Kitty reached out and pulled her friend into an embrace, then released her. The subtle change in Gwynnie's body made Kitty critically aware of the difference between them. Gwynnie—married to a dear man, and now carrying his child. Mistress of her own household.

Gwynnie's eyes brightened with tears. "Oh Kitty, I cannot tell you how sorry I am about how my mother treated your family so horribly. I shall spend the rest of my days trying to make it up to you. And I will."

Kitty smiled, and squeezed her friend's hand. "Do not trouble yourself. For a long time I thought the fault was mine."

"But how on earth could that be? It was my mother who was responsible."

"Do you remember the day before we left, and you and I played that game of hide and go seek in the orchard?"

Gwynnie's mouth fell into a frown. "I could scarce forget it. I soiled my dress. Mother locked me in my room for a month."

"A few days earlier you had shown me some trinket your father had given you." Kitty paused and waited until Gwynnie shook her head, clearly not remembering. Kitty continued. "I was envious, you see. And I wanted to show you my treasure—the Boxford family jewel."

"I didn't know your mother had any jewels," Gwynnie replied. "Not that she didn't deserve them. Sara Boxford has always treated me far better than my own mother."

"She kept it in a small wooden case. It was a beautiful brooch, with shiny stones in the top and a larger one, hanging beneath."

"Shiny stones—do you mean diamonds?" her friend asked, her brow dipping in confusion.

Kitty laughed.

"Don't be silly, Gwynnie. Where on earth would she get diamonds? They were probably glass or paste that she'd received as a gift from an employer." She paused, still remembering the way it dazzled in the light. There had been something absolutely magical about it. "I took it to show you because I wanted for once to have something wonderful that belonged to me. And then…I lost it." She had been climbing up in one of her beloved apple trees to hide from Gwynnie when Lady Snowdon's voice, angry and tight, cut through the air. Startled, she lost her grip and fell.

A boy had caught her—he and his parents were visiting with the countess at the time. He was older than Kitty and his dress was very fine. Terrified by the approaching sound of the countess's voice, she'd jumped out of his arms and run into the trees to escape. The brooch, which she'd pinned to her frock, had torn free. By the time Kitty had raced home, she'd realized it was gone. The next day, she, her parents, and all their belongings were packed up into a cart and shipped off the property.

"But how could losing a piece of jewelry mean it was your fault you were tossed out of Gorland Park?" Gwynnie asked. "It was my mother's fault for being such a horrible, petty woman."

"Mother told me it was special and that it would always bring her luck, which was why she never wore it but kept it safe."

"Katherine Boxford, the heavens could not deny such a beautiful creature the love you so clearly deserve," Gwynnie said, crossing her arms and rising to her feet. "You cannot believe that a jewel—and one made of paste no less—could affect your fate?"

Kitty certainly didn't want to. But nothing had been right after that moment. And the Romani woman's reading of her palm only confirmed it. She'd let her happiness slip through her fingers. The very day Edmund and Gwynnie had gotten engaged, she'd found it— or found what was left of it. A twisted piece of metal, with only a single paste stone left in place. She'd dug it out of the ground with her fingers. It only added to the despair that had gripped her, knowing that the man she'd imagined herself in love with was proposing to her very best friend. The heavens, it seemed to Kitty, appeared quite content to deny her happiness.

"What is this?"

The surprise in Gwynnie's voice drew Kitty back from that awful moment to see Gwynnie picking up the note Kitty had left on her desk. Kitty rose, but could not move quick enough to snatch it from her friend's hands.

"It's nothing."

Gwynnie's eyebrows rose. "Do not tell me this is what I think it is."

"I just said it's nothing."

Gwynnie handed the note to her, and looked at Kitty anew, Gwynnie's usually playful countenance replaced by something else. Something far worse. Pity.

"Are you advertising for a…husband? Why?"

"Maybe. I do not know." She took the paper from her friend, folded it, and carefully tucked it away in her apron pocket. "It's not like it hasn't been done."

"By widows, perhaps."

"It was just a thought, Gwynnie. A little plan. I cannot rely on my parents, nor you, forever," she replied.

"I understand what you are saying, and I am trying very hard not to lecture you on how much I love you and that you would never, ever be a burden to Edmund and me," Gwynnie said in that way of hers that told Kitty she would brook no opposition. "But as for a husband, this is not the way to do it. It is completely, utterly unromantic. You deserve better."

"It is not so very different from Lord Ellsworth's ball," Kitty countered. "With much less fuss and expense." Not that she wouldn't mind a little fussing. No one would ever have a ball for her.

A knock came to the door.

"Miss Boxford, my lady has awakened from her nap."

Kitty breathed a sigh of relief at the servant's interruption. She had

had quite enough talk of husbands and balls for one afternoon, no matter how well she loved her friend.

"Shall I assist you, Kitty?" Gwynnie asked.

"I shall be fine. If you would ring for tea, that would be lovely."

The two girls parted, Kitty grateful for the rest from Gwynnie's well-intentioned, if somewhat overbearing manners.

"Good afternoon, Mrs. Pembroke," Kitty said brightly as she entered the lady's bedchamber, taking her wheelchair and adjusting the pillows. "Did you have a pleasant nap?"

"Naps are always pleasant," the lady replied, her somewhat grouchy tone made less severe by the smile that teased the left side of her face. Kitty approached the bed and in a routine they'd perfected since she'd arrived nearly three years ago, the servant turned away while Kitty carefully examined Mrs. Pembroke's skin for bedsores. Satisfied, Kitty, with a servant to help, pulled on Mrs. Pembroke's overdress for tea.

"Gwyneth is here," Kitty said cheerfully. "She'll be waiting for us with tea."

"Wonderful," Mrs. Pembroke said. "And no further news from Stormount?"

"None that I am aware of," Kitty replied. "Though Gwynnie's head is already turned to dancing."

"At least hers is. Poor Lord Ellsworth will be dancing quite against his will, I suspect," Mrs. Pembroke said, though Kitty could not think of a single thing that was poor about him. "His head has always been in the clouds, that boy. Imagine being more concerned with finding a new assistant than a bride."

Kitty could not imagine. After the news of his broken engagement, Kitty could only assume Lord Ellsworth was horrendously disfigured or had a countenance that betrayed cruelty or reprobation. Of course, during his mother's visits to Mrs. Pembroke, he was spoken of as if the very sun and moon rose and set on his perfection, but mothers were occasionally given to the fault of seeing their children as they wished to see them, rather than as they really were. But he was, indeed, quite pleasant to look upon, and if his manners were somewhat awkward, there was nothing about him that seemed remotely like the type of man one would toss aside.

He didn't have that carefree way about him that Edmund did. Lord Ellsworth was most definitely proper, his manners restrained. Still, when she'd asked him about his telescopes, his manner brightened considerably. She found herself smiling at the thought of it. It was refreshing for a man with every comfort and whim available to him to be so enthusiastic about something more than lands, connections, and power.

"Heaven knows he is more fixated on the stars above than the world around him," Mrs. Pembroke continued. "He would lock himself up in Lofton Tower if he was left to his own devices. I suppose after his marriage, he will be."

Lofton Tower. The name loomed in her imagination, the old Romani woman's accented words as fresh in her mind as the rainy night she'd taken a young, frightened Kitty into her wooden caravan and read her palms. It was impossible that Lord Ellsworth, who'd dismissed the entire idea of palm reading outright, would have anything to do with good luck brooches.

How much coin could one make scribbling down a note or two? She could look after Mrs. Pembroke during the day and make extra wages at night. And then, perhaps she could save enough to post for a husband. If it came to that.

Kitty gazed out Mrs. Pembroke's window, streaked with drops of a light summer rain. In the distance, she saw Edmund and her father walking along, both unbothered by the weather. The sight of them brought up memories of their time together at Falls Lodge, when Edmund had first come to stay with them. An unnamed panic gripped her again. She tore her gaze away, swallowing deeply.

"Is this something a woman could do, do you think? Be an assistant?" The thought exited her mouth before she could stop it.

To Kitty's surprise, Mrs. Pembroke took hold of Kitty's arm and gently squeezed.

"Miss Boxford, I am quite certain that if they possess the qualities Lord Ellsworth require, the right person, regardless of their sex, would make him an excellent assistant. Still, it would have to be handled with discretion." She released Kitty's arm and signaled for the servant to leave. "I would suggest that if you in fact know anyone of interest, you would direct their application to Mr. Holland, who is Lord Ellsworth's man of business. I believe he has an office in Hilsburn."

Kitty stilled, curious as to Mrs. Pembroke's position on the subject.

"Thank you, ma'am. I will pass that on."

"This move is going to be difficult for you, Miss Boxford."

Mrs. Pembroke's bald statement was softened by the curious expression on her face. Her eyes were soft, creased with what Kitty could only categorize as sympathy.

"It should not be too difficult, my lady," she replied. "My parents are already moving their belongings to Silver Cross. The property has a very fine stream running along one of its borders and my father is eager to indulge himself in a bit of fishing. And Gwynnie has offered me my pick of rooms, though of course I will choose one near your chambers, so I can be close by if needed at any time."

"That is not what I speak of, my dear, and I respect you well enough not to pretend otherwise."

"I don't—"

"You still love him. Or, perhaps, what he represents."

Kitty had not felt so trapped since the day Countess Snowdon had caught her by the arm in the wood when Kitty was a child. It took all of her strength to stay fixed in her place.

"I don't love anyone," she replied, swallowing, trying to keep her voice light and matter-of-fact. "Except my parents, of course. And Gwynnie." She was very careful not to mention Edmund.

"Miss Boxford," Mrs. Pembroke continued, a small sigh occupying the pause. "You are a smart girl. Do not disappoint me. I may be confined to this chair, but I am not blind. You have not been the same since Edmund and Gwyneth have returned."

Kitty forced a smile on her face, and inwardly cursed her fair complexion she could feel warming from the force of the emotion she was tamping down. "Of course not. Gwyneth is my best friend in all the world, and Edmund is dear to me as well. And now they are next door. I see them every day."

Mrs. Pembroke stretched out and took Kitty's hand, a movement Kitty could see took great effort, and smiled sadly.

"Miss Boxford, I will say this and no more on the subject. You have a proud heart. Whatever you tell yourself, your heart can only contend with a lie for so long. If you do not heed it, your heart will harden or twist so that you will not recognize it or yourself."

What do you know of my heart? What does anyone know? Kitty's heart slammed in her chest as heat prickled up the back of her neck. However mortified she felt when Lord Ellsworth had pointed out the dirt under her fingernails, she would have gladly repeated the act a hundred times rather than taste the deep embarrassment of this moment. She had never felt so exposed.

Once upon a time, she'd fallen for an illusion. A man who'd turned out to be someone else. Her parents had tried to warn her about the apprentice gamekeeper that had come to stay with them, but Kitty had chosen not to listen. They'd said that Edmund Hanley, as she'd known him, was not who she thought he was. And though he'd never once treated her with any more affection than a dear friend or even a brother, she had stupidly ignored all the warnings and fell in love with him anyway. He liked the outdoors, just as she did. He even liked to dance. He had a lovely smile and he worked hard. And he didn't seem to mind that she wasn't graceful or elegant.

But he didn't love her, either. Not like that, anyway. That love had been for Gwynnie. And Kitty's heart was sad and happy and sometimes a little angry, too.

"Edmund and Gwyneth are together and they are in love and I couldn't be happier for them," she said, taking time to steady her voice. And it was true. But it was a truth laced in an uncomfortable lie —that she'd successfully buried those feelings, that forbidden hurt, safely away.

"I said you had a proud heart, my dear, not a selfish one," Mrs. Pembroke replied. "I do not wish to see you living in the shadow of a life you had thought for yourself. Resentment is a horrible thing. Left to fester, it can lead to anger and bitterness. Bitterness destroyed Edmund's father. It nearly destroyed my family. I will not have it destroy you."

Kitty stood, frozen to floor, aware of only the touch of Mrs. Pembroke's hand and the pit opening up in her belly. Nodding, she patted Mrs. Pembroke's hand before the woman blessedly released it.

She took her position behind the chair and wheeled Mrs. Pembroke into her favorite parlor, all the while wanting to do nothing more than disappear to her room. If she couldn't hide her feelings from Mrs. Pembroke—Edmund's mother—who else did she think she was fooling?

Later that evening, Kitty sat on her bed, finally alone with her thoughts. She ran her fingers over the coins she'd poured from her little wooden box onto her bed, the little metal discs clinking gently against each other.

Eighteen pounds.

Eighteen pounds, one crown and a sixpence, to be exact. She'd counted her savings three times, just to be certain, but the number hadn't changed.

Only four thousand, nine hundred and eighty-two pounds to go.

She let out a low breath, heavy with resignation. Five thousand pounds was, of course, an impossible sum. At the rate she's managed to save her coin, even five hundred would take several lifetimes.

She could not move to Silver Cross. She could not be in the house with them, knowing that Edmund's mother, of all people, knew of her feelings. It would cost her the friendship with both Gwynnie and Edmund. It would cost Kitty her self-respect.

Kitty put the coins away, went back to her little writing table, and pulled out a sheet of paper. Lofton Tower might be the key to finding her happiness, impossible a task as that may be.

But if she could secure the position and earn a little coin, it was, at least, an opportunity to save her dignity.

AFTER A SOGGY DAY, the stars had come out at last. Colin walked along Long Pond, a lamp in his hand. The artificial lake had been his father's great engineering project to improve an otherwise perfect property. Within view of the front part of the great house, it teemed with fish, and due to careful planning, looked as though it had always been a part of the estate—a shining example of artifice masquerading as nature. It was, Colin could not help but consider with some bitterness, a perfect metaphor for the circus about to take place at Stormount; the host of activities his mother was planning all in order to create a "romantic" backdrop to what was, in the end, a transaction between families.

A light breeze brought only the smallest ripples to the otherwise glassy top of the lake, which reflected the stars and the sliver of a moon overhead. Colin had spent the better part of the day with Mr. Holland, his secretary, reviewing application letters for an observatory assistant. It had been an exercise in futility — there had been only a handful of applicants, and after Mr. Holland's initial interviews, none had been suitable. Colin had been tempted to pull the advertisement entirely, but for the clerk's insistence that the deadline be observed.

If only finding the right assistant were as simple as he felt it would be to find a bride. In less than a day, more than two dozen ladies and a similar number of gentlemen, plus chaperones and miscellaneous guests, would descend on Stormount. The house, and his mother in particular, were in full marriage mode. It was to Colin's great surprise, then, to find his father at his favorite spot in all the kingdom. Standing on a small pier overlooking Long Pond.

"A little late for fishing, your Grace?"

The duke turned to him, a contented smile on his face. Colin searched for any sign of distress, and though he saw none, he could not help but notice a certain weariness in his father's features. Had he suffered another fit? Or, Colin thought, was he worried about the fate of his beloved Long Pond if Colin didn't marry?

"Just listening to them jump," his father replied, his voice low as to not disturb his beloved calm. "My boy, I have been your father for the past twenty-eight years. You may save the formalities for when the guests are about."

Colin looked out over the still water reflecting the stars in the near cloudless sky.

"It's a good thing it's dark. If Mother sees you out in that hat, she might have a few creative names for you," Colin said, looking at his father's straw hat, which had seen far better days. And though he could easily afford to replace it a thousand times over, he rather insisted on keeping it. For luck.

"That is why I pay Campbell an excellent sum to look after it," he replied, speaking of his gamekeeper. "I never fail to catch something when I'm wearing it."

"Perhaps I should borrow it, then," Colin replied. "I am having no luck at all finding an assistant."

His father let out a low laugh then shook his head. "There will be a throng of what I am certain will be very lovely ladies descending on this estate, and that is your concern?"

"Finding someone to marry should be easy enough. And since I assume you and Mother will be invested in the choice, you will have your favorites. I will simply pick from among them."

His father grew strangely serious then.

"No, my boy," his father said. He took in a breath, as if he was about to say more, when his attention was drawn away by the sound of a fish jumping in the water.

"No? Are you not invested in an heir?"

"Of course we are invested. I have been invested since you were born. And since that monster came after you, we are more invested than ever."

There were too many days when Colin wished he'd never spoken of that ill-fated January night with his parents. The look on their faces when he told them of it—which he had carefully edited to save them the worst of it—was something he would never forget. He'd been their only surviving child of five, and it reminded him that despite their occasionally suffocating manner and hovering, that he was dear to them. Amongst his acquaintances, he might have been singular in his relationship to his family, and he cherished it.

"That is past now," Colin said. "Time to consider the future. You will be pleased to know I have already spoken to Mother about a token for my future fiancé. I sent it off to be set in a pendant. It should be ready the night of the ball." He'd found the gem, a moonstone with a remarkable star illuminating the center, over a decade ago. Though he was never one for trinkets, Colin had found himself uncommonly drawn to the piece. He'd kept it with him for years, a symbol of his love of the stars. In a fortnight, he would give the stone to the woman who'd become his wife.

He pulled his spectacles off, and after breathing on each lens, gently wiped the glass clean with a handkerchief.

"I am glad to hear it. But choose wisely, Colin," his father said. "Because your mother and I are invested in something else, as well."

His father's statement made Colin pause. What else was there?

"Your happiness," his father concluded, answering Colin's unspoken question.

Colin put his spectacles back on, hooking the frames behind his ears. For his eyes, the world became clearer. The rest of him, however, was anything but. Peers did not marry for happiness. They married for what would most politely be called business reasons. That his own parents had found happiness with each other was nothing short of miraculous. But his own engagement, made while he was but an infant, was like any other joining of his class. That he'd fallen in love with Amelia had been pure coincidence. And definitely not mutual.

"I don't understand," Colin said, attempting to brush off his surprise at his father's proclamation. "What about connections and blood and all that?"

"All of the ladies attending will of course have sterling connections and be from excellent families. But we will stay out of it," his father replied. He shook his head. "We have watched you retreat into yourself. That is our fault. Your mother and I have discussed it, and this time the choice is up to you. Do you have any ideas of who might interest you?"

Colin was stunned. He had a very small list of attributes to consider—primarily, he supposed, someone who would be perfectly indifferent to him. "In truth, I have not given it too much thought."

His father shrugged his shoulders. "Start with a face you might find appealing. It is not where you should end of course, but find someone who is pleasing to you. There may be a spark when you meet them. Someone on whose neck you might like to see that jewel of yours."

A spark? In the time since Amelia had broken the engagement, he could recall no such woman who'd created any reaction he could even remotely call a spark. Indeed, the only female who'd manage to linger in his memory at all was Miss Boxford, and Colin owed that to the fact she'd commented on his poor eyesight. It had nothing at all do with the lushness of her curves or the gentle pink flush in her cheeks when she smiled.

"Perhaps," he said at last. "Perhaps I should borrow your hat. It might bring me luck."

"Or the wrath of your mother, and neither of us want that," his father said on a low chuckle. "But do consider it, Colin. Many of the ladies coming are those you've met before. Surely amongst them you will find one that will provide you with companionship and this estate with an heir. Your mother and I are not getting any younger. And that damned Mumford seems to have a gift for making heirs. I would hate to see him install one of them here. They'd probably drain the lake, kick off the tenants, and fill the place with sheep."

Colin's gaze shot to his father, and for a moment, he worried that the duke might be having another attack. Instead, there was just a loving smile.

The two men sat in companionable silence when a shimmer of lights moved in the distance. Colin straightened, pushed his spectacles further up his nose, and peered into the darkness. It was impossible to make out anything in detail, except for the suggestion of lamps moving slowly along the landscape.

"Do you see that?" Colin asked, pointing at the mysterious lights, which were definitely earth bound. "Please do not tell me that is the early arrival of guests."

"I doubt that," his father said, peering toward where Colin pointed. "I shall ask Mr. Campbell to investigate. 'Tis probably a moving caravan of Travelers. Nothing to concern ourselves with."

Colin watched them for a time, his thoughts settling somehow on Miss Boxford, studying her palm, and her story about the Romani woman who'd supposedly read her entire life in her hands. Silly notion. Perhaps he should find another Traveler willing to read his palm and save him the taxing business of having to talk and dine and dance his way to a bride.

How would he choose? By the cut of a collar? The quality of the smile? Amelia had always been a picture of elegance and demure manners. Whatever qualities she'd had, he supposed, could be found elsewhere. And, it hardly mattered when he did find them. He would not suffer that loss, that humiliation, and that frantic longing ever again.

He'd given his heart once. And he didn't want it back.

CHAPTER 4

*E*velyn Pembroke shuffled in her wheeled chair, pulling herself to the window in her favorite parlor, looking for signs of her daughter in law. It was not the easiest of tasks when only one leg worked properly, but circumstances required the effort. Normally Miss Boxford was here with her in the mornings, but she'd asked permission to go off into town to run some errands.

Breakfast had been an unusually quiet affair. Instead of lively conversation, Miss Boxford had passed the time stirring her porridge with unusual focus. Certainly she smiled and spoke when spoken to, and was as helpful as any other moment, but there was something in her manner that was restrained.

It had been all Evelyn's fault, of course. Perhaps she should have kept her suspicions to herself. But she had been correct. Miss Boxford's affections for Edmund still lingered. Even if the girl was truly happy for Gwyneth and Edmund, which Evelyn believed to be the case, being forced to live in close quarters with them would be trying at best. At a distance, surrounded by new people, those affections might have the chance to wither and die and leave room for new opportunities to blossom. If she stayed at Silver Cross, the constant reminder of unrequited affection she would face daily would ruin her. Katherine Boxford needed her own life before she was consumed by regret and misspent hope.

Not that Evelyn wanted the girl to leave. Katherine, along with her parents, brought more than help. They brought companionship. Perhaps even friendship. Indeed, her parents, Harry and Sara, were close in age to Evelyn, and they, along with the addition of Gwyneth's father, who'd come to visit, brought a much loved element of maturity and camaraderie to Kennington Grove. And, thanks to the Boxfords, she thrived as much as could be said for a woman of seven and forty who'd been written off as a cripple by so much of society. Her condition offered her ample opportunity to watch, to listen, and, just maybe, cook up a bit of an intrigue.

Evelyn scanned the front park of her beloved Kennington Cross, with its tidy gardens. No sign of Miss Boxford. She did not expect the girl back until at least one o'clock. Along with whatever business she had for herself—and she dearly hoped it involved a visit to Lord Ellsworth's man of business—she'd given the girl a longer than normal list of errands. Evelyn needed the time.

The door creaked open, and there, her face lit up with the glow of pregnancy and no doubt the heat of midday, was Lady Gwyneth.

"I came as soon as I got your note. I hope all is well." Gwyneth scanned the room. "Where is Kitty?"

"Miss Boxford went out to run some errands in Hilsburn," Evelyn replied, pulling herself away from the window.

"Errands?" Gwyneth said as she walked toward Evelyn, her face falling in a concerned frown.

"What is it, my dear?" Evelyn asked, taken slightly aback by concern that stretched across her daughter in law's face. "Is something the matter?"

Gwyneth's smile brightened, as if caught, but the tightness on her expression told Evelyn that something was amiss.

"Shall I ring for some tea?" Gwyneth asked.

Evelyn nodded, unsatisfied by Gwyneth's deflection. She waited for the girl to ring the bell.

"Something troubles you," Evelyn asked again, her tone a little firmer this time.

"It is probably nothing," Gwyneth replied, taking a seat on a nearby bench, her gaze straying out the window. "But I can't help but wonder if Kitty's gone ahead with her plan."

It was Evelyn's turn to be surprised. "What plan?"

"She has scheme to post an advertisement for a husband. She made herself a list—I saw it only yesterday. I had thought it a bit of a joke, but now…" She shook her head. "I am not so certain."

List? Evelyn shifted in her chair. "Tell me."

"Kitty is quite convinced she is not going to find a husband on her own. She lost a special piece of jewelry when she was a girl, and cannot be persuaded that it was merely a cruel coincidence that her luck has been bad ever since." Gwyneth proceeded to tell the tale as she knew it.

"That is a remarkable bit of business," Evelyn agreed, turning over the details in her mind. Dear heavens. Her remarks about Edmund—and the move of the Kennington Grove household to Silver Cross—must have only reinforced the idea that luck was not in Miss Boxford's favor.

"You don't believe it, do you?" Gwyneth asked.

"I do not disbelieve it," she replied, idly drumming her fingers on the arm of her chair. "Belief is its own sort of magic, my dear. My nephew believed he was a Beast for far too long. Once a belief settles on a person, it can difficult to refute, regardless of any evidence to show it to be untrue." Evelyn smiled. "To dislodge it requires even stronger magic."

"Magic?" Gwyneth asked. "A wish isn't enough, my lady."

"Of course. Sometimes the magic needs help to move it along. And that is what we will do." She looked to Gwyneth, and though they were alone, lowered her voice in a conspiratorial whisper. "That is, if you are up for the notion of an intrigue."

Gwyneth brightened immediately. "I long for one. Especially a happy one. If there is anyone who deserves happiness, it is Kitty."

"Then we are of the same mind. She uses that pretty smile of her to cover a thousand petty hurts and unmet needs. And I find I cannot bear it any longer." Evelyn paused, so unexpectedly taken aback by a hit of emotion that she took a moment to swallow. "How well do you know the Boxfords, my dear?"

Gwyneth shrugged. "Perhaps not quite as well as I should. I had not seen them for nearly a decade. They are a lovely pair and always seemed very devoted to each other and to Kitty. And they were ever so good to me. Mr. Boxford has family in Essex, I believe. Kitty speaks of having family there. Edmund knows them better, of course, having lived with them for some time."

"I have had the good fortune to get to know the Boxfords myself. Indeed, I was speaking at length with Sara about my concerns. And I learned something very interesting just yesterday." Very interesting.

"About Kitty?"

"About Sara. Tell me Gwyneth, have you ever listened to Mrs. Boxford speak?"

"I have, but I don't—"

"What did you notice about it?"

Gwyneth, raised in the ballrooms and parlors of society, paused, her brow furrowed. Evelyn watched the girl clearly searching her memory.

"Her speech is quite refined," she replied after a time, clearly taken aback by her deduction. "And her manners..."

"Did you know that she was born a gentlewoman?"

Gwyneth's countenance answered for her. Evelyn couldn't help but smile—being confined meant she often was the last to know about intrigues. But this time...she was the first.

"Did she tell you this?" her daughter in law asked.

"When I pointed out to her that I had never encountered a servant —not even a ladies' maid—with such refined behavior, she relented at last."

"Who?"

"She would not say—she is very discreet. And very proud, as it turns out. She told me she ran off with Harry Boxford quite against her family's wishes. She was utterly disowned and disinherited, and does not regret a moment of her life." Evelyn could not help but admire Sara Boxford's circumstances. Perhaps if she had been so bold, she wouldn't have found herself in her current situation—the crippled widow of a thoroughly horrid man who'd ruined one son completely and nearly destroyed the future of her second. Though having Edmund and Gwyneth in her life had perhaps made it worth the pain in the end, there were moments when she could not help but wonder what her life would have been like if she'd chosen differently. For love. "But she would not reveal her parentage."

"Could you get no information from her—not even a clue? Her speech is more refined than her husband's. In the beginning I paid it no attention, and thought she might have had work as a lady's maid at one time. Perhaps it is from the south of the country. I will listen more carefully next time we are together." Gwyneth thought hard. "Kitty does not know."

"No. They have never told her."

"The brooch!" Gwyneth said, nearly hopping from her seat. Her eyes lit up as she spoke. "Kitty dismissed the idea that the gems were real, but now I am not at all certain they weren't." Gwyneth paused, sipping on her lemonade. "If her mother was from a family of means, it might have been one of a few pieces she'd taken away with her. If it was substantial enough, it might have provided a clue as to her parentage."

Evelyn smiled, thoroughly pleased with her daughter in law. "I believe we have an acquaintance to the north who might be able to provide us some assistance in this regard."

"Sir Richard Hamilton?" Gwyneth's mouth fell into a small frown as she puzzled over Evelyn's question. Sir Richard worked for the Home Office, had been Edmund's employer for a time, and was well connected to intelligence circles both at home and on the continent. He was also Gwyneth's godfather, and very protective of her. "Do you think he would trouble himself with something like this?"

"I think for you and Edmund, he would. Indeed, he might provide us some valuable insights. Remember he brought the Boxfords to Westemere once he learned of their eviction from Gorland Park. I wouldn't be surprised if the man knew exactly who Sara Boxford's family is."

Gwyneth toyed with the small pendant around her neck—a gift, in fact, from Sir Richard himself. While it was clear she was considering Evelyn's suggestion, something troubled her.

"But do you think it wise to tiptoe around the Boxfords like this? Perhaps there are excellent reasons why Mrs. Boxford, if she was the daughter of gentry, decided to cut ties with them."

"We shall find out, and we have no time to lose. We do not wish Katherine to do anything rash, do we?" Evelyn chided herself for her miscalculation. If Miss Boxford posted that list of hers before they had a chance to find out more—which was entirely possible now given the impending date of the move, any possibility of making a good match for her might be lost.

"Do you mean more rash than posting an advert for a husband?"

"Exactly to my point, my dear." She pulled herself forward and pointed in the direction of Stormount. "There is a grand party happening not two miles from here any day now. We are all invited. There is no reason at all why Kitty Boxford should not be able to have her opportunity. And if she is a gentlewoman's daughter, this can only help her prospects."

"Do you mean her for Lord Ellsworth?" Gwyneth replied. "As delicious an idea as that may be, I'm not certain that, regardless of her mother's family, it would be good enough for the duke and duchess. And Colin is a lovely man, but a good match for Kitty? His temperament is far too constrained."

Evelyn paused, suddenly weary. Her leg ached, as it often did after a rain. Did she mean Kitty Boxford for the Marquess of Ellsworth? Aside from their vastly different circumstances, Evelyn could not imagine two more different souls. Kitty was exuberant, vital, and loved the outdoors. Ellsworth was a good man, certainly, but word had it that he was still hopelessly in love with his former fiancé. That would not do for Kitty. She needed someone who would heal her broken heart and love her for who she was.

"Of course not. But there will be at least twenty young bucks there, and one might do very well for her. Perhaps a nice young man meant for the church, perhaps. We should try, don't you think? Before she is forever put on the shelf? Or posts some ridiculous advert that throws her at the mercy of some ne'er do well who senses a kind heart and a desperate wish?"

Gwyneth rose out of her chair, and gripped Evelyn's hands. "Very well. We shall send word to Sir Richard at once."

"Excellent. You may advise Edmund but no one else. I would like to be able to lend a little aid to a creature in need, but I do fear Miss Boxford would not wish this sort of help. And I think I fancy a bit of an intrigue on my own."

"Well then," Gwyneth said, walking to a small desk and pulling out a small sheet of paper, "let's begin."

CHAPTER 5

*K*itty hurried along the road leading her to the nearby village of Hilsburn, dodging the shrinking puddles and muddy patches left from rain that had fallen for much of the night. The air was sweet and pleasant as the sun rose toward midday, the combination of water and sunshine adding lushness to the landscape. Bright yellow marigolds skirted the meandering wooded path she'd taken to hasten her journey. The exercise and fresh air was just the thing to revive her after a restless night.

Mrs. Pembroke knew. Knew about her unresolved longing for a man she was never meant to have. Knew how her heart squeezed every time she saw Gwynnie and Edmund together. There was nothing malicious in her employer's remarks, but the mere acknowledgement was an unmasking like Kitty had not felt since she was a child, when she'd learned that to be invisible and compliant was safer for her and her family. The idea that she'd somehow exposed herself in this way was nothing short of devastating. Though her employer had made no further mention of it, it had been so difficult for Kitty to look Mrs. Pembroke in the eye over breakfast. Pretending all was well was so much easier when no one else knew the truth.

Did her friends know her secret? She was sure the answer was no, at least for now. If either of them discovered her feelings for Edmund, it would be the end. The awkwardness of it would further separate her from her friends in a way that might well be irreparable. She couldn't allow that to happen. Her fingers gripped the edges of the folded letter in her hand. A letter she hoped might persuade Lord Ellsworth to take her on as his assistant.

Until the wee hours she had toiled, writing and rewriting her application, laying out in exacting detail why she was the right candidate for a position that she'd had no direct experience doing, but quite suddenly meant everything to her. If she could earn enough funds for a small dowry, as securing this position would promise, her advertisement would be a greater inducement to applicants. Once it was posted, she could find a suitable husband, and be resettled as soon as possible. Before anyone else was the wiser.

Except for Mrs. Pembroke.

When at last the letter was finished and as perfect as she could make it, she'd signed it *K. Boxford*. Not Katherine.

She'd spent what little remained of the night listening to the rain falling outside, and fretted over that signature. Was it a deception not to sign her entire name? Perhaps. But as the night wore on, giving way to first light, another morning signaled another day closer to moving day. She knew enough of the world to know that an overeager secretary might instinctively pull the letters from male applicants first, and she was not about to lose her opportunity because someone thought her incapable merely because of her sex. Someone who didn't know how much she needed this opportunity.

Even before the path merged with the main road to the village, the sound of bustling carriages intruded on the birdsong and the quiet rush of leaves lazily tossed about by the air. Indeed, as she approached, Hilsburn was humming with activity. Carriages laden with trunks trundled by, pushing Kitty further and further to the side to avoid the muck churned up by all the comings and goings. She wore her second best frock and her very best bonnet in order to make a good impression, and had done a fine job of keeping her hem pristine.

"Move out of the way, you silly girl, before yer trampled."

The harsh bark of the driver shocked Kitty, and she dashed to one side as a tremendous carriage pulled into the square. The gilded post-chaise came to a gentle stop not five feet from her. Two footmen, in fantastically colorful livery, moved in almost synchronous motion as they hopped down, one opening the door.

An elegant woman, perhaps nearing fifty, stuck her head out the door, cast a keen eye across the village, and seemed to find her surroundings somewhat wanting. Her fading blond hair was crowned with the most elaborately decorated bonnet Kitty had ever laid eyes on. Kitty spied two younger girls sitting across from her, the eldest perhaps twenty. Both of them with pale, flawless skin. Neither of them smiled.

"You."

The woman's voice cut through the hustle of the square. Kitty thought it sounded quite like a goose in heat. She turned away, ready to continue on with her errands so she would make the deadline and be home in time for her afternoon tea with Mrs. Pembroke.

"Ahem," came the goose.

Kitty slowed.

"You gel," the goose called out, louder. "Turn around."

"You have to speak up, Mother. The girl could be deaf. Or simple."

Kitty's breath caught, and a rush of heat rose in her chest. Letting go of the indignation in a slow steady breath, she turned slowly on her heel, and dipped into a quick curtsey.

"My apologies, ma'am. I did not realize you were speaking to me."

"Well, who do you think I was speaking too, you silly girl?" the woman crowed, obviously incensed.

Kitty cast an eye around the street. There were any number of people around, many of them female, who might have been "you." None of them so silly as Kitty to answer the call of an entitled crone with the nose of a hawk and the personality of an angry badger.

"How may I be of assistance, ma'am?" Kitty asked, taking a few steps toward them and swallowing her pride along with her exasperation. She was eager to have the encounter over with, and the best way to do that was to push through it.

"Are we very far from Stormount?"

Kitty groaned. Of course. Lord Ellsworth's bride hunt must be nearing commencement, drawing ladies and fine carriages from near and far. Kitty considered the two young ladies, no doubt the daughters of the goose. They were both exceedingly well dressed and beautiful. Or they might have been, if not for the expressions on their faces.

"No ma'am. Stormount lays just beyond the town gate." Kitty pointed to an equally fine equipage, pulled by two chestnuts, turning down a road out of town. "If you follow this road, you will find yourself there very shortly."

"Mother!" Kitty heard one of the girls carp. "You promised me we would arrive first!"

"Do not worry, girls. We shall make an entrance."

As quickly the carriage door had opened, it closed again, so close Kitty could feel the rush of wind as it did so. The footmen resumed their posts, and the goose pounded a large walking stick on the roof of the post-chaise, sending it off in a flurry, wheels spinning in the mud. A flurry of dirt lifted into the air and landed with an unceremonious splash onto Kitty's frock.

Perfect.

Mud splattered up the front of her skirt. Not even her bodice was spared. The fabric of her dress, a light blue print, was dotted with ugly brown spots.

Of course it was. Blinking back tears of anger and frustration, she clenched her fists at her sides and fought the urge to say some very unladylike things under her breath.

So much for first impressions. Taking a moment to collect herself, she tucked the letter away in her pocket and started to pluck the larger pieces of mud from her clothes.

"May I be of assistance?"

A familiar male voice was paired with the black boots that had come into view in front of her. Unlike Kitty's footwear, his boots were miraculously free of even the smallest hint of dirt. Tilting her head upward, she came face to face—or rather, face to chest—with Lord Ellsworth.

My heavens, he was tall. Or more to the point, she was rather short.

She dipped into a quick curtsey, suddenly feeling a little more self-conscious. Why was it that this man always seemed to be present when she was at her very worst?

Her entire body seemed aware of his presence, though she supposed it was simply because he was so very tall and so close she could touch him. She clasped her hands in front of her.

"I am fine, if a little—besmirched. Thank you, my lord."

He looked her up and down, his expression one of restrained bemusement. After what felt to Kitty like an agonizing moment of silence, eager to make her appointment and application, already waylaid by the aristocracy enough for one morning, she smiled as a way of signaling her leave.

"I am certain you are quite busy," she replied.

"Indeed." He appeared quite unaware of her signal, and instead pulled a handkerchief out of his pocket. "You have a spot of mud...right here."

Kitty remained fixed to the ground as a terribly odd but utterly pleasurable sensation wound through her body. It began at her nose, where Lord Ellsworth held up his handkerchief and wiped what must have been a splatter of mud from her nose and cheek.

They stood awkwardly for a moment, before the bells from the church struck the hour. It broke whatever spell had befallen Kitty.

"Thank you," she said. "I should not take any more of your time."

"Of course," he replied. "I have my carriage if you wish to return home to change."

"That is very generous," Kitty replied. "But I would think it is more important that you return unsplattered." Kitty pointed to yet another carriage heading in the direction of Stormount. "Your guests are soon arriving."

Lord Ellsworth's mouth crinkled, as if he was suppressing a frown, and Kitty could not help but notice the little lines around his eyes as they narrowed, ever so slightly, before he replied.

"That they are," he said with all the enthusiasm of a man confirming the day of the week.

"You are not anticipating the occasion?" Kitty replied. "Not even a little?"

"I am anticipating its conclusion."

Kitty frowned. "If you are so disagreeable to the notion, why wouldn't you simply pick a name from amongst a list of candidates and save yourself, and them, the trouble?"

"I thought all women loved parties. I have yet to meet a female that does not."

"Perhaps it is because it is one of the rare times they can be out in company, so the opportunity is to be seized, regardless of how much one truly enjoys a crush," Kitty said. "Men, on the other hand, do not have such limitations upon them."

He tilted his head then, as if she'd said something rather curious.

"I had not considered that, Miss Boxford," he replied. "Do you enjoy balls and parties and such?"

Kitty blinked. For half a second she could not help but wonder if he was toying with her. He was to be a duke, for heaven's sake—why on earth would he require her opinion on the subject? Especially since she was never invited to such things. Which was fine, really. Better not to be noticed.

"A large room with many people would be, I admit, the most taxing," she replied after a moment. "But I suppose in a large crowd it is easy to be invisible if one chooses."

"Not for me."

His answer was not boastful. Indeed, there was a distinct hint of exasperation in it, because Kitty had the distinct feeling that if Lord Ellsworth could choose, he would be invisible. Though why, she could hardly imagine. He was a man of great status, and his looks were pleasing.

"The most arduous of occasions may seem less so if one is in pleasant company," she said, refusing to indulge him. "And the finest of picnics could be spoiled by dour, disagreeable people."

"And which am I?"

Another question, this one unnaturally beguiling. Lord Ellsworth wasn't disagreeable. Dour? Perhaps. Or maybe he was simply shy.

"I have not had the pleasure of knowing you well enough to say," she replied, deflecting the question. "But this week is I assume an opportunity to assess the suitability of a potential bride. Use it to your advantage. Consider any dances, for example. Merely look for the contented girls sitting down during the minuet. If she despises dancing, then you will be well suited."

His mouth twitched a little just then, and he cocked an eyebrow. "I didn't realize you were an authority on matchmaking, Miss Boxford," he replied.

Kitty wanted to throw her head back and laugh at the very thought. "I am most certainly not. 'Tis just a bit of logic."

He smiled then, which brightened his countenance considerably. It struck Kitty with the horrifying realization she could do nothing but watch him smile. Which was certainly not logical in the slightest.

The bell from a nearby tower starting ringing the noon hour, breaking through whatever enchantment had kept her from delivering her precious letter. If she missed this deadline, whatever meager chances she had at being the successful applicant would be lost forever.

She was tempted to shove the application into his hand directly, but uncertainty stopped her. What if he mistook her gesture for forwardness? Lord Ellsworth seemed like a man who put much stock into how things should be done, and Kitty wanted to make sure she demonstrated her ability to take direction by following the application requirements to the letter. She looked off in the direction of the clerk's office and curtsied. The time for smiles and pleasantries was over. Mr. Holland's office closed at noon, and she needed to provide her application. Unlike Lord Ellsworth, she had no time to spare. She had a dowry to earn.

"If you will excuse me, I must take my leave, my lord. I am afraid I am already late."

She raced down the road, her frock a complete and utter mess. But she had a date with opportunity.

COLIN FOUND HIMSELF TEMPORARILY MESMERIZED. As she ran along, Miss Boxford's bonnet loosened, sliding off her head and resting on her back. Freed from its containment, a halo of dark brown curls caught his eye. He was completely unable to account for the forces that had fixed his feet to this spot, but his gaze followed her until she disappeared from view. He was due at Mr. Holland's office precisely at noon, to gather and review the last batch of applications. He could only hope that he would finally be able to find a worthwhile assistant to help him with his observations.

Would it be as simple to find his match as Miss Boxford suggested? Have the orchestra play a tune and find the girl who quite deliberately disliked dancing? It was a simple enough deduction. Funny such logic would come from a woman. Women were creatures of passions, weren't they? Or, at least, Amelia certainly was. Rather than seeing what was by all standards a logical pairing, she had cast Colin aside for a man who was far from her equal in social status or countenance.

And if she'd stayed, he would have married her, their child would have been baptized at St. Paul's, Colin wouldn't have a sprained wrist, and he wouldn't have to be dodging puddles on the way to see his man of business looking for an assistant. He definitely would not have spent the last few minutes somehow entranced by a conversation with Miss Boxford. He stuck his hand in his pocket, the soft linen of his handkerchief in his fingers. The one he'd used to wipe the mud from her cheek.

The sound of the last bell marking the hour roused him from his wool gathering. He'd been extremely distracted of late. Truth be told, he'd been distracted since that awful day at Barronsfield this past January, when he'd received the parcel of letters from Amelia—letters he'd sent her after she'd left him. They had catalogued her beauty and refinements, the reasons why she should return to him and all the ways he would ensure her happiness. That pretty little parcel of unopened letters tied in a white ribbon had shut the door—a door that indeed had been shut long before, despite Colin's ridiculous hope that somehow she would throw everything off and come back to him.

He would never make a fool of himself over love again.

Colin soon arrived at the office of Mr. Holland, a local solicitor who handled much of Colin's business affairs. He opened the door, and who stood across the desk from Mr. Holland's clerk but Miss Boxford. The pink in her cheeks, along with the furrows across her brow betrayed her irritation despite the tight smile on her face.

"I am afraid that this round of the competition is closed," the clerk said.

"But it is only two minutes past the hour."

"His Lordship's instructions were quite clear. Noon was the end of the competition. Punctuality is highly regarded by his lordship."

"It was his lordship that kept me from being punctual!"

Colin could not help but smile. No wonder she was so eager to get on her way. But why was she here?

He cleared his throat and stepped in the room. The clerk shot to his feet, and Miss Boxford turned to him as well.

"Is there a problem?"

"Not at all your lordship," the clerk said, clearing his throat. "I was merely explaining that the competition for the role of observatory assistant is now closed."

"My lord, 'tis but two minutes."

Colin saw the letter in her hand, the smooth paper crinkling ever so slightly where she gripped it.

"The observatory assistant position is not suitable for young women," Colin replied.

Her eyes widened slightly, she opened her mouth, and Colin watched as the pink in her cheeks deepened to red. Was she offended by his proclamation? Though why on earth she would be, he could hardly imagine. Positions like these were not meant for women. Of course, Miss Boxford had been raised in a very untraditional way, if she had seen to the rearing of bitches at her father's side.

"With respect, your lordship, I fail to see how note taking is a particularly masculine vocation," she said. "The task involves sitting still and listening, which is of course what women are expected to do."

He stilled, quite unprepared for her argument.

Colin shook off his surprise. He'd taken part in countless numbers of scientific debates over the years in his London clubs, or over dinners at the Royal Society. Certainly he could trade barbs with a gamekeeper's daughter.

"And how equipped are you to sit and listen, Miss Boxford? Given our very short acquaintance I have seen you do very little sitting. Indeed, you are always in motion."

Her lashes fluttered slightly at his verbal riposte, and for a moment he'd wondered if he'd said too much. That is, until she recovered.

"I am a servant, my lord. Servants do not sit unless we are bidden to do so." Her posture stiffened with something akin to indignation. "We are too busy attending to the whims of our employers who do nothing but speak all day long. And to do that…we must listen."

She brightened, a rather smug smile on her face. It made him want to rise to her challenge. And she was…challenging him. It was fascinating and provocative.

"The females of my general acquaintance are hardly quiet little mice, Miss Boxford." Indeed, his mother's voice was by far the most commonly heard throughout Stormount.

"You confound being silent with being attentive," she replied. "But women, regardless of rank, do what is expected of them. And it is expected that they are quiet when asked, and heed the orders of the men in their life. Therefore, we are back to my original argument."

"And…back to mine. Propriety would not allow a lady to sit with me for several hours each night, unchaperoned. Regardless of the qualities required by the position, the very nature of the position excludes them." He looked at her anew. "Are you applying for the position, Miss Boxford?"

"I already have a position," she replied, then nodded to no one in particular, then held out the letter. "I am sending this on behalf of—of my cousin."

Colin accepted the letter, unsealing it. The missive was well written and tidy. The writer had extensive experience cataloging horticultural pursuits, which, while not in the sphere of astronomy, were still of a scientific nature. At the bottom it was signed, K. Boxford.

Colin read the letter twice, casting the occasional glance at Miss Boxford, who was equally fixated on watching him, but otherwise betrayed no emotion.

"K. Boxford?"

She smiled tightly. "Kenneth. My cousin. I mentioned the competition to him after I learned of it. He leaves nearby, in Aylesford. He is always mucking about with seeds and plants which I have used in my garden to great effect. I thought he would be an excellent candidate, so I encouraged him to apply."

"I see. And why did he not send the post directly here?"

"I—we were together when he wrote it, and since I always have errands for Mrs. Pembroke in the village, I promised I would deliver it for him."

"And you were late."

Her shoulders sagged and it was clear she was not a little frustrated by him, which amused him. The only animated expression he normally received from women were prim smiles, nods and stares. If he danced on the moon, or launched into a lecture on refracting lenses, the interaction was always the same. Miss Boxford seemed unable to be prim in any measure.

"Only because you kept me from being on time, my lord," Miss Boxford replied. "Which I realize is something of an excuse, but I believe, as you were witness to it, it's an acceptable one."

Her eyes flashed then, and yet again Colin found himself uncommonly entranced. She was standing up to him, challenging him, this strumpet with the whiskey eyes and her skirts dotted with mud.

The bell on the front door tinkled, intruding on Colin's thoughts.

"Excuse me."

The voice was soft, low, and feminine, and drove all thoughts of observatories, balls, and Miss Boxford from his mind. He straightened, and turned to it.

Colin's heart froze in his chest. Impossible.

"Oh Lord Ellsworth, my apologies. I should have realized you would have been engaged at the moment."

Colin opened his mouth, but it took him a moment to find his voice. He was so very tempted to adjust his spectacles. He remained speechless for a moment. A moment that it took for him to realize this vision in front of him was not Lady Amelia. And yet…

"I am not engaged, at present." He handed the letter to the clerk.

"Package this one up with the others, and send it to my office," he said over his shoulder, then brushed past Miss Boxford and bowed. "I do not believe I have had the pleasure of your acquaintance?"

The lady curtsied.

"Lady Mariah Stapleton, my lord. My father is the Earl of Bedford. I have traveled here with my sister and my mother. They are waiting for me now, in a carriage just outside."

Colin regarded her very carefully. The resemblance between Lady Mariah and Amelia was striking. Not perfect, of course. But there was so much about Lady Mariah that felt familiar. Was it the way she stood? Or the polite, pensive smile on her lips? Or her favored colors, which were similar to ones Amelia favored?

"I know it is most untraditional, but I saw you enter, and I was compelled to come and thank you personally for the invitation to Stormount. Our family is honored by the attentions of the Duke and Duchess of Weymouth."

She paused, then held out her long, elegant, gloved hand. Colin took it and kissed it gently.

"Not at all", he replied, releasing her. "Indeed, the person who deserves your gratitude is my mother. But I am pleased at your gesture." He could not help but cast a glance sideways at Miss Boxford who was standing to one side, uncharacteristically quiet as a mouse, her mouth crinkled in what he was certain was a stifled grimace. He returned to Lady Mariah, whose bewitching blue eyes were fixed on him, her smile unwavering. Though the color of her hair was not the exact shade of yellow as Amelia's, she wore it in a very similar fashion. Everything about her was elegant, graceful.

"Thank you, my lord." She curtsied again. "Well, I shall take my leave. I am most eager to see the storied Stormount Hall."

"I was returning myself," Colin said.

"If it pleases your lordship, you are most welcome to ride with us. Our humble carriage has more than enough room."

A curious sound erupted—like air escaping from a cracked pipe. Colin cocked his head sideways, only to see Miss Boxford, her brown eyes wide, her hand up to her mouth. Slowly she lowered her hand, her countenance serious as she made a display of clearing her throat.

"Apologies," she said as she regained her composure. "I must have a little something caught in my throat."

He regarded her another moment before turning back to Lady Mariah. It suddenly seemed like a rather sound idea to be out of Miss Boxford's presence. The girl was entirely too distracting. Which was remarkable, given she was everything Amelia was not.

"I thank you for the generous offer, Lady Mariah," he replied. "But I come to town on my own horse. However, I shall ride back behind you. My business here is concluded. But before I go, perhaps you can introduce me to your family."

The girl's face barely moved from its placid demeanor. "I am honored, my lord."

"Mr. Holland, have you gathered all the applications?"

"Indeed, there is only one."

Colin balked. "One? Are you quite certain?"

"Quite, my lord."

"Even though you raised the salary?"

"I am afraid so," he replied. "Perhaps you have exhausted the local supply of potential assistants."

Colin pulled his lips together in a tight line. "Very well."

"It did come in after the deadline."

"Which was, I believe, my doing." He looked over at Miss Boxford, her hands clasped in front of her. "I will review this thoroughly today. And if your cousin is the correct candidate, how shall I reach him?"

"I am expecting him to visit on the morrow, my lord," she replied. "If you send it addressed to him care of me at Kennington Grove, I will ensure he receives it."

Colin methodically folded the letter and tucked it into his pocket. If Miss Boxford's cousin was not suitable, he would have to look even further afield, and Colin found himself becoming impatient with the idea.

"Excellent. Now if you will excuse me." He turned toward the door where Lady Mariah was standing most expectantly, waiting for him to make his leave. He'd spent most of the morning avoiding the house, but, curiosity piqued, he found himself wanting to return.

Colin threw one last look over his shoulder, where Miss Boxford stood, their gazes meeting for but a second before she looked away.

One application for an assistant. And now Lady Mariah.

Perhaps this would not be so taxing after all.

CHAPTER 6

"Somethin' wrong, Miss Boxford?"

Kitty practically jumped out of her own skin at the sound of Charlie Pembroke's voice. The twelve year old adopted son of Gwyneth and Edmund stood in the door to her bedchamber.

"Sorry, miss," the boy replied. "I'd been knocking for some time. It sounded like you were a bit out of sorts."

Kitty's shoulders sagged slightly even as her fingers clutched the note she'd received from Mr. Holland's office yesterday afternoon, unable to determine if the fates were laughing at her or offering her a chance. Incredibly, she'd been offered the position.

She'd been panicking ever since.

"I am fine, Charlie, thank you," she said, folding up the note. "You startled me is all. Am I needed?"

"Papa had just come to take Mrs. Pembroke out for a walk, and bid me tell you that the afternoon was yours," he replied, clearly taking note of her. Little escaped Charlie Pembroke's notice. Edmund had rescued the boy from the London slums years ago, and while the boy flourished under the attentions of his adopted family, moments such as these reminded her of the skills he'd no doubt learned to survive his earliest years.

"Thank you, Charlie," she replied with a tight smile. In truth, she wasn't at all certain if the time to herself was welcome or not.

The boy doffed his hat, about to turn away and close the door when he stopped and turned back again.

"Are you certain nothin's wrong, Miss? 'Cause you look as white as a sheet in a lord's bed chamber."

Kitty sighed, unable to hold in her panic any longer, and plopped down on her bed.

"To be perfectly honest, Charlie, I'm not entirely certain."

She cast a glance once more at the letter in her hands, written in a tight script and addressed to the quite fictitious Mr. Kenneth Boxford care of Kennington Grove. Mr. Holland was pleased to announce that Mr. Boxford's application had drawn the interest of Lord Ellsworth, and an interview and discussion of terms would take place in Hilsburn this evening.

Kitty didn't know whether to laugh or cry at her own foolishness. What had absolutely felt like a logical scheme to expedite her removal from Silver Cross, at least in the moment, was, now that the opportunity had landed in her lap, absolute madness.

She'd gotten the job. Or more to the point, *Kenneth* Boxford had, and was now expected to meet with Mr. Holland this very night. Kenneth Boxford. Not Katherine. Not a girl.

The weight of her folly seemed to pull her lower and lower into the mattress. She had no cousin named Kenneth, nor could she conjure one. She'd imagined, somehow, that if she had actually secured the position, she would arrive at the observatory, present herself, and make Lord Ellsworth see reason. And of course, in the fairy tale she'd spun in her head, they would work together until his arm healed, he would pay her, and that would be that. She hadn't worked out the ending entirely. Maybe he would find her so helpful she could do the work permanently, and then perhaps she could find a room in Hilsburn and wouldn't have to move to Silver Cross at all. Maybe she could even find a space with a little garden she could tend. Not too far from her parents, not too far from Edmund and Gwynnie and Mrs. Pembroke, but a safe, comfortable distance for her heart.

She let go of a long, low breath and fought back tears brought on by frustration at her own foolishness. Why did she tell herself such a fantastic story? It made her doubt any of the good sense she would have otherwise claimed for herself.

This was bad luck...entirely of her own fanciful, impulsive making.

Now she was in the thick of it. Kenneth Boxford? Of course, Kitty had cousins, all on her father's side—several of them that she knew of —but not one of them was named Kenneth, and most of them lived at least three counties away. If it hadn't been for the unexpected arrival of Lady Mariah, hopelessly distracting Lord Ellsworth with her little sighs and brilliant blue eyes, she would have been tempted to blurt out that K. Boxford was, indeed, Kitty. She was a horrible liar. Her face got red in all the wrong places at even the thought of it.

The content of the application letter was absolutely the truth at least, and Kitty was quite confident she could do everything required of the position. She just happened to be capable of doing those things as a woman.

But, apparently, if she wanted the job, she could not present herself as one.

To Charlie she gave a much more abbreviated version of events, but at the end of it, the boy let out a low whistle and cocked a single eyebrow—a trait he no doubt learned from Edmund.

"That is a bit of a stew, Miss Boxford," he said, and Kitty took some curious comfort in the fact the boy appeared in equal parts amused and impressed with her. "Unless you plan on finding some breeches."

"I'd need more than that to pretend I'm a man, Charlie," Kitty replied.

The boy shrugged, apparently unmoved by her protest.

"Father pretended he wasn't a gentleman and no one knew," Charlie said, "and he's bloomin' quality. People usually see what they expect to see. As long as you don't act all prim and quiet and lookin' down at your feet. Do you want me to find you some clothes? I can probably find some in Papa's closet. He wouldn't mind for just one night."

Kitty looked down at the letter once more and back to Charlie. He was right…she'd known Edmund for years before she'd realized he was a gentleman. It would be dark. It would mean a bit of play acting at first.

"Right then," she said, at last. "I will try. But—Charlie—please keep this between us for now. If I make a complete fool of myself tonight I would rather the fewer people know of it, the better. I know where I can find some things to wear."

The boy nodded, and was about to leave when Kitty sprang from the bed and took his hand.

"Thank you, Charlie. I am very happy we are neighbors once more." She released his hand. "And remind me to buy you an extra sweet next time I go into Hilsburn."

The boy smiled widely, nodded as if slightly embarrassed with the attention, then left.

Kitty ran to her parent's little cottage, which was once a small stable attached to one wing of the small manor house. They were nowhere to be found, but already there were trunks and crates open, ready to accept the contents of the cottage for the move to Silver Cross. Among them were her mother's favorite crockery, and the watercolor that Gwynnie had painted for her father of Falls Lodge, where they had lived at Westemere.

Kitty went to their bedchamber and started searching through a cupboard where her father kept his clothes. Certainly there would be something she could borrow for a single night. Carefully she pulled out a shirt, frock coat, trousers, and an old pair of shoes that she could never even recall her father wearing. They looked a little large, but a bit of cloth in the toes would be just the thing.

She closed the door and had bundled up the fabric and boots in a small sac when a small box caught Kitty's eye. Nestled in a small trunk amongst coverlets and a linen tablecloth, the box's rich dark wood contrasted with the more delicate, soft fabrics beside it. Her heart leapt into her throat as recognition dawned. The family treasures. This was the box that once held the brooch. If her mother ever wondered about its whereabouts, she'd never mentioned it to Kitty.

Perhaps she'd thought it lost during the tumultuous eviction from Gorland Park, or the journey up to the Lakes.

Setting down her bundle, Kitty reached into the trunk, her fingers reaching for the box. It, and the contents, had come from a faraway land, her mother had said. It had only added to the magic of it all. Unable to help herself, she pulled the little box out of the trunk. The wood was smooth and dark, and the hinges made of brass. It was square, no longer than the length of her hand, and covered with intricate carvings of leaves, a bluebottle prominently displayed on the lid.

"There she is!"

Her father's voice called out from the threshold, his face bright and happy. Her mother stood alongside, carrying a bowl of fresh strawberries. Kitty set down the box, quickly nestling it back where she found it and went to meet them.

"Are those for me?" she asked playfully. "Or has Gwynnie talked you into making another one of your strawberry cakes?"

"She may have asked," her mother replied, kissing her daughter on the cheek, then walking toward their little kitchen. Kitty followed. "I'm surprised to see you here at this hour. Is Mrs. Pembroke napping before dinner?"

"No," she said. "Edmund took her for a walk, which freed me to come to see if you needed any help." Kitty winced at the lie.

"We are working our way through it," her mother replied. "Help will be sent for the heavy things. Edmund was here earlier, fussing over us."

"Fussing over my flies." Her father shuffled to a chair and sat down near next to Kitty, making no pretense about how pleased he was about Edmund's interest in his skill. "That boy is eager for me to set up a shop over there. And I'm keen to do it. The fishing is quite good. Almost as good as at Long Pond."

"Long Pond?"

"Aye. At Stormount. Mr. Campbell is the gamekeeper there. Fine sort," he said. "Someday you'll have to come with me, my daughter, to pay Mr. Campbell a visit and see if his fish are as good as Edmund's."

Kitty shook her head. Due to the injury that put his gamekeeping days largely behind him, Harry Boxford's interests had focused on angling. "Stormount is about to be inundated with ladies, Father. I don't know if there will be time for fishing."

"At least for carp," her mother laughed. "I feel almost sorry for poor Lord Ellsworth."

Kitty frowned. "There is hardly anything poor about the marquess, Mother."

"No," she replied. "I suppose not. But he is about to be chased like no other man in the kingdom, and that is not an envious position to be in."

"Well, I shall have to take your word for it," Kitty replied. Kitty couldn't imagine being chased, though it would be lovely, for a moment, to be pursued. It didn't matter, perhaps. In the end, she would have to do it for herself. "Are you pleased with your situation at Silver Cross?"

"Oh yes," Kitty's mother replied. "The rooms are lovely. I believe Lady Gwyneth is quite eager for you to choose one for yourself."

Kitty forced a smile. Gwynnie was so excited.

"Yes." Kitty shrugged. "Though, I have been thinking about that…"

"About what?"

Her eyes strayed to the bundle of clothes she'd nicked from her father's cupboard. "I just wonder if I am a burden to you. I am four and twenty, and have not a prospect in sight." Despite Gwynnie's best attempts at matchmaking. "I wonder sometimes if I have been a disappointment to you."

"Now where on earth would you get such a thought?" her father said, patting his brow with his handkerchief and stuffing it back in his pocket.

"Perhaps it has just been the change in our circumstances. It has me thinking, is all." She cast her eye over the boxes, and though they were in far better and happier circumstances now, for just a second Kitty could imagine herself back at Gorland Park in the chaos of that awful day when they'd been forced out.

Her mother, as if reading her mind, sat beside her. "You have been nothing but a gift to your father and me. A gift. Years ago a miserable woman told me that your father and I would be barren, and yet, here you are. Strong, beautiful. Any man would be lucky to have you. You just need to decide what you want."

An unwanted mix of envy and guilt settled uncomfortably in Kitty's stomach. She thought she knew what she wanted, once. But it wasn't for her. Edmund wasn't for her.

Kitty rose, gave her mother a firm hug, and her father too.

"I should be off and see to Mrs. Pembroke," she replied, scooping up her bundle and heading for the door.

"What is that?" her father asked, motioning to the bundle.

"I found some of your clothes that could use some mending before they are packed away," she said.

"You don't need to do that," her mother said, frowning.

"No, but I want to," she replied, feeling like the worst daughter in the world. "'Tis only a few shirts."

After Mrs. Pembroke's early supper, Kitty feigned ill and tore away to her room to look over the clothes she'd carefully laid out. After wrapping her chest, which was more uncomfortable than the tightest of corsets, she pulled on her father's shirt and a pair of trousers, which felt peculiar to say the least. The coat was a bit oversized, and along with the shirt and waistcoat, skirted her hips. Her curls had been tamed with a thick layer of pomade, brushed with a thick boar bristle brush and pulled into an artful queue. The hairstyle was somewhat out of date, but effective enough.

Kitty turned around, looked in the mirror, and let out a long sigh. At best, she looked like a very lumpy boy. She could not imagine Charlie would be the least impressed with her efforts.

"How does this ever work in stories?" Kitty asked aloud, unsure whether to throw her head back in laughter or bury her face in her hands and cry. Maybe all those characters in Shakespeare or in folk tales had remarkably bad eyesight, Kitty decided. William Shake-speare had a far better imagination than she.

It would be dark, she told herself. And often people only see what they wished to see. Hopefully Mr. Holland would wish to see an eager boy who knew the Great Bear from Perseus, the phases of the moon, and something about notation. *Don't be quiet. Don't be prim. Don't look at your feet.*

Gwynnie pressed her lips together and pulled a hat with a large brim over her head and looked straight ahead, a bemusing bit of irony pulling her lips into a wry smile. This was the longest she had ever spent preparing for an evening with a gentleman.

In trousers and a frock coat.

Hardly romantic.

CHAPTER 7

olin sat in his carriage as it rumbled along toward Hilsburn, idly watching the sun's descent below the horizon. A swath of orange and purple stretched across the sky, save for a heavy blanket of cloud encroaching from south. He'd left the festivities at Stormount behind him and was now traveling toward Hilsburn to interview the lone suitable candidate for position of observatory assistant. He'd warned his parents of the appointment, and perhaps because Colin had spent the last two days doing his damnedest to be engaging, which did not come naturally to him, the duke and duchess did not complain too much about his absence at the card tables this evening.

He pushed his spectacles up with his fingers, rubbed his eyes a moment, and let out a yawn. The past two days had been positively exhausting. Smiling, nodding, trying to comment in novel ways on the same rotating subjects of weather, changing fashions, and race horses. He was never good at that type of polite conversation so often the centerpiece of social occasions. That had always been Edmund's specialty.

And people were so eager to speak with him. To impress him. To ask his opinions on topics as diverse as the shade of pink on Lady

Charlotte's gown—more of a rose, or a salmon—(rose, for certain), what was his favorite dance (the minuet, he lied), to whether he preferred cold pork or mutton when dining al fresco (definitely mutton). Two days of inconsequential nothingness, with more to follow. Tomorrow, if the weather favored it, a grand picnic was planned on the west lawn of Stormount, where, he surmised, he would be treated to more of the same, merely out of doors. If this was what marriage held in store, he could only hope deafness found him.

His mother had indeed made certain every eligible female within five counties had been invited. He'd stopped counting at twenty-four. How he would ever choose from among them he could not fathom. Lady Mariah's impression on him was still strong, but lessened when he realized there were at least a half dozen ladies of fair coloring that had styled their fashion in a similar way. Eager to replace the woman who'd come before them all, it seemed.

The carriage made the last turn into the town. It had been Mr. Holland's intent to see to this meeting, but he'd been struck down by the most miserable of colds and offered to reschedule. Colin, excited by the opportunity to escape Stormount for few hours, and decidedly curious about meeting Miss Boxford's relation and his suitability for the position, decided to take his place and do the job himself. They were to meet at precisely quarter past ten at the local inn. Colin was not expecting greatness. He'd already interviewed, hired, and subsequently let go two other candidates since returning from London.

Colin had not been in his observatory for nearly a week. He missed the serenity of the night—just he, his telescope, and the night sky. They did not care if he was to be a duke. And when Amelia had thrown him over and run north, they had been there for him, asking nothing of him. They were constant, and possibly eternal.

The carriage came to a stop outside the Brookside Inn, ingeniously named over two centuries ago for the brook running alongside the establishment. The place was remarkably quiet, which suited Colin as well. He took a seat at his favorite table and pulled out his pocket watch. It was ten past ten. Before he'd put the piece away, a shadow crossed him. He looked up—not too far, he noted—to find a youngish man, little more than a lad, standing nearby. The boy was well enough dressed, though it looked to Colin as if his clothes didn't quite fit. He looked lumpy, if such a thing could be said. His face was obscured by a hat with a rather large brim. Colin could not help but notice he did not remove it.

"Lord Ellsworth?" the boy said in a low voice. "I—I had expected Mr. Holland."

"Mr. Holland was unable to attend."

The lad bowed, his manner stiff, which Colin dismissed as nerves. "Kenneth Boxford."

"Please, Mr. Boxford." He held out his hand and gestured to the seat opposite him.

The boy did so, nearly tripping over his own feet as he landed heavily in his seat, almost knocking the candle that lit the table. Colin straightened, immediately put on his guard.

"You will be working around sensitive—and expensive—equipment," Colin began. "Do you regularly have trouble with the placement of your feet?"

"I—borrowed the shoes, my lord," he replied. "They are a tad large. My own are being repaired. I assure you I am very careful."

Colin nodded, impressed by the lad's honesty on the matter. Indeed, he wondered how much of his attire had been borrowed. Not that it was of consequence. What mattered was if he could do the job.

"It was good of your cousin to post your application on your behalf," he said.

A nod was the only reply.

"Your application letter made no mention of any experience in an observatory," Colin continued. "But it did make mention of experience with record keeping and observations. I am most keen to understand how this could translate to astronomical work."

The lad grimaced then cleared his throat—which was the most unusual of sounds, Colin couldn't help but note—then pushed a small, well-worn journal across the table toward Colin.

"These are some of my own recordings," he said at last. "I hope you find my work to your standards."

Colin pursed his lips, then flipped open the book. It was page after page of entries. Dates. Weather conditions. Even moon phases. And it was almost entirely about…botany.

Colin pursed his lips, confusion furrowing his brow. Irritation rankled.

"Mr. Boxford," Colin said, trying to keep the impatience out of his voice, "in case the advertisement was not clear, the position requires you to be staring at the sky…not concerning yourself with what is at your feet. I am sorry, but Mr. Holland may have wasted your time."

Colin started to hand the book back to the lad, when the boy, to Colin's surprise, gently but rather insistently pushed it back in front of him.

"I know all of the main constellations. You may test me." He reached over and opened the notebook again, pointing out pages filled with little tables of dates, temperature, weather conditions. "These are not astronomical observations, but if you study my notes you will see that they are filled with detail, and quite orderly. I even keep an index by season, so I can easily find and compare notes from one year to the next. I would think that is the far greater skill for an assistant."

Colin pored over the pages, which contained the tidiest writing he'd ever seen. Neat columns. Clear notation. They may have even been more detailed than comparable work he'd done himself.

He skimmed a few more pages, and begrudgingly agreed. His last two attempts at finding an assistant yielded two young men who boasted of being able to name the stars and had a good grasp on Newtonian law, but were sloppy in work habits. Mr. Boxford clearly did not suffer the latter…and just perhaps Colin could teach him everything else that he'd need for the job at hand.

Colin closed the book, but kept it in front of him. "And besides the constellations, what else do you know about astronomy?"

The boy shook his head. "I've never looked through an eye piece. But I am willing to learn."

Colin nodded, his gaze going back and forth between the young man, and the pages in front of him. Colin did need an assistant, and young Mr. Boxford seemed to fit the bill, even if there was something a little strange about him. Locally the pickings were non-existent. Mr. Boxford, he guessed, from the awkward manner, smooth chin, and the lack of depth in his voice, was young. Barely fifteen at most, Colin surmised. But he clearly had the interest and inclination—traits absent in his former assistants, who were generally young apprentice clerks looking for a little extra coin.

Colin sat back, regarding the boy, who still had not removed his hat. His eyes fell to the boy's hands, which might have been boy's hands, except there was something about them that seemed soft. And his lips...perhaps a boy could have a mouth like that, but it didn't seem to fit.

Perhaps it was merely the strong familial resemblance he bore to Miss Boxford that made him deliberate on the boy's features so.

Or, perhaps, it was not a boy at all. Dark shadows be damned.

He stilled, suspicion welling inside him.

Colin gave himself a mental shake. It was a theory, after all. In school he had known a couple of boys whose features were some-what more delicate. Some of them had been horribly teased about it. And maybe this was such a boy in front of him, which may have been why Miss Boxford applied on his behalf. Maybe she was protecting him. It seemed like something she might do. He could hardly imagine her stealing out at night dressed as a lad to meet with Mr. Holland. She would have too easily given herself away with her feminine curves and her propensity to avert her gaze when spoken to.

It most certainly could not be Miss Boxford. Ladies didn't engage in this sort of nonsense.

But then, he reminded himself, Miss Boxford was not a lady.

This was all theory, and an absurd one. But theories demanded testing.

"Excellent," he said, abruptly, pushing the book back across the table. "We shall do a trial. Come to my observatory tomorrow night, an hour before sundown. I will show you the equipment, as you should become familiar with it."

The boy balked. "Before sundown?"

"Is there a problem with that?"

"No, my lord."

"If you do well, you could have a promising future."

Relief relaxed the boy's shoulders. "Thank you, my lord. If it not too untoward, may I ask the wage?"

The baldness of the question took Colin aback, and for a moment it made him doubt his assumption. Women never talked about earnings in such a direct manner.

"Of course," he said. "As advertised, a crown per week to start. But if you do well and are a quick study, I may see fit to raise it. Do we have an agreement?"

"We do, my lord."

Colin extended his hand across the table, to seal the agreement. For a moment the boy hesitated, then extended his hand. The grip was firm but…soft. Bloody hell.

He released his hand, and Colin sat back in his seat.

"Remove your hat, Mr. Boxford," Colin challenged. "It has just occurred to me I haven't gotten a proper look at your face."

Slowly, the hat came off, the shadow disappearing from the lad's face. Though the hair had been pulled back and matted with some curious wax, Colin could not help but notice the stray, insistent curls that no pomade could tame. Or the full lips that most certainly did not belong on any lad.

Colin didn't know whether to be amused, horrified or angry. He did know that he was sitting across from one Miss *Katherine* Boxford.

"So Mr. Boxford," he continued, careful to keep his countenance steady. If Miss Boxford intended to make a fool of him, he had no problem at all returning the favor. "Shall we drink a toast to our new arrangement?"

"I don't—"

"Come now, Mr. Boxford. We are men of the world, you and I." He summoned a bar wench and called for two servings of whiskey. He pushed one in front of the imposter. "Let us make a pact."

He pushed a cup in front of her, but she merely stared at it. Colin picked up his.

"I do trust that everything is in order with your application, Mr. Boxford. Misrepresentation of the truth is a hanging offence in Cheshire."

The girl's eyes widened slightly before she managed to compose herself. She cleared her throat in that ridiculous lower register she'd attempted. "I've heard no such thing, my lord."

"It's a little known fact, but alas, 'tis a fact nonetheless," Colin replied, finding that he was enjoying this sport immensely. "Come— we are wasting some of the best spirits to be found in these parts."

With that, Colin grabbed his glass, raised it and brought it to his lips, and tossed it down, ignoring the fire in his throat, before setting the cup down and gesturing to his companion to do the same.

Her fingers wrapped tentatively around the glass, and then her eyes narrowed, as if suddenly eager to meet his challenge. With an equal amount of bravado, she drank the spirits in a single gulp, and put the cup down.

In an instant, her eyes watered and began to sputter and cough. And those cheeks…even in the dim light they colored a delicious pink.

Colin leaned forward, his voice lowered. "Perhaps if you were a man, you might have the constitution for such pursuits."

She looked up at him then, her eyes wide, brightened from the tears brought on by her coughing fit.

"I am not—"

"Do not toy with me, *Miss* Boxford," he continued in a low voice.

Her eyes widened, brightened with tears from her coughing, which subsided after he produced a glass of beer for her to swallow to sooth her throat. She took a sip, then recovered, her shoulders slumped in defeat.

"When did you know?"

"I suspected something from almost the moment you sat down. You need to broaden your reading beyond sensational novels," Colin said. "Women cannot simply throw on a pair of trousers and fool another into believing they are male." He stiffened then, realizing her legs were practically exposed under the table beneath him.

"Shakespeare put women in disguises all the time," she protested. "In Twelfth Night, a woman managed to fool a duke and work for him as a man. For seven years, I might add."

Colin waved her argument aside. "Most fictional characters are fools. Duke Orsino included."

"They are not all fictional. Have you not heard of Hannah Snell? She dressed as a soldier and fooled the entire army." She sat back with a smug smile that was entirely female in character.

"Well, that woman either did a superior job of hiding herself," Colin snapped, "or else she did not have your shape, Miss Boxford."

"Shape?" She leaned forward, her whisper nearly a hiss. "What shape? Other than being a lump." She gestured to her oversized frock coat that practically hung from her shoulders.

What shape? Miss Boxford was blessed, if one had bothered to notice, with a lovely shape. Soft hips and a lush bosom, both of which were clumsily covered with some poor fellow's frock coat. And he had, in fact, noticed.

"Needless to say, there will be no agreement of employment," Colin continued.

Her face twisted then, bitterness marring her otherwise pleasant features.

"No. Of course there isn't." Miss Boxford grabbed her hat and placed it back on her head, then hastily stuffed her journal into a jacket pocket. "Heaven forbid a man could see beyond the blindness of his own sex. Good evening."

She turned on her heel and stalked out. Even through the heaviness of her costume, the feminine movement of her hips were unmistakable. Colin shook his head and turned way, his gaze falling on the empty whiskey glasses. What was she thinking, attempting to fool him with such a disguise? It was obvious to anyone who gave her a second look that she was female.

A female now walking at night.

Alone.

She couldn't be alone, could she? Surely to heaven she wasn't that daft to come unaccompanied. Of course, she'd been daft enough to apply for a position she clearly wasn't qualified for, then tried to disguise herself to get it.

Bloody hell.

THERE WAS BAD LUCK, Kitty thought, and then there was this. She'd congratulated herself on managing not to turn around and bolt the moment she saw Lord Ellsworth sitting at the table, waiting for her.

She should have bolted. Should have hid herself away, made herself invisible. And escaped to safety.

This night was turning into an absolute, unmitigated disaster. And it was all Lord Ellsworth's fault with all his silly notions about what she could or could not do. And she could do it. She'd seen the surprise and delight in his expression as he reviewed her work. But it was not enough. Once again, she was not enough.

The air, which had been merely misty when she'd arrived, had progressed to a heavy drizzle as she took her first few steps toward the arranged meeting place for her hired coach. Charlie had offered to drive the cart for her, and while Kitty had no illusions that the boy could both secure the cart and drive it well enough, he already knew far too much about her exploits this evening and she wasn't about to involve him further.

The dampness of the air made the woolen coat she wore even heavier on her shoulders. Her breasts were aching, confined in those bandages, and her father's shoes made walking awkward. She'd nearly tripped down the stairs of the inn, earning her the stares of passersby who probably just wrote her off as a young lad who'd had a pint or two too many. Now, all she wanted to do was go home, pull off these ridiculous clothes, wash that horrid wax out of her hair—which would probably take most of the evening—and go to bed. She should have known better than to get her hopes up.

Disappointment was her oldest and dearest companion, and it was keeping her in fine company tonight.

She shuffled along as best as her oversized shoes would allow, conscious that with every step the mist was more and more like rain. Just a little further along this street and around the corner to a small lane, where the cart she'd hired to take her back to Kennington Grove would be waiting.

Except it wasn't.

A flash of doubt and panic warred in her as she walked more purposefully now down the road, and then up again and around another corner, looking for the onepony cart and driver she'd paid in advance to wait for her. But it was nowhere to be found.

Her belly clenched and panic prickled at the back of her neck. It was over a mile to Kennington Grove. In the dark.

Oh Kitty, you silly, silly thing.

She pulled off her hat and looked up at the sky a moment, which mocked her further by opening in a steady rain. She wanted to cry. But she would give neither the heavens, Lord Ellsworth, nor anyone else the satisfaction.

"What in the blazes do you think you are doing?"

Lord Ellsworth's irritated voice broke through the darkness. He stood but a few feet in front of her, a lamp in his hands. It lit up his face, and cut through the rain with a warm glow.

"Shouldn't you be on the lookout for a bride?" Kitty asked, perfectly aware she was speaking to a peer in a most inappropriate way but entirely too angry to restrain herself. "Or are you having me hauled away to the gallows?"

He paused, clearly taken aback by her manner. "At the moment I am on the lookout for a wayward strumpet masquerading as a boy in the misguided attempt to see her home safely. Because that is what a gentleman does."

Kitty unceremoniously plopped her hat back on her head, and ignored the discomfort of the wet felt.

"What a gentleman does is not allow a woman to do work she is perfectly capable of," she said. "If you are not in need of my assistance when you so clearly need it, then understand when I do not feel the need to avail myself of yours. Good evening."

She brushed by him, walked right by that impervious look he wore, and tried to ignore the carriage that was patiently waiting nearby. Even in the dark, Kitty could see its quality. She picked up her pace, determined to continue on before her foul mood disappeared and the temptation to give in overtook her. She didn't want his help. She wanted the position.

She had not gone two steps, however, before he stood in front of her again. Curse the man and his long legs.

He gestured to the carriage driver, and the conveyance pulled alongside. "Get in, you silly girl."

Silly girl. Lord, but he was right. She'd been a silly girl. Silly to think she'd escape her fate. But, as she stood there, facing down this impossibly powerful man who she had, without a doubt, impressed with her work, a new rebellious thought struck her.

She would have been far more silly if she had not tried at all.

"Come, Miss Boxford," he said, his exasperation growing. "Mr. Allan is a loyal driver, and I do not wish to see him out in the wet any longer than he need be."

Kitty swallowed her pride, nodded, and allowed Lord Ellsworth to lead her to his carriage. He opened the door, held out his hand, and guided her inside. As she gripped his hands, a shock of warmth took her aback, and as she settled in her seat, the echo of his touch lingered.

She sat across from him, though not directly. She wasn't eager to see the look of condescension in his eyes. He knocked on the roof, and soon they were off. Her body was cradled by soft seats, traitorously enjoying the lush velvet and the smooth ride of the well-sprung carriage. Kitty would arrive home far less drenched, and far sooner—well before midnight, when the doors to Kennington Grove were locked for the night. The sooner she arrived, the sooner the sting of this miserable evening would be behind her.

"You don't have a cousin Kenneth."

Kitty closed her eyes a moment, prepared to swallow the bitter medicine of contrition. "No. At least, none that I know of. I made him up."

"Like your portfolio? Your qualifications?"

Kitty straightened, incensed. How dare he?

"The only qualifications that seem to matter to you, Lord Ellsworth, is my gender. Everything else on that list was true. I only lied because I didn't see it explicitly written as a requirement of the position, and when you announced it so suddenly in Mr. Holland's office, I…became creative."

"That is one word for it," he replied. He held his face steady, but if she didn't know better, Kitty was tempted to guess he was suppressing a smile.

"My note taking you saw. My father taught me the constellations, and one of the farmers near Westemere taught me about planting with moon phases, so I started tracking those as well when I became more serious about my garden. I spent years assisting my father with his record keeping, especially when it came to breeding, or organizing coveys for shoots. If all you need is a temporary assistant to record your observations until your arm heals, I am more than qualified."

He was still for some time. Though his gaze was on her, his mind was clearly somewhere else.

"I apologize for my…bullishness on this matter. I meant no disrespect to you," he said, his voice lower, softer. "But I cannot have a single young lady with me, alone, through the night. You must see it cannot be done, Miss Boxford."

Kitty willed herself not to be mollified by the softening of his manner. "Mr. William Herschel has had a female assistant through his entire career. And the talk is that Miss Caroline is a very accomplished astronomer in her own right."

"You do know Miss Herschel is William's sister, I assume."

"I do."

"Then I should not need to point out that you are not my sister. Which brings me back to my original point."

"With all due respect, Lord Ellsworth, if I were employed in your household, I could very well be cleaning your room or stoking your fires while you were in your bed, quite alone, and no one would say a word about it one way or the other."

"But you are not. You are in the employ of Mrs. Pembroke, and Lady Gwyneth's closest friend. That still makes you—"

"A nobody." Kitty turned away, swallowing deeply. It hurt to say, but in the end, it was true.

He reached out, and put a gloved hand on hers, his countenance earnest. "Not at all."

Her breath caught in her throat, and even in the dim light of the carriage, she found herself entranced by the shape of his mouth, and the expressiveness in his eyes. If she hadn't stopped herself, Kitty would have found herself reaching out to touch him.

He pulled away, as if he'd only realized himself what he'd done. "Are you unhappy at Kennington Grove? If you are, I can raise it with Edmund—"

She shook her head. If anyone had found out about this stunt, there would be some terrible explaining to do.

"I am quite satisfied there, thank you. I have my own reasons for attempting it, and none of them have to do with my situation at Kennington Grove. I merely thought I'd like to try something new, and earn a bit of coin on the side." She sighed, then smiled sheepishly. She was not about to share her reasons with Lord Ellsworth. She could barely think about them herself.

"That is one of the more fanciful tales I have heard of late."

"Excuse me?"

"No one would go to such extraordinary measures to earn extra money if the situation wasn't desperate."

Kitty swallowed. Maybe she should rethink being so close to Lord Ellsworth. "Not desperate. Just determined."

The carriage continued on, the two sitting in an uneasy silence in the dark.

"What is that ungodly smell?"

"Hair wax." Kitty grimaced. "I thought it would work to tame my hair. Make it more masculine."

"There is no substance on this planet that could accomplish that."

He was smiling at her. She could tell, even in the dark. It made her want to smile, too.

"It will take me half the night to wash it out. Serves me right for being so foolish." Kitty shook her head. "Every time something good happens, the heavens seem to intervene and take it away. Tonight was no different. It was folly to believe it could be otherwise."

"It wasn't the heavens, Miss Boxford," he replied. "You tried to hide who you are. There is no man alive with a working set of eyes that would have mistaken you for a man. Your sex betrays you."

Kitty laughed, unable to stay the bitterness she felt. "My sex doesn't betray me, your lordship. It is the male view of my sex that betrays me."

Tension hung in the air, tightening the space between them. Kitty found herself on the edge of her seat, chin tilted up toward Lord Ellsworth, who held her gaze steady with his green-gray eyes. She thought then, impossibly, that she was going to kiss him and that he, impossibly, wanted to kiss her too.

A strong rumble of thunder and a flash of lightening broke whatever spell had entranced them.

"You have some remarkably bold opinions, Miss Boxford," he said, settling back into his seat.

Bold? Kitty could never recall being accused of being bold. And she was, until tonight at least, so very good at hiding herself away. For whatever reason, her best attempts to do so failed when it came to Lord Ellsworth.

They rode along in silence as the approached the front park of Kennington Grove. It was still nearly a hundred yards before they'd reach the house, but it was close enough. Kitty knocked on the roof of the carriage and soon it came to a stop. The rain was still falling steadily, pattering on the roof.

"We have not yet arrived," Lord Ellsworth said, and though it was dark, she heard the question in his voice.

"This is a safe distance," she replied. "I do not wish to wake the house."

"I see." He raised his eyebrows and smiled in a most infuriating way. "At least I am secure in the knowledge that Mrs. Pembroke had enough good sense not to condone this charade of yours."

Mrs. Pembroke, Kitty thought bitterly, was far too aware of Kitty's charades. But not this one. She did not dignify his jab with a response. He was far too eager and able to see more about her than she wished to reveal, which gave her all the more reason to quit his presence as soon as possible. The front lamps were lit, allowing just enough light for her to see her way. She put her hand on the door latch when she felt his on her shoulder.

"Where do you think you are going? I must at least show you to the door."

Kitty paused, aware of the warring sensation of desire and annoyance at his touch.

"I am going home. While I appreciate your generosity, I think for the sake of the delicacy that you feel necessary to uphold with regards to your assistant position, it would be better for us both to part ways right here."

Not bothering to wait for an answer, she pushed open the door, took a step, her oversized shoes catching on each other, and started to fall forward onto the muddy park. At the last moment she regained her footing and what remained of her dignity, and fled toward the house.

She turned back to the carriage only once, when she was safely on the other side of the door. She left the door open just enough to see the carriage was still waiting, no doubt to ensure she'd arrived safely.

She closed the door quietly, heart pounding. Fumbling in the dark, she lit a lone taper. The bells chimed the hour.

Look aloft... The Romani woman's words played, unwelcome, in her head. Lofton Tower was out of her reach, wasn't it? Just like Kitty's fanciful notions of unlocking the meaning of those words and earning herself some coin in the process.

Kitty pulled off her father's shoes and started toward her bed chamber, trying to avoid every creak on the staircase and eager to put this entire disastrous, humiliating evening behind her. Unfortunately, with an entire fortnight of festivities at Stormount ahead, and Mrs.

Pembroke invited, the marquess would still be, if only from a distance, in her immediate future.

...and see what is unseen...

She'd been dressed in men's clothes. Her breasts had been bound. But it was Lord Ellsworth who'd seen through her disguise.

Who'd seen more of her, perhaps, than anyone ever had.

CHAPTER 8

$\mathcal{C}$olin stifled a yawn while he waited for his valet. It was past midday, but he'd had a wretched sleep after his shocking and somewhat provocative encounter with Miss Boxford.

Alone. In a public house. Dressed as a boy.

Good heavens.

He'd spent far too much of the evening replaying the encounter in his head. Her determination to have the position. Her legs, free from layers of petticoats and whatever else ladies had under their skirts, mere inches from his own. The flash of anger in her eyes when he doubted her abilities.

She had also wasted his time with her fanciful notions, cost him a good night's sleep, and had falsely given him hope he might have an assistant.

Enough of Miss Boxford. It was a wife he needed today.

Any fears that this afternoon's garden party would have to move indoors to save delicate hems and slippers from a squelching lawn proved unfounded. Sun fell over the garden, and the only water to be seen poured from the large cascading fountain that provided the centerpiece to the festivities. The grass, lush and green, provided a verdant backdrop to the sea of pale and white muslins gowns wore by the ladies waiting for Colin to arrive.

In moments he would be among the throng, wearing what charm and sociability he could muster. All in the service of finding an heir and alleviating his parents' worries about the security of the title in his family line. Not that he wished for the title anytime soon. Colin had been watching his father closely, looking for even smallest whisper of another episode since that fitful day in the study. This morning, his father had come down to breakfast well past his usual hour, and though the duke gave no hint that anything was amiss, Colin found himself on edge. Now that Stormount was full to the brim with guests, his father would have little time to rest and recover. And there was no warning when it might strike again. It may have been nothing but sheer luck that had kept the duke alive thus far.

How was it, Colin wondered, that a man such as he, so invested in logic and study, could owe so much to sheer luck? Lucky enough to survive to adulthood, the only one of his siblings to do so. To be born into such a privileged family. To survive the attempt on his life this past winter. Perhaps the need to observe and record the heavens had less to do with astronomy and more to do with his need to understand fate. More magic than celestial motion.

Miss Boxford had an uncommon belief in luck, didn't she? Except she was convinced that hers was entirely misfortune. Poor judgment, perhaps. His eyesight was not perfect, but he would have been blind not to notice that, regardless of trousers or oversized frock coats, Miss Boxford was undeniably female.

Colin's valet reappeared, having found a cloth that was a suitable match for his burgundy coat. Gingerly he untied the sling from around Colin's neck, then helped Colin into a new coat. A fresh shot of pain shot through his arm, reminding him that not only did he need a wife, he needed a bloody assistant for his observatory.

Carefully the valet managed to get his arms in without too much jarring of his wounded wrist, and as the jacket slipped over his shoulders, the tight seams pulled Colin's shoulders straight across his back. The sling was re-secured around his arm, and he was presentable at last. Taking a breath, he checked his watch and glanced out the window one last time, a flash of color catching his eye. There, amongst the pastel colors and white gowns was a young woman in a deep rose-colored dress. And it was most decidedly rose, and not some pale imitation of it. The style was a little dated compared to the others, but it suited the wearer very well indeed. She walked along, deep in conversation with Edmund and Gwyneth Pembroke. Colin fought the smile the sight of Miss Boxford brought to his lips.

He pushed his spectacles up onto his nose. She looked undeniably feminine today. He could not help but chuckle to himself at the impossible costume she'd worn last night. Perhaps there were women who could disguise themselves as a boy and pass muster, but Miss Boxford was not one of them. Strange that she was so desperate for the position of assistant that she'd gone to such trouble to try. Was she in some sort of trouble? If so, it was clearly of such a nature that she'd dared not share it with anyone. Damned if he didn't want to help her, if that were the case.

Her notation was remarkable—precise, detailed. Even though he knew little of the study of plants, it demonstrated, just as she argued, that she was capable of doing the work. But it was not her capacity to do the work that was at issue, though there seemed no possible way to make her see his rationale.

She could not be alone with him, especially at all hours of the night. It wouldn't be proper in the slightest. And yes, even though there was a bevy of female servants in his parents household, who entered his rooms to tend to his fire, bring him breakfast, and tend to his room while he was in it quite alone, this somehow wasn't the same. Stormount belonged to the Dukes of Weymouth. To the family...to the ages. The observatory, in contrast, was small. Intimate. And, more importantly, it was his. Being alone with any woman did not feel quite right. And, given the very nature of the work which happened at night...it would have been too much of a risk to her reputation as well.

A quartet of musicians struck up a tune, drawing Colin out of his wool gathering. Enough of this. He needed a bride. He gazed turned to Mariah—or, at least, on the several women with her coloring and manners. He had two weeks until mid-summer, when he'd promised his parents he'd make a proposal. His father's good health was dependent on it. There had to be a logical solution to the problem. He could leave it to chance. He could put all the names into a hat and pick one. And it had a certain appeal. Leave it to fate. Except fate had landed him in this position. And he wasn't about to allow it to rule him in the end.

And, certainly, there was Miss Boxford's sound logic when it came to dancing. Merely find the ones who disliked to dance. Did Miss Boxford dislike dancing? No. Lady Gwyneth had mentioned she loved to do it, but never had the chance. He wondered why.

And then he wondered why he was wondering about her at all.

Kitty had clearly lost her sanity. There was no other explanation for why she was walking across the grass of the storied estate of Stormount. The hall, with its gabled red brick façade, stood shining in the afternoon sun. On the lawn, edged by expertly trimmed topiaries and borders bursting with every color flower, were small huddles of elegantly dressed young ladies. Somewhere, Kitty thought, Lord Ellsworth was lingering in amongst the crowd, no doubt turning his critical eye over woman after woman, deciding which one would be his bride. She was surrounded by at least two dozen who would have practically sold their soul to be his wife. Or at least be the mistress of Stormount.

The very notion saddened her a little.

As friends of the family, Edmund and Gwynnie had been invited. Mrs. Pembroke was too, though she decided at the very last minute not to come. That decision had initially given Kitty great relief, as the only reason she would have been obligated to cross Stormount's gates was in her capacity as Mrs. Pembroke's companion. She was certain she had escaped the humiliation of having to face him again.

Instead, Gwynnie begged Kitty to come with her and Edmund, and Mrs. Pembroke had practically ordered her to go. Did the lady know about her late evening escapade into Hilsburn, and if so, was this her punishment? It was just as likely that Gwynnie had been convinced this was a matchmaking opportunity too good to miss, which produced the same sensation in Kitty—punishment.

Regardless, Gwynnie had appeared at Kennington Grove with a lovely pink gown that she'd found in the back of her closet she thought would suit Kitty very well. And, as if by magic, even though Gwynnie was six inches taller and shaped differently from her friend, the dress suited her perfectly. It was meant to be, Mrs. Pembroke said, and so Kitty had to go to the garden party, so as not to waste the opportunity to wear it. It had all sounded remarkably suspicious to Kitty. Then, most traitorous of all, Kitty's mother gave her her prettiest fichu, while her father wore a ridiculous proud smile and told her how lovely she was.

So here she was, in a rich pink gown in a sea of white and pale colors. There was nowhere to hide, she thought, though ducking behind one of the larger topiaries seemed like an option if the situation became desperate.

"Would either of you fair ladies like an ice?" Edmund asked, looking decidedly dashing in his blue coat and breeches. It had been a shock when she'd first seen him this way—dressed as a gentleman. It made her realize that the man she'd thought she'd loved was someone else entirely. But it suited him. Edmund was absolutely besotted with Gwynnie, and they were perfect for each other. She was a lady, and he was a gentleman. Kitty's heart squeezed with a pang of regret. Not for what Gwynnie had found, but for what Kitty had lost. How could she ever hope to find someone as perfect for her as the man she thought Edmund had been? His presence was the constant reminder of a once pleasant dream that in the end was never intended for her.

"Yes, thank you," Gwynnie replied. He smiled in return, then made his way through the crowd. Kitty watched Edmund disappear, then unfurled a fan her mother had lent her. It was an exceptionally warm day, even for June. Her face would soon match her dress in this heat.

Kitty swallowed a small sigh. "Edmund is very attentive to you."

Gwynnie's stare followed him through the crowd for just a

moment. "I am very lucky to have him." Then she patted Kitty's hand, a motion that surprised her. "We shall have to find you someone just as attentive."

"Gwynnie," Kitty said. "I am here for you. Not for a husband. Besides, the gentlemen here are…well, gentlemen. And I am certain none of them are looking for a gamekeeper's daughter."

Gwynnie merely shrugged at that, as if Kitty's rather pragmatic assessment of her social situation was unimportant.

Amongst the ladies there were a number of gentlemen, all finely dressed, though none quite so handsome as Edmund. Except for Lord Ellsworth, perhaps. There was something about his manner and countenance that lingered in Kitty's imagination. But it hardly mattered. He was a duke in waiting, after all. And she wasn't even a lady.

"Poor Lord Ellsworth," Gwynnie said, looking positively radiant as she always did. She scanned the field, using her practiced eye to assess the crowd.

"Everyone keeps calling him that," Kitty replied, then lifted her gaze to the soaring heights of Stormount manor, large enough, she wagered, to house half of Cheshire. There was not a thing poor about him.

"Should we wager on who will win him?"

"If I was a betting sort," Kitty said, "I would put a crown on Lady Mariah."

"Mariah Stapleton?" Gwyneth pulled a face. "What makes you say that?"

"I saw her in Hilsburn when she first arrived, in active pursuit. I've spent far too many years helping father bait traps. Lady Mariah is a serious hunter. She seems quite determined."

"I suppose we shall all know the night of the grand ball," Gwynnie said. "Edmund said that's when Colin will announce his choice. Kitty, we are going to have to get you a gown for that."

Kitty looked askance at her friend. "I hardly think that will be necessary."

"And why ever not?"

"Because it's unlikely I will be invited, Gwynnie." And after last night, she was most happy not to be.

Gwynnie took a sip of her lemonade then glanced up at her friend. "You will have to come as our guest. You know Edmund would dance with you."

Kitty pasted a smile on her face. At one time, Edmund had danced with her, back at Falls Lodge, just for fun. And she had gone and fallen in love with him. Part of her was still trying not to be. And though he would do it willingly, because he loved her as a sister, it was too awkward. She did not wish for a pity dance.

"I am touched, Gwynnie, but truthfully, I would much rather be at home. I would be a pigeon amongst the peacocks." It was bad enough she was here, after that disastrous encounter with the marquess.

Gwynnie laughed. "Oh my dear Kitty, I thank the heavens you are back in my life. But come now, let's find you a husband."

Kitty shook her head, quite emphatic. "You are not to do any such thing. I told you, I have a plan."

Gwynnie's brow fell into a deep frown. "Do not tell me you are going to post that notice?"

"I—"

Gwynnie shook her head in that helpless aristocratic way of hers. "No. You may pine over lost trinkets all you like, but my best friend is not putting up a notice for a husband. It is the singularly most unromantic thing I have ever heard. You deserve better."

"And this is better?" Kitty asked, trying to mask her exasperation. "There are at least two dozen ladies lining up, jockeying for position just like Lady Mariah, in the faint hope that they will catch his affection." She curled her lip. "No, thank you. Besides, he doesn't like to dance."

Not that Gwynnie was asking about Lord Ellsworth, of course.

"True, but still, I do not like it." Gwynnie pursed her lips, her eyes narrowed slightly.

Kitty knew that look. Gwynnie was quietly scheming. Though her friend lived a much simpler life, she was still the daughter of an earl, and it was in these moments that Gwynnie could not help but be the princess she was raised to be.

"But do you really need to post an advertisement?" Gwynnie asked after some time. "It is not commonly done. Perhaps not ever."

"I saw one, not long ago, in one of the London papers Edmund had brought for Mrs. Pembroke. A widow, looking for a new husband. Certainly it is not conventional, but it might work. And then, I get to choose...not unlike Lord Ellsworth with the assistant for his observatory."

Gwynnie took her friend's hand in earnest. "If you insist upon this, please show it to me before you post it. I want to make sure you have the best match possible. He must have a dazzling smile."

"Or at least a kind one. One that is eager for a help mate."

"Should he be tall, do you think? He certainly must be handsome."

"Gwynnie!" Kitty started to laugh. "He doesn't need to be too tall. Handsome might be nice. Certainly not a requirement."

"For you, I insist upon it. Anything else?"

"A good heart. And maybe someone who might, after a time, might be able to look fondly upon me, and perhaps I can do so in return."

"Oh Kitty, my sweet Kitty," Gwynnie threw her arms around her friend and gave her a big hug. After letting her go, Kitty was shocked to see Gwynnie's eyes bright with a sheen of unshed tears. "I wish you nothing less than the truest love. You deserve it more than anyone I know."

Kitty drank in her friend's fierce, protective love. She had missed Gwynnie dearly when they were separated, and thanked the heavens for the remarkable set of circumstances that had reunited them. That was a remarkable bit of luck she would be grateful for.

"Look who I found," Edmund called out, reappearing from amongst the crowds. In either hand he held an ice, which he passed to each of the ladies. Next to him was none other than the very man Kitty had hope to avoid. "Or rather, look who I rescued."

Kitty forced herself to smile. She loved Edmund dearly, but at the moment she wanted to throttle him. Lord Ellsworth didn't need rescuing. If anyone needed rescuing, it was she. It was not only Lord

Ellsworth's fault she had to endure this spectacle, but she had to do it after she'd spent half the night washing that ridiculous paste out of her hair. She was certain she was beet faced except for the dark circles under her eyes from a lack of sleep.

Adding insult to injury, he looked positively dashing. The sun danced on his red-gold hair, and his lean, muscled legs, clad in doeskin breeches, were met by beautifully polished boots. His dark burgundy coat fit perfectly across his shoulders. Indeed, she could not help but think that there was nothing about Lord Ellsworth that anyone would consider "lumpy." Even with his right arm in a sling.

Lord Ellsworth approached, his gaze lingering on Kitty for but a moment, before he bowed to Gwynnie. To Kitty, he merely nodded. And for that, given their awkward encounter, she was grateful.

"This is quite the challenge your mother has put before you, my lord," Gwynnie said. "So many pretty young ladies to choose from."

"That there are," he replied. Kitty could not help but notice his gaze straying across the crowd. "I am certain in the end I will make the right choice."

"Speaking of choices, have you been successful in finding an assistant at least?" Edmund asked.

It took all of Kitty's self-possession to not roll her eyes.

"I thought perhaps I had the right person," he replied, looking at Kitty. "But alas, I was mistaken."

"Well, I hope you are having better luck in the marriage department. I assume there are no running favorites?" Edmund asked.

"If there are, it would be ungentlemanly to discuss it. And I am a gentleman," Lord Ellsworth said, his gaze sliding over to Kitty, "unlike some."

Kitty did not miss the jab. No doubt she deserved it, but it stung nonetheless. Even in the heat of the afternoon, a warm rush of blood flooded her cheeks.

"Tell me, Lord Ellsworth," Gwynnie asked, "have you had a chance to dance with any of the ladies yet? When two bodies can work in unison, perhaps their temperaments can as well."

"Lord Ellsworth dislikes dancing, remember?" Kitty interjected.

"But there is much to be said for a woman who would rather spend her time with a wall than a gentleman."

"And there is something to be said about a lady who would rather bob around a room to music than engage in civil discourse with a gentleman," Lord Ellsworth replied.

"When the time comes that a gentleman provides either civility or meaningful discourse, ladies might stop bobbing around the room," Kitty replied, her gaze locked with his, her heart thrumming in her chest.

"Kitty, your ice is melting."

Kitty blinked, her attention pulled away from Lord Ellsworth. It took a moment for her to register that it was Edmund speaking to her. He was smiling, and nodded down to her hand. Inside the elegant glass cup her lemon ice was quickly becoming a slurry in the heat. She pasted a smile on her face, and as delicately as she could, she slurped the melted liquid before it threatened to spill over the side, then took a spoonful. It was cool, refreshing, and almost sinful.

It also gave her the most immediate blinding pain across her forehead. It subsided quickly enough, but distracted her enough to allow Gwynnie and Edmund to engage Lord Ellsworth further in conversation.

Kitty, determined to be civil, tried again. "What do you wish for in a partner, my lord?"

"I need a wife, Miss Boxford. If I was looking for a partner I would be going into business."

"I see." Kitty smoothed her skirt, and blew out a low breath of exasperation. So much for civility. "No companionship then?"

Lord Ellsworth pursed his lips, as if giving the idea genuine thought for the first time. "A little, I suppose, would not be unwelcome."

Kitty scanned the crowd. Every manner of respectable young lady, accompanied by mothers, elder sisters, aunts and chaperones, were present.

"What other characteristics? Good teeth, straight back? What do you wish for in your children?"

"Healthy ones," he said, without hesitation.

"Interesting," she said, taken aback the ease of that answer. "And boys, I suppose. At least two."

He cocked his head, then looked at Kitty anew. It made her more than a little self-conscious.

"Yes," he replied at once. He paused, shifting his weight, then regarded her anew. "Miss Boxford, I have to ask the nature of these questions."

"It's quite simple, really," she said. "Your requirements for a mate are going to be primarily about breeding. I know a little about that."

Lord Ellsworth's eyes widened at the remark but Edmund burst into laughter, the sound drawing more than a few looks in their direction. Oh dear. Kitty wanted to do nothing more than sink into the ground.

"Kitty Boxford, you rascal," Edmund said, recovering, wiping a tear from his cheek. "You might want to consider her help, Ellsworth. Aside from being one of the finest anglers you'll ever meet, Harry Boxford was one of the best dog breeders in the western counties. I think Kitty's learned a trick or two about his methods."

"With respect, Miss Boxford." Lord Ellsworth, not nearly as amused by Kitty's assessment as Edmund, pulled his mouth into a tight line. "I am not a spaniel in need of a bitch."

"Oh heavens," she said, taking another spoonful of the ice. It was tempting to feign a headache and run the three miles all the way back to Kennington Grove. "I didn't mean it that way. My apologies, my lord. I merely was trying to apply some parameters to what seemed like a logical problem to solve."

"There is nothing logical about love," Edmund said. "Though I believe poor Lord Ellsworth is not interested in that."

"You are quite correct," he said, an edge of bitterness that piqued Kitty's interest. He stilled for a moment, his gaze turning to the crowd, until whatever thought had demanded his attention was satisfied.

"But Miss Boxford, you have given me something to think about," he said, his gaze sliding over her. "Much, in fact."

"Here he is, hiding away."

The buoyant sounds of the Duchess of Weymouth filled the air. Lord Ellsworth's manner relaxed ever so slightly.

"Mother," he said, with a note of affection Kitty sensed was genuine. "I was saying hello to the Pembrokes, and Miss Boxford."

His mother's gaze dropped affectionately on Edmund and Gwynnie, before grazing over Kitty and back to her son. It was clear that the duchess thought highly of her son, and though her attentions might wear on him, Lord Ellsworth did return his mother's affection.

"Good afternoon to you all. I have the tremendous pleasure to introduce the Countess of Bedford, and her daughters, the ladies Mariah and Belinda," she said.

All three nodded in unison, and while the countess acknowledged the Pembrokes, Lady Mariah's gaze never left the marquess.

"It is a pleasure to meet you again," Lord Ellsworth said. "I hope you are enjoying the ices."

Kitty pressed her lips together to keep herself from smiling too much. She sometimes became clumsy when she was nervous, but poor Lord Ellsworth seemed to be stifled by his own tongue.

"I am, thank you, my lord," Lady Mariah answered, doe-eyed. "I understand it was your idea to offer both lemon and strawberry. You must know both are my particular favorites."

"I am quite glad to hear that," he said, and the way the color rushed into his cheeks at that moment, Kitty was absolutely certain he was. Heavens, men were funny creatures.

Kitty watched the exchange between Lady Mariah and Lord Ellsworth. The way she tilted her head, so that she presented what Kitty was certain was her best side, smiling at every word the marquess said, regardless of how clumsy his conversation. If there were any awkward pauses, she did not register a one, and indeed where there was silence of a second or two, it was filled by either the duchess or the countess. Edmund offered his own benign opinions on the weather, the dresses, the ices, and all the details with ease. But Lady Mariah's gaze rarely left the marquess.

After some time, a curious sort of unease filled Kitty's belly. She wasn't certain of the sensation, but each time Lady Mariah reached out to touch Lord Ellsworth's hand, no matter how lightly, at something he said that was amusing—to her at least, for she was the only one who laughed—it grated on every last ounce of her good mood.

It must have been the lack of sleep. Or knowing she had bags resting under her eyes. Lady Mariah looked as fresh and sunny as the flowers in the garden. And Lord Ellsworth definitely did notice.

After what felt like entirely too long, Gwynnie put a hand to Kitty, who was nearby. It was her signal that she too was spent and ready to leave.

"You must excuse me, your Grace," Gwynnie said during one of the awkward pauses that the duchess did not fill. "I would like to thank you very much for your gracious hospitality, but I think I may need to rest. The ices were delicious."

"Of course! I am thrilled you could attend." The duchess alerted a passing servant, and then made her goodbyes to both the Pembrokes. Kitty, of course, was not given such attentions, and for that she was quite grateful. She was suddenly in quite a surly mood. She curtsied, her gaze flicking up to Lord Ellsworth for a second, then locking eyes with Lady Mariah. She pressed her lips in a tight smile and turned away.

When the conversation fell to a natural conclusion, Edmund and Gwynnie strolled back to the main park, where their carriage was brought around. They were ahead, speaking with another group of acquaintances, while Kitty trailed behind. She found herself quite exhausted from the afternoon.

"You have not left yet. Excellent."

Kitty's heart leapt a little at the sound of Lord Ellsworth's voice. She looked up and saw his hair was tousled ever so slightly. He must have run to catch up with them.

"Edmund and Lady Gwyneth are just ahead," Kitty said, gesturing to her friends.

"It is you I wish to speak with," he said, giving the footman a look that dismissed him. "If that is acceptable."

"You are a marquess, my lord. If you wish to speak with me, then I suspect I have little choice but to listen. I believe we established this only yesterday."

His eyelids fluttered, and Kitty was surprised by the idea that she might have hurt his feelings. Not that she should have cared, given how easily he'd dismissed her last evening.

"In some ways you have come to the heart of my challenge," he replied. "I have given some thought to your earlier words about finding a mate. And, as straightforward as your assessment might have been, I believe there is value in your methods. I would like to hire you, perhaps in a consulting role, to provide some guidance as to how I might choose a bride."

Kitty stilled, blindsided by his words. "Truly?"

He nodded, his firm expression melting into a somewhat sheepish smile that had the most remarkable effect on her mood.

"Why not ask Edmund?"

"I have asked Edmund to tutor me on small talk, and even how to shoot properly. As you may have noticed on the first account, his methods did not prove useful." He shuffled his feet, looking down at his boots a moment, then up at her.

"You have no trouble speaking to me," she countered.

"But we are speaking on particular matters. Will you help?"

Kitty paused but a moment. "I think not, your lordship."

He blinked, clearly taken aback by her answer. "Why not? You have the expertise, and due to your position, you could observe me without being noticed. I am offering you some extra pocket money. It would be a good sum."

She shook her head, then squared her shoulders, a fresh hurt bubbling up in her chest.

"Do you have no appreciation for irony, my lord? I came to you yesterday, offering my expertise on something that is truly important to me, and you rejected me out of turn. How does it feel, your lordship, to be rejected for no particularly sound reason?"

His eyes narrowed and a flash of anger went across his brow. "Not that it is any of your business, Miss Boxford, but as you are no doubt aware I have been rather publicly rejected."

"I can't imagine why."

"The lady in question gave me quite an itemized list, in fact, if you are so interested."

A list? "She must have been a fool, then."

"What did you say?"

"I said she must have been a fool." Kitty gestured to the grandeur of the house that towered over them. "I mean first of all, you're probably as rich as Midas. Your back is straight, you have all your teeth, and you are quite handsome, but of course you know that. And you are interested in interesting things, not just betting on horses or whatever it is rich men do to pass their time. You think well of your parents. You have good men as friends, which says something of your character. So, I say to you again, whoever she was, she was a fool."

He stilled then, and Kitty silently chided herself for her impulse to say exactly what was on her mind without any thought to how it might be received.

"Thank you, Miss Boxford."

"Not at all." She began to turn away, when inspiration struck. Maybe, just maybe, there was a way to get to Lofton Tower after all. "Perhaps we could make an arrangement?"

He tilted his head slightly. "I am listening."

"I will help you with this at no cost, if you will let me work as your observatory assistant."

"I explained to you why that is impossible. It is outside the boundaries of society."

"I am outside the boundaries of society. The rules do not apply to me," Kitty replied. "When Edmund was in danger, Gwynnie—who is neither a soldier nor a spy, and quite female—set aside those rules to save him. She is a respectable woman, and no one would think less of her. No one knows about what happened last evening. You came alone. If anyone asks, and no one will, you can say that your assistant is Kenneth Boxford, Harry Boxford's nephew."

He took off his spectacles and clumsily attempted to clean then lens with his handkerchief when he lost his grip. Before they landed, Kitty caught them in her hand.

"Let me help you," she said, then, without saying another word, took his handkerchief and gently cleaned the lenses, then handed them back to him. His eyes were quite remarkable. "Hire me, pay me at the wages you offered, and I will help you find a wife."

He put his spectacles back on, slowly, deliberately, then took the handkerchief she'd folded neatly back into a square. He toyed with the edged of it with his well hand, clearly deliberating.

"Very well, Miss Boxford," he said in a low, but businesslike voice. "You will arrive at the observatory at sundown each night unless you receive a notice from me. Our observation times may vary. I will see to your safe transport to and from Lofton Tower. We will trial it for a fortnight."

"At the wages you specified?"

"The wages specified were for an observatory assistant."

"Which is how you are hiring me."

"A male observatory assistant," he challenged.

She crossed her arms. "Unless you are expecting me to do less work, you will pay me the wages offered."

He shook his head. "Done. You drive a hard bargain, Miss Boxford."

Kitty could not keep a smile from breaking across her face. Perhaps, just for today, her luck was changing.

"You will not find a better one, Lord Ellsworth."

CHAPTER 9

Colin sat in his favorite chair in his favorite corner of Lofton Tower and gazed absentmindedly toward the window. The hour of Miss Boxford's arrival was imminent, and he found himself unable to concentrate. Normally this was a place where he quite selfishly locked out the world; his parents, society, politics—all were banished from this most jealously guarded space. Though it was not terribly large, especially by the standards of Stormount Hall, the observatory allowed him the privacy to work for days at a time if he chose. Aside from the largest room, which functioned as his study, there was a small bed chamber, a modest kitchen, and a pantry. Above it was the observation tower, crowned with a rotunda that provided him an unobstructed view of the sky. He could sit, tinker, observe, make notes, read, and forget about the world.

It was here he'd retreated after Amelia had left him. If he couldn't disappear off the face of the earth entirely, like Edmund had done following his confrontation with his father, Lofton provided Colin refuge to get through the worst of those god-awful days. The stars, at least, were non-judgmental company, and the rest of the world was out of his view.

Until tonight.

What in the blazes had come over him at the garden party? Whether it had been the heat, desperation, or simple madness of two endless bloody hours of having to comment on musicales and necklaces and heavens knows what, he did not know what it was that inspired this agreement. Perhaps it was the way Miss Boxford's amber eyes distracted him, or the way her head tilted slightly when she spoke, causing the rich brown curls of her hair to bounce against her skin. Or perhaps it was the logic, unorthodox as it was, that intrigued him. Regardless, it would be of short duration. By the end of the month his arm would be sufficiently recovered to take his own notes. And, more immediately, he might very well be married, and most definitely engaged, by mid-summer. Despite whatever promises Miss Boxford made with those bewitching eyes of hers, it would definitely no longer be appropriate to have a female assistant and a wife. If her advice did prove helpful, then she'd be gone even sooner.

To distract himself, he started poring over his notes from his visit to Wold Cottage, where a piece of rock had fallen out of the sky and landed there around Christmas time. He'd visited while he was in Yorkshire this past winter, eager to get a good look at what on the surface looked to be an unremarkable piece of rock. But it had come from the same space as the moon, stars, and planets. It made him want to find more. Finding comets was a tricky business that required patience and time. In nearly a decade of observing, Miss Caroline Herschel had discovered only five. It was like hunting for treasure with no map, and a target that never stayed in a single place for very long.

The sound of carriage wheels in the distance pulled him from his reverie. It was precisely ten o'clock, the agreed upon hour in which Miss Boxford would arrive. He pulled himself to his feet, negotiated the piles of books and papers and ephemera he'd collected over the years, and went to the door, an unexpected sense of anticipation brimming inside him. He owed it to the fact that he might at last have a true assistant who could help him with his observations. And, perhaps, a better end to the misery of having to find a bride.

Miss Boxford's matter-of-fact inventory of his merits earlier today had taken him completely off guard. Especially considering they were all at Amelia's expense. His parents had stopped speaking of her, for his benefit. Most people carefully avoided the subject. But not Miss Boxford. She spoke about her as if she was speaking of Sunday breakfast. As if it was a truth so obvious that all the world could see. Of course, his wealth and title were a matter of public record. But her comments about his character was something quite different. And he found he could not stop thinking about it. Or her.

The gentle rumble of the carriage emerged from a dark wooded path that led to the observatory. The sound contrasted with the hum of crickets rising from the verge on this warm evening. The driver brought the carriage to a gentle stop, and Miss Boxford quite unceremoniously hopped out. It took a moment for Colin to register what he was seeing. Was that—a tricorn on her head?

"Pray, Miss Boxford, what costume do you have on this evening?"

He stepped closer. She did indeed have a tricorn hat on her head, and the lumpy frock coat from their ill-fated meeting at the Brookside Inn had made an unceremonious return. Blessedly, she'd appeared to leave the trousers at home.

She shrugged. "You seemed concerned about being seen with a woman here, my lord. I assumed this might be enough to throw off the suspicions of anyone who might see me drive by. Unless of course, people are accustomed to seeing ladies come here in the evening."

Colin frowned. "What the devil are you suggesting, Miss Boxford?"

She blinked, apparently shocked by his reaction.

"Well..." He could tell her mind was racing. "This is a rather perfect place for a romantic liaison, my lord. When we met in the inn, you seemed unduly concerned about my reputation. I just thought, perhaps—"

Colin rolled his eyes and held up his uninjured hand to silence her. "You can stop thinking at once, Miss Boxford. At least about that." He dropped his hand back to his side, and cast a glance up to his driver, who quite wisely, was ignoring the entire conversation. He stepped closer, lowering his voice. "But, since you clearly know nothing about my reputation, allow me to inform you that the observatory has never been used to entertain women." Or anyone. He shook his head. Colin Middleton as Lothario. He could almost hear Edmund laughing across Cheshire at the very idea.

She bowed her head and dipped into a quick curtsey. "My apologies, my lord. I did not mean to assume. Keeping track of the lives of dukes-in-waiting is not how I spend my time."

Colin stifled a chuckle. "Do not trouble yourself, Miss Boxford. But I think next time you can leave the disguise behind." He nodded to the driver, bidding him instructions to return precisely at midnight.

Her gaze went straight to the rotunda, her mouth falling open in undisguised wonder. Colin could not help but be pleased with her response.

"This is quite remarkable," she said. "I cannot say I have ever seen a building quite like it."

"Thank you," he said. "The original structure has been here for some time. I merely added onto it, to make it more useful for my needs."

"You must be able to see all of Cheshire from here," she said, turning on her heel and casting her gaze around.

"Not entirely, but a good chunk of the western part." He paused and pointed west. "Wales is over there, and you can see it clearly most days. This is one of the highest points in the area."

"Indeed. The stars seem to be right on top of us."

"Technically they are."

She turned at him with a funny look on her face. "That is not what I mean. This is truly a magical place. I can see why it means so much to you."

He stood, somehow transfixed by this unusual woman in her ridiculous frock coat, the glow from the lamplight inside lighting up her nervous smile.

The hum of the crickets filled the silence.

"My lord?"

"Yes, Miss Boxford?"

"You have sent the carriage away. Are we going to stay here and do the observations outside?"

Colin shook his head. "Of course not. My apologies, Miss Boxford." He stepped aside, and ushered her in the door. "Just mind where you step. And don't touch anything."

She smiled stiffly, then walked past him. She took perhaps two steps into the room, then turned around. She shrugged off the lumpy frock coat and removed the tricorn hat and put them on an empty hook by the door. Though she'd whipped her hair back into a knot quicker than he could say "'Copernicus," he'd gotten a glimpse of the dark brown curls that fell down her back. His mouth went dry and the rest of his body…paid attention.

She turned around, her hands clasped in front of her, an expectant smile on her face.

"Where do you want me, my lord?"

It was the most innocent and yet suddenly complex of questions. As she stood there in her simple blue frock, her cheeks flushed, and the smallest bit of exposed skin from the most modest of necklines, unadorned with jewels or any other trappings save eyes bright with anticipation, Colin was struck by the most illogical of all thoughts. Where did he want Miss Katherine Boxford? Was it in his arms, so he could put his fingers through her lush sable curls, touch what he was certain was warm soft skin, and taste her mouth? Or perhaps in his arms was not enough. Perhaps where he wanted her could not be answered by a gentleman. Certainly not by a duke in waiting.

But perhaps, by a man.

It was a dangerous thought.

He blinked, trying to cast aside whatever spell he was under. He should never have invited her here. Whatever his need to pick a bride, he could have pushed through and done this without her advice. But there was something about Miss Boxford that was creeping through the rigid rules he'd made for himself.

This was a mistake.

"My apologies, Miss Boxford," he began. "I—"

"Where is your telescope? Is this it?"

She pointed to the looking glass on his desk.

He shook his head. "I use it for more casual observations. I sometimes take it with me, as it folds up quite nicely. My larger telescope is on the upper deck of the observatory."

"My heavens," she exclaimed brushing past him, blessedly unaware of his discomfort. She turned and looked at him with undisguised incredulity. "You are truly alone here, aren't you?"

Alone? He'd been alone his entire life. And he quite liked it that way.

"The servants have strict instructions not to disturb me when I am here."

She dragged a finger along a shelf, leaving a trail where dark walnut wood was newly exposed. "I think some of this dust requires a little disturbing."

He tried to cross his arms, but the gesture was defeated by his sprained wrist, still supported. "The servants have more than enough work at Stormount. I bring them here when it is necessary. And I prefer to be left alone."

"With respect, Stormount looks to have enough rooms that you could hide for weeks without being found," she said.

"My mother has a remarkable gift for finding me," he replied.

"She does seem to dote on you," she said, without judgment.

"My parents had an heir and several spares, of which I am one," he said. "None of the them, save myself, survived childhood. My parents are heavily invested in my wellbeing."

Her face fell a little, concern lowering her brow. "How horrible a thing for them to endure," she said. "In those earliest days they were probably afraid to lose you as well."

Colin nodded. His parents spoke occasionally of his elder siblings, and he had only the faintest memories of some of them.

"I suppose they were. But once I am married and give them a few sons of my own, their worries shall be over." Which would, he hope, mean that his worries about his father's health would be over as well.

His assertions did not lighten her countenance. "I cannot imagine that to be entirely the case."

"In case you have forgotten, there is a rather large spectacle being thrown simply to achieve that goal, Miss Boxford."

She tilted her head ever so slightly. "I would think your parents would be concerned for you always, given you are their son. Mrs. Pembroke seems heavily invested in Edmund's wellbeing, even now that he is married and with children."

"It is the continuity of the line that matters in the end." Indeed it was only through the most remarkable set of circumstances that Colin's grandfather had become Duke of Weymouth at all. And Colin had survived, luck on his side, childhood illness that took his siblings, and a further attempt on his own life earlier this year. "And it will."

"I have heard your mother speak of you, my lord. One would have thought that the very sun rises and sets just for you."

Colin nodded. Given all that Edmund and Gwyneth had endured as a result of their sires, Colin was more than ready to endure a little matronly smothering.

They fell silent, the only sound the ticking of a nearby clock. It was a reminder that Colin had some business to attend to.

"Right." He rubbed his hands together and looked about for a spot for Miss Boxford to sit. He reached for the pile of scientific letters piled on a stool. Clumsy from his injured arm, some fell to the floor. He bent to pick them up when the shock of Miss Boxford's touch slowed him.

"Let me help you, my lord," she replied, her face inches away from his. He could smell the scent of her perfume. She paused but a moment, her lips parted slightly, and in that moment Colin was utterly tempted to taste her. Tearing himself away, he rose as she gathered up the rest of the papers. She stood and put them aside, and for a moment she seemed as flustered as he.

Most definitely an error.

In a firm and most businesslike manner, he took the chair, found a spare bit of floor to plant it in, and gestured for her to sit, which she did. Her posture straight, sitting on the edge of the seat, her expression neutral, it seemed she was equally eager to get down to business.

The sooner, the better.

"Let's begin." He looked over at the clock, which read fifteen minutes past the hour. It had at once seemed like only seconds, and on the other like an eternity since she'd arrived. He settled into his chair. *Focus, Colin.* "I was very interested in your approach to selecting a bride. And while it might be somewhat unorthodox to speak of traits and selection as one would with race horses and dogs, I do believe the theory behind it is sound. You were among the crowd this afternoon. Of the ladies that you observed at the garden party, is there any direction you can provide as to who might be the right one? Or perhaps it is too early to narrow down the field so quickly. What do you think?"

KITTY'S SMILE FROZE. What did she think?

Instead of getting ready for bed after a very full day, she'd scrubbed her face, put on a fresh dress, brewed and drank two cups of coffee to keep herself bright eyed, then snuck out of the house, lying to her parents and Mrs. Pembroke in the process. And she did all this so she could come to the observatory and give the marquess her opinions on animal husbandry? Or wifery? She knew exactly what she thought.

But by some miracle or another, she managed not to share those thoughts with him.

She blinked, looking for any sign of a joke. Certainly, she knew she would provide him advice on this subject. It was part of the bargain. But this was not at all what she had in mind.

Perhaps it was some sort of test she had to pass. To show him that she could uphold her part of the agreement. That she would be everything he'd hoped an assistant would be. Which meant, of course, being more than he'd expected, because she was a woman.

"Well," she began, eager to fill the air that was laced with the marquess's expectation of an answer. Well what? She turned her mind to the days when her father would carefully look over Sir Richard's dogs, looking for traits that he would consider might make good offspring. But surely, the marquess was looking for more? "I suppose you must consider what qualities you desire. What is the outcome you are looking for?"

His eyes narrowed, and a passing expression of disgust, or discomfort perhaps, flashed over his face, but he recovered himself quickly.

"Healthy children," he replied. "I require someone who will bear healthy children."

Kitty caught herself leaning forward, waiting for more. There was none.

"Right then," she nodded, as she attempted to hide her confusion. "I suppose you might choose a woman who has many healthy siblings. That is not a guarantee, of course. But a start."

He nodded, apparently satisfied with her answer.

"And presumably," he added, "a woman with many brothers."

"Of course," she said, smiling, and looked to her feet. "Heaven forbid a family full of girls," she muttered under her breath.

He looked at her and chuckled. "Perhaps I need a woman who knows how to hold her tongue, then. Heaven forbid."

Kitty's head snapped up, and she froze.

"Do you truly have no control over your voice, Miss Boxford?"

She pressed her lips together, and swallowed her panic. "I-it is a failing of mine, unfortunately. I have a thought and sometime I catch them before they come out, but not all. It, as Edmund can attest, makes a position in a house somewhat difficult for me. I am very lucky Mrs. Pembroke is a generous employer. If I had your qualities perhaps, I would have had a different future."

"I don't understand." He had a curious expression on his face. It had gone from surprise to dismay to amusement in the blink of an eye. The Marquess of Ellsworth was a curious man. And a deeply guarded one.

Kitty exhaled slowly, forcing herself to consider every word. "Some people have the gift to say volumes without saying a word. My father is such a man. He might seem to be dull or taciturn, but the careful observer will know he is conveying a great deal. It appears to me, my lord, you have a similar way of expressing yourself."

He stilled then, and it felt as if he'd become very self-conscious. "Well, perhaps I shall visit your father one day, and enjoy a quiet drink. But back to the subject at hand."

"Of course," she nodded, eager to move away from what had suddenly felt like a personal moment. "Again, linking yourself to a woman of large family, including many brothers, is no guarantee of success. I remember a time when my father had bred two lovely spaniels. The mother came from a litter of puppies whose mother was renowned for the size of her litters, and a good mix of male and female. But the dog's litters were of normal size, largely female. The male pups were all sickly."

"That is not reassuring."

"Are you certain there is nothing else?" she asked. "Good potential for large families and a distaste of dancing? Beyond lands or titles, which is simply a matter of maths, and you hardly need my input for that. A cheerful temperament, or perhaps, as you suggested, a more subdued one."

"It would perhaps be better if both of us were not subdued." He regarded her carefully, then pulled his attention away, and shook his head, as if he was having an argument with himself. "Solitude, Miss Boxford. Solitude and an heir. That is what I seek."

"Right. Well, then you need a woman who won't need you—beyond the biological necessity of creating your offspring, as it were." Heavens, but this was painful. "If this is the case, then whether or not the woman is subdued or likes to dance is of little consequence."

He gaze snapped back to her. "I suppose you are right."

"Well then, there you have it. Look for the woman with many siblings who isn't fawning over you. Your requirements are simple enough," she said. She folded her hands in her laps. "Is that what you were hoping to hear?"

"I don't know, frankly, what I was hoping to hear. But this does give me some way of narrowing the field as it were."

"Wonderful. Are we done then?"

He brightened then, and rose. "Yes, I believe we are."

"Excellent. I am most eager to get to work."

"I think the best thing would be for you to begin by reading through some fundamentals."

Kitty blinked. "Fundamentals?"

"Of course. If you are going to be taking notes, you need to know what you are taking notes about."

Kitty turned that over in her head. She didn't want for a moment to gainsay Lord Ellsworth. She needed this opportunity. So she bit her tongue, and nodded.

"I see no reason to delay," she replied, eager to demonstrate her willingness.

"Right." He stopped and looked around. He bent over book shelves, and dug through papers. After what felt like an eternity, he pulled out a book and handed it to her.

A Catalogue of Constellations. The volume was large, not unlike a book of plates Mrs. Pembroke had of flowers.

"With respect, my lord, but I think perhaps I can read something a little less fundamental," she replied. "I am quite familiar with the sky. Indeed, I am certain if we went outside right now, you could test me."

"Perhaps another time. I am not appropriately prepared for that at this time."

"I do not understand what preparation is needed." She pointed to an open page in the book. "When I came in, Cygnus was rising high in the sky. And there is a waxing moon that will rise in a few hours."

He paused a moment, rose again, and took the book out of her hands, casting it aside on a nearby pile of papers. "Right then. Well, what do you know about comets, Miss Boxford?"

"Comets?"

"Indeed." Her question seemed to satisfy him. He rooted around and pulled out two papers. "Comets are celestial bodies that move through the sky in their own orbits. Not planets."

"You mean like Mr. Halley's comet."

"Yes. I am scanning the sky for comets," he replied. "As I do that, I am recording anything I find against established charts."

"That is absolutely fascinating." And it was.

"Yes," he replied, his lips inching up in a smile. "So it is imperative that you understand as much as you can about them before we begin."

Kitty pressed her lips together, and nodded. "Well then, I will do that."

He pulled out a tattered journal and handed it to her. "Do you think you can manage this?"

"Of course." What else could she say? It appeared, at least, to be written in English and not Latin.

"You will need light to read. I will be in the viewing room, adjusting my instrument and making some preliminary viewing. I'll come down and check on you shortly."

He grabbed a lamp, and disappeared upstairs.

Kitty had been dismissed in some spectacular ways in her life. But this was something new.

She sat down in her chair and began poring over the notes. Some of it was fascinating. Some of it, she had to admit, was as dry as salted fish in winter. She read through it once, then twice. She looked at the clock. It was a quarter to eleven.

She rose, and went to the stairs. "My lord?" she called out. "Is there something else I can do?"

"A moment, Miss Boxford," came the muffled replied from above.

A moment passed. Followed by ten more. Letting out a low breath, she cast her eye around the room and marveled at the idea of Lord Ellsworth bringing anyone, let alone a lover, to this place. It had potential, of course. But it was a mess. He seemed so orderly. So in control. But this was clearly an outlet for his otherwise structured life.

Maybe this too was part of the test. Many apprentices did menial work to show their dedication to the craft, she reasoned. Her father allowed Edmund to do nothing but clean up after the dogs for weeks before showing Edmund how to tie a snare. Was this what Lord Ellsworth was playing at? If so, she would show him how useful she could be.

The observatory was lit on all sides by sconces. On one side was a small hearth, though the season was so warm that it was unlit. Its presence suggested that Lord Ellsworth must make use of the space for much of the year. There were two bookshelves, and a large table which was piled with papers, books and curious looking instruments. One she recognized as an astrolabe. There was also a compass, a small looking glass, and a fantastical little machine that showed the sun and all the planets.

"Remarkable," she said, the word coming out under her breath. It was also remarkably untidy.

Aside from the mounds on the desk, there were more piled on a nearby chair, which might have been a comfortable place to sit if one was so inclined. On the wall was a print of Isaac Newton, his face looking out at her from a decidedly lopsided angle. She was about to straightened it when a squeaking sound drew her attention downward. At her feet, she discovered a curious book open on the floor, a mouse nibbling at one edge. As she scooped it up, the creature scampered away. The volume's insides were hollowed out in order to hide a treasure or one sort or another. She scanned the floor, but whatever it was meant to hold was nowhere to be seen.

Kitty worked away, tidying, organizing books, and dusting. She'd gotten so involved she hadn't even heard the creaking of the steps as Lord Ellsworth had come down to meet her.

"What happened here?"

Kitty whipped around, and any sense of satisfaction instantly evaporated when she spied Lord Ellsworth. He was stone faced.

"I finished reading, so I tried to make myself useful. I assumed that's why you left me here." She slid past him and pointed out what she'd done. "First, all the dirty crockery is washed and out of the way. Then I took all your books and put them back on the shelves—by subject matter and then alphabetical order. Except for ones that had papers sticking out of them. Those I kept with all your notes. But now, look…you can walk around and not trip over anything. You can even sit down if you like, and work. I even swept out your hearth…it looked like it hadn't been done for a while."

She clasped her hands in front of her, expectant. His gaze kept bouncing from her, to his bookshelf, to the walls.

"I didn't touch any of the instruments. Though I do think the astrolabe deserves a polish."

"Miss Boxford, you were hired to be my assistant. Not my housekeeper."

"No, but I thought—"

"I do not pay you to think."

Kitty clasped her hands together, and she swallowed deeply.

"I assume you must have to think," she said. "And how anyone can when they are surrounded by such piles of clutter is beyond any thinking person's comprehension."

His eyes narrowed. "Do you know to whom you are speaking?"

His condescension rankled and loosened her tongue.

"A self-indulgent lord who does not care to look after his things, I would say. Only a person who does not care for the value of books and knowledge would treat them so carelessly." Kitty picked up the strange book with the hollowed interior, her anger rising. "I rescued this one from a mouse who was chewing on the edges of it. It was on the floor."

He took it out of her hand, his skin brushing up against hers, which were soiled from her toils. A flash of heat and embarrassment swept through her. She pulled her hands away.

"Whatever it had that was valuable is gone," she said. "Or at least, I couldn't find it."

Even in the dim light, she could see his face flush as he swallowed. He stared at the book a moment, then tossed it carelessly aside.

"Nothing you need to concern yourself with."

The clock on the mantle began to chime. Midnight had come.

He cleared his throat. "This is clearly not going to work, Miss Boxford. I should not have made such a ridiculous offer of employment. It was a lapse of judgment on my part."

"We had an agreement. You would hire me on and I would give you the advice you sought. I have upheld my half of the agreement." Panic began to rise in her. Panic, and anger. "You do not understand what this opportunity means to me. I asked for direction. And you gave none save to wait. And so I waited, as a good assistant might. Because you gave me no further direction. And you, a great lord with every opportunity and advantage, would take it from me because I was simply trying to do my best to read your mind?"

A hush fell over the room, the only sound the bells chiming the hour. A knock came at the door. The carriage ready to take her home was at the door. She blinked, fiercely trying to keep tears at bay, and grabbed her coat and hat.

"You do not understand what this means to me, Miss Boxford. No idea."

"Perhaps not. But perhaps Lady Amelia did. And that is why she chose someone else. Or perhaps she wanted a man of his word."

He took a step back, his jaw tight, his cheeks reddened from anger.

"How dare you speak so. I am absolutely a man of my word."

Kitty, emboldened by her own hurt pride, stepped forward. "Then to what should I attribute your behavior this evening? Aristocratic whim? Because it is obvious you clearly had no intention of actually allowing me to fulfill the commitment. I am a woman of my word. I have done my half, and more, and you repay me by toying with my life as if there is nothing for it. Go ahead and be angry because I decided to pay this place the respect you claim for it but do not show. But be angry with yourself."

Their gazes locked as the last bell rang out, and then Kitty tore out the door. She jumped into the carriage, but he did not follow her.

And she did not care.

CHAPTER 10

"Katherine?"

Kitty's eyes fluttered open, vaguely aware of a hand on her shoulder. Waking took nearly all her energy this morning. She was exhausted. And someone was calling her name. Who on earth called her Katherine?

Her mother.

"Are you ill, child?"

It had taken her far too long for sleep after she arrived home. Kitty rubbed her eyes, fatigue making it difficult even to focus. Her stomach was a little queasy from being so tired and heartsick.

"Mother?" she asked, confused. She rubbed her eyes with her hands. "What are you doing here? Shouldn't you be helping Father?"

"Kitty my dear, it is nearly ten o'clock," her mother replied, a look of concern across her brow. She sat down on the edge of the bed. "I think the poor servants thought you were dead."

"Ten? Are you certain?" Panic pushed aside her exhaustion and she sat up. Dear heavens…Mrs. Pembroke took breakfast at nine. And normally Kitty was in her room by eight, helping her get ready to meet the day. She looked down—still in most of the clothes she wore last night. "Mother, can you tell Mrs. Pembroke I'll be down as soon as I can?"

"Mrs. Pembroke is doing well enough today with my company, my dear." Her mother looked at her, reaching out and gently pushing Kitty's hair out of her eyes. "Are you ill? You do not seem yourself."

Was she ill? In her heart, yes. She'd thought she'd done Lord Ellsworth a kindness, or at least proved her worth by cleaning up his papers and dirty crockery. Instead, he seemed to be perturbed by her very presence. There was nothing she could do correctly. She was either too quiet, or too loud. And he let her nowhere near his instruments, much less record a single mark.

And then he'd decided that she was not the person for the position after all. Even though she'd fulfilled her part of the bargain.

She wanted then just to throw her arms around her mother and cry a bit. Cry about the pendant she'd lost and the good luck that she'd let slip through her fingers. Cry about being tossed out of Gorland Park. Cry that she was going to live with her best friends and felt like a traitorous person for the reasons why she didn't want to. And, just when she thought, just perhaps, she'd found a way out of her predicament, she'd tried to impress a man who, she realized, did not wish to be impressed by anyone. Least of all her.

But doing that meant telling her mother everything…and she wasn't brave enough to do that.

"I am, perhaps," she said, inwardly kicking herself for yet another lie. She forced a smile. "But I am certain if I get up and dressed, I will recover. It is a nice day, is it not?"

"In fact, it is a very lovely day. But if you are not well, it would do well for you to rest, my dear," her mother said. "I am sure one of the servants can attend to Mrs. Pembroke today with my help. Unless there is another event at Stormount."

"I dearly hope not. I have had enough of society." Kitty could not help but roll her eyes as she pulled off her blue dress, thoroughly crumpled from being slept in, and pulled a fresh one from her cupboard. If she ever had to lay eyes on Lord Ellsworth again, it would be too soon. "I do not understand why a man with such resources is so afraid to marry. He could have whomever he wants."

"I suspect the problem is that the person he wanted did not want him in return. And that nothing he could offer her was good enough. Regardless of who you are, that rejection is painful."

Kitty stilled. Though Edmund knew nothing of Kitty's affection for him, nor had given her even the slightest hint of attentions beyond those of friendship, the simple fact of the matter was that he had not the affection for her she'd carried for him. And while the sharpest sting of the pain had passed, the dull ache remained.

"And he feels he was not good enough."

A stone sunk deep in Kitty's gut. Last night she'd unknowingly found his wound, hadn't she? Found it and drove a knife right through it. No wonder he was angry.

Her mother nodded. "To Lord Ellsworth's credit, he has done everything ever asked of him. Not all men would, or do. But he must marry. That is his duty, like his forefathers. So he endures this spectacle because that is what it means to be a duke in waiting. When Lady Amelia broke with him, he did not bind her. He did not challenge her new fiancé to a duel. The papers would have been vicious about the scandal. And he bore it."

There was something about the way her mother spoke that caught Kitty's attention. As if she was speaking about something she knew.

"I did not realize you followed the society news so closely, Mother," she said.

Her mother pursed her lips, and her cheeks reddened slightly. "I am not impervious to gossip, Katherine. It has been whispered about in the shops here in Hilsburn as well as in the London rags."

Kitty sat quietly, watching her mother very carefully. "Mother, how did you know Father was the person for you?"

Her mother smiled then in that way of someone still in love. It made Kitty's heart happy and ache all at once. "I didn't, in fact. Not at the beginning. But perhaps my heart knew, somehow, that happiness lay at Harry Boxford's door. It just took a little while for my head to realize it."

"A little while. How long?"

"Not too long, I suppose. But when both my head and my heart knew, there was no stopping me from being his wife."

"You sound like Gwynnie," Kitty replied.

"Lady Gwyneth is a strong minded girl, Kitty. And I love you very much, but I think you could do with a little of her confidence."

"Gwynnie was raised a lady."

Mother took one of Kitty's hands in hers and gave it a gentle squeeze. She smiled, though a hint of sadness had crept in to her voice for just a moment. "Being a lady is about breeding, I suppose, but it is more than that. It is about knowing one's worth. In that way, every woman has the potential to be a lady. Know your worth, Katherine. And don't for a moment let anyone else trample on it." She pulled Kitty forward and kissed her on the forehead. "Now, shall I tuck you into bed and tell Mrs. Pembroke you are ill?"

Know your worth.

Kitty Boxford was not blessed with riches, or even great beauty or grace. But she was blessed with good friends and good parents. People who believed in her, and helped her to believe in herself. For just a moment, she wondered if Lord Ellsworth had such support. And then she decided she did not care if he did or not. Kitty, for once, was going to worry about Kitty. And she was not going to let Lord Ellsworth and his self-indulgent moroseness trample on it. He might be happy to be unhappy, but she was determined not to be.

It was, perhaps, her one gift.

Fatigue fell away, the empty feeling inside replaced with another much more robust emotion. She would show Lord Ellsworth that Katherine Boxford was an excellent observatory assistant. Perhaps the best one he'd ever had. And he wasn't going to toss her out like every other person who didn't live up to his imaginary, impossible—and she sensed—ever-shifting standards.

"Mother, can you tell Mrs. Pembroke I shall be down shortly?"

"Of course. Are you certain, Katherine? If you need to rest—"

"I find myself quite recovered, in fact." She put her arms around her mother, hugging her tightly, then after a moment, released her.

Kitty Boxford might not be a lady in the proper sense, but she knew her worth. And she was determined to show Lord Ellsworth she knew it, even if he couldn't see it.

IT WAS JUST past ten o'clock at night when Colin arrived at Lofton Tower. The visit followed a full day of organized games of boules, croquet, and other polite sport, that finished with a late supper and cards. His need for solitude had warred with his desire to simply have a good night's sleep. He'd had little the night before after his most provocative encounter with Miss Boxford. How could such a strumpet of a woman get under his skin this way? Not even Amelia had managed to do that.

Bringing Miss Boxford to Lofton Tower had been a serious misstep on his part—his desperation to solve his marriage conundrum interfering with his normally careful judgment.

Colin shifted in his seat, thinking back on last evening. Perhaps he had been unfair to her. He'd given her meager direction, and she'd taken it upon herself not to be idle. She'd expected to be working in his observatory. But as the hour drew near, Colin had found himself quite unwilling to allow her there. The last woman he'd taken there was Amelia. And she'd rejected him.

But in the end, Miss Boxford's inability to listen to direction, her insistence on disturbing his space all the while daring to pass judgment on his methods—clearly they were not what he needed or desired in an assistant. Everything about her livened some unwanted sensation in him. And her barb, before she parted. How was he to know he was trampling on her chance at happiness? What on earth did he have to do with that? He swallowed, pushing off the remorse the crept upon him as he recalled the mix of indignation and panic in Miss Boxford's face when he'd ordered her not to come back. He was supposed to be looking for a bride.

Or, as Miss Boxford so plainly put it, a breeding partner. Which is all he needed, in the end. Solitude and the production of heirs. It was dispassionate, as Miss Boxford had pointedly said, but passion's only reward had been a broken heart and battered pride. Indeed, he'd been treated to the unhinged passion of one of his kin earlier this year that had nearly gotten him and several innocent people killed. Passion was best left for poets and painters. Not for dukes.

Dispassion and method would be his guide. So when he did manage to tear himself out of bed this morning, he focused on the two qualities that suited his needs.

After careful consultation with his father, he learned there were several ladies present who met his basic requirements—at least a dozen were from families that had four children who all lived to adulthood. One, a Miss Rosamund Peck, was from a family of nine. Lady Mariah, he could not help but notice, was from a family of five. She had three brothers. And Lady Mariah, unlike Miss Boxford, seemed to know exactly when to speak and when not to.

As his gig rounded the last gentle curve that let up to the observatory, Colin found himself extraordinarily unsettled. Above him, the stars were thick in the sky and an entire cast of constellations were on display. Constellations Miss Boxford was more than eager to identify to prove herself. Too eager, perhaps. True, she had tidied up much of the old crockery that should have been washed up long ago. He could have been nicer about that, he supposed. But then she'd gone and cleaned and moved and generally did exactly what she was told not to do, which was to touch everything else. He simply could not have an assistant who could not take direction.

The encounter made him reconsider his entire decision about allowing her to be his assistant. That she'd even made the attempt to disguise herself as a boy made the entire situation worse. Of course, who had the worse judgment? He didn't know, given his rash decision to make a bargain with her at Stormount after a single afternoon of bride hunting. In the end, he'd let emotion get in the way of good sense, which was certainly not at all like him.

She had that sort of effect on him. Best to be rid of her.

As the gig came to a stop, he hopped down and gave instructions to his driver to fetch him at sunrise. A gentle glow came from the lower windows, where a servant must have come ahead of him and opened up the tower. An immediate sense of calm came over him as he walked in. The neat piles still stood as Miss Boxford had laid them up the night before, and Colin could not help but grudgingly admit to himself that, just perhaps, this may have been better. The Orrey his father had given him stood proudly on the center of a worktable normally piled high with papers and books. A smaller viewing telescope — the first one he'd ever purchased—stood on the mantle over the hearth. He'd pointed a similar one at the moon when he was little more than a boy, and saw another world with hills and valleys, ghostly and wondrous. He'd pointed it at a patch of sky and had seen more stars than he thought possible. And until last night, it had gotten lost in the frantic piles that had somehow accumulated in the past few years. He climbed up the stairs, two at a time, eager to get on with his night's viewing. He would only do an hour or so—he was exhausted from the endless socializing, but he figured this would do him a world of good.

Except there was someone standing at his telescope. Not just someone.

Her.

She swallowed, and though the light was low, he could tell she was nervous. Good.

"Unless there was some mistake, this arrangement had been terminated, Miss Boxford," he said, keeping his voice steady. "Instead, I come here to find you not only present, but touching my telescope."

"I gave it some thought, and decided to give you another chance."

Colin started. He couldn't have heard her properly. "You what?"

"You said you wished to hire me to assist you to find a wife. But, unless the news has not yet reached Kennington Grove, you are still without a fiancé." She looked at him with a curious expectation.

"I remain quite unattached at the moment," he said with equal parts relief and regret.

"Well, then," she said, holding out her hands as if all was settled. "My help is still required. And, assuming you are a man of your word, which you claimed to be last night, that agreement is contingent on me continuing to work as your assistant."

"I think you overstep yourself, Miss Boxford. I recall releasing you from our agreement."

"Well, if that is the case, then I am owed two weeks wages."

Colin frowned, then let out a small, exasperated laugh. "Excuse me?"

"I fulfilled my half of the bargain, and did everything asked of me. And then you reneged—"

"Because you did not listen to direction."

"No, in fact. I did listen and abide by the very little direction you provided. So again, you may pay me for the duration, or I can work for my wages and continue to offer advice. And since your arm is still bandaged, and this work is clearly important to you, I believe the second option should suit us both."

Colin blinked. Caught between being thunderstruck at Miss Boxford's impertinence or impressed by her bearing, he let out a low breath. He ran a hand through his hair, then adjusted his spectacles. He may have even uttered a curse under his breath, which he could not recall having done in recent memory.

"You wish to hunt comets," she continued. "I will help you in whatever way I can. But before we begin, I do wish to apologize, my lord."

"For touching my things when you were not invited to?"

"I suppose." She paused, tilting her head a little to one side in the most beguiling way, then continued. "But if I may, you were extremely vague as to the duties of the assistant. I merely assumed they were part of them."

"Your lack of contrition is remarkable, Miss Boxford, but I suppose I see your point."

"But—my words about your fiancé were heartless and inexcusable. I was angry, and scared, and I lashed out in a way that was beneath me," she said, her manner softening considerably. "I know nothing of the circumstances between you. But, if it means anything at all, I am very sorry for my words. They were ill considered."

Colin stood, uncertain what to say. No one spoke to him the way she did. Like he was a human being. She flitted over to a basket that was sitting on a nearby table, and smiled broadly.

"I brought some refreshments—strawberries from my garden. Would you like some? And a bit of cheese as well. I would have brought something to wash it down, but I didn't know what was appropriate."

"Brandy sounds good at the moment," he muttered.

She blinked at his words, then smiled. "Was that a joke, my lord?"

"I think it might have been," he replied, an equal measure of surprise and delight lightening his mood. A strange sort of relief washed over him. "I am generally not known for my humor."

"And I am not known for being so horribly unfeeling to another," she said. "I am truly sorry."

"Apology accepted, Miss Boxford," he replied. "Now, let us leave the strawberries for another time and get down to work, shall we?"

"Of course, my lord."

"But we will do this on these terms. And I will be clear. Your job—your only job—is to record my observations."

"Of course."

He walked over to the telescope and beckoned for her to follow, holding up the lamp to ease her passage. Normally he had as little light here as possible, but she needed to become familiar with the surroundings. Though she was never to use the telescope, it did not hurt to show her how it worked.

"This is a reflecting telescope." He pointed to the eye piece. "Unlike a refracting telescope, like the sort used by Galileo, this uses mirrors to gather light and project it to the eyepiece right here. It is a Newtonian invention, though others have been perfecting his design."

She nodded, and Colin could not help wonder if she understood. He'd explained this to many before, and none seemed to take the slightest interest. Of course, Miss Boxford's interest may have been solely the crown per week she was earning.

"Like Mr. Herschel."

Colin blinked and looked anew at Miss Boxford. "Yes. That is quite…correct. Mr. Herschel's genius is the mirror itself. The quality of the mirror, even more than its size, is the most important piece."

"So what is it exactly that you wish for me to do?"

He led her to a small table containing some writing instruments, his observation book, and a clock.

"I need light, as well as a good arm, to record my observations."

"And the light ruins your vision for the darkness," she said. "I see."

And she did. She did see. There was something incredibly comforting about that.

"The stars move through the heavens over the course of a night, just as the sun moves through the day. I am doing a scan of a particular piece of the sky. To track the position of an object, the telescope is aimed at the meridian. When one of the larger stars crosses the field, I will call out which one. At that moment, you must look at the clock and record the time for that object. Do you think you can do that?"

"I know I can."

A sense of buoyancy filled Colin's chest. He rubbed his hands together, set the lamp down on the little desk, then pulled out a chair for her. She sat and picked up the pencil.

"Shall we begin?"

It took several bits of back and forth of Colin making his observations, and going back to check on Miss Boxford's recording of them to ensure that she was doing them correctly. She was an extremely quick study, and soon he was able to concentrate fully on his work.

Perhaps not fully.

He pulled his glasses off, gazing through the eye piece, waiting for his sight to adjust and allowing the heavens to reveal themselves to him. The mirror on this telescope was the best he'd procured to date, designed exactly to his specifications. Wisps of white light, along with shimmering points, revealed themselves. Knowing he could give his full concentration to the task was delightful.

The only other sound in the room was that from the pencil in Miss Boxford's hand, along with the occasional clearing of her throat.

"Would you like some refreshment, my lord?"

Colin started at the sound of Miss Boxford's voice.

"Refreshment?" he asked, bewildered by the question. He had not moved from his position.

"Refreshment. Food. You have been at this for nearly two hours."

Colin stood, stretching his back, and rubbing his eyes then placed his spectacles on. He had no idea that so much time had passed. He turned toward Miss Boxford, who still sat at her little desk, holding up the small basket she'd brought. She took out a small box full of strawberries.

"Would you like some?"

"No, thank you," he replied. "It is nearly midnight. I want to get as much work done before the carriage comes to get you."

"Very well," she replied. "I will leave these here for you. I would think you might benefit from some fuel for your occupation. My mother always ensured my father had plenty to eat before he went out on his daily rounds."

"Your father's work was more physically strenuous that this. This requires brain power."

"And gamekeeping does not?" she replied, and Colin could not miss the edge of sarcasm in her voice. "I suppose you can mind the location and breeding habits of two thousand coveys?"

Colin grimaced. His back did ache, and if Miss Boxford kept bombarding him, then his brain would. too.

"My apologies, Miss Boxford. I admit to being not as well versed in the art of gamekeeping as others."

"But you will inherit a great estate. Surely you should know something about it."

"That is why we have a steward, Miss Boxford. And a head gamekeeper."

"Mr. Campbell. His Grace wishes my father to meet with him."

Colin shifted uncomfortably in his boots. "Really? On what topic, pray?"

"On how to breed your coveys and keeping your father's fish stocks healthy."

A queer sensation settled on Colin then. Like he was being set down by a gamekeeper's daughter. Who, quite possibly, knew more about the functioning of part of his estate better than he did.

"Point taken, Miss Boxford. I would be honored to share your feast."

He shook his head, then put the stool nearby her. She put the book aside for a moment, unwrapped a small chunk of cheese and opened a wooden box full of strawberries. Carefully considering the contents, she plucked one from the top, and put it to her lips, which may have been the most distracting thing Colin had seen in a long time. His body reacted almost instantly to the sensation.

He pulled his gaze away, and helped himself to a berry, eager to divert himself from the quite illogical desire to wrap his fingers in Miss Boxford's thick brown curls and bring her mouth to his. To run his lips along her neck. To lose himself in her lush bosom.

Dear Lord, he thought. He walked to the window, allowing the fresh air to bring him back to his senses.

"These strawberries are very good," he replied, determined to keep himself focused on more mundane subjects. "Mrs. Pembroke is very lucky to have your parents in her employ."

"She has Edmund to thank for that," Miss Boxford replied, letting go a small sigh. "He is the reason why we are here at all."

A twist of something—bittersweetness perhaps—caught his attention.

"My understanding is that your parents were in the employ of Sir Richard Hamilton for some time," he said. Sir Richard had been Edmund's employer too—when Edmund had run away from his family. He'd worked as a spy for a time, before throwing off the mantle and settling as a gamekeeper at the estate.

"Yes," she replied, cutting several pieces of cheese off a small chunk. "We had been there since I was thirteen. A few years ago, my father injured himself at Westemere, and he was unable to keep up with the significant demands of the position. I offered to help him, but it is frowned upon for a woman to be a gamekeeper. And he wanted better for me, though I fail to see what could be better than that."

Colin was struck by her declaration. He had blessed little interaction with women, and most of any consequence had been with those from his own social sphere.

"Marriage? Isn't that what most women want?"

Miss Boxford looked at him as if he'd declared the sun to be the moon. "If the only other option available to us is abject poverty, then I suppose so. When you have only two choices before you, then I suppose marriage is the preferable one. If we could be gamekeepers and observatory assistants, maybe we would be less inclined."

"You are a bluestocking, Miss Boxford. I hadn't pegged you for a radical."

"If being a radical is pointing out a simple error in men's logic, then I suppose I am. You don't have to marry to be a duke," she said, "but if you didn't have to be duke at all—if you could choose from all the immense choices before you, what would you do? Would you marry?"

"It is a pointless question, Miss Boxford," he replied. "'Tis merely a business transaction, in the end." There was a harshness in his reply he did not expect. Perhaps he was merely convincing himself of it, so he did not have to dwell on his heartbreak.

"Fifty guests and a fortnight of parties? My goodness, is this how the peerage conducts all business transactions?"

"My parents…are heavily invested. In the end, I am certain I will pick the right woman."

"And who is the right woman for this transaction of yours?" Miss Boxford sat back in her chair, thoughtful. "It can't be someone who might fall in love with you."

"Why ever not?"

"Well, primarily because it appears love is not on your list, which would leave one of you in misery if your partner was interested in that," she said in a matter-of-fact way. "You also want someone who will leave you alone to pursue your studies. So it must be a woman who is able be parted from you. Who would view you as a pleasant, if detached, acquaintance in her life."

"I suppose." It sounded horrid spelled out so plainly.

"What else?" she said. "Or perhaps it doesn't matter. Perhaps there is someone who, in the quiet moments, can share your joys and hardships. Someone you wish to support in return. Someone who will support your work. A great patroness of whatever scientific endeavors you chose to support."

"Patroness?" Colin took a sip of the tea. "In truth, I had not considered such an idea."

"Well, I don't see why they wouldn't be," she said so bluntly it almost amused him. "The lady in question does not need to share all of your passions, but she should, I hope, support some, as you would do for her in return."

"I do not have passions, Miss Boxford."

She looked at him most strangely, as if he'd said something illogical.

"My lord, you keep saying this. And yet, we are sitting in a building you designed and oversaw the construction of, which houses a telescope you guard more jealously than any dragon guards a horde of gold. And when I tried to touch any of it, you lost what little temper I have seen you betray. I would say you are quite passionate. It's just that no one has bothered to notice. You most of all."

"You noticed."

She picked another berry out of the box, examined it, then looked at him with a smile that threatened to disarm him completely.

"I suppose I have." She paused, her countenance thoughtful. "I am passionate about my garden, and very protective of it."

"You love to garden," he said, inexplicably interested. "But it is more than gardening, judging by your extensive note taking."

"Gardening is active for the mind and body. If I were a man I supposed I would love to be a gardener for an estate." She looked at him, but he could tell her mind was somewhere else. "It is always constant, and never constant all at once. Like the sky, I suppose." She let out a small sigh and her shoulders sagged ever so slightly. "And even if I have to leave it behind, I can take seeds and plantings with me."

"Do you often have to leave it behind?" Colin asked.

She shook her head. "No. But we are not landowners, my lord. My father's occupation is as a servant to the landed class. We are subject to the whims of the gentry, for good or ill."

Whim. She'd used that term before, when she was angry at him. No wonder.

"I hope the whims have been more of the former," he said.

"Mostly, yes," she said, her mouth turned downward. "Indeed, I will be uprooting the garden again very soon."

It was now Colin's turn to frown. She was moving?

"Where? When?"

"Not far—just to Silver Cross," she said, then proceeded to reveal the circumstances. "As to when...very soon. Indeed the move itself has already begun."

Realization dawn on him. Was this why she was so eager to earn some coin?

"Is this situation not amenable to you?"

She shrugged her shoulders. "It simply is. And really, what choice do I have at present?"

"This is why you want a position here."

"I wish to be less of a burden to my parents. I am four and twenty. I have a bit of a plan, but if I could earn some extra wages, I might be able to expedite them," she said. "And maybe one day, I will have my own little garden somewhere that is mine. That I never have to move."

The clock began to strike the hour.

"Right then, Miss Boxford. I will hire you to be my assistant, and you can remain in my employ until I find a bride."

Her eyes widened then and she looked at him with such appreciation he thought his heart would burst.

"Thank you, my lord," she replied, jumping to her feet and gathering her things as the bells continued to chime. "You will not regret it, I promise you."

She looked at him with such gratitude and joy. It made him want to hold her. Indeed, it made him want to do more than that.

"One moment," he called out as she ran toward the steps that led down to the first floor. "I will pay you a little more so you may continue to help me choose the right woman to be my bride. I will pay you more because it will demand more of your time. There is to be a picnic tomorrow, and more events to come. I recognize attending most of them might not be possible, but I will require your presence as much as is possible. Do you think you can do that?"

She paused, pursing her lips, then nodded.

"I trust you to be discreet, of course," he said.

She laughed. "Worry not, my lord. To nearly everyone I will be quite invisible."

The last bell chimed, and she hurried down the stairs and out the door she went. Colin went to one of the windows in the tower, and watched the carriage until it disappeared down one of the wooded paths that let away from the tower.

And then he kept watching.

CHAPTER 11

There were picnics. And then there were *picnics*. The scene before her on the shores of Stormount's Long Pond was an intoxicating mix of nature, spectacle, and wealth.

"Stunning," she said, gripping the arm of her best friend as they walked along. Edmund and Mrs. Pembroke were alongside, as he pushed his mother down a path through a formal garden alongside a small lake. Sunlight glistened on the water, creating a thousand tiny lights that danced on the surface. Open tents had been erected to allow for shade, and large tables were set out with the finest pastries, cheese, and other refreshments. Bunting and garlands were strung from poles and nearby trees, and flitted prettily in the light afternoon breeze. Kitty marveled at the spectacle. If this was a picnic at Stormount, a formal ball must be an unimaginably remarkable event.

"The duchess has outdone herself," Mrs. Pembroke concurred. "We are in for a treat."

Kitty was somewhat surprised that Mrs. Pembroke wished to attend; not because she was unwelcome, but she rarely traveled beyond the confines of Kennington Grove and Silver Cross. Perhaps she was concerned about Kitty's presence alongside Edmund and Gwyneth. Her employer had not said anything more since their earlier conversation, nor had given any indication that she disapproved of Kitty. But the fact that Mrs. Pembroke knew of her feelings was still troublesome. And embarrassing.

No matter. Kitty was on a different mission entirely, which was to assist Lord Ellsworth. Provide him that sort of female intelligence about her sex that might have been lost on a man, and especially one so clumsy in his manner. When she'd left Lofton Tower last night, she'd truly wondered, for the first time, what she had gotten herself into. Every moment she spent with him played with her emotions. It must simply be that he was a lord, and a terribly important one, she reasoned. And, perhaps because he was the key to her happiness. That he was giving her this opportunity was no small thing. The extra wages should push ahead her plans. It wasn't five thousand pounds. But it would be enough.

The Pembrokes and Kitty found a comfortable place amongst the crowd, higher on a gentle slope, near a small stand of trees that offered shade. It also afforded Kitty an excellent view of the crowd.

"Gwynnie, why don't you and Edmund take a turn through the gardens? I will stay with Mrs. Pembroke."

"Kitty," Edmund said in that way of his. She shouldn't like it so much when he said her name after all this time. "Do not make Gwyneth subject me to a thirty minute fashion review."

"I am sure it is a small price to pay for a private stroll with your lovely wife," Kitty said.

"And we can also take stock of all fine young gentleman present," Gwynnie said, looking squarely at Kitty. "Come, Edmund."

"Alas, my lady calls and I must answer her," he said, giving his mother a kiss on the cheek. "And don't worry, Kitty, I'll restrain Gwyneth as much as I can."

Kitty watched her friends go off, that familiar pang of regret in her chest lessened by her new-found mission. She turned her gaze to the crowd. Finely dressed ladies and elegant gentlemen were clustered in small groups. If any of the gentlemen here were distressed about the fact that they were the absolute second choice, none seemed confounded by it. She lifted herself up on her toes, watching for any sign of Lord Ellsworth. At last she found him, speaking to a small crowd surrounding him. She was too far away to make out the expression on his face, but his posture betrayed him. Despite the cheer of the afternoon and general frivolity surrounding him, it was clear he was not at ease. Had he not listened to a word she'd said?

"Ask them a question," she found herself saying under her breath. "Just ask."

His stance changed then, and it seemed, somehow, that he'd noticed her. What his expression was, she could not tell, but a bolt of awareness shot through her, straightening her spine, and she found herself pulling a stray curl from her cheek and tucking it behind her ear. Though she was supposed to be watching the crowd, she found herself watching him. Rather intently, in fact. Which was not the point of the exercise at all.

"Miss Boxford."

Mrs. Pembroke's voice broke through Kitty's concentration. She turned her attention toward her charge, taking a moment to refocus her thoughts.

"Yes ma'am?" she asked, smiling.

Over the years, Kitty had become accustomed to Mrs. Pembroke's expressions, which to those who did not know her, could be difficult to read owing to the injuries that had left one half of her face without movement. She'd trained herself to watch the right-side of Mrs. Pembroke's face only, as her mouth on the left side had fallen into a permanent frown. But today she found Mrs. Pembroke quite unreadable. Was it surprise? Dismay? Or something else?

"If you would be so kind as to fetch a glass of lemonade for me, Miss Boxford, I would be forever in your debt."

"Are you certain?" she replied, searching the lawn for her friends. "Perhaps I should wait until Edmund and Gwyneth return."

"I find myself quite comfortable here at present, and you should only be a few minutes," she replied, with a firmness of voice that Kitty knew would brook no opposition.

"Very well, ma'am," she replied, then started off toward the refreshments. She hadn't taken too many steps when she found a servant and asked her to keep an eye on Mrs. Pembroke and to find Kitty immediately if she was needed. From there she made her way through the crowd toward the refreshments tables.

She spied Edmund and Gwynnie conversing with several ladies and gentlemen, looking very much at home in their surroundings. Kitty moved on, quite invisible to them all. Within minutes, she arrived at a refreshment table. There several ladies spoke in excited conversation about the man of the hour.

"He stood with me for at least five minutes," one of the ladies said. She was a young, pretty thing with light brown hair fashionably done, perhaps no more than eighteen. "It was positively painful. One can only speak on the weather for so long."

"True, Marianne," her friend replied. "But he is terribly rich. You wouldn't have to spend more than five minutes with him each day. And the title has several estates. You would only need to see him several times a year."

"But our children..." Her mouth fell into a small pout. "What if they had that horrid orange hair? I am not a fan of gingers. They get so terribly freckled. I do not know if I could look upon them favorably then."

Kitty walked among them and ladled lemonade into a cup, taking a sip or two for her own refreshment, then cast her eye around the crowd. She saw him again, walking with another lady, again his manner stiff. The lady in question wore a tight attentive smile, but Kitty could see in an instant the woman was bored beyond measure. Something needed to be done.

She looked for Edmund and Gwynnie. Perhaps she could communicate through them? But there was nothing for it, as she couldn't tell them about their agreement.

Kitty put down her cup, let out a low breath, smoothed her skirt, then moved toward him, a plan hatching in her head. She was a servant, after all. Servants could speak with anyone if they had a reason to do so.

"My Lord Ellsworth," she said, coming upon him and stopping in a quick curtsey. He was in the middle of another strained communication with another young lady who she recognized as the sister of Lady Mariah. The lady, of similar coloring but perhaps lesser beauty than her sister, regarded Kitty with a narrow gaze that lasted only seconds before returning to her placid expression.

"Excuse me, Lady Belinda," the marquess said, confusion coming over his face. "Yes?"

"I am to deliver a message on behalf of my employer, my lord," she said.

"Right," he said, an almost visible relief resting on his face. "If you would excuse me a moment, Lady Belinda."

Her eyelids fluttered, and the smallest hint of annoyance marred her otherwise placid countenance. "Of course, my lord."

The girl strode past Kitty, not sparing her a glance as she went by.

"What is Mrs. Pembroke's message? Please do not tell me she is ready to leave, as I am certain you arrived but ten minutes ago," he said.

Kitty blinked, surprised by his statement. Had he, in fact, seen her the moment they'd come? How was that even possible amongst so many taller, more elegantly dressed women? Or was it the plainness of her dress that had called attention to her in some way? Self-consciousness threatened to steal her confidence. She looked to her feet a moment.

"When I said my employer, my lord, I was being...imaginative. I was speaking of yourself."

He nodded then, his serious countenance betraying the hint of a smile.

"You do have a penchant for imagination, Miss Boxford. What seems to be the problem?"

Kitty let out a low breath, then dared to look him in the eye. This was, in fact, what he'd hired her to do, she reminded herself.

"With respect, my lord, it is you."

"Me?"

"Well, I am not having a problem with you. But you are having a problem...with yourself." She clasped her hands together, uncertain how to say it nicely. She leaned forward and dropped her voice, fearful anyone, perhaps even Lord Ellsworth himself, hear a game-keeper's daughter criticize a marquess at his own picnic. "With apologies, my lord, you are not that easy in conversation."

He let out a small chuckle, and looked out over the crowd, before returning his gaze to her.

"Miss Boxford, I hardly needed you to tell me that," he said. "I believe, aside from the debacle with Lady Amelia, it is the thing I am most famous for. Or infamous."

He smiled in earnest, and it quite transformed him. It made Kitty feel curiously happy inside, and she could not help but smile at him in return.

"Perhaps it is because I have rarely seen you in a public forum such as this," she replied. "You seem to have little trouble conversing with Edmund or Lady Gwyneth. Or me, for that matter."

He paused, pursing his lips slightly in thought before he spoke again. "I had not quite considered that."

"It is because you are not trying to court me, and I am most certainly not trying to court you."

He looked almost hurt then. Which was ridiculous, of course. Gamekeeper's daughters did not court the sons of dukes.

"May I offer some advice?" she asked. "Ask the ladies about themselves. It is so rarely done. But you will find out more about them, and then you will not have to speak as much."

He stilled, tentative, and she could see he was turning over her suggestion in his head.

"Ladies learn early to converse prettily—to ask a man to talk about himself. Indeed, Gwynnie was being schooled on this when she was just a little girl. But I am certain it must work in the reverse."

"So you suggest I speak to every woman, and do nothing but listen."

"You look as if that is a completely novel idea."

He reddened slightly, as if embarrassed that he'd not considered it before. "I suppose it is. This is not something, alas, boys are trained to do."

"Consider it observation, like you are doing now. You sit at your telescope and watch, and note what the heavens have to offer. Pretend the ladies are the stars, and note what you discover," Kitty replied.

He nodded slowly, realization dawning on this face. "Yes, of course," he replied. "Excellent Miss Boxford. Thank you. I shall try it."

He put his hand to the brim of his hat, quite an unnecessary gesture, then excused himself and continued, where he was quickly pulled away by a gentleman who was, no doubt, eager to introduce Lord Ellsworth to his daughter. She watched him for a short while, before she realized she was quite overdue to return to Mrs. Pembroke with her lemonade. Having one charge at a gathering was responsibility enough. Having two was quite another thing.

After securing two glasses of lemonade, Kitty carefully maneuvered through the crowd, keeping one eye on her drinks so as not to spill them, and another ahead of her. As she was nearly free of the crowd, she was sharply jostled, freeing the contents of one glass and pouring it down the front of her dress.

"Oh dear," said Lady Amelia, who was standing in front of her. Her expression went from detached to unapologetic in an instant.

Kitty looked down the front of her dress. The light blue muslin was darkened from the middle of her bodice to the upper part of her skirt.

"I am sure it will be fine," she said, eager to make her leave. "If you will excuse me."

Kitty stepped to one side, but Lady Mariah, it seemed, was not interested in letting her pass. "I will, once you apologize."

"Apologize?"

"For bumping into me so ferociously. I don't know if anyone has told you, but you move like an absolute bear. If my ladies' maid did thus, she would be turned out of the house."

"Indeed," Kitty said, swallowing the anger bubbling inside her. She knew what it was to be turned out on the whim of a privileged, heartless woman. "If I was your maid, I think I would rather serve a bear. They have better manners."

"I cannot believe that the duke and duchess would entertain the presence such a low-born, hapless creature at such an important occasion," she said, her indignation and anger marring the normally benign, placid look on her face. "You forget your place."

"I know exactly where my place is," Kitty said, "and it is not to stand here and subject myself to the poor manners of one of my so-called betters."

Kitty stalked off, her entire body prickling with indignation. By the time she returned to Mrs. Pembroke, Edmund and Gwynnie were with her. She handed Gwynnie Mrs. Pembroke's glass to hold, then pulled out a handkerchief take the worst of the dampness off herself.

"What happened?" Gwynnie asked.

"Nothing at all," Kitty answered, not willing to discuss her unpleasant encounter with Lady Mariah. "Just clumsiness."

"Perhaps we could take a moment," her friend said, "and try to fix it? Here, take my shawl."

"It's of no consequence, Gwynnie," Kitty said, accepting the yellow silk shawl and sliding it over her shoulders despite the warmth of the day. "Lady Mariah did not even see me. I do not think anyone else will either. Regardless, I will stay with Mrs. Pembroke and watch the show from here."

"Lady Mariah?" Gwynnie narrowed her gaze and turned toward the crowd. "I will have words with her."

"No, you will not," Kitty said. "She is beneath our concern. And I am most definitely beneath hers."

Gwynnie looked at her friend anew. "If she intentionally spilled lemonade down your dress, I would say she is immensely concerned about you. But we can't fuss about this now," Gwynnie said, catching Kitty's eye and darting her gaze toward the crowd.

Kitty turned her head and to her absolute horror, the Duchess of Weymouth was approaching. The affected manner of her walk suggested to Kitty that despite her desire to appear otherwise, the duchess was nervous.

Kitty and Gwynnie lowered themselves in a deep curtsey, while Edmund and his mother bowed. Kitty clasped Gwynnie's shawl around her front, but the stain down her dress made itself known regardless. Not that Kitty need be troubled by it. Her Grace barely spared Kitty a glance. Indeed, she turned her restrained smile to Mrs. Pembroke and most especially Edmund.

"Good afternoon," she said by way of introduction, louder perhaps than was required. "I trust you are enjoying the afternoon? We have been fortunate as to weather."

"Indeed," Edmund said. "I think you may count this as another one of your successes, your Grace."

Kitty marveled at how easy Edmund was in conversation. When he first came to Westemere, he had been much more reserved, no doubt still haunted by the events that had led him there. But, as Kitty suspected, something larger loomed on the duchess' mind, for she smiled tightly at the compliment, which was not her usual way.

She lowered her voice. "Indeed, I hope it remains that way. But I have just heard the most troubling rumor…and I am appealing to you, Mr. Pembroke, for your assistance. You know my poor boy better than anyone."

My poor boy. Kitty could barely stifle her smile. Only a mother could look on a man like Lord Ellsworth and brand him thus.

Edmund nodded, concern creasing his brow. "I am, as always, at your service."

She settled down on the bench and begged Edmund to sit next to her. "You must convince the marquess to choose a bride. Quickly."

"I spoke with him only days before the party started," Edmund replied. "He was most insistent on doing so. Has he given you any indication to the contrary?"

The duchess cast a look across the crowd. Kitty followed her stare and found Lord Ellsworth sitting on a blanket. She could not help but smile a little. He seemed to be listening intently to a couple of ladies and gentleman. Perhaps he had taken her advice after all.

"Not yet. But I have just heard it from Mr. Harnish, who lives but a mile from Stormount, that a group of Travelers have set up camp in the wood just past the river. Is this true?"

"Indeed," Mrs. Pembroke said in a tone Kitty often heard her use to calm her neighbor, "but I fail to see the concern. They have not troubled us in the past."

"They were camped in that very spot but a fortnight before Lady Grafton so carelessly trampled on my boy's heart." The duchess clutched a fleshy hand to her breast. "I fear it is an omen."

"Mayhap it is a good omen, your Grace," Mrs. Pembroke replied.

With a flick of her wrist, the duchess opened her elaborate lace fan, madly fluttering it as she was clearly deliberating Mrs. Pembroke's suggestion.

"Perhaps you are right." The movement of the duchess' fan slowed, then sped up again. "However, it unsettles me. Why come to Stormount, of all possible places?"

"Fear not, your Grace," Edmund said. "If the need arises, I will speak to him."

"Thank you, Mr. Pembroke," she replied, the relief palpable in her manner. "And pray do not speak of this to his Grace. I fear if he finds word of it—"

"Ah, here is my lovely bride."

Kitty's attention was drawn to an older, well-dressed gentleman walking toward them. Though he was not quite as tall as Lord Ellsworth, his graying reddish hair and green-gray eyes marked him as the Duke of Weymouth. After an exchange of civilities, he turned, remarkably, to Kitty.

"Good afternoon, Miss Boxford," he said, his eyes kind and curious. "I have been quite eager to make your acquaintance."

Kitty's eyes widened. She smiled, flustered, as all eyes in the party fell on her.

"Th-thank you, your Grace," she replied, bewilderment staggering her words.

"I have heard that your father is one of the best anglers in this part of the country. And has been offering advice to Mr. Campbell on a number of matters."

Kitty nodded. "We are most thankful to Mr. Campbell for his interest in my father's assistance."

"While I do not wish to tread on my gamekeeper's toes, I would be most interested in Mr. Boxford's opinions on my fish stocks. Campbell, much as I appreciate his work, is much more focused on his beloved fowl," the duke continued. "Perhaps he could visit, once we have Stormount to ourselves again."

Kitty was overwhelmed to nearly the point of tears. "I believe I can speak for my father when I say he would consider it a very great honor, your Grace. Thank you."

"Excellent," he said, beaming in what Kitty could only consider to be genuine happiness at the prospect. And it occurred to Kitty, for some strange reason, that if Lord Ellsworth smiled more often, he would share the same joyous expression as his father.

He turned then and spoke to Edmund, Gwynnie and Mrs. Pembroke at length.

After the excitement of having spoken with the duke and duchess, the heat became too much for both Gwynnie and Mrs. Pembroke, and they prepared to take their leave. Kitty cast one last glance toward the crowd, looking for Lord Ellsworth. She'd found him, speaking—or rather listening intently—to a young woman who was quite animated in her conversation.

She smiled, relieved to see not only that he accepted her advice, but that it appeared to be working well. Lord Ellsworth seemed far more at ease, and so did the ladies he spoke with. Perhaps he had already found his bride.

"Is something wrong, Miss Boxford?"

Mrs. Pembroke's question cut through Kitty's reverie. She shook her head, and pulled her attention away from Lord Ellsworth.

"No ma'am," she replied quickly, before realizing the Pembrokes were starting to make their exit. She picked up her pace and fell in step with them.

"Colin's manner with his female company seems to have markedly improved," Edmund said. "Indeed, toward the end I believe he was actually enjoying the chase. I wonder what on earth happened to him?"

Kitty stifled a smile, congratulating herself on how well he'd taken her counsel. But as she took one last look over her shoulder and watched him smiling and nodding at one of the many ladies vying for his hand, that satisfaction faded, replaced with an uncomfortable sensation that tightened her chest.

Never mind Lord Ellsworth, she wanted to say. What on earth was happening to her?

It may have been something of a miracle. Or, Colin corrected himself, a discovery. Taking Miss Boxford's advice, Colin spent the afternoon talking to his female guests. Or rather, listening to them.

Women, it turned out, had something to say, if one bothered to ask. Damn it if Miss Boxford wasn't right.

He could still picture her, walking toward him, a curious mix of trepidation and purpose. If nothing else she'd distracted him from his woeful attempt at conversation with Lady Belinda Stapleton. That had been painful beyond measure.

He'd been a tad nervous at first, taking Miss Boxford's advice. Over the years he'd worked hard to improve his discomfort in large social occasions. When he became duke, he would take on the role as one might put on a jacket, and he needed to be able to manage it. People would ask after his injury, and he would reply. Ladies would ask after his parents. And he would tell them his parents were in excellent health. But instead of letting the answers hang in the air, he'd done the unthinkable today. He had asked about their parents. What they liked to do on sunny afternoons. What books they liked to read. And then he closed his mouth and made mental notes of the answers.

He'd begun with Miss Lydia Peckford. Her answers were uninspiring but informative, and it did allow Colin a reprieve from the endless questions about himself. And then he moved on to Lady Mary Cross, then Miss Patricia Winslow. And on and on, through the crowd he went. His plan was to spend precisely ten minutes with each girl. In some cases the conversation faltered in half that time. Colin had occasionally taken a break from the courting, getting swept into conversation with a number of gentlemen. Some of them were fathers, eager to negotiate the worth of their daughters. Some were young bucks, eager to pick up what Colin would not. After more than two hours of this, it had become exhausting. And, Colin could not help but admit, distasteful. But it had been far easier.

Conversation wasn't hard with Miss Boxford. Perhaps it was because there was, in fact, something to speak about. And he wasn't going to marry the girl. He didn't need to assess every word for a hint of compatibility. She was just…there.

Of course, he'd also learned something else this afternoon. His mother's unfounded fears about the encampment of Romani in the woods outside Stormount. Colin didn't believe in omens, or fate, or other such nonsense.

"My lord."

Lady Mariah Stapleton stood before him, a vision in a pale blue dress, her flaxen hair braided and twisted into an elaborate knot. She held out her gloved hand, which Colin took, gently kissing it before releasing her.

"A great pleasure to see you, my lady," he said. And it was. Though he was trying to be methodical in his approach to picking a bride, he could not help but admit to himself that Lady Mariah had much in her favor. Thus far, nothing had changed his opinion. "I trust you are enjoying the afternoon?"

She wore a serene smile. "Very much. The duke and duchess are very generous hosts."

A compliment to his parents. "That they are. My mother adores parties, and takes every opportunity to throw one." He cleared his throat. Time to ask about her. "Do you enjoy soirees, Lady Mariah?"

"I do, yes. Indeed, I have been assisting my mother to plan all our teas, back in London. Though nothing quite so elaborate as this." She smiled in the way Amelia did, and suddenly Colin felt at once familiar and wistful.

Lady Mariah was young—barely eighteen, according to his mother's intelligence. He had met the Earl of Bedford several times, but those occasions were primarily at his London club. Society had familiar names, but new faces emerged as daughters came of age. Since Colin had been engaged to Amelia, he'd not had occasion to seek out new faces. And in the two years since she left, he'd been quite determined not to.

"If I am not being too bold, my lord, can I entice you to partake of the strawberry ice? It is quite delicious."

"Of course. I would be delighted." Colin smiled to himself at her use of the phrase. An image of Miss Katherine Boxford found his way into his head, clad in trousers, a hat pulled down over her hair in an effort to disguise herself, as she tried to negotiate for a job, in the center of town, past dark. That was bold. And then, returning to his observatory last night, announcing that she would give him a second chance. He didn't know if even his mother would have been that bold. Of course, that sort of boldness was not the stuff of ladies.

He offered his arm to allow Lady Mariah to lead him to a tent where servants were scooping bowls of ice for the guests. As they walked along, past picnic blankets and garden chairs, he found himself looking for a sign of Miss Boxford, but she, along with her company, must have departed. Disappointment rushed through him, slowing his gait.

"My lord?"

Colin's smile froze on his face, and he realized she'd been speaking to him while his thoughts and attention were elsewhere. "Excuse my woolgathering, my lady. I was merely looking for one of my mother's acquaintances, but she may have left before I had the opportunity to make my greetings."

"Perhaps I can help," she offered. "Can you describe her?"

"Easily done. It is Mrs. Pembroke. She generally is in a wheeled chair."

Lady Mariah's mouth fell into a little sad pout.

"Was she the lady with the peculiar face?"

Mrs. Pembroke's injuries had left most of one side of her body with a type of palsy. It also made her mouth droop on one side.

"You are correct."

"She departed only a few minutes ago," she replied. "If I may be so bold, I think it is very charitable of her Grace to invite her. The poor thing must barely get out owing to her condition. Especially given the earlier scandal to befall her family."

"Scandal?" Colin felt himself stiffen slightly. He was not one for gossip. Especially after more than a year of being on the receiving end of it.

"The unfortunate events surrounding her husband and eldest son. And to be left alone, crippled," she said. "Very sad."

While he could not detect malice, there was a note of salaciousness in her tone that rankled. "Mrs. Pembroke has held herself very admirably given the circumstances that have befallen her. Lord Barronsfield himself holds her in the highest regard, and he shows great affection and loyalty to his aunt, as does her brother, Viscount Ainsley. Her physical condition is unfortunate, but we value her sound judgment. My mother has found Mrs. Pembroke's dignity in the face of great trials to be a virtue. As I do." And she'd always appreciated Colin. At Kennington Cross, when Edmund was at home visiting and not with his father in London, they were free to be themselves. For that, he would always be fond of her.

"Of course," Lady Mariah replied, checking her manner. "I was merely suggesting that your mother does her an honor bestowing her friendship on a woman of her circumstances."

Colin nodded, but said nothing. Lady Mariah was very young, and for that, her ill-chosen words were probably nothing more than an eagerness to display her loyalty to the duchess. He let it go.

After nearly three hours of walking, eating, commenting on the way the water shone on the lake, or hearing about the particulars of the bits of people's lives, it was over. The blankets were folded, the plates cleared away, and the musicians had tucked their flutes and violins into their cases. People strolled back toward the house, or allowed themselves a bit of solitude by wandering through some of Stormont's impressive gardens. Colin wanted nothing more than to steal away and immerse himself in silence.

Later that evening, Colin stood outside the front entrance of Lofton Tower, looking up at the sky. Heavy cloud had settled in the area, making viewing impossible. By agreement, he would only send for Miss Boxford if the viewing conditions were favorable, and though he'd been quite spent by the endless socializing, he found himself peering into the blanket of cloud, willing the stars to reveal themselves. He, despite his frustration that the sky would not heed his wishes, had convinced himself the reason he wanted to see them had nothing at all to do with the fact that as long as they remained hidden, Miss Boxford would remain at home. It was all science.

He turned away, closed the door behind him, and settled in his favorite chair. He took off his spectacles and released his frustration in a long, low breath. He should have been happy for the solitude. He'd had so bloody little of it of late.

But, quite unexpectedly, he simply felt alone.

CHAPTER 12

Kitty lit the lamps on the main floor of Lofton Tower while she waited for Lord Ellsworth to arrive. After only a week in the position, she was becoming accustomed to arriving a few moments before he did. Despite his best efforts, the pull of the activities at Stormount were becoming too great, even for him. He was to be married. And despite Kitty's growing theory that Lofton Tower was a refuge not only from the crowds but his need to commit to a wife, in the end, he and another woman would be promised to each before the festivities were over. Given his determination to see the business done, she could not help but wonder what was truly keeping him from merely picking any of the ladies present and having it over with. Something kept his decision at bay. Was he afraid to make the wrong decision?

Fear drove people to do many things. It had once driven Edmund to hide away from his name and family. Gwynnie's mother had planned horrible crimes against her daughter because she feared her daughter's beauty and the attention it garnered. Indeed, it had driven Gwynnie to be as good a girl as possible when she was in her mother's sights.

What was Lord Ellsworth afraid of?

Kitty gave herself a mental shake. Why on earth did it matter? Kitty had her own fears at present, and she was the only person in the world to manage them. This is why she'd lied to a peer, and dressed up like a boy to get a chance to work in Lofton Tower. This is why she snuck out of Kennington Grove after her employer went to bed, and endured too little sleep in the morning. She was tired of having to manage her fears alone. Tired of having to pretend all was well when it really wasn't.

Kitty yawned. Her topsy-turvy schedule was beginning to take its toll. She wasn't sure how much longer she could keep up her unusual hours and sneaking away before it caught up with her. Before someone noticed.

Look aloft and see what is unseen.

The curious words the Romani woman had spoken all those years ago rushed back to her. Those words were meant to be a comfort, but at the time they shook her to her bones. How on earth was she to find what she had lost? It did not help, of course, that she had not even the slightest inkling of what she was seeking. And the only thing that came to mind was her brooch, and she'd found it—or what was left of it. She had to make her own luck now.

She'd been tempted to have the coach that brought her to Stormount stop alongside the Romani camp that had set up nearby, in a vain attempt to find the woman who'd read her palm and uttered those curious words, but that was silly. There were many Traveler groups in England.

See what is unseen. What in the blazes did that even mean?

The telescope? No. She couldn't touch that. But perhaps something else. Lord Ellsworth's smaller looking glass, perhaps.

Kitty straightened, her gaze sweeping the room with a new-found purpose. Past the books and notes and the magical contraption on the desk with the sun and planet. The looking glass had to be here somewhere. She'd cleaned it herself. But it was nowhere to be found. Had she let that slip through her fingers as well? Or, as usual, were the heavens playing tricks on her once again...giving her a hint of what might be, before taking it away?

She put her hands on her hips and looked up to the heavens.

"Would you please, for one moment, stop making things so bloody hard?"

"Language, Miss Boxford."

The sound of his voice, firm but with a hint of levity, brought a tingly, warm—and quite forbidden—sensation that slid straight down into her belly. She closed her mouth, dropped her hands, and spun around on her heels. There, standing on the opposite side of the room was Lord Ellsworth, his lips pulled into a bemused smile.

"My apologies, Lord Ellsworth. It will not happen again."

"I think I am rather sorry about that," he replied, pulling off his hat. "There is something quite amusing about such a small person with such grand expressions."

She crossed her arms and dipped her eyebrows. "I am not certain if that is a compliment or an insult."

"Heavens, Miss Boxford, I have suffered through an entire day of miss-ish tittering and sly looks. Trust me when I say I find your enthusiastic response to be a balm."

"Thank you, I think," she said. "Although, in fairness to your female guests, they were trained to communicate that way. Do not slight them for exhibiting the mannerisms they were told to adopt for a man's society."

"You are a bluestocking, Miss Boxford, whether you admit it or not," he said, closing the door behind him. "So you will be pleased to know that I have been taking your advice and listening more than speaking. And more."

He walked to the desk and planted a small box on the table, then opened it. The small brass looking glass she'd been looking for.

"You will see I am still a bit indisposed at the moment," he said, gesturing to his bandaged arm. "Would you be able to put it there, in its usual spot on that shelf?"

"Of course," she said. She reached out for it, almost afraid to touch it.

"I trust you won't drop it, Miss Boxford."

She took a deep breath, then screwing up her courage, took it from him.

"Would you mind if I looked through it?"

He paused a moment, which was just enough to make her regret even asking.

"Never mind, my lord," she said, heat rushing into her cheeks. "I should not have asked."

He tilted his head slightly, and scratched the back of his neck, a deep furrow in his brow.

"Miss Boxford, you are a puzzle to me."

"How so?" She swallowed, unsure of his demeanor. Did he like puzzles or not?

"You offer your opinions on certain subjects freely—solicited or not. Your very presence here, we can both agree, is based on some rather bold actions on your part. And yet you seem to fear asking the smallest favor directly."

Kitty tried to hold his penetrating gaze as he approached her, but found herself unduly affected by it and his observation.

Because everything I have ever really wanted has always been taken away.

"What do you wish, Miss Boxford?" he asked, suddenly closer than ever.

I wish to know I can be happy.

"I wish to look through the telescope, my lord."

He opened the fine wooden box that housed the brass telescope, and removed it. Then he gestured for her to follow, and they made their way outside, walking along under the canopy of stars to a bench not far from the tower. In front of it lay much of the countryside. Peepers chirped their evening summer melody, while fireflies created their own starlight in the nearby trees.

He beckoned her to sit, then placed the telescope in her hands, which he'd extended to its full length. Then, he sat next to her, not too close—heaven help her, perhaps not close enough—but she was overcome with awareness of his tall, masculine form.

She swallowed. This was it, at last, she thought. Somehow in the next few moments, she might uncover what on earth the Romani woman's words meant. Whether she had in fact a second chance to recover her good luck.

"Now, see that bright light there?" He pointed toward a light, one among many, though she could tell that its light was somewhat different from the others. Firstly, it was very bright, and yet did not seem to shimmer. "That is Jupiter. See if you can point the instrument toward it."

Kitty took a breath and pointed it toward the sky. It took a moment for her eye to adjust, but where she'd seen some stars with her eyes, so many more miraculously appeared before her. Some dim, all shimmering a bit.

"There is so much that cannot be seen with the eye that this reveals," he said. "Have you found Jupiter? It may take a moment to get your bearing."

"I'm not certain," she replied, taking the instrument away from her eye, then back to it.

"The light you see is that of the sun, reflecting on it, just as it does the moon," he replied.

It took her a moment, but at last she found it. And a small bout of wonder filled her chest. "I see it! I see it! It looks a bit like a disc."

"Excellent. Now, steady yourself and look at it again."

"What am I looking for?"

"I want you to discover that for yourself."

The earnestness of his voice caught her off guard a moment, and she felt herself lowering the instrument and looking toward him. It was dark, and his face was heavily shadowed, but there was something that caused her heart to flip over in her chest.

"Jupiter is that way, Miss Boxford," he said at last.

She nodded, as if struck dumb, then went back to the telescope. She pointed it to the sky, and this time, it took her much less time to find Jupiter. Soon she had the bright white disc in her sights and waited.

It took a moment or two, but then they started to appear. Four smaller lights, discs themselves, near the planet. Two on either side.

"Oh my goodness."

"Now you and Galileo have something more in common, you see?" he said. "How many do you see?"

"Four. Are they..."

"Jupiter's moons."

She stared at them a moment longer. They shimmered a bit, and even now it was becoming difficult to hold the telescope steady enough not to have them bump around in her eye piece. But she'd seen them.

"The joy of astronomical observation, for me, is simply being open to looking at the sky and discovering it," he said. "There are the things we know to be there, and then things we do not. Some are fixed, like Jupiter. Others are comets that fly through the sky. But we cannot know unless we look and be open to the possibility of discovery."

She lowered the telescope and turned to him, taking him by the hand.

"Thank you," she replied. Tears pricked at the corners of her eyes. "Thank you for sharing that with me. I know how special this is to you."

"Miss Boxford," he began, his voice restrained.

She pulled away, as if she'd touch a hot coal, and stood. "My apologies, my lord. I did not mean to take such lib—"

He stood then, and put a finger to her lips, which had the effect of dazzling her into silence, then put his non-injured hand in hers. "Despite my best attempts at maintaining masculine nonchalance, I cannot always manage it when my injured hand is being squeezed in such an enthusiastic way."

She nodded, opening her mouth to apologize again when she became aware of nothing but the sensation of his thumb, gently stroking her hand.

"Especially," he continued, his voice deepening, faltering, "when the person touching me is as lovely as you."

Kitty's heart pounded in her chest so loudly she wasn't certain she'd heard him properly. She tilted her head, instinctively leaning closer, drawn by the intense need she saw in his eyes. It mirrored her own growing desire. It was new. Terrifying. And beyond thrilling.

And she knew, inexplicably, that she was going to kiss him. Which was not, she realized, how it worked in those fairy tales she'd read in Edmund's book. Or any books that she knew of. And, having never been kissed before, she wasn't even sure she knew how. But then she'd never dressed up like a boy before, or looked through a telescope or hunted for comets, and this—kissing—seemed like it shouldn't be quite as hard.

And before she could think about it another second, she lifted herself to her tiptoes, and kissed him.

It was only a second or two, her lips on his, warm, glorious, before she pulled away, absolutely certain she was done for.

"My lord," she said, her breath coming out in a rush, her bottom landing back on the bench. She was about to look away in embarrassment when he cupped her chin gently with his hand.

He tilted her chin back, then brought his lips to hers. Gentle, exploring. The kiss was clumsy at first. Wonderful, but clumsy. But desire was a powerful instructor, and soon the awkwardness melted away until Kitty's toes curled from the splendor of the moment. The taste of him, the sensation of his lips against hers, his tongue in her mouth—it was heady and wonderful all at once.

The rattle of an approaching carriage intruded on them, and they both broke the kiss. Kitty, still dazed, looked in the direction of the road, where, even in the dark she saw a fine carriage coming up the road.

"Damn," Lord Ellsworth muttered, his formality returning. Before he even spoke the words, she knew what was coming. "Miss Boxford, I know it is most awkward, but I think it is best if you make yourself invisible at the moment."

It was always that way in the end.

COLIN STRODE across the grass toward the front entrance to the tower where the carriage came to a halt, the taste of Katherine Boxford still on his lips. A flash of anger fueled his steps. Could he not have a single bloody uninterrupted moment?

Then again, perhaps he should have been thankful for the interruption. That unexpected and completely unintended kiss was a heady mix of hunger, need, and soul-healing delight. And it needed to never happen again.

The telescope in his hand, he arrived at the entry just in time to see the driver jump down from his perch and open the carriage door. He'd assumed it might have been a few of the gentlemen, eager to escape the ladies and find refuge—if not alcohol—at the tower. But the rather feminine ankle that was already reaching for the step suggested otherwise.

"Good evening, Lord Ellsworth."

Colin swallowed. "Lady Mariah." His gaze went past her toward the carriage. There was a servant in the carriage with her...a rather meager form of guardianship, he could not help but notice. "This is unexpected."

"An unexpected pleasure I hope," she said, holding out her hand for him to take it. He poked the telescope under his arm, then took her hand.

"Of course," he said. "You are alone."

"Not entirely," she said. "Don't worry, Lord Ellsworth, you are quite safe. I found that after an evening of cards and the like I wondered where you had disappeared to." She looked up at the tower. "I take it this is the competition."

"Lofton Tower is where I spend time making my observations."

"I see. Would it be ungracious of me to ask for a little tour while I am here?" she replied. She gazed at him, doe-eyed and inviting in ways that should have made a man fall over himself to be beside her. Striking, then, it had no such effect on him. This should have been a mark heavily in her favor. Should have been. "I promise to keep this between us."

Colin smiled tightly. The situation was tenuous, though why should it be? Lady Mariah was number one on his list of choices to be his duchess. He cast a quick glance around.

"Oh dear," she replied. "Perhaps we are not alone. I thought I saw someone as I approached, but maybe it was a trick of the light."

His attention snapped to her. "Of course we are alone. Occasionally there is a servant here of course, to see to my needs. But they should have gone by now. Come," he said.

She took him by the elbow, apparently enthusiastic at the invitation. Her chaperone stayed in the carriage, he could not help but notice.

"Your mother and sister did not think to join you?" he asked as he opened the door. He glanced around the room but Miss Boxford must have been tucked away in another part of the tower.

"Mother cannot manage to stay up later most of the time, and my sister decided to stay behind."

How convenient.

They walked inside, and Colin kept the door open. Perhaps Lady Mariah was merely an enthusiastic observer, but a man couldn't be too careful.

"This is wonderful," she said, her voice that placid tone that never seemed to waver. "So many books."

He put the telescope back into its case and placed it on a nearby shelf. "Do you enjoy reading, Lady Mariah?"

She looked at the spines of the titles, then back to him. "Occasionally, if I am very bored and have nothing better to do."

"And what do you enjoy?"

"Many things. What do you enjoy?" she asked.

"I am here to learn about you. A friend of mine has encouraged me to ask questions and talk less, so I will endeavor to do that now." Was Miss Boxford a friend? Not really. Of course he had no idea what she was to him.

She blinked and it occurred to him she was blindsided. "Well, I am sure I would enjoy whatever you would enjoy."

"Reading," he replied.

She smiled tightly, then after a rather painful moment, spoke. "I am a great lover of games. Cards, of course. And I do enjoy the occasional game of croquet."

"Excellent. And what do you enjoy about those games?"

"Winning."

The muffled sound of something falling from a nearby shelf broke the silence that had followed her telling answer.

"What was that?" she asked.

She was looking around now, more closely. Would she notice the brown satin capote and shawl hanging from a peg by the door?

Colin coughed, then took her elbow, refocusing her attention on him. "I will check. Why don't you sit right here and wait?"

He stalked off toward the where the sound had come from. The porch was dark, but there was Miss Boxford sitting next to a mop and bucket that had fallen over. He peered at her.

"Sorry," she mouthed, clearly unhappy to be stuck in a cupboard.

He shook his head, barely unable to contain the smile on his face, then closed the door again, returning to his guest. She'd risen from where he'd asked her to perch and stood near the door.

"'Tis nothing but a stray animal that had gotten in through an open window in the back porch. I have showed him on his way," he replied.

"Sometimes the servants are so careless," she replied, then gestured to the shawl and capote hanging near the door. "I thought they might have been here," she said, gesturing to it.

"No," he replied. "That belongs to Lady Gwyneth," he stammered. "She must have forgotten them here the last time she and Mr. Edmund Pembroke came for a visit."

"She must have left in a hurry," she replied, still wearing that blithe smile Colin realized was permanently pasted on her face. He was quickly tiring of it.

Eager to distract her, Colin gestured to the staircase that led to his telescope.

"Lady Mariah, I assume since you came here you must be interested in the stars. Would you like to see some?"

She nodded. "I would, thank you."

He grabbed a lantern and took her upstairs.

She smiled approvingly at the space. "This is very remarkable," she said. "And you spend every evening here?"

"Most, yes," he replied. "And I will continue to do so once I am married, as business allows me to be."

There he said it. Would she complain?

"What about your duties in London?"

He stiffened a little at the insinuation. He spent hours of each day reading over the papers, speaking with his father and keeping himself informed on matters of state so that he would be ready to assume his role in the House of Lords when the time came.

"I will always do my duty."

She nodded but did not have anything more to say in response.

"The hour is getting late, Lady Mariah," Colin replied, impatient. He offered his arm, which she took, then led her down the stairs, to the carriage and opened the door. It was nearly midnight. "I believe the duchess has a full day planned, and I am certain you would appreciate your rest."

"Could I offer you passage back to Stormount Hall?"

Colin forced himself not to laugh at her request. He could not help but wonder if at the end of the ride, she'd have made all the arrangements for a special license and a minister waiting for them.

"I thank you, but under the circumstances that would perhaps not be the best idea." The sound of another carriage rumbled up the lane, and Colin wanted to thank the stars for the timing. Though this coach would take Miss Boxford back to Kennington Grove, Lady Mariah would be none the wiser for it's true purpose. "And as you can see, I have transport already prepared, and I would hate to keep my driver up late for nothing."

She frowned in a rather pretty way, but Colin held firm.

"Thank you for the tour, Lord Ellsworth. It was most…enlightening."

He closed the door and stepped away, then signaled for the driver to leave before she could make another move. Breathing a sigh of relief as her transport disappeared down the hill, he then signaled for his driver to wait as he fetched Miss Boxford.

She was still there, hiding in the cupboard, her countenance one of restrained discontent.

"You can come out now," he replied. He held out his hand and assisted her to her feet, savoring the moment before she released him. "What on earth did you trip on?"

"Another pile of your books you obviously missed," she replied, then brushed a pile of dust from her elbows and shoulders. "You are lucky I didn't unleash a torrent of sneezes in there."

"Your carriage is here," he replied. "And Lady Mariah is gone."

"Is she still your number one?" The girl went to the door, grabbed her shawl and hat. "Because she is most definitely aiming to be yours. What did she think of all this?"

"It was as I expected," he replied.

"But not, perhaps, as you had hoped?"

He paused then. Indeed, her reaction was exactly as he might have hoped. Entirely dispassionate. And yet, it was curiously lacking. Especially in light of the sheer delight he'd experienced with Miss Boxford only moments before her arrival. The delight she'd expressed after looking through the little telescope. The riveting sensation of their kiss. What had he done to deserve such a moment? In all their time together, Amelia had graced him with nothing so wonderful as that. And he'd promised her so much more.

The image of Amelia settled him like a cold rush of water. It was not riveting sensations or delight he'd desired. It was dispassion. Just as Lady Mariah had offered.

"What I hope is to get this marriage business over with, Miss Boxford."

She regarded him with a pensive expression, then turned away. Colin suspected she was biting her tongue. She pulled the shawl off the peg and draped it over her shoulders. Colin found himself fixated watching her.

"She noticed those, but you don't have to worry," he said. "I told her they belonged to Lady Gwyneth and they'd been left here."

She looked up at him and laughed, tossing her head in such a way that was intoxicating.

"I am not the least bit concerned about Lady Mariah. I have stood in her presence more than once, and I do believe I am quite beneath her notice."

"To her perhaps," he said, then swallowed and recovered himself. "But you do recall my concerns about your reputation. I take my role in this with utmost seriousness, Miss Boxford." Which is why, he added silently to himself, he was absolutely not supposed to be thinking about kissing her.

She stood in front of a small mirror by his door, adjusting her capote to her satisfaction, then turned to him.

"There is one part of this I don't understand," she said. "You are in a rarified position, my lord. To choose your way to be happy. Why wouldn't you? Instead, you have allowed other people to dictate the terms of this most important decision."

"This is often how it works, Miss Boxford."

She sighed and shook her head, unable to contain her exasperation with him, then spread out her arms to engulf the space. "You have this magnificent passion. Why on earth would you not want to find someone who shares it, or at the very least, is happy that you indulge in it? Instead of picnics and dancing—as lovely as they may be to some —why isn't this part of the itinerary? Do you have any idea how ridiculous that is to —" She faltered then, her eyes alight with a passion that could not be contrived. "—to most men? Those whose happiness is dictated entirely by the whim of others?"

Her question hung in the air, waiting for an answer.

Miss Boxford had curious opinions. Her rather fanciful view of life was perhaps remarkable. Made all the more remarkable because though she spoke of "most men," he knew perfectly well she was speaking of herself.

And she was right.

Her eyes were bright as they locked gazes. A nameless tension hung in the air. He found himself wanting to reach out to her. Claim her mouth. Claim much more, in fact. Drink in whatever enchantment she offered that made him feel that who he was, who Colin Middleton was, was enough.

The bell chimed the first stroke of midnight.

"I must go," she said, perhaps to fill the space and sunder whatever spell the evening had woven. He opened the door and assisted her into the carriage that waited patiently outside.

"Thank you for showing me Jupiter," she said as she climbed into the waiting carriage. "I don't think I shall ever forget that moment."

He was damned sure he wasn't about to either.

THE NEXT MORNING, Colin sought out the one person he knew would provide him with advice on how to plan—heaven forbid—a party.

"Good morning, Mother," he said as he entered her dressing room. She was at her dressing table as her ladies' maid was attaching her cap to her hair.

She turned her gaze just enough, clearly shocked by his appearance. The last time he'd come looking for advice from his mother, he'd been a child.

"Is something the matter?" she asked. "Has your father fallen ill?"

"When I left him, he seemed perfectly well," he replied. "Indeed, I have something I wish to speak to you about."

"Of course." She paused, looking him up and down, unable to mask her surprise. Indeed, his mother was as naturally expressive as he was restrained. When her cap was in place, she thanked her maid, who excused herself. "I hope this is good news? Have you chosen at last?"

"Not yet," he replied. "But I have not given up."

"I suppose that is something. But honestly, is there not one of them to tempt you?"

Colin reviewed the mental notes of everyone who'd been invited. Miss Peckford with her polite smiles and devoid of opinion on any subject save weather. Miss Russell, who enjoyed poetry. And, of course, Lady Mariah Stapleton, whose manners and looks reminded him of the woman he'd given his heart to so long ago.

But then, quite inexplicably, the image of another woman, crouching in a closet and staring at him with a mix of exasperation and indignation pushed all of that aside. A woman whose lips he'd tasted, lips as plump and sweet as the strawberries she'd grown in her garden.

Colin gave himself a mental shake and pushed the image aside, tempting as it was.

And it was tempting.

"Alas Mother," he said, "you have done such a stellar job with the guest list, you may have made it more difficult, rather than less. But I have been inspired to find an opportunity to help it along a bit. I would like to throw a party."

The relief on his mother's face was replaced by confusion.

"Colin, my dear," she said. "What do you think all of this is?"

He took his mother's hand and kissed it, and as he did so, he realized it had been too long since he'd expressed such open affection for her.

"This is you and father doing your very best to ensure your wayward son marries. And he will. But I have been inspired to put my own efforts in."

"Well then, I am intrigued," she said. "What do you propose?"

"A viewing party."

"With your telescope." His mother paused. "Are you certain?"

"Absolutely," he replied. "Anyone who will share my life should, if not share my passions, at least understand them. A viewing party might be like a picnic, but out of doors, in the evening. It can be done right before the ball."

His mother grew silent, clearly wrangling with the notion. She was quiet for a moment, and then her face lit up.

"Yes. I can see it." She put out her hands, as if attempting to draw out the scene in front of her. "Oh Colin, it would be so romantic! I didn't know you had such notions, my dear."

She rose, kissed him on his head, then started pacing the room. Colin could not help but smile. The General was in the room.

"We could have some musicians—I believe a quartet would do nicely. And some lanterns, strung on poles and in the trees, just far enough away from instruments that they would not interfere with the viewing. Some light refreshments, followed by a midnight ball. It would be weather dependent, of course."

"Of course," Colin said, himself entranced somewhat by the idea. "See? I knew I could trust this to you. I will see to the set up of the instruments." Perhaps Miss Boxford would assist there. "I am certain I shall discover the right lady that night...and we can announce the proposal at the ball."

"This will be close, but it can be done," his mother replied. "I will speak to your father. We shall see what is possible."

Suddenly, Colin thought, anything was.

CHAPTER 13

Kitty slumped onto the bed in the room that would be hers in only a week. The move from Kennington Grove to Silver Cross was now imminent, and Kitty's best attempt to see the upside of it was becoming more and more difficult by the moment.

Kitty and Mrs. Pembroke had been invited to Silver Cross for tea and refreshments, and to discuss particular issues regarding accommodations. Almost as soon as they had arrived, Evelyn Pembroke had been lovingly greeted by Charlie and Fanny—a meeting made even more enthusiastic by the knowledge that soon the children would see their adopted grandmother every day. Surrounded by her grandchildren, Edmund's mother came alive. It was easy to see why Edmund and Gwyneth were so keen to have her come to live with them.

Gwynnie and Edmund were in equally cheerful moods. Gwynnie had practically led Kitty by the hand and taken her from room to room, reviewing every detail, her excitement palpable. Silver Cross was a very modest home by the standards of Gorland Park where Gwynnie grew up, but a much happier one.

When the conversation about furniture and windows were concluded, the conversation at tea turned to Lord Ellsworth's marriage woes. The subject did not improve Kitty's mood. Every time Gwynnie and Mrs. Pembroke suggested another Miss So and So or Lady Whatshername as a possible candidate to be the Marchioness of Ellsworth, Kitty forced herself to smile and offer a civil opinion. She had yet to see a lady amongst the crowd who had been his equal in manners or interests.

He'd been clear that companionship was not amongst his requirements. Was his connection to Lady Amelia so very strong that he could have no other but her? It was possible. She'd read about that kind of one-sided love in books, and it seemed so terribly tragic. Even her own infatuation for Edmund, as embarrassing and hurtful as it had been, did not dim her soul's need for love. It only served to remind her of what she desired. And, perhaps most painfully, what she was missing.

And then, as if Gwynnie had been able to read Kitty's mind, she'd wondered aloud about having a small gathering to welcome Kitty and Mrs. Pembroke to the house. It hardly seemed necessary until Gwyneth and Mrs. Pembroke began considering a perspective list of guests that included, Kitty couldn't help but notice, a disproportionate amount of local gentlemen. She'd been tempted, for just a moment, to present her advertisement and suggest they cross reference the qualities she desired with the men on their list. At least then, perhaps, she'd have something of a say in her own life.

She sat, gripping the beautifully turned wooden post at the foot of the bed, knowing logically that it was more than a girl like Kitty could hope for. The room was lovely, and just the right size. Gwynnie had picked it for her especially. The bedchamber had a pleasing prospect that included a view of the back garden. The windows faced southeast, which meant she would have generous light in the early part of the day. Gwynnie and Edmund had taken great care to point out a part of the garden she could use for her own plantings. It was a much larger space than her little cottage garden she now used. Much of that garden she would be forced to leave behind.

It was perfect. Except for a curious resentment that rolled in her belly. And she hated herself for it.

"There you are."

Kitty rose abruptly to her feet, and turned to see Edmund standing in the door, his adopted daughter Fanny standing beside him, a wide smile on her face.

"Here I am," she said, forcing a smile.

"Do you like it, Miss Boxford? Do you?" Fanny asked, bounding toward her. "We picked this 'specially for you."

"You did a spectacular job of it," Kitty answered, stealing some of Fanny's enthusiasm for herself as she tousled the child's hair. If Lord Ellsworth had children, maybe some of them would have lovely ginger hair like Fanny. "I do not think I have ever had a nicer room."

"I am so glad you are coming to live with us! Aren't we Papa?" the girl said, turning to Edmund.

"We are indeed. Very happy," he replied to the girl, before turning to Kitty. "Tell me truthfully, does it suit you? I know Gwyneth can be somewhat enthusiastic."

Kitty smiled, thinking of her friend. How excited she was for Kitty to be close to them. And she could picture Gwynnie fussing over every detail to make sure she'd picked the perfect place for Kitty. Truly, she was blessed to have friends such as these.

"It will suit very well, thank you," she replied. She smiled, but inside, wished Edmund away. She was tired of pretending to be happy. Instead, he turned to Fanny.

"Mama and Grandmama are in the parlor. Why don't you run along now, as I am certain they are missing you? Miss Boxford will be along shortly." The girl hugged Edmund, then waved to Kitty before skipping away. Kitty's heart squeezed a little.

"I can join them now, Edmund," she replied. "I am your mother's companion. I have neglected her long enough."

"Kitty Boxford," he said, in that knowing way of his. They'd been friends, after all, for four years. And for two of them, in her mind anyway, they had been much more. "Something is not quite right."

She waved off his concern. "I am tired is all. Your friend's marriage festivities have me quite drained." Never mind the late evenings at

Lofton Tower. And the early mornings at Kennington Grove. And the growing number of restless nights in the middle.

He walked over to where she sat, pulled a chair opposite her and sat down. "Kitty, you are one of my dearest friends. Indeed, you are like a sister to me."

She nodded, suddenly weary and readying herself for the sibling-like lecture to come. "I know."

"So please take my next sentence with all the affection I have for you, which is considerable. You are an open book, Kitty Boxford. And the book I am seeing before me is not...happy."

"I am happy," she replied, suddenly self-conscious, and slightly indignant. Besides, it wasn't a complete falsehood. She was tired. She turned to a nearby mirror, supremely displeased with what she found there. She pointed to the darkish circles under her eyes. "Just tired. It's a ghastly business, all this upper class frivolity. No wonder you chose to run away and set traps instead."

Edmund shook his head, and gave her a wry smile. It was the smile he gave Gwynnie when he was not about to let her have her way.

"You have many singular qualities, Kitty Boxford. Among them is the most expressive pair of eyes in the kingdom. It was how Gwyneth knew her mother had been lying to her. The countess had hinted you were in on my supposed schemes to gain her fortune, and Gwyneth knew from the look on your face that no such thing could be possible."

Kitty blinked, cocking her head to one side.

"She never told me that. Of course, you didn't tell me you were a gentleman until almost the moment we left, Edmund. I could barely get over the shock of it." Kitty remembered that day with perfect clarity. Everything she'd assumed about him was wrong. And everything she thought her life might be—with him—was wrong too.

"I should not have lied to you," he said, his mood growing serious, "and I have never apologized. I was a selfish man and very much afraid of my own truths. I am sorry for that."

For all the years she'd known Edmund, it was now, sitting with him, she realized that she hadn't fallen in love with Edmund

Pembroke. Not who he truly was. What she wanted had been an illusion. And it had taken Gwynnie's love to break through it and heal him. She had to let the illusion go, once and for all.

"Edmund," Kitty said, her mood lightening a little, "there is nothing to forgive. Thank you, but truly, do not think on it. It was another time." And it was, she realized, as a weight lifted from her shoulders.

"Thank you." He rose and looked out the window. Kitty let out a small sigh of relief when she thought he was leaving her alone. Instead, he turned, leaned against the window, and crossed his arms. "My days of hiding are over—and I pretended to be something that I truly wasn't for a very long time. So, in that spirit, I have to tell you, that despite the smile you have pasted on your face, I know something is wrong."

His expression was so earnest it nearly hurt Kitty to look upon it. Because he was right. Something was wrong. Many somethings. She felt completely out of sorts. And some of it had to do with moving to Silver Cross. But not all.

"I am just tired, Edmund. That is all. Truly." She rose and went to the window, resting her hands on the deep window pane. She took in a deep breath and gazed down at the daisies dancing in the summer breeze, before turning around. "The room is lovely, and I am quite thrilled to have Gwynnie spoil me so."

"I will not press you further on this subject." He rose, and looked upon her with kindness. "I will leave that to Gwyneth and Mother."

"And their matchmaking," Kitty said to herself as she watched Edmund leave. Gwynnie had caught her handsome prince and was determined that Kitty must have one too. Except Kitty didn't need a prince. She just wanted to be happy. Whatever that meant.

Right now, it meant getting some fresh air and away from this room.

WHAT STARTED as a well-intentioned stroll to her garden quickly became a longer more rambling walk along one of the roads leading toward Hilsburn, Silver Cross at her back, her feet leading her nowhere in particular, her thoughts racing. The air had grown cooler, and a ridge of darker, heavier cloud had moved in on a swift breeze. She could have turned back, she'd supposed. After all, it was part of their agreement that the marquess would not send for her if the weather was not tenable for viewing. But after an afternoon talking about Lord Ellsworth's marriage prospects, followed by that far too candid discussion with Edmund, and ending with a light supper where she'd been peppered by relentless questions from Gwynnie about possible matches of her own, she'd needed the escape. The journey here reminded her of the long rambling walks she had taken with her father around the grounds at Gorland Park, and then Westemere. And it made her heart ache.

Indeed, Kitty's heart seemed under assault from all sides. Maybe there was merit in Lord Ellsworth's approach to marriage. But Kitty knew enough to know she couldn't be alone. She'd had that experience—being alone in a room full of people. Maybe, at last, she'd grown tired of pretending that it did not matter.

Because it did.

You are an open book, Kitty Boxford.

See what is unseen.

Kitty chuckled to no one but herself at the paradox, her voice thick and heavy with melancholy. She threw her head back, blew out a heavy breath, and looked up to the sky, which was shrouded by gray cloud.

"How can I be so transparent and yet invisible? I don't understand."

"Because you are the riddle, my child. And the answers to riddles are hidden, but always before us if we care enough to look."

Kitty halted, her heart pounding at the unexpected reply.

Not half a dozen steps ahead of her stood a Romani woman of dignified bearing, who seemed bemused by Kitty's question. Threads of silver shot through her thick black hair, her eyes dark, a brilliant purple cape hanging from her shoulders. She balanced a basket on her hip, her fingers bedecked with numerous silver and gold rings.

Kitty put a hand to her chest, surprise catching her breath. She found herself studying the woman intently, searching into her own memory for the image of the fortune teller who she had met so many years ago. It was impossible to know, and so very unlikely they were the same person. And she'd probably been staring quite enough.

"My apologies—you startled me," she said at last, her eyes falling to the basket, which appeared heavy. She gestured to it. "May I help you with that?"

The woman dismissed her concerns with the smallest of shrugs, then set the basket on the ground.

"I can set my burden down and refresh myself. I am not certain you can say the same."

Kitty's mouth fell into a frown. She was quite tired of platitudes at the moment.

"Everyone wants what is best for me, yet no one trusts that I know what is best," she said. "Why does no one trust me?"

"Perhaps you do not trust yourself? Will you continue to let happiness slip through your fingers?"

There was no anger, no taunt in the woman's voice. And yet, Kitty took a step back.

"I...found the brooch," she protested. "Nothing has changed."

"Nothing has changed because you have not changed."

Kitty wanted to reply. Something pithy that would refute this woman's claim. A claim Kitty's heart could not deny, but wounded nonetheless.

"Your heart is calling to you," the woman continued. "Do not resist its call. It will reveal itself in time if you let it."

"I did not resist its call once. And it was wrong. I was wrong."

The woman laughed out loud, her rich accented voice climbing into the trees.

"Do you believe yourself so special, child, that you cannot make a mistake? That is being human. It is our capacity for forgiveness—of others, of ourselves—that makes us more."

She thought back to the time she'd met Edmund. Edmund Hanley. A man full of secrets. Not the man he was now. But it had still hurt.

Kitty fought the urge to roll her eyes. She'd had enough lessons for one evening. About to turn on her heel and retreat to Silver Cross, the woman interrupted her thoughts one last time.

"Your heart is calling to you," she repeated. "And its call is not coming from that direction."

The sky grew even darker then, and the rain fell in earnest, fat drops sliding off leaves and quickly forming puddles along the dips in the road. The Romani woman pulled her hood over her head, picked up her basket, and disappeared into the woods as silently as she appeared, leaving Kitty quite alone with a choice.

She kept moving forward toward Lofton Tower. What drew her there she didn't know, or at least she was not at all prepared to acknowledge it. She simply craved the solitude of it, she told herself. Away from the Pembrokes, even her parents. A place that was hers.

Which was a most peculiar feeling to have, given it wasn't hers at all.

By the time she reached the observatory, she was soaked through. She pushed on the heavy oak door, the weight of it groaning on its hinges. Kitty rushed in, shutting the door behind her. The place was dim, owing to the heavy grayness of the sky, and no lamps were yet lit.

Kitty cast a glance down at her dress and shook her head in disgust. However useful the walk was in driving away some of her tumult, her hem was heavy with mud, and her shawl dripped on Lord Ellsworth's floors. She opened the door and wrung out the edges of her clothes in the doorway, before shutting the weather out once more.

A shiver slid down her spine as she hung her shawl on a nearby hook. It was frightfully damp. She was frightfully damp. And Lord Ellsworth had not arrived. Nor was he likely to, given the state of the weather and his other responsibilities.

She should have been grateful for that, but she could not help but think about his calm, warm smiles, rare as they were. And that kiss that warmed her even now. His steady presence would have been an antidote to her restless mood, and the work a welcome distraction. Much of her time with him was spent watching a clock, but she'd had plenty of time to watch him as well. The fiery color of his hair in the candlelight. The line across his brow as he poured all his concentration into that small eyepiece. The enthusiastic smiles when he'd look over at her, and share what he'd seen. And, best of all, his warm, masculine presence close to her when he would call her to the telescope, and invite her to look up at some fuzzy patch in the sky.

Another shiver flooded through her then. But it had nothing to do with the damp.

Kitty went to the hearth, which had been prepared and begging to be used. Finding the tinderbox nearby, she lit the kindling and soon had a fire blazing. A pleasing glow filled the room. She took off her boots and set them nearby to dry.

Despite the heat, a deep chill began to set in. What a fine mess she'd put herself in. She would hardly be useful to Lord Ellsworth or Mrs. Pembroke if she fell ill, and she was already a bit worn down. She rose and went to the window, peering out into the growing dark. It was raining even harder now, and not a patch of sky was visible. He would hardly come now. And she was both sad and relieved by that idea.

She went back to the fire, seeking its warmth. Unpinning her frock, she took off her heavier outer layer, which was the wettest, hung it over a chair, and placed it near the fire so it might dry. She then untied her garters, peeled off her stockings, heavy from the wet, and hung them next to her dress.

Freed from the heaviest and wettest of her garments, she was finally able to feel some comfort from the fire. If only she had something warm and dry to pull over her shoulders. Even though she was quite alone, and quite likely to remain so, she felt more than a little exposed in nothing but her chemise, stays, and petticoat.

Rubbing her arms briskly, she rose and looked about the room for anything to cover herself, but there was not a blanket to be found. Surely Lord Ellsworth occupied the tower in more than the summer season, Kitty reasoned. Aristocrats didn't suffer from inconvenience or discomfort. A search of the small kitchen and pantry, where she'd hidden away when Lady Mariah arrived, yielded nothing.

Kitty came back into the study and tried a second door, which opened with a rather satisfying click. Lighting a taper, she walked through the entry, the light cutting the darkness to reveal a bed, a nearby table stacked with yet more books, and an empty hearth.

The air in this room was not stale—and indeed, it seemed entirely likely that Lord Ellsworth would often spend the night here. The bed was of modest size, but its linens were fine to Kitty's touch. At the foot of the bed was a small chest. Kitty knelt in front of it and pushed up the lid with one hand, her curiosity rewarded with the discovery of several woolen blankets. She pulled out the top one, which was dark blue and a lovely, fine quality, and placed it at her feet. To her surprise, a small wooden box tumbled out of its thick folds, its contents spilling out on the floor.

She set down the candle beside her, chiding herself for not being careful. She scooped up the box and a small packet of letters, tied prettily in a white ribbon. Beside it lay a small miniature. Gingerly she picked up the piece, studying the portrait. With her fine features, blond hair, and elegant countenance, at first she thought it might be Lady Mariah, though the resemblance was not that strong.

She placed the letters and the miniature back in the box, her eyes lingering on the address. Lady Amelia Grafton, Templeton House, Grosvenor St., London.

Kitty froze, aware she'd become privy to something she should not have seen.

"I believe we discussed that your sole responsibility was to record my observations, Miss Boxford."

The edge of undisguised anger in Lord Ellsworth's voice cut through Kitty like a knife. In one fluid motion, she shut the box and the lid of the blanket chest.

"I—" She scooped up the blanket from beside her, clutched it to her chest, picked up the taper, then turned to face him. The scant light revealed the clenched muscles in his jaw and a stillness to him that, given the circumstances, she found quite unnerving. He was close. So close she could smell his cologne. He was like a wall of maleness in front of her.

She clutched the blanket even tighter. What could she say? She had clearly trespassed on his privacy, no matter how unintentional. And, to make matters impossibly worse, she stood only inches away in naught but her petticoat and stays. Away from the fire, the dampness crept into her bones, but the heat from her embarrassment pricked the back of her neck.

CHAPTER 14

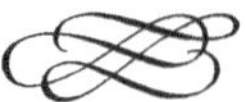

"*I*—"

Colin looked down at Miss Boxford, her cheeks flush with embarrassment, her hair damp and hanging loose. Her lower lip trembled. Her vulnerability threatened to wick away his anger and the indignation that tightened his jaw and filled his chest.

She'd found his letters. The ones he'd written to Amelia in desperation after she'd left him. Letters cataloging her beauty. Her elegant manners. How much he would honor her. How much he would care for her. She'd sent them back. Most of them she'd never even bothered to open, he'd discovered.

They were his private shame.

When they'd first been returned, Colin's friend Bastien DuMont told him to burn them. They were, if nothing else, fodder for the rags and certainly the opportunity for scandal. The Frenchman, who'd long lived in the shadow world of secrets and the power they held, was right, of course. Instead, Colin had hidden them away, buried deep where he was certain no one would find them. But he had not counted on Miss Boxford, who had a gift for forcing him to face those uncomfortable sensations he'd thought he'd locked away.

"Get out."

"But—"

"You will collect your things and leave."

He turned away, before he could take another moment of those brown eyes and their gift of looking right through him. Before she saw past the anger to what really lay there.

Humiliation.

He stepped away, expecting her to brush by him. Instead, a single word, clear and commanding, filled the air.

"No."

Colin blinked, then turned on his heel.

"What did you say?"

As his gaze settled on her once more, he watched her back straighten and her eyes narrow. Surely he had misheard her.

"No." Her cheeks were flushed with anger and perhaps embarrassment, but there was steel in her manner that took him aback. "I believe I am quite tired of being told where I belong and where I do not."

She pushed the taper at him, forcing him to take it. The light fell on her neck and chest, which he realized, for the first time, was practically bare.

"Miss Boxford," he repeated, a different sort of heat rushing through him as the gentle, generous swell of her breasts was evident before him. "Where on earth are your clothes?"

She drew the wool blanket around her shoulders, and it was only then he'd noticed it at all. She must have retrieved it from the blanket box. He'd not even seen it, so blinded by his shock at seeing her with those letters.

"Drying," she said at last. "I didn't feel inclined to sit around in wet clothes and catch my death. So I went looking for a blanket. That is all."

He was silent, considering her words, when he noticed her lower lip trembling again. Damn it.

"Come," he said, walking out into his study, "before you catch your death." He threw another log on the fire, poked at the embers and brought the flames to a roar, and tried not to be completely distracted by the sight of her stockings and garters hanging nearby to dry. Which was ridiculous, considering they were quite plain and rather muddied at the feet. He pulled his armchair close to the fire and bade her to sit.

"But I might stain it," she protested.

"It is just a chair," he said, perhaps more tersely than he intended. "Sit."

She looked at him, her expression difficult to read. Her feet were bare, and her ankles as well. It seemed almost indecent to look at them as she settled in the seat and stretched her toes toward the hearth. And then, to his chagrin, she tucked them under her.

He took a second seat and settled in nearby. The only sound was the rain pelting hard on windows and the dry logs crackling in the heat of the hearth. But the air was filled with an unnamed tension.

She turned to him, the flame illuminating one side of her face, which wore a painful expression. "I'm sorry. The box fell open, and I should have just scooped it up without stopping to look. I have no excuse to justify my actions. When my dress is dry, I shall pack up my things and return home." She looked away then, an expression on her face he found almost unbearable in its sadness.

"I may have been hasty in my anger," he replied at last. "Clearly you are in distress, and I fear I am the cause."

She threw back her head and let go a curious mix of laughter and a stifled sob. Her expression was one of such utter sadness it threatened to shatter him. She'd always seemed determined. Happy. Joyful. Even grumpy. But this...this bordered on despair.

He went to the cabinet that held a modest quantity of brandy and poured each of them a measure.

"I did not expect you this evening," he said, eager to distract her troubled mind.

"I walked from Silver Cross. Gwynnie and Edmund were showing me my new room."

Her voice became almost brittle then.

"And it was pleasing to you, I hope?" He replaced the stopper on the bottle and placed it back on in the cupboard.

"It is suitable in every way," she replied, the emotion gone from her voice entirely.

Which was entirely unlike Miss Boxford. Indeed, it reminded him of someone else. Himself, in fact.

"Except?" he prodded.

"Except when I looked out that window—and over that lovely view—I just had the most intense feeling. Of being trapped. That once I settled there, I would be there forever."

He turned to her and placed the brandy in her hand, allowing himself the fleeting luxury of the touch of her fingers brushing up against his. His body was already alive with awareness—from the hint of her bosom underneath the folds of his blanket, to her toes, peeking out from under the hem of her petticoat. Their gazes locked, her amber eyes rimmed with tears she seemed to be holding back with the sheer force of will.

"Drink. It will help warm you a bit."

He took another chair and pulled it beside hers, stretching out his legs.

"You do not wish to move," he said after a short while.

"What I wish is of no consequence," she said. "Mrs. Pembroke is my employer, and if I want to remain employed, I must go."

"And she is good to you, I trust?"

She smiled wryly, then took a sip of brandy. "I could not wish for better."

"Well then, I have some work to do."

She looked at him, her lips teasing a smile, which made Colin far happier than he realized was possible.

"I believe you just made another joke, my lord," she said, taking another sip of brandy.

"I believe I did." He stared into the fire. "And Edmund, Lady Gwyneth. You count them as friends, I understand. Are they eager to have you?"

"Very," she replied, then let out a long, low breath.

"I see." And yet, he did not. "Actually, Miss Boxford, I do not see. I am afraid I am not talented in the way of intimating what another person thinks. Edmund is far better."

"Not always," she said, bitterness lacing her answer. "You are an excellent listener, my lord. That is a skill far more rare, and more valuable. Anyone can talk."

He looked at her anew. Was she actually complimenting him on his shyness? "You are a remarkable woman, Katherine Boxford. A remarkable woman indeed."

She blushed then, and dipped her head. It made Colin inexplicably annoyed.

"Why do you do that?"

"Do what?" she asked, turning toward him.

"Look down. Look away."

She shrugged. "Because I do not know how to be passive in my manner. I do not have that way about me to easily keep inside what I am feeling, as others do. And perhaps I am a little embarrassed by it."

"You should not be," he grumbled. "Do not deprive the world of the finest pair of eyes I have ever beheld. You deserve to be seen. Be damned what they think."

She looked up then, as if he'd spoken in an unfamiliar language. The shadow played with the firelight on her face, her eyes lighting up, and he could tell she was using all her will to hold his gaze and not, as was her way, look down at her feet.

"Thank you," she said at last.

"Not at all," he replied, clearing his throat and gripping his glass in an attempt to bring himself down to earth. His chest was so damn full of something approaching giddiness because of Katherine Boxford's stunning, joyous smile. "And Edmund, Lady Gwyneth," he continued. "Can I assume you have been able to disguise your lack of enthusiasm from them?"

He caught the subtle flicker in her eyelids at his question. The happiness that had buoyed her but a moment ago evaporated. He'd unknowingly hit upon something raw—just as he'd felt when she'd discovered his letters.

"Not entirely. I know they wish the best for me. But it is... complicated." A tear rolled down her cheek. It was the first time he's seen her so unhappy. "I don't even know what is best for me anymore."

A imagine of another time, and a woman on her knees in the tall grass amongst the apple trees in Gorland Park, flashed in his memory. Her eyes were puffy, her cheeks, which she'd madly wiped when she realized he was near, had been streaked with tears. The same eyes looked at him now.

"You were the lady I saw that day, in Gorland Park, last summer."

Her eyes widened slightly for but a moment, then she gave him a wry smile.

"You did remember."

"I could not forget those eyes." Or the heartbreak he saw there. He remembered it because he knew that pain all too well.

"Indeed, when we first met I certainly hoped you would," she said, then shook her head. "It was not one of my finer moments. Although I believe I have probably outdone myself this evening."

She laughed, but there was not an ounce of cheer in it.

"I can't stay at Silver Cross. I love them all. They all mean the world to me. But I can't stay there and pretend that I am happy. I will always be someone to be concerned about. Someone to entertain. I don't want that."

"Have you thought of telling them? They are your friends."

She turned to him with a look of undisguised incredulity. "Of course not. That afternoon—" She swallowed. "That afternoon that you saw me in the orchard, I vowed that I would bury that feeling so deep no one would ever find it. Including myself. And I would not betray that vow. Because I would be betraying the two people I hold most dearly."

"Love denied is a horrible thing."

"The fault was entirely my own. I fell in love with an idea of a man, instead of the man himself. And in the process, I allowed myself to believe—quite foolishly—that someone like me could be worthy of a man like that, regardless of how fantastical a notion it truly is." She shook her head. "I am, as one cruel lady once said to me, five thousand pounds too poor and a stone too heavy to make anyone a proper wife.

So I will find myself a new position, or at the very least, earn enough coin to advertise for a husband on my terms. It may not be a love match, but it will be someone I can, I hope, come to find some companionship. A gamekeeper, perhaps. Or perhaps a farmer."

She took a very long sip of brandy, and pulled a face before wiping her cheeks unceremoniously with the heels of her hand. She placed her feet on the floor, and straightened her back.

"Enough of that," she said, more to herself than to him. Her voice changed then. It did not waver. Indeed, it sounded rather firm. "I have made an utter cake of myself. Wallowing in one's own misery is like brandy. A little is a tonic. Too much is unseemly."

Setting down the glass, she grabbed the arms of the chair and forced herself to her feet.

Dear heavens. The floor beneath Kitty's feet was off kilter, and the room spun. The blanket around her shoulders began to slide down her back, but reaching for it seemed far too dexterous an action at the moment. So much for tonic, she realized too late. She'd become unseemly.

She'd had too little to eat today, and drank an entire glass of brandy far too quickly. Clumsily she reached for one arm of the chair, eager to regain her balance, when a firm, steady hand reached out and caught her. Her fingers gripped his upper arms and she found herself savoring the sensation of his hard, muscular body next to hers.

He regarded her with a most peculiar expression. It wasn't pity. Thank goodness for that. Neither was it anger, sadness, or even happiness. It was something else. Something she'd never seen before —at least, not directed at her.

Desire.

His lips were parted slightly. He had a gorgeous mouth. And whether it was the swimming in her head from the brandy, the warmth of his body mere inches away from hers, the scent of him, or the sensation of his arousal, Kitty found herself being swept away somewhere new.

She lifted herself on her toes, and curled the fingers from one hand around the back of his neck, stroking it. As she did so, he sucked in a quick breath. He pulled her closer then, so that her breasts were more firmly against his chest. And though the blanket was at her feet, the heat growing between her legs twirled up into her belly.

When she'd left Silver Cross—fled it—she'd had no intention of coming to Lofton Tower. Was he the thing that was calling her heart, as the Romani woman suggested? She certainly had no dreams of being held in the arm of a powerful, handsome man as Lord Ellsworth. Was it his quiet, steady way she'd craved? Because the man who held her now seemed a different person altogether. Passionate. Bold.

And she wanted him.

He brought his lips to hers. These were not the gentle, clumsy kisses they'd exchanged under the stars. These were hungry, urgent. She parted her lips, kissing him back, tasting the brandy on his lips, exploring the warmth of his mouth. As she did so, his lips pressed harder, pushing her back until she lowered herself in his chair, wrapping both hands around his neck, pulling at his cravat while he ran his mouth down her neck and across the top of her bosom where her skin met her stays.

"Katherine."

Her name on lips—that name, that no one seemed to call her—was utterly enthralling. It sounded almost foreign, like it belonged to another woman. Indeed, it almost seemed like he was another man. His voice was thick and heavy with desire. But as he raised his head and gazed at her, she knew it was she that he was speaking to.

She put her hands in his hair then cupped his face, and brought her lips to meet his, while his hand explored her chest. Her legs. Even the way he dragged his fingers up the back of her calves sent waves of pleasure rippling through her body. Every touch was new, every sensation magical.

Then he stilled, teetering as if on an edge. He broke the kiss.

"We must stop, now," he said, his lips pulling back as if he were almost in agony.

"Must we?" she asked, driven by something new, foreign, and absolutely exhilarating.

He stood, pushing himself away. As he did so, she could not help but notice his arousal had not subsided. "I cannot dishonor you this way."

Frustration—physical, carnal—coursed through Kitty's body. She felt woozy, and not all of it was from the brandy.

"I am not feeling particularly dishonored," she said, trying to keep the frustration out of her voice. "Quite the contrary."

He picked up the blanket that had fallen to the floor, and drew it over her shoulders. "You say this now, but in the cold light of day, when your head has cleared, and this moment is but a memory, there may be consequences that neither of us are prepared for."

She could see the two parts of him warring with each other. One logic. The other passion.

Just for once, she wanted the passion to win.

"My lo—"

He put a finger over her mouth. "Please do not use that term with me after what has passed between us."

What had passed between them?

He rose abruptly. "I shall return in but a moment," he called over his shoulder as he practically bolted for the door. He threw it open, then disappeared into the darkness. Cool air had snaked into the room, which aided to slow the urgent throbbing in her body. After a few moments more, mesmerized by the fire, overwhelmed by any number of conflicting emotions, and a glass of brandy in her veins, she allowed sleep to take her.

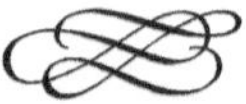

olin was no longer certain of anything. And for a man who quite enjoyed being certain, it was a most disconcerting sensation.

He'd been a man who'd prided himself on his logic, his control. And yet he'd allowed himself, at the slightest temptation, to throw that control aside. That he'd regained it, at the end, brought only the smallest measure of comfort.

She'd tempted him. This gamekeeper's daughter who talked passionately about everything, this woman who was everything Lady Amelia had not been. Like no one he'd yet met at one of Stormount's many parties—and most especially not like Lady Mariah and her cool, detached manner and excellent pedigree.

And yet he could not define Katherine Boxford by her deficits.

At the last he'd regained his senses. He would have liked to think it was solely because he was a gentleman. Rather, it was a less dignified truth. At the merest touch of her, he damn near spilled his seed in his own breeches. Instead, he'd torn himself away, leaving her for a moment to stand in the cool evening rain. It managed to stem the worst of his passion, leaving him heavy and uncomfortable. By the time the worst of it subsided, and he was able to return inside, Miss Boxford was fast asleep.

He unhooked the sling supporting his wrist and then, ignoring the pain, carried her to the very modest bed in the guardroom. He lit the hearth to provide some warmth, and let her sleep. His lower arm throbbed after weeks of being unused, but the discomfort was worth the effort. Then, he'd retreated to the chair where he'd wanted so desperately to lose himself in her, swallowed another healthy dose of brandy, and sat alone with his thoughts.

Five thousand pounds too poor. A stone too heavy.

Horseshit. She was perfection.

Were these the measures by which Katherine Boxford counted her entitlement to happiness? He could see nothing wrong with her stature or shape. She was neither tall nor elegant in the way of many ladies, though elegance was in some ways a matter of training. Katherine Boxford was the daughter of heartier folk, and her upbringing, largely spent, by her own admission, outside, traipsing through the woods…not unlike the girl he'd caught all those years ago. That child had been confident and free in a way he had never been. Until Countess Snowdon's voice cut through the stillness of that moment, and the child had disappeared.

Colin sat up, jolted by the memory.

That child. Was she Katherine Boxford? They had the same eyes—like whiskey in the firelight. But she'd been looking up then. Not down.

Did Edmund realize the heartache, however inadvertent, he'd caused her? Colin shifted, an unexpected flash of anger tightening his jaw. He doubted it very much. Edmund had a naturally carefree way about himself that ladies found attractive, but he was not a Lothario. Given his father's troublesome, and occasionally abusive relationship with his mother, Edmund was indeed very thoughtful of the women in his life. But for someone like Katherine Boxford, who at the time would have been young, impressionable, and presented with someone she'd believed to be in her sphere—his natural charm may have been interpreted as something else. He must have seemed perfect for her.

Not unlike Amelia. Of course, Amelia had been perfect for Colin because she'd been there. And in truth, that was all. He'd woven her into the fabric of his existence, of his future, without ever truly asking if they were a fit.

Unlike Colin, however, Katherine Boxford did not bother with despair. She knew she had to act. No wonder she'd gone to such remarkable lengths to secure the position as his assistant. She was looking for an escape. It also explained her frustration at Colin's inability to get out of his own way—to allow others to determine his happiness. He shook his head and chuckled bitterly at his own expense. What a self-indulgent ass he could be.

His gaze went to the door where she slept. It took all of his will not to want to lay with her. Touch the lush softness of her skin. Play with the curls at the base of her neck, trace her lips—

The bang of a fist pounding on his door tore his attention away and brought him immediately to his feet. He strode to the door, placing his glass down on his work table as he passed. Colin opened it, peering into the darkness. On the other side stood Edmund Pembroke, the lamp he held revealing his face, uncommonly serious.

"Is she here?" he asked, before Colin had a chance to speak. His voice was as hard as his manner.

It took Colin a moment to register the question. "Who?"

Edmund looked Colin up and down and it was then that Colin became brutally aware of his disheveled appearance. No jacket, waistcoat opened, cravat gone, and if Edmund cared to examine more closely, the last of his lingering erection. Thankfully, he did not.

"Do not toy with me, Ellsworth. I don't care if you're about to inherit half the bloody kingdom. If you have so much as touched her —" Edmund pushed past him, into the room, his eyes going immediately to the fire, where a simple frock and two stockings hung over a chair, drying.

It didn't look suspicious. It looked positively damning.

Colin let out a low breath.

"Edmund, this is not what it appears."

Edmund whipped around, his eyes narrowed. This was a man who'd spent time working for the Home Office, Colin reminded himself. Who worked with Bastien DuMont and Sir Richard Hamilton, hunting down men working against the Crown. Often, Colin found it incredulous that Edmund could have done such work. Until this moment.

And yet, this was the same man who'd unknowingly broken Katherine Boxford's heart.

"How does this look?" Edmund challenged. "Because it looks pretty goddamn bad."

"This past winter your colleague Bastien DuMont had decided, based on his own erroneous conclusions, that I was the head of a terrorist organization," Colin said, his own anger rising. That was a remarkable night indeed. Bastien, a spy working for Sir Richard Hamilton, had come searching for *Le Veneur Rouge*, the loathsome head of an organization that had committed crimes across England—and France—in the name of a single man's lust for power. A man, it turned out, who was Colin's long-lost kin. Bastien and Colin had come to blows, but in the end, Colin had gained something he'd had few of. A friend he could trust. "He was wrong. And so are you. I have not dishonored her. I would not."

At that moment, the door to the guardrooms creaked open, and there stood Katherine Boxford, his jacket pulled around her shoulders, looking beautifully bleary-eyed. Edmund's gaze went from Katherine to Colin, and hardened.

"You bastard," he growled at him, before softening slightly and turning his attention to Katherine Boxford. "Kitty, get presentable and then into the carriage."

"Edmund—" Colin began, holding up a hand.

"You." Edmund pointed a finger. "Don't speak, lest I am responsible for turning your wedding party into a funeral."

"Edmund," Katherine Boxford called out, her voice firm, and undeniably edged with anger. "Go home."

"Not without you," he replied, his gaze darting between Colin and Katherine Boxford. "Everyone is worried sick about you."

She blanched slightly at that, but remained where she was. "You can see that I am quite well."

"Did he touch you?"

"Whether he did or not is none of your concern. You are neither my father or my brother." The authority in her voice was unmistakable, mixed with indignation. "But let's not dance around the subject. My virtue is quite intact."

Edmund blanched for but a moment, and Colin suspected this may have been the first time Katherine Boxford had ever spoken to him in such a manner. Edmund softened. Clearly, he did care for her.

"Right then," he replied at last. "We should go."

Miss Boxford, however, did not move.

"How did you discover I was here?" she asked.

"One of my mother's kitchen maids. She told me you'd been sneaking out at night."

Sneaking?

"Miss Boxford is in my employ," Colin interjected. "Surely Mrs. Pembroke knows this. 'Tis but a temporary measure."

Edmund became even more angry, if such a thing was possible. "This is not helping your case."

"What kind of man do you take me for?" Colin shot back, his own anger pushing through. "I am currently seeking a bride. A future duchess. Why would you think I would dally with a local girl? Especially one with your protection? Especially the daughter of such a well-respected man?"

"Because you can."

An unknown anger broiled in Colin's chest, and he shoved Edmund away from him.

"Whether you realize it or not, your insinuations are dishonorable to Miss Boxford, and I will not stand here idly while you make sordid accusations about her character, which is, like the rest of her, flawless."

"Kitty—" Edmund said, looking past him toward Miss Boxford.

"Not. One. Word." Colin felt his uninjured hand ball into a fist. "Or so help me Edmund Pembroke, I will risk a second sprained wrist by putting my fist into your jaw."

Edmund's eyes widened a moment, and the two stood in a tense silence.

"Oh for heaven's sakes." Miss Boxford's exasperation broke through the silence. She unceremoniously threw off Colin's coat, strode across the room, and grabbed her stockings and dress. "The two of you will stop this nonsense at once. You are acting like children, and, may I remind you, that neither of you have a say in my life. Edmund, I will come with you. Lord Ellsworth, I apologize for imposing on you. It seems your fears were in fact quite justified."

Colin nodded and watched her disappear into his room. The two stood, stunned to silence, before Edmund started at him again, this time in a harsh whisper.

"Your fears? What did you fear? That your little tryst would be discovered?"

"She is my assistant, you arse, and she is a damned good one. I hired her a fortnight ago. She told me your mother endorsed the arrangement."

"Your assistant?" Edmund lowered his guard somewhat, clearly trying to take in what Colin was telling him. "For the observatory?"

He nodded. "She learned of it when we met at Silver Cross a fortnight ago and applied. She was by far the best candidate."

"Why on earth would you hire a woman?" Edmund grated. "Not that I doubt Kitty's intellect for a moment, but you must know how this looks."

"Of course I do," Colin replied. "I refused her application twice for that very reason. But she was quite determined, and assured me your mother would have no qualms about it. I relented, against my better judgment so it would seem. But she has proven herself quite useful."

More than useful, in fact, though he kept that to himself. Her presence was ever more necessary in his life. He found himself more and more impatient, not just to escape the crowds, or resume his observations. He was becoming impatient to see her.

"She came in the early evening," he continued. "On foot—unscheduled. Normally, as your kitchen maid would attest, I send a carriage for her to ensure her safety to and from the observatory. Because of the weather, our normal viewing session would have been cancelled. When I found her, she was quite upset. And very drenched. I was going to see her back to Kennington Grove at first light. You know me. I am not in the habit of breaking society's rules."

"I am wondering if I know you at all, Middleton," Edmund said. "Or Kitty, for that matter. We had spoken earlier, and she did seem unsettled. Apparently I underestimated her."

"I suspect everyone does," Colin said. "Including myself, in the beginning." His gaze strayed to the door where she was getting dressed, then looked back to Edmund. "But she is far more than she appears. Far more."

Edmund shook his head. "Her parents. Mother. Gwyneth—we were all worried when she disappeared before dinner. And I can assure you they have absolutely no idea about this." Edmund looked up at Colin then, his eyes narrowing slightly. "If she was a lady, you would be obligated to marry her. Regardless of what happened here."

"I am well aware of that," Colin replied. If she were a lady, she would never have been here. Instead, she occupied some curious space between the titled and the common, and to label Katherine Boxford as common felt unseemly and beneath her.

The door opened, and Miss Boxford, now properly attired, her hair tied back in a simple knot, walked past both of them, her bearing steadfast. She nodded toward Colin, gracing him with a smile he saw did not quite meet her eyes, then turned to Edmund.

"I am ready." She pulled her shawl off the peg by the door, then walked out to the cart waiting to take her home.

Edmund exchanged a solemn nod with Colin, then hopped up into the cart, and the two disappeared into what was left of the night. He waited until he could no longer hear the sounds of the horses, then closed the door and sank down into the chair where she'd sat. The blanket she'd had around her shoulders was there. He picked it up and put it to his nose, drinking her subtle perfume that lingered in its fibers.

If Miss Boxford was a lady, he would have married her. Those were the rules.

But she lived on the periphery of those rules. Like that shooting star that had landed in Wold, she was something outside his sphere, crossing into his sights, fascinating him at every turn.

If things were different—if she had been born a lady, would he have made an offer? Even then, he was not sure. Falling in love was a violation of his first rule in this game of marriage he was playing. Not that he was falling in love with her. He was merely testing an hypothesis.

A rather dangerous one.

THE NEXT MORNING, Kitty sat on the edge of her bed, still in her nightdress, watching the sun break over the horizon. She'd arrived at Kennington Grove only a few hours ago to the deep relief of her parents, Gwynnie, and Mrs. Pembroke. The very sight of them all sitting in the parlor, their faces a mix of relief, curiosity and—to her great shame—deep disappointment, was almost impossible to bear. Still, Mrs. Pembroke suggested to the agreement of everyone, that it was best if everyone got some sleep, and the matter could be dealt with in the light of day. Kitty was left alone to dwell on her own tumultuous thoughts. She spent a few miserable hours tossing and turning in what little of the night remained, and she supposed she deserved the misery.

Would she lose her position with Mrs. Pembroke? Would they want her out of the house? Would Edmund and Gwynnie no longer welcome her at Silver Cross? Horribly ironic, given everything. And her parents…Kitty could hardly bear it. The look on her parents' faces when she'd arrived at Kennington Grove was almost enough to finish her.

What explanation should she give for why she'd gone to Lofton Tower? That she'd taken a position none of them knew about, save Mrs. Pembroke, for reasons she dare not convey? Because a mysterious Romani woman appeared on the road and told her to follow her heart?

How could she even begin to explain why she first sought out the position? Even if she could, it was not why she'd gone there last night. If she could bear to own it, it was Lord Ellsworth she'd been in search of. Which was remarkable, she supposed. She hadn't wanted to like him so much, especially since he'd been so determined, early on, to dismiss her simply because she was a woman. And because he'd seen her once at her most vulnerable. Until last night. That was something perhaps far more intimate. Even before he'd kissed her.

She could picture him now, even without her eyes closed. His smile made her smile, and his eyes, even with his spectacles on, seemed to look right into her. What did he see there?

More than anyone else, and it was both thrilling and terrifying.

It felt dangerous that anyone should know her as anything but Kitty Boxford, the sturdy, happy girl who did what she was asked and kept her complaints to herself. But he had seen her that horrible afternoon at Gorland Park, and he'd remembered. How was it possible that he could remember her when she was practically invisible to the rest of the world?

He'd called her remarkable. Remarkable! And then, when he'd kissed her, tenderly at first, it was followed by an eagerness so intense that even now the memory of it brought a rush of sensuous heat between her legs. He'd wanted her in a way that no one had, and she would not regret that. Nor would she regret her choice to work for him. That had opened her eyes to a countless number of wonders. To other celestial bodies, possibly other worlds beyond her own very confined one.

A knock at the door snapped Kitty's attention, and her heart started beating a little faster. Though it was light, it was not quite six o'clock, and she had not yet dressed. She could hardly imagine Mrs. Pembroke was awake already, especially after such a long, distressing night at Kitty's expense. Pulling her robe tightly around her, she checked herself in the mirror, ignoring the dark circles under her eyes. Would they turn her out? It was entirely possible, she supposed.

As long as her parents' security was not threatened by her actions, Kitty would live with the consequences of them.

Letting out a low breath, she went to the door. Better to get the horrible business over with. But it was shock that greeted her when she saw Gwynnie at the door.

"Kitty," she said in a low voice, and pulled her friend close for an embrace. "Thank heavens you are all right."

Her friend released her, then came inside and shut the door before each taking a spot on the bed.

"I am well, Gwynnie. Up to my neck in trouble, but fine otherwise."

"We were so worried," she replied, concern marking her brow. "After you disappeared, we'd thought perhaps you'd returned to Kennington Grove with a headache. Indeed, Mrs. Pembroke was convinced. But when you didn't return there, we became worried. We searched everywhere. And then Edmund questioned the servants."

"Heavens," Kitty said, a stone sinking in her gut. "I am so sorry to cause you all such worry. I went for a walk, and got caught in the rain."

Gwynnie pursed her lips and narrowed her eyes. "A walk all the way to Stormount? Edmund told me you took a position as Colin's observatory assistant. Is it true?"

Kitty nodded and waited for censure. Instead, a wide smile broke across Gwynnie's face, and then she grabbed Kitty's hand and took it in her own. Suddenly, Kitty felt like a girl again, conspiring with her childhood friend. It was a wonderful feeling.

"Tell me everything," Gwynnie demanded in that encouraging way of hers.

"Aren't you upset with me?" Kitty asked.

Gwynnie became a bit circumspect. "I suppose I was shocked. I don't know if you are unhappy with your position with Mrs. Pembroke, or if you were doing this on a lark, or you are genuinely interested. I am, perhaps, a little surprised you didn't tell me. I know we have been parted for many years, but you are my best and dearest friend. There is nothing I would not do for you, especially after all you have done for Edmund and me."

Kitty held up a hand to her dear friend's face and smiled sadly.

"I'm sorry I didn't tell you. I didn't want you to have to keep a secret from Edmund, or his mother, and I didn't want anyone to know. Especially as it is only temporary. I didn't want to upset anyone and I'm afraid I've done quite the reverse."

"Did Colin make that demand? To keep it secret?"

Kitty recalled the shock on his face when he'd realized that no one at Kennington Grove or Silver Cross knew about the arrangement either. "No. He had no idea that it was a secret." She paused, wincing at the surprise when he'd been caught unawares by her lie. "Not that he wanted it known either, I suppose. He is very concerned with propriety. And I didn't want Mrs. Pembroke to think I was unhappy."

"Are you unhappy here? Is this about your list? Because if you needed money you know you can come to me."

"It is about the list," Kitty began. "And at the same time, it is not about the list at all." There was so much to tell. But only so much Kitty felt safe to reveal. Kitty was the older of the girls by two years, and as children, she had in some ways been the one to shelter and protect Gwynnie. Now it felt quite the reverse. But she could not carry this alone any longer. "I feel…stuck, I suppose. You have moved on with your life, and I am very happy for you. I have no great plans for myself, but I thought I'd find myself a gamekeeper and we'd be happy. Indeed, when I first met Edmund—"

"You thought it might be him."

Kitty nodded. "Or at least, I imagined myself with someone very much like him. Don't you remember? You were going to marry a prince, and I was going to marry a gamekeeper, like Papa."

The two sat in silence for some time, Gwynnie holding Kitty's hands and never letting go.

"I remember how silly I was, thinking I knew what the future held. But those were not my dreams, really. They were my mother's. Because I knew no other dream for myself." Gwynnie looked at her friend. "What do you dream for yourself, Kitty?"

A terribly forbidden thought entered her mind. An impossible dream. A dream that involved a tall man with red-gold hair, spectacles, and a warm smile. A dream she didn't know she'd had until that moment. But he was a marquess. And so a dream it would remain.

"I don't know," she said, unwilling to speak it aloud, lest the heavens hear her. "I used to, once. But now…everything feels very upside down. I am a spinster, Gwynnie. And a burden to my parents."

Gwynnie smiled. "Kitty, you are a burden to no one. Mrs. Pembroke thinks very highly of you."

"After last night, I think that is no longer the case." Kitty shook her head. "I have done her and Lord Ellsworth a great disservice by not being truthful with either of them." She closed her eyes, the true ramifications of her actions rushing down on her. "Oh Gwynnie—what if we are tossed out again? I don't know if I could bear it. And it would be my fault. Again."

Gwynnie blinked, clearly stunned by Kitty's worries.

"Kitty Boxford, you know that you and your parents will always have a home with Edmund and me. Always. And I cannot imagine Mrs. Pembroke would even entertain such a drastic notion." Kitty felt herself being pulled into an embrace. "I am so sorry for what happened all those years ago at Gorland Park. What was done to you then was unconscionable. But it was not your fault. Nor mine. How could you even think that?"

"How could I not? I'd broken every rule and my family was punished for it." Even now, the fear of those awful uncertain days after the Boxford's unceremonious eviction from Gorland Park came rushing back with perfect clarity. "I'd been in the orchard, picking some of the drops to put out for your father's prized deer. It was later in the day, and I probably should have been home. Your mother was having guests, and I was to stay out of sight. But I didn't."

"Oh, Kitty."

"I'd been climbing a tree—I can't even remember why now. I was probably playing some silly game or another." Kitty shook her head. "Your mother—somehow—saw me. I have no idea what she was doing there, and I suppose it doesn't matter now."

"And that's when you fell and lost your brooch. You were lucky you weren't hurt."

"There was a boy there. I hadn't seen him before—but he must have belonged to your mother's party of guests. He was older than I. I don't remember much about him, except for his hair, I suppose. It was—"

Kitty stopped. His hair was ginger. And his eyes were a remarkable shade of green.

"Oh my," she said to herself, blinking in amazement.

"What?"

"I think it might have been Lord Ellsworth."

"Colin? Are you certain?" Gwynnie paused, as if searching her memory. "It is possible. It's not like England is teeming with ginger-haired aristocrats." Gwynnie rose, idly rubbing her swollen belly before brightening again. "Perhaps he found your brooch?"

Kitty's shoulders slumped, then she rose and went to a small chest at the end of her bed. In amongst the woolen blankets was a small piece of silk—a scrap she'd managed to save years ago. She unwrapped it and put it in Gwynnie's hands—little more than a broken scrap of metal, a single paste gem in the setting. Alongside were three hollowed out spaces where the others had been, and the link that had once held a beautiful stone with a star inside.

"I found it. Last summer. That day Edmund proposed to you. I dug it out of the ground."

Gwynnie frowned, examining the piece carefully, holding it up to the light, turning it over, and examining the back.

"Remarkable," she said, more to herself studying it intently, before turning back to Kitty. "That is, remarkable that you had found it after so long." She folded it up and handed it back to Kitty.

"I suppose it is."

"And even more remarkable that Colin was there!" Gwynnie replied, clearly tickled by the idea. "You will have to ask him if it was him."

"My parents or Mrs. Pembroke might forbid me even speaking to him," she replied, placing the pin back in her chest and closing the lid.

"They won't. I promise you. Heavens, I disappeared from my family for an entire fortnight. And during that time, I made so many blunders."

"Did you spend a night unchaperoned in a the company of a marquess in only your stays?"

"Not quite," Gwynnie smiled, her eyes mischievous. "But tell me, what did Colin do when he found you?"

Kitty's thoughts went back to yesterday evening. His indignation when he'd caught her with his letters. His understanding. His smile. And, heaven help her, his touch. Just thinking about it brought a smile to her face.

"He was surprised. And not pleasantly so, in the beginning."

"But it became pleasant after, I would say," Gwynnie said. "You like him, don't you?"

Kitty rolled her eyes, cursing herself as she felt the heat rising in her cheeks. "He is an amiable gentleman."

"Not stiff? Or uneasy? I like Colin, but he seems forever on guard. How he and Edmund ever became friends eludes me."

"He is nervous, I think, in company. And it may manifest itself as brusqueness. But he is not normally like that."

"With you."

"Gwynnie, I see what you are doing," Kitty said, slightly exasperated at her friend's manner. "It is largely when it is at Lofton Tower that he is more...himself."

Gwynnie sat up and gave Kitty an incredulous look. "I saw you two speaking at the picnic. He looked quite comfortable then and there was not a telescope in sight. And you looked lovely and quite at home with him."

"Until Lady Mariah dosed my dress in lemonade."

Gwynnie threw her head back in laughter. "And look what it got her. Not a night with Colin."

Kitty was hardly going to mention the fact that Lady Mariah did indeed arrive on his doorstep later that very night, forcing Kitty to hide in a pantry.

"Gwynnie, it's not funny! Lord Ellsworth is quite taken with her."

"Of course he thinks he is. She no doubt reminds him of his old fiancé," Gwynnie said. "But it doesn't matter."

"Why ever not?" Kitty thought back to his letters and the miniature of Lady Amelia he kept with his things. "It seems to matter a great deal."

Gwynnie lifted her head in that impervious way of hers. "It doesn't matter because you like him. And I suspect, dear Kitty, he likes you."

"I do not," Kitty replied, and probably too forcefully. "And even if I did, it hardly signifies. I am not even a gentleman's daughter. And he is going to be a duke."

Gwynnie shrugged.

"And I fell in love with a gamekeeper. Anything is possible."

"You are the daughter of an earl, and Edmund was raised a gentleman. His uncle is a viscount and his cousin a marquess. It is not at all the same for me."

"Edmund has a book his cousin-in-law gave him. Full of stories of milk maids who marry princes."

Kitty smiled. "I remember that book." Edmund had kept it with him, and even read from it from time to time. "But those are fairy tales, Gwynnie. Geese that lay golden eggs, magic beans, and fairy godmothers that turn pumpkins into carriages and create gowns out of thin air."

"Well," Gwynnie said, "it all depends on how you look at it. I had a fairy godfather of sorts. And a prince masquerading as a huntsman."

Maybe, just maybe, the heavens would change its mind and allow her, just once, to have what she wanted. And rediscover her happiness. But she had to change. But how could she change? She had no pixie dust or magic potions to change her into something else. She was just Kitty.

Except when she was with Lord Ellsworth.

She bit back her wish. For now, she focused on more immediate worries—her parents. Mrs. Pembroke. Her job.

Happiness would have to wait.

CHAPTER 16

Early the next morning—not early enough, but earlier than he typically rose—Colin found himself on the front steps of Kennington Grove, knocking on the door. He had no idea what he was doing here beyond the inexplicable sense of requirement he felt to speak to Katherine Boxford's parents and Mrs. Pembroke and apologize for his extreme lack of judgment.

He should have turned Katherine Boxford out on the spot last night. Not only had she arrived on an evening outside the boundaries of their agreement, but she was only half dressed and rooting through his personal affects. His bloody letters from Amelia. Only this past winter he'd dressed down a servant at Barronsfield Manor on the suspicion of stealing them. Those letters were his very private shame. And a reminder to himself that falling in love only led to humiliation and pain. Better to stick to logic. To science.

And she'd found them. Even now, the mortification of that moment rolled in his gut. He should have tossed her out on the spot. Regardless of the rain, or the state of her clothes. Hell, he never should have bloody well taken her on in the first place. And then, of all things, to discover that she'd been working without the permission of her parents, her employer? He was perfectly within his bounds to leave Katherine Boxford to whatever fate and punishments set for her.

He'd spent the rest of the night recalling all the reasons why he should have been angry with her. Why having Edmund remove her from Lofton was absolutely the right thing to have done. Why her return to Lofton Tower was absolutely impossible. After all, she'd broken almost every rule society had laid out for her, and there was a cost for breaking rules.

But he couldn't manage to be angry with her. Instead, he was angry with himself, for wondering what might happen if he broke them as well. If he'd taken her in his arms, and made lov—

"My Lord Ellsworth." The crisp voice of Mrs. Pembroke's long-time manservant, Vincent, saved Colin from having to finish that most unsettling thought.

"Good morning." He cleared his throat and adjusted his spectacles. Bloody hell but he was nervous. "I would like to speak with Mrs. Pembroke, if it's convenient."

The manservant betrayed the smallest hint of a smile, which was enough to remind Colin that the man, along with the rest of the household, knew exactly the topic that had driven Colin to the doorstep.

He removed his hat and stepped into the entry of the quaint manor house, waiting for Vincent's return. A moment later, he was led to a parlor where he found Mrs. Pembroke, who smiled and nodded as they met each other's eyes. She was sitting in her chair, near a small fire which kept the room warm despite the fine summer day.

Two women kept her company. The first was Lady Gwyneth, whose barely contained curiosity almost made Colin want to turn and run. The third woman he had not yet met. She was perhaps forty or a little older, her dark hair streaked with silver. Much of the woman's features carried a similarity to Katherine Boxford, leaving him in little doubt she was the girl's mother.

She regarded Colin with suspicion, as was her due.

He bowed deeply and waited for Mrs. Pembroke to invite him to sit. It did not escape him that she regarded him very carefully before she did so.

"Thank you for seeing me, ma'am," he replied, then cleared his throat and turned his attention squarely to Mrs. Boxford. He was nervous. "I came to beg your apology, Mrs. Boxford, over the distress I have caused with regards to Miss Boxford's whereabouts yesterday evening."

Mrs. Boxford straightened, and though she was the wife of a gamekeeper, she held herself with considerable poise.

"It is very good of you to come, my lord. Mr. Boxford and I spoke with Kitty at length yesterday, and we are satisfied with her explanation. Not happy." Her mouth pulled back into a tight smile. "But satisfied."

"Still, I should have made a more earnest effort to send word of her whereabouts," he replied. "And for that, I do beg your forgiveness."

"I had no idea that my daughter had taken it upon herself to gain a position in your observatory," she continued.

"Indeed, I had no notion you were unaware," Colin replied, pushing aside the sting he felt at the news. "But if I may, Miss Boxford has exceeded my expectations. She is a quick study, and has taken to the work as if she has always done it."

Her mother nodded, her pride in her daughter showing through her guarded countenance.

"Her father has been teaching her the constellations since she was a little girl, and she is well acquainted with moon phases. She claims it helps with her gardening." She offered Colin a small, folded piece of paper. "This is a note to you, my lord. We were getting ready to send it when you arrived."

Colin accepted the paper, carefully unfolding it. In her careful, tidy script, she wrote,

Lord Ellsworth,

I regret to inform you that I can no longer continue as your assistant. Given the duties with my current position, it is best that I focus my attention at Kennington Grove. I apologize for the inconvenience and disregard for propriety as a result of my unexpected visit to Lofton Tower the last evening.

Best,

Katherine Boxford

P.S. Thank you for showing me the moons around Jupiter. I shall remember that always.

Colin read the note. He read it twice. He cleared his throat, then read it again.

No one had ever thanked him for sharing his work with them.

He swallowed and took a deep breath to stave off the heaviness in his chest. Of course it was right and appropriate she resign her position. It had been foolish to allow her to take it.

But he suddenly didn't give a damn about what was right or appropriate.

"Please sit, my lord," Mrs. Pembroke said, breaking Colin out of his reverie. "It is early yet. Vincent has brought some coffee. You appear to need some refreshment."

Colin gave himself a mental shake, then folded the note and tucked it in his pocket. All three ladies were watching him closely. Too closely.

He sat between Mrs. Pembroke and Mrs. Boxford and gracefully accepted a cup of coffee. After spending a restless night, he needed it.

"You understand of course," Mrs. Boxford began, "that Kitty cannot continue. It was her decision."

"Of course." Colin nodded. "Though I admit to being dismayed by it. I confess I had doubted her abilities in the beginning, but she has become quite valuable to my work. That is selfish, I realize."

His self-deprecation brought a much needed break in the tension that had settled in the room.

"Since we are in a confessing mood," Mrs. Pembroke said, "it was I who first encouraged her."

Colin stilled as all heads turned toward her, shock evident on their faces. Mrs. Pembroke seemed quite pleased with the joke.

"And I suppose given that we are laying out our apologies, I will add mine," she said, waving her hand in the air, "though in truth I do not feel terribly apologetic about it."

"You encouraged her?" Colin said, flabbergasted. Though, given the expressions on Mrs. Boxford's and Lady Gwyneth's faces, he was not the only one taken aback. "Did you know she was successful?"

"I had a notion, yes," she replied. "The girl is four and twenty. Lively. Active. And as much as I value her—" her eyes fell to Mrs. Boxford then— "and I value her very much, she needs more. More than any of us can give her." She gestured to Mrs. Boxford and Lady Gwyneth, who looked positively gobsmacked. "The girl is far too careful to spare our feelings at the expense of her own."

The room fell silent. Colin's mother visited on Mrs. Pembroke from time to time, and sitting with her now, he fully understood why. Most assumed it was charity. Now, he realized, it was far more. Astute observation and brutal honesty. He could not help but wonder what opinions she'd given Mother about him over the years.

"The employment is of short duration," Colin began, finding himself moving toward the edge of his seat. "Just until my hand is fully healed. Her role was to take notes of my observations while I view, and indeed, Mrs. Boxford, your daughter is quite talented and has a keen mind. She is a credit to you and your husband."

"That she is, my lord," she replied. "Mr. Boxford and I thank God every day for her. But I cannot pretend to be pleased about her behavior, or that she is spending a portion of her evenings, unchaperoned, with a powerful man."

We come to it at last, Colin thought, and thank goodness for that. For all the reasons he'd considered himself.

"I understand perfectly," he replied. "Indeed, I had rejected an earlier application from her for those reasons you have just stated. And I would agree with you under normal circumstances. But these are not normal circumstances."

Mrs. Boxford crinkled her brow.

"Surely to heaven you can find another person to help you?" Mrs. Boxford said.

"I have tried, ma'am. None I have met are her equal—in talent or temperament," Colin replied. "But if I might beg your patience for moment a longer. I need Miss Boxford to help me with a very special night."

All three stilled, and Mrs. Boxford looked positively thunder-struck. Lady Gwyneth's eyes widened to saucers, then pressed her lips together in an attempt to stifle her laughter. At least one person in the room was enjoying Colin's discomfort immensely.

"That—did not come out right," Colin said. Heavens, this was more nerve wracking than presenting at the Royal Society. "That is to say, I am planning a viewing party two days hence—the night of the ball. We will have a couple of small telescopes and a looking glass. The moon will be coming to full, so it provides some opportunity for guests to partake of a pleasurable evening."

Visible relief settled on Mrs. Boxford after Colin's ill-chosen words, which he took as permission to continue.

"It was Miss Boxford's idea, and it's a jolly good one. I would like to ask if Miss Boxford can assist me with the planning—during the day, in the full company of servants and my mother—and then off course, the evening itself."

"Sounds fascinating, Lord Ellsworth," Mrs. Pembroke said. "To what end is this viewing party?"

"To help me select a bride," he said, though the words seemed suddenly distasteful. He shook off the sensation. "The night itself will be full of guests, and indeed, Mrs. Boxford, I would be most pleased if you and Mr. Boxford would also like to attend. I do not think I can do this without her. She has become…invaluable to me."

Colin quieted, the ticking of a nearby clock adding more unwel-come tension to his tightening nerves. Toying with the rim of the hat in his hand, he studied Mrs. Boxford. It was impossible to tell if she would relent, and questioning why it mattered so much to him that she did. Though they were vastly different in station, she did not appear the least intimidated by that fact.

Mrs. Boxford replied at last. "You must not look only to me, my lord. Mrs. Pembroke is her employer."

"I am certain I will make do," Mrs. Pembroke replied, waving her hand in the air as if she were swatting away a fly. She looked at her daughter in law. "And I am certain Gwyneth will be eager to keep me company."

"Of course!" Lady Gwyneth replied, an over-enthusiastic smile on her face. "Most happy."

"If it pleases Mrs. Pembroke, I will return to my husband and Kitty and discuss this with them," Mrs. Boxford said at last. She awaited a nod from Mrs. Pembroke, then stood. Despite her diminutive height, Katherine Boxford's mother held her herself in a manner that was quite regal. Her back was straight as a board, her shoulders square, her chin up. She turned and looked straight at Colin. "My daughter is likely in the garden with her father, my lord. If you care to walk with me, we can discuss the particulars of this arrangement."

"I would very much like that, thank you." He rose, seeing this as progress, but not allowing himself to relax. He bowed to Mrs. Pembroke and Lady Gwyneth, then followed her out.

The two walked in a silence that Colin could not say was easy.

"Miss Boxford speaks of you and your husband with great affection," he offered as a way to break the silence.

"Kitty is a very special girl," she began. "Something of a miracle, perhaps. I was told early on that I would never have a child, and still she came."

Colin chuckled at that. "It is my observation that she is very determined, once she has decided upon something. Indeed, if it were not for that determination, I believe we would not be speaking now."

She looked up at him then.

"So this scheme to be your assistant, it was hers?"

"Indeed. In fact, I did not wish to hire her at all." He could hardly think of that first meeting at the Brookside Inn without smiling. "She was determined to change my mind. And I am glad she did."

"I am not certain I wish to know how."

"In a word—tenacity. But she remains my assistant because she is excellent. It is the very reason I am here." Certainly not because he enjoyed being with her. He did. But it could not be the reason.

"This pleases me," Mrs. Boxford said at last, a smile teasing her lips. "But it is also worrisome, my lord. Kitty is a girl of easy temper. Eager to please. She has a good heart. But it could be far too easily trampled on. Especially by a powerful man."

"Mrs. Boxford—"

"The whims of the powerful have directed Kitty's life since birth. Far more, in fact, than even she can appreciate. She is your assistant for a fortnight, and then? Your arm will heal and Kitty will return, restless for a world that she has tasted, but cannot have."

"I see that you are trying to protect her, ma'am, and I honor that." Her mother spoke the truth. Their arrangement skirted the rules of polite society, and Colin found himself struggling against them for the first time. "The terms of our arrangement were clear, and I am determined to honor them. Three more days. It is all I ask of her, and you. Then Miss Boxford will receive a generous remuneration and a letter or recommendation, so she can explore a future of her own making."

They turned a corner, and came to a rather spectacular garden already in bloom.

"If it were up to Kitty, her future would be spent in a garden. She has always had a gift for nurturing things. My wish for her future is for someone to nurture her."

It was, quite inexplicably, Colin's as well.

A day in the sun digging in among a row of peas and carrots was by far the best antidote to almost any ill, Kitty decided, though the crushing regret for her ill-considered actions still lingered. Every time she closed her eyes, an image of her parents' disappointment appeared in her mind as clear as if they stood in front of her now. It was that image that had given her the strength to write Lord Ellsworth and end their agreement. Funny how it felt like far more was ending than that.

Maybe it was for the best. Before she got her hopes up.

She looked over her little plot of earth, considering what was worth transplanting, and what she would leave for the whims of the new tenants. An old resentment bubbled up inside her as she thought about it, but she pushed it from her mind. She would move to Silver Cross without complaint, then continue with her plan. She might never discover the meaning of the Romani woman's words...those from years ago, and the equally challenging phrase from yesterday. But whatever the meaning, it was not worth the respect of the people who loved her most.

She was grateful to Mama and to Mrs. Pembroke for giving her a day out of doors to recover from her "ordeal," as her mother described it. Of course, when she recalled the softness of Lord Ellsworth's lips, and the heat of his breath on her skin, and the hunger in his eyes and how it made her feel all very warm and achy in all sorts of places, Kitty could hardly say spending time with him was any sort of ordeal at all.

Her true ordeal, perhaps, was that she'd been heartsick, and that was entirely of her own making. She checked over the tender sprouts of her beans that were already beginning their climb up the poles she'd staked in the ground. It was not likely she would see Lord Ellsworth again. At least not before he'd announced his marriage.

Papa and Mama—Mama especially—insisted that she give up the position, and she could not in good conscience refuse them. Mrs. Pembroke, for her part, was shockingly amused by the entire affair. But perhaps she knew better than anyone that for Kitty to remain in the house with Edmund and Gwyneth was not a good idea. Though, she realized, whatever longing she'd had for Edmund was gone.

Kitty moved on from the peas to her prized pumpkin patch. This was her first attempt at a new, larger variety of pumpkin after she'd tried crossing some last year. Would she be able to transplant it? She pulled a few weeds that had found purchase in the soil.

"Here you are, Kitty."

Kitty breathed a small sigh at the sound of her mother's voice. She had disappointed them terribly, and it was that disappointment in their expressions that had been almost impossible to bear this morning.

Dropping the weeds into a nearby basket, she wiped her dirty hands on her apron and ran the edge of her sleeve across her brow. Squinting in the midday sun, she caught the unmistakable form of Lord Ellsworth. Her heart slammed in her chest and she swallowed hard, unable to disguise her surprise at seeing him.

"Miss Boxford," Lord Ellsworth said, smiling as he walked along next to her parents. If Kitty didn't know better, he seemed…happy. "It is good to see you."

Even when she had dirt under her fingernails and a face that probably resembled beetroot?

"I—" she turned to her parents, who seemed remarkably at ease with him. "—was just seeing to my pumpkins."

Kitty wanted to bury her head in her hands. How absolutely ridiculous that must sound to him.

"The marquess came to speak to us, Kitty, and apologize for our distress," her mother said. "He also spoke with Mrs. Pembroke."

"That is very kind," Kitty said, looking from her parents, to Lord Ellsworth and back to her parents. "I believe I'd made it clear that Lord Ellsworth bears no responsibility for what happened. It was my folly. The marquess has been a gentleman in every respect."

"While I thank Miss Boxford for her assessment of my character," he began, his mouth falling to a familiar, serious line, his gaze lingering on her for the briefest of moments, "I insist on bearing the responsibility for what happened. The power differential between us is too great for it to be otherwise. I insist upon it."

Kitty blinked. He was utterly commanding in his voice, without being harsh or oppressive in his speech. Her gaze went to her parents, and in particular her mother, who, she could not help but notice, seemed moved by his manner. Mama turned to Kitty, a hint of a smile on her face.

"Lord Ellsworth has asked for your assistance, Kitty, with his viewing party. He has been very generous in cataloging your skills as his assistant."

Kitty's gaze darted between her parents and Lord Ellsworth, uncertain of what to make of her mother's declaration. He must have received the note. Her parents had made it quite clear that being in the private employ of a man such as Lord Ellsworth was dangerous.

"I thank you, my lord, but under the circumstances—"

Kitty's mother smiled, and looked to her father. "We have discussed it, and reconsidered, my dear. Given that the employment is of short duration, and we have Lord Ellsworth's assurances you will be not be privately tucked away, it would be an honor for you to assist in this way.

"You have?" Kitty looked from her parents to Lord Ellsworth. "And Mrs. Pembroke?"

"I will help in your stead," her mother replied. "It is but three days."

Kitty clenched her hands together. She dearly wanted to continue with him. It would give her the means to become less reliant on her parents. She could advertise for a husband almost immediately. And even before her mind could rest on that idea, a far more traitorous thought popped into her head. It meant she could spend just a bit more time with Lord Ellsworth.

"Of course," her mother continued, "if you would rather not…the choice is yours."

It was a heady thing, choice.

"I would very much like to continue," she said, her heart drumming so rapidly she thought she might not catch her breath. "Thank you."

He smiled then, which had the remarkable effect of making her giddy and quite possibly weak in her knees.

"Miss Boxford," Lord Ellsworth said, "would you do me the honor of showing me your garden?"

Kitty's eyes widened.

"You…want to see this?" she said, gesturing at her plot. She was suddenly embarrassed for these little rows of onions and cabbages for a man who would someday have ownership of more lands than she could imagine.

"Indeed," he replied, with an eagerness that seemed genuine. "One can only listen to mini-lectures on moon phases and planting for so long and not at least be curious at the result."

Actually, it was entirely possible, she thought. But there was something about the way his eyes twinkled that pushed aside her doubts and made her want to show him every leaf and flower.

The garden was not large by many people's standards, but it was fruitful. She showed him rows of peas, beans, and the onions she was trying. He asked questions and she answered them.

"And these?" he asked.

"Pumpkins. Or they will be. I have been trying to cross a few varieties," she said, then crouched down to highlight a few plants. "I am hoping to grow a few past the expected size."

"I did not realize you were a horticulturist," he replied.

Kitty shook her head. "Hardly that, though I would dearly love to be one. It seems men have claimed the heavens and the earth for their own."

He paused then, thoughtful. "That doesn't seem logical, does it?"

"Because it is not," she said. "If only I'd been born a man, perhaps I could have been a horticulturist, or even a gamekeeper."

"But then you would have been only a man. Instead, you are a very remarkable woman. Which I realize is selfish. But there is nothing about you that isn't…"

He swallowed then, and he looked away, before returning his gaze to rest on her.

"…perfect."

Kitty almost stopped breathing. "What did you say?"

"I was just thinking," he stammered a bit, "about that nonsense about five thousand pounds and whatnot. And it really is nonsense. Truly."

Kitty blinked. Was she truly standing in her pumpkin patch with a dirty apron and a sweaty brow, with a marquess who had the most remarkable smile who thought she was—

"Perfect," she mimicked under her breath, then burst out laughing because it was all so wonderful and ridiculous and she didn't know what else to do.

"Did I say something amusing?"

Kitty shook her head. "Not at all. I'm just tired still, from my little 'adventure.' You need not have come, my lord. This mess was of my own making."

"My arrival here, you will be pleased to know, was a bit of selfishness on my own part," he said as they started to walk again. "I spoke with Mrs. Pembroke and your parents to beg permission for you to assist with my viewing party. I find myself quite adrift without you, Katherine Boxford."

Kitty knew very well that Lord Ellsworth was speaking about his party. But an uncomfortable yearning opened in her heart as he spoke, and her name on his tongue, the name only he used, was a pleasurable, if somewhat forbidden melody.

The sound of bushes rustling from a nearby hedge distracted them both. A second later, two small field mice scurried out from underneath the boxwood hedge and through her pumpkin patch. It was enough to bring her down to earth.

"If you agree," Lord Ellsworth continued, "I will pay your salary in full and provide additional funds. Not five thousand pounds—though your value is many times that. But a respectable sum that may allow you a greater view of the world than from your bedroom window."

Kitty blinked. He was offering her a future. Something that seemed impossible only a few moments ago.

❧

SHE WAS in the middle of an intrigue, and this was even more delectable than she could have dared dreamed.

Evelyn Pembroke's life had been, in some respects, a series of regrets. But what she had learned over the years was that some of life's misfortunes had a peculiar way of mending themselves if allowed to do so. Edmund, driven by a misguided need to prove himself, had spent years in some of the more dangerous parts of London and France, doing work that, if she had known the details of it, would have kept her awake at night. But much good had come of it, for him, and in truth, for her as well. And one of them was adopting Charlie Cochrane.

He'd scooped the boy, now twelve, out of a slum in London, and soon the child had become part of Edmund's life. And when he'd brought the boy here, proclaiming him his son, Evelyn was at once surprised, and then grateful.

The two had formed a particular sort of kinship. Both, in their way, had been betrayed by the people who were supposed to protect them. They were fiercely loyal to those who did. In the eight months since he'd arrived at Silver Cross, Charlie had become Evelyn's eyes and ears. And today, once again, he'd used them on her behalf.

He now stood in her parlor, red-cheeked and out of breath after he'd given her a blow-by-blow account to her and Gwyneth of what had happened after Lord Ellsworth had left with Sara Boxford.

"Excellent, Charles," Gwyneth said, reaching out to the boy and cupping his cheek. "Go to the kitchen and ask Mrs. Coleman to fetch you some lemonade and biscuits."

The boy smiled, nodded to his adopted mother, and left.

Evelyn turned to Gwyneth, who was as wide-eyed as she'd ever seen her.

"Well, my dear, what do you make of that?"

"I am not certain, Evelyn," she replied, "what to make of you. I had no idea you had encouraged Kitty to apply to be Lord Ellsworth's assistant. I thought you were trying to find her a husband."

"I know she is very dear to you, and that you feel a great responsibility for her," Evelyn replied. "But that girl has dreams, and they are bigger than tending to me. She needs to find her own way. I was merely helping her."

"By throwing her in Ellsworth's path," she replied. "I don't know if that is genius or folly."

"Actually I had not considered him for her," Evelyn said. "But I cannot help but try."

"Did you see him? He was practically on the edge of his chair speaking about her." Gwyneth put a protective hand over her belly and smiled. "The only time I've ever seen him so animated is when he's speaking about his telescope. And he loves his telescope."

"Exactly." She held out her hand, and Gwyneth took it. "Exactly."

"What are we going to do?" Gwyneth replied. "I am all for love and fairy tales, but Kitty is a gamekeeper's daughter and Colin is to be a duke."

"We are going to work a little magic. Have you heard anything yet from Sir Richard?" She'd asked him for any information on Sara Boxford. There was, Evelyn was convinced, far more to the woman than she admitted. Even the way she'd handled Ellsworth today was quite remarkable.

Gwyneth shook her head. "I will ask Edmund. Still, I have something else to share. I think Kitty has a diamond in her room."

It was Evelyn's turn to be shocked. "A diamond?"

"The brooch Kitty lost, remember? She found it—what was left of it—just last year. I cannot be absolutely certain, but the setting appears to be silver and the remaining stone, I am convinced, is neither glass nor paste. I would have to get a better look at it to be certain."

"That is very promising." Very promising indeed.

"But we do not have much time."

Evelyn pursed her lips. There was much to do.

"We have two days to find a suitable gown for Kitty and make her the belle of the ball. He is already in love with her, the fool just doesn't know it." Evelyn tapped her fingers impatiently. "Everything else is merely a detail."

"And Kitty? What if she is not in love with him? Or his parents do not approve?"

Evelyn paused. She knew perfectly well about Kitty's unresolved feelings for her son. Whether she was still infatuated with him, or with the ghost of an idea, she didn't know. But the fact remained that on a day she sought solace, she found herself at Ellsworth's door. Her heart had led her there. Evelyn was certain of it.

"We will work our magic, my dear. That is all we can do. They will have to do the rest."

A cool breeze teased at the strings of ribbons of Kitty's bonnet as she alighted from the carriage Lord Ellsworth had sent for her. Was it her imagination, or did the soaring towers of Stormount look especially daunting today? In a vain attempt to steady her nerves, she let out a low breath even as heat pricked at the back of her neck and her stomach was uneasy. While Lord Ellsworth wished for her help, Kitty had not a clue what his parents must think of this curious arrangement. Though they no doubt humored their son in many things, Kitty could not help but wonder if planning a party with the daughter of a gamekeeper was beyond the borders of their indulgence.

The gravel on the front park crunched under her feet. She'd worn slippers instead of her regular sturdy boots—Gwynnie had positively insisted, and her mother agreed the more delicate footwear was far more appropriate to meet with the duke and duchess. Not satisfied with concerning themselves only with her footwear, they'd sent her off in her finest day dress, which was a lovely light blue and, Gwynnie had gushed, complimented her skin and brown hair. When Kitty had reminded her friend that traipsing around the grounds and creating lists would be the sum of Kitty's activities for the afternoon, Gwynnie merely shrugged her shoulders in that way of hers. There was no point in pressing the point further. And, Kitty admitted, she did look very nice. Almost ladylike. When Lord Ellsworth's carriage arrived—a carriage she'd taken many evenings to Lofton Tower—both Gwynnie and Fanny squealed with unabashed delight.

Kitty may have had a similar reaction, inside, but she tamped it down, deep inside. Of course, she'd been inside his carriage many a time in the past fortnight, but it had always been under the cover of darkness. Now, even on a cloudy day, the vehicle was impressive with its shiny brass fittings and even a footman to see to her comfort. It was dazzling. But Kitty knew this could not last. She was here to help Lord Ellsworth find his bride from among the many ladies vying for the position and the title, and the deadline for that announcement rapidly approached.

Kitty Boxford was not one of those ladies, nor was she ever going to be. It shouldn't have bothered her in the slightest. After all, when this was concluded, he'd promised her remuneration enough to forward her plans along nicely. It had been the very basis of their agreement. She was coming to the ball as an employee, not a guest. And then, perhaps, with Lord Ellsworth settled on his path, she would be able to consider hers.

Would the heavens frown on her attempts? The Romani woman's words echoed in her ears. *Look aloft.*

But before she could think on it more, another set of words flooded into her memory.

Do not deprive the world of the finest pair of eyes I have ever beheld.

She walked across the park and through the doors of the massive brick structure that was Stormount, led by a servant in full livery. It was difficult not to look agog at the ornate Jacobean ceiling that stretched toward the heavens, or the intricately carved timbers, or the fine tapestries that hung on the walls.

After what felt like a very long time, and traveling up stairs and around corners, the servant paused at a set of doors. Kitty swallowed, smoothed her skirts, and took a deep breath. The doors opened, silent on their hinges, and the servant announced her.

"Show her in, Davis," came an older, but familiar voice. The Duke of Weymouth.

She took two steps inside the door and looked straight ahead. There, sitting near an empty hearth, was the Duchess of Weymouth, whose eyes narrowed as she spied Kitty. She was looking far more impervious today than normal, if such a thing were even possible. Perhaps it was because the duchess was looking directly at Kitty for the first time, rather than glancing over her as she might with a servant. Beside her was the duke himself, who regarded her more as a curiosity. And their son was nowhere to be found.

Kitty dropped into a curtsey, gripping the edges of her bonnet until her knuckles were nearly white. *Where was he?*

"Davis, relieve Miss Boxford of her bonnet before she mashes the brim entirely," the duchess said, holding out a velvet-covered box. "And please take this and lock it with my other jewels in my bedchamber. We shall have need of it very soon."

Mortified, Kitty handed over the bonnet to Davis, who bowed to his mistress, accepted the parcel, then exited the room. Fixed to the floor, completely uncertain what to do next, Kitty could do little but stand there and be appraised. For years she'd been quietly overlooked by the duchess when her Grace made her calls to Mrs. Pembroke. But no longer.

"Mrs. Pembroke sends her regards, your Grace," she began, her words catching in her throat. She took another breath, then continued. "And I wish to convey, if I might, my sincerest gratitude at her invitation to the festivities at Stormount."

The duke and duchess exchanged the briefest of looks.

"Mrs. Pembroke is quite welcome," the duchess replied. "Indeed she sent a note early this morning quite singing your praises, Miss Boxford. Since then I have been most keen to meet you. Most keen."

Kitty blinked. She certainly hadn't expected a letter of recommendation or introduction, especially after all the trouble she'd caused.

"I understand," the duchess said at last, "that this notion of a viewing party was yours."

Kitty swallowed. "Yes, your Grace."

"And that you convinced our son to use the occasion to choose his future wife," she continued.

"Yes," Kitty nodded. "That is, if he has not yet chosen."

"He has not," the duke said, exasperation sharpening his tone.

"And how, pray, did you concoct this notion of a viewing party?" the duchess continued, ignoring her husband.

"I merely suggested to him that he might wish to share something he is clearly passionate about with the person who will spend the rest of her life with him," she said. "That is all."

"That is hardly 'all,' Miss Boxford," the duchess continued. "I have rarely seen my son so taken with an idea. His sudden enthusiasm for the task of finding a duchess is a revelation. Even though the deadline for making the decision is at hand, this vigor is something I have never seen. I am also quite curious to know *when* you made this suggestion."

Kitty swallowed, her lips pulling into a tight smile. *You are an open book, Kitty Boxford.* But telling the entire truth was impossible.

"I can't recall exactly," she said. "Perhaps Mr. Edmund Pembroke shared it with Lord Ellsworth. His wife and I are very good friends."

The duchess unfolded a fan she kept nearby, waving it near her face as she was clearly considering it. But doubt lingered.

"My father once shared with me how you used a fishing trip to woo your bride, your Grace," Kitty continued, turning her attention to the duke, excited by the flash of inspiration and hoping the flattery might distract the duchess from further inquiry. "Fishing is something you clearly have a passion for, and that her Grace appreciates your love of it must be fulfilling. I believe Lord Ellsworth is looking for the same requirement, though he might not have articulated it. So I suggested it to Ed—Mr. Pembroke, who must have passed it along. That is the beginning and the end of all the credit I can take."

The two exchanged a glance, and between them the warmth of their attachment was evident, even after so many years.

"Excellent deduction. Though I am still at a loss for why he felt your assistance was essential," the duchess continued, her eyes narrowing.

Kitty shook her head. This time, at least, she could be honest. "I cannot say, your Grace. But I am honored to be of assistance."

"Well done, Miss Boxford," the duke replied and rose. "I will leave you two to start."

Kitty swallowed again. She was going to be *alone* with the Duchess of Weymouth?

"Come, Miss Boxford," the duchess said, folding up her fan and pointing it a Kitty. "Do you know how to write?"

"Yes, your Grace."

"Excellent," she replied, then pointed to a nearby writing table. "Mrs. Cooper is overseeing preparations for dinner this evening. You may take the notes."

Kitty walked to the table that was situated near the duchess, conscious of every sound she made as she pulled the chair out from its place and sat down.

"I admit to knowing far less about my son's passion for astronomy than I should," she began. "I can plan balls and picnics with little fuss. This is something altogether different. I am not sure what one does at such a thing."

"Well," Kitty began, clearing her throat and steadying her nerves that threatened to shake the quill right out of her hands. "I suspect it would be very similar to a picnic in many respects. The main activities would happen in the dark, and lead directly into the ball, which could begin at the stroke of midnight. Perhaps it could start with a lovely dinner, and then usher guests to the lake by lamplight. Once there, you might have some light refreshments, and some music. And Lord Ellsworth could have one or two of his instruments set up, and people could take turns viewing through the telescope. The moon will be full, so it will be easy to see."

"And that is all?" the duchess asked.

"I imagine Lord Ellsworth might like to say a few words, and of course he would speak with the guests as they took their opportunity to view the sky with the instruments. It would beget conversation, and it is in that conversation he might find the spark of interest that would make a match apparent." Kitty paused. "It is what one might wish for…a common interest of the heart."

The duchess was silent for a time, but while Kitty was far from relaxed, her heart quieted from a pounding to a mere thumping.

"It would have been far easier for me if his heart was open to dancing," her Grace said, shaking her head and letting go a sigh.

"Perhaps the right woman can tempt him," Kitty said.

"If she can do that," the duchess replied, "she will be a magical creature indeed."

COLIN RUSHED toward into his mother's favorite parlor, damnably late. He'd fully intended to meet Miss Boxford in the courtyard upon her arrival, only to be held up by the Countess of Bedford, who'd insisted on a private tour of the west wing of the house. Perhaps it was her opportunity to size up Colin as a man, or rather, to size up the apartments of Stormount. Regardless of her motives, by the time he'd made it to his appointment, Miss Boxford had already arrived and had been in the company of his parents for ten minutes.

He met his father just outside the doors.

"Your Grace," Colin said. "My apologies for my tardiness."

His father waved a hand to signal his lack of concern. "No need. Miss Boxford has arrived, and I left her with your mother."

Colin blinked. "You left her with Mother? Alone?" His gaze darted toward the door. "How was she?"

His father raised an eyebrow.

"Your mother? Or Miss Boxford?"

"You know that regardless of the room, Mother is the most commanding presence in it," Colin replied, cursing himself for appearing too eager. "I wanted to ensure Miss Boxford was prepared."

"The girl comported herself very well," his father replied, then regarded Colin closely. "I believe I am more curious about your interest in her."

Colin smiled sheepishly, and shrugged his shoulders, groping around for an appropriate answer to the question. It was, he supposed, entirely natural his father would ask this question. But it was also entirely natural for Colin to want to avoid answering it. For his father, and for himself.

"Miss Boxford has agreed to help manage the viewing party," he said, keeping his voice polite, but direct. "My only interest is that with her assistance, it will be successful, and you will not have to worry about an heir. That is all."

The duke stood silent a moment, then shook his head as if in silent conversation with himself. "Very well. You will be pleased, I hope, that your stone has been set. I viewed it only a few moments ago. I am eager to see you place it around the neck of the right woman."

Colin nodded. He'd held onto that stone for so long—a little more than a decade. A remarkable gem, hidden in the long grasses beneath the apple trees at Gorland Park. He'd found it not long after he'd caught the girl who'd fallen from the apple tree. The girl he was certain now had been Katherine Boxford. It was, like the stone at Wold, something of a fallen star. And even though it was of earthly origin, he'd taken it as confirmation that his passion to study the heavens was the right one.

"I am certain in the end I will make the logical choice," he said, pushing down the growing sense of dread that gripped him as he pictured draping it around a lady's neck. "It all comes down to logic in the end, does it not?"

His father smiled, when, quite suddenly, a stricken look came over his face. He paled, and gripped Colin's sprained arm so tightly it would have made him wince but for the distress his father was in.

"Your Grace—Father," Colin said, taking hold of the duke's shoulder to steady him. "I will call for your physician at once."

He was about call out for assistance when his father shook his head and released his grip. Beads of sweat formed across his father's hairline. Pulling a handkerchief from his pocket, he covered his mouth and breathed into it, then mopped the perspiration from his head.

"Father—"

His father straightened slowly, the color slowly coming back to his face. "I'm fine, my dear boy. I must have over indulged with cook's Scotch eggs this morning. 'Twas merely a sudden bout of biliousness," he said, attempting a smile. "I shall ring for Davis to bring a bit of brandy and loosen my cravat. All will be well."

His father's protests did nothing to calm Colin's concerns.

"Father, perhaps I—"

"I am well." His father pointed a finger at Colin. "And I will be much better when I know you are married." He started walking away, and called over his shoulder. "A wife, my boy. Find your Miss Boxford and get yourself a wife."

Colin watched for a moment as his father strode down the hall and disappeared into his study. A grim determination came upon him. In a little more than a day, he would choose his bride and the matter would be done with. And hopefully then, his father's health would improve.

These episodes had started not long after Colin had returned from Barronsfield Manor this past winter. His doctor was convinced it was his heart. Or that his humors were somehow misaligned. Whatever the cause, Colin knew he had to make a choice. For years his parents had spoken about their desire to see Colin married before their deaths, but Colin had disregarded these as the idle words of two parents who were quite vocal in their feelings about Colin's love life. Now that banter had turned into something more urgent.

He opened the doors to his mother's parlor, where, upon entering, he came upon a most remarkable sight—his mother and Miss Boxford in animated conversation, Miss Boxford with her little notebook in her hand, scribbling something with a pencil. The very sight of her, with her brown curls springing against her cheeks as she spoke, her dress hugging her curves and skimming over them in just the right places, put him at ease.

Until he had a most illogical thought concerning a gemstone that held a star, and how beautiful it would look hanging from Katherine Boxford's neck.

"If she can do that, she will be a magical creature indeed," his mother said.

"Who is this creature you are speaking of?" Colin asked, only to find the two women staring at him, wondering where on earth he'd come from.

Katherine Boxford's face went from relief to curiosity to concern in seconds. Did she see that he was worried?

His mother, as always, greeted him with her normal conviviality, but it was tempered with a bit of restraint. For the first time, Colin felt that perhaps he had intruded.

"We were wondering where you had gone," his mother said. "Though Miss Boxford and I are making great progress."

"My apologies to you both," he replied, nodded to them. Unwilling to worry his mother and cause her distress, he chose to wait to speak to her about his father's episode. "I had hoped to introduce Miss Boxford to you, Mother."

"We have taken care of that ourselves," his mother replied. "Though I do believe Miss Boxford is not unknown to me. I hope you will extend my thanks to Mrs. Pembroke on allowing us to have Miss Boxford's help for these next two days."

"I have, but will do so again," Colin said, relief flooding through him. He had been far more nervous about this than even he'd realized. "Mrs. Pembroke impressed upon me that she was quite pleased to have Miss Boxford at your service."

"And she is that. Why don't you go and see to our guests, my dear."

"I have already, hence my tardiness," Colin said. "Given the short amount of time we have to prepare, I had hoped Miss Boxford could begin without delay. Would you wish to join us, Mother? Or perhaps Mrs. Cooper?"

His mother shook her head. "Mrs. Cooper is engaged in other matters at present, and I have promised the Countess of Bedford and Mrs. Strickland that I would come and listen to the piano forte recitals this afternoon. A lady should have some accomplishments in the musical arts, don't you think?"

His mother was a great lover of music, but could hardly play and her singing left much to be desired. But Colin wisely kept his opinions to himself.

"I suppose she should. But they may have other accomplishments," Colin replied. "Like the ability to grow strawberries or climb trees."

He looked at Miss Boxford, whose eyes widened suddenly then narrowed, as if in warning. It put a smile on his face and warmed his heart. He enjoyed teasing her. He enjoyed her. And whether or not she could sing or play an instrument was inconsequential.

"Climb trees indeed," his mother said, clearly not amused. "Once you are done with your tour I expect you back to listen to the performances. You do not want to disappoint them, do you?"

"Perhaps, your Grace," Miss Boxford said, "if we leave directly, we can accomplish all that needs to be done in a very short period of time. Then, Lord Ellsworth would be free to enjoy the concert, and I can discuss some of the arrangements with Mrs. Cooper. Would this be acceptable?"

His mother seemed perfectly happy with the plan. Before departing, he quietly shared with his mother the episode that had struck the duke. She became solemn but resolute, eager to see to him. Despite their titles and place in society, they were still man and wife, and had much affection for each other. Colin gave her strict instructions to send for him immediately if something was amiss.

Colin and Katherine Boxford walked along to the shore of the lake, a small group of footmen in tow. Despite the grayness, it was a pleasurable afternoon. Together, they worked out the details of exactly the right placement for the equipment. Because the moon would be near full, its brightness would wash out many of the other stars. And it was an easy target to spy, making it less tedious for the guests. She gave instruction to the workmen about where the musicians would be housed, and two small platforms. Under a smaller tent, they would set up his Orrey.

"Would you agree to tend to the smaller telescope?" Colin asked. "We could have the two Gregorian scopes here. The ground is flat and they should be steady. The moon will rise over those trees," he said, pointing to the south east.

"Me?" she replied. "Are you certain? I am far from an expert."

"Neither am I, in truth. But you are interested, and you can help others who are."

"I am not at all certain that any of your guests will have the least bit of interest in what I have to say," she replied.

"I do."

Her lips turned up then in a smile that brought a thrill to Colin's insides. No one smiled at him the way she did. It was genuine. Everything about her was genuine.

"I will do my best," she said. "As it is part of our agreement."

"Of course," Colin said, feeling quite suddenly deflated. This was a business transaction in the end. She was helping him find a wife because that was part of their bargain. And with Father having another episode, he needed honor that bargain.

After thirty minutes of careful consideration and contentment that the plans were in good order, they turned their way back to the house.

"All we have to do now is make some kind of sacrifice to the weather gods for a clear evening," Colin said.

"You shall have to do the asking," she replied. "The heavens are not particularly generous when I ask it for favors. But if not, here are my thoughts about how this could be done, to similar effect, in one of the galleries. And it will lead right into the ball. Not quite as spectacular, but still very nice."

They walked side by side, while she outlined what mitigations could be made if the weather was not as promising. She had considered every possibility, and Colin marveled at her creativity and dedication to the idea. Her hands moved in an animated way, mesmerizing him. He was aware of every inch of her—the swish of her skirts, the little mole below her left ear, the smell of her lavender soap. His fingers positively itched to reach out and touch her elbow, but it was not to be done. And it was a bloody agony.

"I am sorry I left you to my mother," he said as they approached the house. "I dearly hope it was not too difficult."

"Not difficult, exactly." She tilted her head, looking up at him, artless, but stirring his blood all the same. "Your parents were very gracious, if a little mystified, by me. I assume they know nothing of my 'duties' at Lofton Tower?"

"No." His parents indulged him, but even they had their limits. "And it is probably best that they stay that way."

"It is bad enough that my parents do," she said. "Soon you will have no further worry about me. You will have your bride, your arm will soon be healed, and you will have no further need of me."

She said it with a smile, but it stung nonetheless.

No need of Katherine Boxford? Impossible.

"Let's not think about that at present, shall we?" It was a question, but he knew it came out more like an order. Eager to delay their parting, he pointed to one of the many lanes that led through Stormount's gardens. "Let's take this path ahead. It's a pleasant walk, along a nice bit of wild garden. You might like to look at some of the plants."

"Not eager to return to hear accomplished ladies play?" she teased.

"I enjoy music," he said. "But I enjoy this more. And you have done nothing but dedicate your time to my pursuits. It is the very least I can do is walk along and show you flowers I don't know the name of."

She smiled then, so expectant he thought his heart would burst. "You have made another joke. You are becoming quite accomplished at it."

He bowed deeply. "I am at your service."

They stood, just the two of them, the lake in the distance. Both holding their breath. And, he realized, surrounded by a half dozen footmen. Colin dismissed them with direction to take the notes of the afternoon's work back to the house.

He led her away from the house toward his father's prized gardens, which were more tamed wilderness than manicured borders. They walked along a gently winding path that led them past soaring trees and borders of ferns.

He could not say that the silence between them was comfortable. Every step bristled with awareness of the other, every brush of her skirts brought another tantalizing dose of longing. The physical attraction he could account for; he was a man after all, and his distinct lack of experience in the matters of carnal love did not mean he did not have that longing. Indeed, every moment he'd spent with this remarkable woman, his gentleman's upbringing warred with his baser, masculine desires. But this longing he felt…this was more. It filled his chest and made it ache, in the most pleasant and yet torturous sort of way.

"How delightful!" The pleasure in her voice broke through his reverie. She pointed to a rough stone structure up ahead. "May I explore it?"

"Of course," he replied, and allowed her to lead the way along a small set of sandstone steps that led toward the object that had caught her eye.

The subject of her delight was a stone grotto, draped in swaths of tiny, elegant white flowers. It stretched nearly twelve feet high, with an image of a cherub perched at the peak of the half-shelled dome. It was one of half a dozen structures placed strategically through the garden to surprise and delight. This one, he would be happy to report, had managed both.

Mists were beginning to encroach on the tops the trees. He settled on a bench while she hovered over a nearby flower border, pointing out each of the flowers—foxglove, hellebore, anemone—with enthusiasm that could not be manufactured.

"This is magical," she said at last. "Truly magical."

And it was magical. She was magical. The way she moved. The way she made him feel.

"Do you know every plant, Miss Boxford?" he asked.

She shook her head, then walked toward him and took a seat on the bench beside him, the two of them cradled by gray stone and soft white flowers.

"Heavens, no. The world is full of fascinating specimens, and new ones are being discovered and displayed every day. It would be impossible to know them all."

They were silent for a few moments, with only a few birds in the distance. She put her hands down beside her, her fingers wrapped over the edge of the bench, and looked down at her feet for but a moment before turning toward him, her back straightening, and a determined smile on her face.

"If I may, my lord—"

"Miss Boxford, I believe, between the two of us, it is not necessary to address me so formally."

She blinked. "Right then. What should I call you? Mr. Middleton?"

Colin smiled at the name. It sounded so blessedly normal. Even tempting. But not…not quite right. Though, quite suddenly and inexplicably, another name popped into his head.

Mrs. Colin Middleton. Kitty Middleton. *No.* Though the truncation of her name was a popular one, and clearly an endearment by those who cherished her, it did not feel right for a woman as bold as she. A woman who'd just sat with a duchess and held her own. Who negotiated for a man's salary to do a job no man had yet been able to do. Who stood in the firelight and set his body ablaze. To Colin, she could only be Katherine.

Katherine Middleton.

With the jewel around her neck.

Dear Lord.

He cleared his throat, pushing the thought out of his head. "If it is not too much to ask, I believe my Christian name will suffice."

"Very well," she replied, nodding her head gently before resuming her question. "Earlier, when we were with her Grace, you said something very curious. About ladies who garden and climb trees."

"Curious? How so?"

"It's silly, really. I feel silly for asking, but I must." She blushed then. She couldn't help herself, and while she found it a source of embarrassment, Colin could not help but be charmed by it.

He could see her tense slightly, then after a quick intake of breath, she spoke again.

"Many years ago, my father worked as a gamekeeper at Gorland Park—where Gwynnie grew up. We lived in a cottage on the estate. It is how Gwynnie and I became friends. One day, I was playing in the orchard. I had been given strict instructions by my parents to stay out of sight, as the countess was having very important guests."

"And I assume you did not."

She shook her head, and her expression grew serious. "I had been climbing one of her apple trees, and somehow she spied me there. I was eleven. She startled me, and I fell."

"And I caught you," he said. "You were the girl in the orchard."

She stopped then, excited. "Yes! I was caught by a boy. A tall boy," she reached up, and living in the memory, brushed a lock of his hair. "With ginger hair. I knew it was you."

"You did?"

"Well, only yesterday. But I was convinced."

"You startled me," he said, letting go a small chuckle. "I was surprised I had the wits to catch you."

"You saved me from a nasty fall and a broken bone or two, I suspect," she replied. "I really should thank you."

"While I appreciate the gratitude, it is hardly necessary," he replied. "Besides, it was simply good fortune. I have been extraordinarily blessed with it."

Katherine's lips twisted into a sad smile. "My fortune left me that day. My chance at happiness."

Colin frowned. "Are you not happy now?"

She looked up at him with a sweet, melancholy smile. "Very. But this won't last, will it?"

"Nothing lasts forever," he replied, then gazed up at the sky, the trees cloaking much of the sky above. "Except for the stars, perhaps. They seem eternal. The constellations we see above us have been noted since the time of ancient Babylonia."

"Is that why you like them?"

"I like them because they remind me there is always more to discover. That my brothers and sister, who I never knew, saw those same stars. That my children will gaze upon them. It allows me to feel connected to a world that I sometimes feel disconnected from."

"That's lovely. Truly." She reached out, her fingers gently tracing the outline of his, her cheeks flushing as she did so. The sensation of her skin against his, even in this most innocent of gestures, was both touching and stirring. "That is why I garden. To stay connected. I have brought seeds from everywhere I have ever been. They have become a sort of home to me."

"You said you lost your fortune that day. What happened?"

"I lost something very dear to my family. A brooch that belonged to my mother. I found it years later, but it was in a sorrowful state of disrepair, though it was something of a miracle I'd come upon it at all. Indeed, I found it that very afternoon last year, when we met by chance in Gorland Park."

Her expression moved from one of grim resolution to wistful sadness.

"Is that…why you were crying?"

"Yes. And no. It had been my mother's good luck charm. Years ago, a Traveler told me I'd let happiness slip through my fingers that day. If I was ever to find it again, I had to look up. Look aloft. And see…what is unseen."

"Lofton Tower," Colin said, realization dawning on him. "I thought you merely wanted to earn extra funds."

"I did. I do." She bent down, and picked up a smooth stone, rubbing it between her fingers. She looked over at him, a wistful smile on her face. "But when you arrived, with this opportunity to gaze at the stars and see…what cannot be seen by our eyes alone, I thought, perhaps, this was my chance to find my happiness."

Colin stilled then. Afraid to ask the question. Selfishly fearful of her answer.

"And you have not discovered it?"

"I think I have."

"What is it?"

She shook her head. "I can't speak it aloud. If the heavens know—it will be taken away. And—I was probably never meant to have it."

What sweet torture this was. He reached for her hand, tracing each finger, feeling the warmth of her skin.

"Can you show me, then?"

"I'm afraid."

"So am I."

Her gaze fixed on him then, their breaths catching at the same moment. She laced her fingers in his, then stood before him. She gently ran her fingers across his brow, down his cheek, tracing his ear. It was the lightest, most teasing of touches, but it set his body on fire. He wanted to lean in to her breasts, mere inches away from his mouth. He wanted to touch her. Taste her. Worship her.

She put her lips to his ear.

"Let's not be afraid. Just for today."

CHAPTER 19

itty straightened, blood pounding in her ears, every ounce of her aching for Colin Middleton. Not his title. Not his lands. The man. This sensation was new, and it was pure, utter want of the most delicious kind. And she had absolutely no idea what to do about it.

But Kitty was always willing to learn.

She pulled off his spectacles, placing them on the bench. Without the glass between them the brilliance of his eyes was even more apparent, as was the desire that lingered there. It was a heady thing to be wanted like this. A glorious, sensuous ache grew between her legs. Kitty brought her mouth to his, and while their bodies may have been novice to this experience, an ancient knowing guided them.

There were no gentle kisses this time. They were urgent, impatient, and hungry. In this moment, she knew what she wanted, and maybe because of that, she also knew this would be her one opportunity to have it. One blissful moment of happiness.

She felt his hands at her breasts, clumsily trying to loosen the bodice of her frock, while she tore at his cravat, ruining the perfect knot his valet tied, which was merely an impediment to his flesh. He pulled her down, positioning her on his lap, his erection plain and firm under her bottom. Freeing him at last of the fine linen, she undid the top button of his shirt, exposing the smallest triangle of chest.

His skin was warm under her lips, the tang of salt on her tongue. She licked, she kissed, she sucked at his neck, pulling his collar to one side, delighting in the ragged breath and low curses he uttered at every touch. He returned the favor, loosening her stays enough to free one of her breasts, taking it first into his hand, running his thumb and fingers over her nipple which was already taut and sensitive to the faintest of touches. But when she felt the warm, soft tug of his mouth, she gasped, calling his name under her breath.

"Colin."

He gave her breasts glorious attention. It made her heady, as if she'd taken far too much wine. Her body loosened, unwound by glorious ribbons of heat, yet fed her need. She shuffled her bottom over him, rubbing herself against him, urged on by every groan coming from deep in his throat as she did so. He claimed her mouth then, his tongue inside hers, his hands on her breasts, then moving down her body. She became vaguely aware of him sliding her off him then. Breaking the kiss.

"We cannot continue, Katherine. I cannot do this to you."

"You are not doing anything to me." She pulled down her hair and loosened her stays. It was freeing, the breeze kissing her skin. And terrifying. She was risking everything now—her body, perhaps her future, and most definitely her heart. "I want us to experience each other. Just this once."

He wanted her for a lifetime.

But for now, he would have her for this moment.

He stood, pushing his flesh against hers. She looked up, her lips parted, already deliciously swollen and dark pink from the attentions they had given him. Frustrated by his restrained wrist, he tore the sling off his right arm, so he could greedily touch her breast with one and lace his fingers in her thick brown curls. Pain shot through his wrist but he ignored it, the cost far outweighed by this carnal delight.

He took one of her arms, guided it around his neck. Then, using his left arm, he lowered himself, grabbing her under her bottom, lifting her so that her legs straddled his waist. She hung on, a gasp of delight as her middle met his, the meeting of their flesh hampered by breeches and layers of skirts. He let out a moan as he felt her push her core closer to him, his erection stiffening even further, his body sensing where its hunger would be sated.

They danced this most intimate of dances as he moved her toward the back wall of the grotto, lowering her bottom on a small ledge that ran the length of the structure. His hands cupping her face, he continued his attentions to her lips, when she took his left hand, guiding it under her skirts. Her fingers led him to where her wool stocking met soft, silky flesh. As he did so, he vowed he would send her a box of stockings made of the finest silk. For only they would have been worthy of her.

His fingers dug into her flesh, as hers toyed with the front of his breeches.

"You are bold, Katherine," he said between hungry, deep kisses. "Who is this woman before me who knows what she wants?"

"I don't know," she replied, her voice breathy, her lips turned up in a devilish smile. "But I think I like her."

"I know I do." *I love her.*

The words, unspoken, still caught in his throat, giving him pause.

"Do you know what else this woman knows, thanks to you?" she asked, running her finger along his bottom lip and threatening to drive him mad with lust.

Colin paused, thrown by the question, his body driving his need, his brain, quite willing to submit to this overwhelming pleasure. "Telescopes?"

She pursed her lips, and dragging her fingers down his front, she unbuttoned the front flap of his breeches.

"How to take off men's clothes."

Whether it was the boldness in her eyes, the pinkness of her flesh, or the exquisite way she teased him, Colin didn't know, but he decided now was not the time to work out the elements of the enchantment she was working on him. He merely wanted to be fulfilled, to be one with her. He pulled up her skirts, pulled her closer to him, and allowed his erection to find purchase in her soft, wet folds.

"Katherine," he uttered, urgent as this glorious sensation engulfed him. She was tight. She was perfect. Everything about her was.

Her breath hitched a moment and he wondered if he was hurting her. Instead, she moved her hips closer to his, rocking slowly.

"Oh Colin," she whispered in his ear. "This is…this is…"

He rocked slowly at first, his body teaching him what to do. He feared he was clumsy, but between them, they found a glorious pairing in motion. Her nails dug into the back of his neck, her rocking becoming more insistent, her gasps hurried and urgent. He responded in kind, his strokes harder, faster, the call of her body dictating the movements of his own.

She stopped then, tightening around him as she froze, then let out a glorious cry that seemed to take her by surprise. His body responded, a glorious ecstasy of oblivion falling over him as he found his release. The two became silent then, clutching each other, only their breathing and faint sound of birdsong surrounding them.

The urgency of the moment fell away, the spell dissipated. She smiled awkwardly at him, adjusting her stays and bodice, hiding away her breasts. He likewise fixed his clothes, picking his cravat off the ground where it had fallen, and put his spectacles back on.

"Let me help you," she replied, her voice breaking the silence as her fingers worked to put his cravat back to rights. "It won't be as good as your valet's, but hopefully will be enough to get you through your door without too much comment."

Her hair was still down, falling over her shoulders. Just moments ago those dark ribbons had cascaded over her breasts. The very thought threatened to make him hard again.

They had coupled. In the light of day, in the mists of a gray afternoon. The very act had broken every rule Colin had kept for himself.

And it had been absolutely incredible.

She slipped the sling over his shoulder, and together they positioned his wrist. Indeed, his arm was much improved in the past fortnight. And then, she pulled her hair up into a simple knot, pinning it in place.

"Katherine—"

"We should return to the house," she said, her voice bright, as if somehow, what had passed between them had not happened. "You will be missed at the recital."

She started to walk away. He reached out for her hand.

"Katherine," he repeated, more insistent this time. "Do not run away. There is too much to discuss. Much—"

She put her fingers up to his mouth, her lips turned up in a smile.

"Let us just treasure this, shall we? I shall always treasure it."

She stole away from him then, back in the direction from whence they'd come.

It was entirely possible, of course, that his seed had found purchase in her body. Damn him for his moment of weakness. For breaking the rules. Of course, many men of his position helped themselves to women to which they had no claim, without another thought as to the aftereffects. But Colin was not such a man. Those rules had been his own.

Katherine Boxford may have been five thousand pounds poorer than every woman currently vying for his hand. But to him, he realized, she was priceless.

Could he break those rules again? He wanted nothing more than to run after her. To be with her. To place that jewel around her neck and claim her for his own.

"WELL," Gwynnie asked, sitting practically on the edge of her chair, Mrs. Pembroke and her mother alongside. "What happened?"

Kitty stood two steps in from the entry to Mrs. Pembroke's favorite parlor, having just returned from her most extraordinary afternoon. Her clasped hands together, she took a breath as three faces looked back at her with anticipation.

"I met with the Duke and Duchess of Weymouth," she started. "And it was quite nerve wracking, though I am very grateful for the letter of recommendation you sent, Mrs. Pembroke. Thank you."

"Think nothing of it, my dear. It was my pleasure. And she was pleased with you, I trust?"

Kitty thought back to the encounter. While she could not say that it had been easy—and the duchess was certainly direct—she was neither rude or dismissive. And in the end, they had worked together quite well. "I think she was pleased with my assistance. She is so eager to have C—" she took a breath. Heavens, this might have been worse than sitting with the duchess. "—to have the marquess marry, that she was very open to my suggestions."

Her mother beamed, clearly proud of her daughter. Whether she would have been proud of what her daughter had done was another matter altogether.

"And the marquess?" Gwynnie asked, Kitty knowing full well what she was aiming for. "Was he pleased with your assistance?"

Kitty nodded, and before she had the chance to say a single word, a rush of heat moved up her into cheeks.

"I think he was very well pleased," Mrs. Pembroke said, her face positively lighting up. "Very pleased indeed."

Kitty glanced at her mother, who was not, Kitty could tell, as delighted as Mrs. Pembroke.

"The marquess and I—and a small army of footmen—spent a very fruitful afternoon outlining the placement of the telescopes for the viewing party, as well as placement of refreshment tables," she said. "I think it will be a magical evening. And by the end of it—"

"He shall choose his bride," her mother said, watching Kitty too keenly for her comfort.

She nodded, immediately crashing down to earth. "That is correct." And it could never be her, could it?

"And we can hope he chooses correctly," Mrs. Pembroke said, looking squarely at Kitty. "I know I shall."

"I should change," Kitty said, eager to change the subject and refresh herself. She should have expected the questions when she'd returned. Peeking her toes out from under her skirts, she displayed her footwear, quite stained by the grass. "My poor slippers are quite beyond repair after the afternoon. I told you I should have worn my boots."

"There is nothing like a first impression," her mother said, an air of authority in her voice that caught Kitty off guard. "The Duchess of Weymouth is an exacting woman. How you present yourself would matter greatly. I am pleased to know the afternoon was a productive one."

Kitty nodded, conscious of a second wave of heat rising into her face. She had to leave.

"I will be down shortly. As soon as I change my clothes." She turned to Mrs. Pembroke. "If that is acceptable, ma'am."

"Of course, Miss Boxford. We were merely discussing some details of our own for tomorrow evening. We wish your opinion on a gown we found that might be suitable for you. Given that you are playing such an important role, it is important that you look the part."

"A gown?" Kitty frowned. Of course she needed something to wear, but she hadn't had too much time to consider it given all that had happened in the two days. "I'm not certain I would need—"

"Everyone needs a gown sooner or later," Gwynnie replied. "You will see it is just something that I found at the back of a closet. I must have had it shipped from Gorland Park. I do not know if I have shoes that will fit you," Gwynnie said, clearly disappointed by it. "One can alter a dress easily enough, but shoes are altogether a different problem."

"I am certain I can find something suitable. It will be dark, after all, and I do not think I will be dancing."

Though what a glorious notion that was. Dancing with Colin. She gave a small sigh in spite of herself.

Kitty gave herself a mental shake. Right now, she just needed to get out of her clothes before someone noticed that her hair was being held up by two fewer pins than she'd had when she left.

She rushed upstairs to her bedchamber, eager to be alone at last. It had been a glorious, forbidden afternoon. And Kitty was determined not to regret a moment of it.

Kitty sat down on her bed and pulled off her slippers. The entire ride back to Kennington Grove, she hadn't known where to put her hands or entirely what to do with herself. A thousand sensations—echoes of those remarkable moments in the grotto—filled her with warmth, and she merely had to close her eyes to relive the sensation of his touch—tender at times, urgent at others—on almost every part of her, from her head to her bottom. Even as she started to untie her stockings, she recalled the sensation of his hands on her thighs, and gripping her backside. She closed her eyes, the mere memory creating an unnamable ache for him to touch her again.

But it was more than his caress she craved. She hadn't just made love to Colin Middleton, she realized.

She'd gone and fallen in love with him.

And that was troublesome indeed.

Kitty pulled off her outer layers, then poured a bit of water in a wash basin and cleaned herself, wiping away the last remnants of their coupling. They would be together only one more time, wouldn't they? And then he would marry.

But they would be together one more time.

Kitty rose, went to her wardrobe, and opened the door. There, hanging from the door, was the most incredible gown she had ever seen. It was the palest shade of blue, and shimmered with what appeared to be countless tiny stones. It was so pretty, Kitty thought, she could hardly bring herself to touch it.

"Do you like it?"

Kitty turned, wiping her eyes, to see her mother poking her head in her door.

"It is the most beautiful thing I have ever seen," she replied, ushering her mother inside, and taking her by the hands and leading her to the wardrobe. "But I do not believe for a moment that Gwynnie found it at the back of her closet."

"It does not matter where it came from," her mother replied, a bright smile breaking across her face. "What matters is that it is a dress fit for someone as beautiful as you."

"Please tell them thank you," she whispered, swallowing back tears of joy. "It is beyond anything I could have imagined."

"It is what I had once imagined for you," her mother said, her smile faltering, her eyes growing bright with tears.

"Mother?" Kitty asked, squeezing her mother's hand. "Is something the matter?"

"Nothing at all, my child," she replied. "I am merely excited for you. But I also have something for you. Something I would like for you to keep just between us."

"Of course," Kitty replied, her brows furrowing, taken off guard by her mother's request.

Her mother slipped a small muslin bag from her wrist. She set it on the bed, and pulled out the most remarkable pair of shoes.

"Mother," she gasped, reaching out, almost afraid to touch them. Even in the light of day, the gray silk glistened like silver. The top of the shoes were encrusted with tiny crystal beads.

"Try them on," her mother said, her eyes lighting up as she picked one up and handed it to Kitty. "Let's make certain they fit."

Kitty wiggled her foot into the shoe, her wool stocking a poor match for the exquisiteness of the shoe. It hugged her foot perfectly.

"Where did you get these?" she asked. The crystal beads on the shoes would have been worth a laborer's wages for a year. And though they were far better compensated, these slippers were beyond the means of a gamekeeper.

"I have had them for a very long time," her mother said. "They have been waiting for the right moment to be worn. This is that moment."

Kitty looked down at her feet, and back to her mother.

"Are they yours?"

"They were. They belong to you now. I think they were always for you."

Her mother rose, kissed Kitty on her head, then went to the door. "I have to go help your father with the last of the packing. Mrs. Pembroke and Gwynnie will be most eager to know if you like your gown. And, knowing Gwynnie, she will be even more eager to know every last detail about your afternoon with the marquess."

The door closed again, leaving Kitty alone, her mind racing. What an utterly remarkable day it had been.

Kitty sat alone for a while longer, looking down at her beautiful shoes, and then up to that magnificent dress. It didn't seem possible she deserved any of it.

Or maybe, for the first time, she dared to think she might.

CHAPTER 20

The evening had come at last, and for once, Colin was not anticipating the stars.

Dinner had finished. It was a stunning affair, even by his mother's standards. The ballroom had glittered with candlelight, crystal, and anticipation. One of the ladies would be a future duchess by the end of the evening, and throughout dinner Colin had been peppered by questions from gentlemen, chaperones, and ladies alike in a vain attempt for him to betray some clue that pointed to the lucky lady. It had been exhausting.

When the dessert course had finished, instead of having the sexes separate into their traditional post-meal spheres, ladies were invited to retire to their rooms to fetch shawls or other vestments they felt necessary to venture out for the viewing party. It was here, Katherine Boxford had insisted, that the right woman for him might present herself. Now, standing alone in his father's study, he peered down at the velvet-lined box in his hands, and swallowed back his nerve. Tonight—in a few short hours—he would give the jewel inside it to his future wife.

Colin was never one for earthly fripperies. He liked his creature comforts well enough, but his tastes ran toward simplicity. So he'd been concerned when he'd sent the moonstone away to be set by one his mother's favorite jewelers. His mother had always delighted in bright, glittering, and occasionally flamboyant pieces, and he'd worried that the simple majesty of this remarkable stone with its glittering star would be lessened by the distraction of other stones and embellishments. He need not have been concerned.

The stone was set in the center of a wreath of pearls of various sizes, which only highlighted the intensity of the jewel itself, without stealing its majesty. In truth, it needed little ornamentation. It only needed the right woman.

Katherine Boxford.

The incredible woman who'd found his way into his life in a lumpy frockcoat in order to make a bit of coin; the gamekeeper's daughter he'd hired to help him find a suitable wife—someone who'd bear him sons and leave his battered heart untouched—had somehow enchanted and healed his. It was not just the subtle curve of her hips, or the brightness in her eyes, or even the way she seemed to turn the deepest shade of pink at the slightest inclination that had come to fascinate him. Though it had. Their lovemaking yesterday was as magical as it was forbidden.

But she was not the woman he was supposed to want. And it was not only because she was commonly born, without fortune or connections. The woman he'd wanted to be paired with needed to bear him children. Something that was quite possible, he realized now. But even if that thing came to pass, marrying Katherine Boxford violated the most important of rules he'd set for himself—that he would not allow another woman to take his heart. A woman couldn't have that much power again. Polite indifference was his plan. He would satisfy his parents, satisfy society, and be left alone. Which was, he'd tried to remind himself, exactly what he wanted. Perhaps he was a coward. Afraid, at least publicly, to break the rules of society and expectations that formed the foundation of Colin's life. His father's health had become increasingly fragile. To throw off his duty and expectation might be the end of him.

"Are you ready, son?"

His father's voice caught his attention, and he looked to see the duke's silhouette in the door. Though shadow obscured his father's face, the gravity in the duke's voice was unmistakable. The ever faithful Davis stood behind them.

Colin shut the box, and went to greet him.

"I am," he said, handing the box to Davis. "Let's get this over with, shall we?"

They walked toward the door, their boots clicking on the polished wooden floors, where an absolute throng was waiting for them. The crowd parted for them, and he took his place with his parents near the doors. His heart pounded in his chest as two footmen pulled the doors open, revealing a splendid summer evening, the last remnants of twilight still visible in the west. Ahead was a series of lamps that would lead him and his guests to where the telescopes were waiting.

Where she was waiting.

The rush of a warm summer breeze greeted him as he stepped out into the night, let go a quick breath, and led the crowd toward Long Pond. He strolled along, his pace measured, anticipation filling him beyond measure. He was soon joined by Edmund and Lady Gwyneth, who looked radiant as always.

"This is going to be a wonderful evening," Lady Gwyneth said, then leaned into him, lowering her voice. "Kitty has told me some of what you've been up to."

"Miss Boxford has been a terrific help to me," Colin replied, trying to ignore the mischievous look in her eye. "She will make someone an excellent helpmate, if that is what she chooses."

"And how will you choose?" Lady Gwyneth asked.

"To be quite honest, I am not at all certain."

"Perhaps you will just recognize it when you see it," Lady Gwyneth said, her eyes twinkling.

"Perhaps I will."

"And if you don't," Edmund said, his matter decidedly less charming. The two had not really spoken since that rather uncomfortable night when Edmund had come to fetch Katherine. "What then?"

Colin had considered that. If, after a night of sharing with his guests that which he held most dear to himself, no one found even the slightest amount of pleasure or interest? There was his original plan of course. Just choose, and move forward.

"Then I will just have to make the best decision I can. Logical, methodical. And leave it at that." Except his heart had already chosen.

"You will know it," Lady Gwyneth said. "I am certain. Just—trust your heart. Trust it. It will not lie to you."

Colin nodded, then looked away, wondering if all women had the ability to see into his motives.

A year ago, Colin had met Lady Gwyneth at a party at Westemere. It was widely accepted that Colin would offer for her, and that Gwyneth would accept. But their hearts were not meant for each other, and while Lady Gwyneth was an amiable woman of terrific character, their temperaments did not at all suit. But she was turning into a very insightful friend.

In the time it took to reach the lake, the indigo sky deepened to an inky darkness, the Rose Moon rising on the horizon. The lamps near the lake had been lit, and the musicians had started to play, the music rising above the trees, carried on the light breeze.

The murmur of voices and footsteps from behind him rose up to meet it. Colin walked ahead, eager to be in place to greet the guests. As he approached, even he was taken aback by how wonderful it had all looked. The two telescopes were perched securely on the dais, pointing at the southern sky. The musicians were near the lake, the water carrying their sound across the estate. Chairs and benches had been placed for those who wished to sit.

And there, standing near the water's edge, he caught a glimpse of Katherine. He caught more than a glimpse, and his heart fairly burst out of his chest.

"Oh my, Edmund," he heard Lady Gwyneth whisper behind him.

Oh my indeed.

She was draped in a simple pale blue gown, shot through with silver thread. The style was perhaps a little older, but it had clearly been altered to fit every curve and did so beautifully. Tiny little stones dotted the skirt, and shimmered like stars where it captured the lamp light. Her only adornments were tiny white flowers artfully placed in her hair.

She was innocence and temptation. Majestic, yet approachable.

It took every ounce of strength he had not to run to her and greet her as if they were something more than indifferent acquaintances. But nearly fifty people were at his back, including his parents.

"Miss—Miss Boxford," he said, jumping the two steps up the small platform to where she stood. "You are lovely."

She blushed in that pretty way of hers and damn him if he didn't want to kiss her then.

"Thank you, my lord," she said, then nodded to him. "Your arm! Is it improving?"

He had not worn his sling tonight, instead wrapping the wrist itself for support.

"It is, thank you," he said, then caught a shimmer from below. Just below the hem of her skirt was the most remarkable pair of shoes. Not that he normally took notice of ladies' footwear, but there was nothing about Katherine that was beneath his notice. The way she moved. That small mole behind her left ear. The way she laughed under her breath when—

"Colin." His mother's voice from below snapped his attention away from Katherine. His mother and father were below looking mildly befuddled and not a little concerned. "I think it is time for you to explain why we are all here."

Colin cleared his throat and looked out into the crowd, ignoring the awful rolling sensation in his gut.

"Your Grace, my dear lords, ladies and gentlemen, I thank you for your patience and am eager to quell your bewilderment at why I have taken you from the splendid ballroom here at Stormount." He pointed to the moon, now well over the trees, its brightness spilling onto the lake behind him. "Some of you may know of my...passion...for the heavens. I wished to share that with you, in some small measure, this evening. There are two instruments here. They are trained on the moon, which is granting us its beautiful light this evening. I bid you, if you are so inclined, to take in its hidden splendor. I shall be at one telescope, and my assistant Miss Boxford shall be at the other if you have questions."

A slight murmur went up from the crowd then. He ignored what was no doubt whispers about her, and continued.

"And while you are waiting, please—we have seen to your every comfort with music and refreshment."

With that line, the musicians began to play, and a gentle clapping went up over the crowd. He threw one last quick look over his shoulder at Katherine, then went to greet his parents.

"Well done, Colin," his father said. "You looked quite at home up there. As did Miss Boxford."

"Thank you, Father," he replied. "If you would excuse me, I will move to take my place at the other telescope."

Colin walked off to the second, larger platform, cognizant that the crowd would be watching every step. Still, in this environment, he felt quite comfortable. If not for the evening's true purpose, he might have almost enjoyed himself.

He stepped on the platform, and turned to see a veritable curtain of silk and muslin waiting for him. Expectant.

He brought his parents up first. They had the same look about them that a parent might have when their child was showing them his first drawing. He was uncommonly nervous, he realized now. While his father bought him his first telescope—the very same instrument he'd used to show Katherine Jupiter's moons—neither of his parents had looked through them. Though they'd supported his plans to remake the old roundhouse into an observatory, he'd never truly invited them to enjoy it. He'd never truly invited anyone into this part of his life. At least, not in a way that would be meaningful to them. He'd talk about focal points and mirrors, declination and ascension. And while those things were important to him and essential to the science, it was wonder and curiosity that were the tantalizing invitation to a shared experience. And if that was all they found in it, wasn't that enough?

And, incredibly, they did.

"This is stunning!" his mother said, bending ever so slightly over the eye piece. "I had no idea the moon looked like powder. Am I seeing…" she paused, and looked up at her son, clearly uncertain, "mountains?"

"Indeed, Mother," he replied. "The surface of the moon is quite irregular."

His mother smiled with what could only be described as utter delight, before turning to her husband. "George, you must procure me an instrument like this. Perhaps Colin can help you select one."

"Of course, my dear Jane." His father nodded, clearly pleased, though equally surprised by her demand. "My dear boy, you will have me out of pocket."

They stood aside, and one by one, ladies came up to the platform, curtsied prettily, smiled coyly, and observed. A few spent only the fleetest of moments looking up, others lingered. Some expressed true delight and even asked questions that betrayed what Colin could only construe as true interest. But none of them, he found, stirred his heart.

But of course, wasn't that what he wanted?

From time to time, his eyes would gaze over to the second platform, where Katherine stood. Edmund and Lady Gwyneth nearby, clearly protective of her. Though she was but fifty feet away, it felt an interminable distance. What wouldn't he give to be near her now? To take her by the hand, lead her to the shore, where he knew the moonlight would be glistening its gentle light on her, and with the music in the background, hold her close. Dance with her. She liked dancing, didn't she?

He wanted to dance with Katherine Boxford under the moonlight.

He wanted to spend his life with her.

"Good evening, Lady Mariah," his mother said. Colin blinked, the name intruding on his rather pleasant thought. He dragged his attention away, falling down to earth again, to see Lady Mariah, her sister and mother firmly in tow, bustling up the steps to the platform.

"Good evening, your Grace," she said in that mild voice of hers, curtsying prettily to his parents, then to him. "This is truly a splendid evening. What a master stroke of planning. I am certain viewing parties will become all the rage."

His mother beamed, clearly pleased. "Why thank you, Lady Mariah. Indeed, I must give credit to Lord Ellsworth, of course, and Miss Boxford, who assisted me in the particulars of the evening. Indeed it was her suggestion to have the little lanterns in the trees. Magical, are they not?"

"Magical!" she said, her gaze flitting over to the second platform before returning to Colin. For the first time ever, he detected the smallest flash of anger on Lady Mariah's otherwise placid expression. If he had looked away for but a moment, he would have missed it.

"You look especially well this evening," he said, as she seemed to be expecting the compliment. And indeed she did. "Do you wish to look up at the moon, Lady Mariah?" He took a quick look in the eye piece, then adjusted it to match the moon's position, which had shifted over the course of the evening.

"I do," she said, her answer a little louder than was necessary given the space between them. "Indeed, 'tis a good thing I suppose that this instrument is small enough to move. I hope I can see as well through it as I could the one at your tower."

Colin froze. Oh no.

"Excuse me, my dear," her mother said, her voice crackling with surprise. "What did you say?"

Lady Mariah's mouth opened in a pretty little 'oh,' and Colin's gut dropped.

"Oh dear," she said. "I suppose I shouldn't have mentioned that."

"Mention what, my dear?" Colin's father said, clearing his throat, the edge in his voice unmistakable.

"That, I," she faltered, her gaze shooting from the duke, to her mother, and resting on Colin. "I visited Lofton Tower. Several nights ago."

"*Night?*" her mother gasped, her stare piercing Colin. He could not decide if her indignation was genuine; panic and contempt warred within, distracting his normally keen sense of observation. What a fool he'd been. "And pray, were you alone when you visited Lord Ellsworth? At night?"

"I took Millie with me, Mother," she replied, a hint of a smile teasing one edge of her mouth even has she attempted a frown.

"Millie," her mother spat. "Millie has all the wits about her of a cow."

"My boy," his father intervened. "Did you entertain Lady Mariah, unchaperoned, at Lofton Tower?"

"'Twas but ten minutes," he said. He did not lower himself to protest that Lady Mariah had arrived of her own free will. Unchaperoned.

"A lot of damage can be done in ten minutes," the Countess of Bedford said in a whisper, her eyes hard, yet clearly aware of the opportunity in front of her. "To reputations if nothing else. The Stapletons are one of the oldest and most important families in Shropshire. This will not do, your Grace. It shall not."

Colin stepped back, the implication of what was to happen next washing over him like ice water. As he did so, the instrument caught his boot and fell to the ground with a sickening smash. He turned to see the eye piece lying separately from the main viewing tube, and the glistening of a broken mirror scattered on the platform. The sound caught the attention of the crowd, and while the music continued, a hush fell over the gathering.

"Oh dear," Lady Mariah said again.

Colin's memory went back to that evening. He should have told his parents of it. Warned them. He did not. His only witness was Katherine, and he did not wish to risk her good name. Mariah had told him her favorite part about playing games was winning.

And she was about to.

"Well, we know what to do, don't we?" Colin said, his wrist aching beneath his bandage. He straightened, his heart hard, and nodded. "It was my folly, allowing Lady Mariah to get out of the carriage. So we shall announce our betrothal at the ball."

"Very well. It is the only solution to this most vexing of situations,"

Countess of Bedford said. "Come ladies, we must get Mariah ready for the announcement."

Colin watched them scamper away, then let out a low breath.

"Colin," his father said, "Are you quite certain of this?"

"What else is there to be done?" Colin turned to his father, trying to bite back his anger. "You should be happy, Father. This is what you wanted, is it not? A bride? An heir? You shall have it. The line will continue."

His father nodded, his movement solemn, then he took the duchess by the arm and walked away.

"I'm afraid this telescope is broken beyond repair," he called out, forcing his voice steady and bright. "We shall be returning to the house soon, but if you wish a chance to view the moon before we retire, please take the opportunity at the second platform. The view will be just as pleasing there, I assure you."

He looked to where Katherine stood. She was watching him. Observing him.

Did she know that his heart was ready to break?

He turned away and stalked off toward the house. Toward his future with Lady Mariah.

He was a marquess. He needed an heir. He'd spent ten unguarded minutes with a lady. Gentleman did not spend unguarded minutes with ladies. Not without consequences. Those were the rules.

And Colin knew the rules.

CHAPTER 21

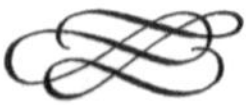

*S*omething was wrong.

Even with the din of people around her, looking up at the telescope, the music playing in the background, she'd heard the clatter of the telescope falling over, and the sound of the mirror shattering.

More than that, she could feel it in her bones.

"Edmund," she heard Gwynnie say, her voice pitched low and full of concern.

Kitty watched a trio of ladies scurrying toward the house. She could not make them out at this distance, but she was willing to bet a crown that it was the Countess of Bedford and her daughters. The duke and duchess were soon in step behind them, when Colin's voice rose above the crowd, informing them that the telescope was no longer available.

He looked across at her then, and she knew. In her heart of hearts, she knew.

He'd chosen.

"Kitty, are you well?"

The stars seemed to spin a little and she felt wobbly, as if she'd

250

drunk too much of Colin's excellent brandy. She stepped forward, then back, vaguely aware of someone catching her.

"Steady on, Kitty," Edmund whispered in her ear.

"Kitty!" Gwynnie said, a little louder, standing right in front of her.

She blinked and shook off whatever weakness that had come over her.

"I'm fine." She smiled weakly at Gwynnie, then glanced over her shoulder at Edmund who was looking at her the way he always did—as a concerned elder brother. And right now, that was exactly what she needed. "I don't know what has come over me."

"I can guess," Gwynnie said, pulling a handkerchief from Edmund's pocket and dabbing it to Kitty's cheeks. "Kitty, do you wish to go home?"

"Why on earth would I wish to do that?" she said, perhaps a little too brightly given that going home and forgetting the night had ever happened, that Colin had ever happened, was exactly what she wanted to do. She looked to Stormount, with its blazing windows, then to the fields beyond it, where the lights of the Traveler's camps lit up the night.

Nothing has changed because you have not changed.

"Because you are not feeling well," Gwyneth said. "I would not wish to put you through the rest of the night."

Kitty took in a deep breath. She had always known how this was going to end. That she'd thought, even for a moment, it might have a storybook ending was entirely her own whimsical doing.

She reached down into that part of herself, that part Colin had awakened, and tried to conjure it. Tried to hold on to it.

"Gwynnie, I know what you and Mrs. Pembroke have tried to do for me. Turn me into a princess. And you have. I feel…perfect." She paused then, the spell fading slightly. "Under this dress I am still a gamekeeper's daughter. But I am a gamekeeper's daughter wearing a dress and a pair of shoes fit for a princess, and there is a ball ahead of me, so I will drink one glass of champagne, and if I may borrow Edmund for at least one pity dance I shall take it."

Her friend reached out, folded her in her arms, and squeezed her tight.

"Let's go then, shall we?" Edmund said, offering an arm to both Gwynnie and Kitty. "I shall be the talk of the ball with not one, but two beautiful ladies on my arms."

The sounds of the ball wafted from windows and the doors were thrown open to the pleasant evening weather. As they approached the ballroom, the air was filled with a hush of muffled voices, then she heard Colin's voice ever so clearly…

"Lady Mariah."

After a cacophony of applause and voices talking over one another, it grew silent again, before a larger "ooooo" sound rose from the crowd, followed by applause so thunderous, Kitty faltered in her step as they approached the ballroom.

It was done, then.

"Kitty." Edmund turned to her. "Are you certain?"

The only thing she was certain of was that she should have never, in her deepest, darkest thoughts, wished for love. Wished for Colin Middleton's arms around her. Wished for his touch. Wished for his affection.

And then she remembered the look on her mother's face when she brought out her shoes. She'd been so hopeful for Kitty. *They deserve to be seen. As do you.*

She looked down at her toes one last time, sheathed in these glistening silk shoes, then nodded.

"I am certain."

They walked into the ballroom and Kitty took a moment to be dazzled by it. Ladies wearing the most elegant dresses, glittering candlelight, and gleaming crystal. Liveried servants walking by with trays of champagne. Gwynnie picked one up and handed it to Kitty.

"You deserve this," she said. "It's wasted on me right now."

Kitty put the glass to her lips, the bubbles causing her nose to crinkle. They moved to one side of the festivities, where Edmund found Gwynnie some lemonade to refresh herself.

"We shall stay as long as you like," Gwynnie said. "The music should begin soon, and I would imagine that Colin will be obligated to dance the first dance with Lady what's her name."

Kitty took a sip of the champagne and decided it was very good. "Mariah," she said, the name bitter on her tongue.

"Let us not use that name in my presence ever again," Gwynnie pronounced, pursing her bottom lip in that habit she had when she was not happy. "Edmund, I am not certain how we can be neighbors with that woman. We may have to move to Yorkshire, and live near your cousin. The winters there are dreadful, but I would rather moody moors to sitting in parlors with that horrid woman and her family."

Before Edmund had a chance to placate his wife, the musicians began to play. The crowd parted, and Kitty watched as Colin led Lady Mariah to the floor. She was beaming. He, she could see, was not. Polite applause filled the room, and then other couples joined them on the floor.

She swallowed her champagne, and before all courage deserted her, she turned to Edmund.

"Come, Edmund," she said. "I promised Mother these shoes would grace the floor for one dance, and I will not disappoint her."

Edmund exchanged a look with Gwynnie, then bowed deeply. "I would be honored to stand up with you."

Edmund led Kitty to the floor, where they were one of a dozen couples. She stood shoulder to shoulder with ladies who had come here hoping to be the woman in Lady Mariah's position. Were they as disappointed as she? Perhaps. Perhaps he had, in fact, had some feeling for her. And perhaps she had imagined it. But these ladies were of his sphere. They had what she did not. A real chance to be his wife.

She dared herself to look over to him. He was looking straight ahead. His jaw was tight. He hated to dance.

She looked back to Edmund who instantly caught her eye and smiled. Kitty blew out a small breath and smiled in return, determined to enjoy it. Determined to ignore the heavy ache in her heart.

On cue everyone started moving in time to the music, polite steps and the lightest of touches and swirls through the queue. Her mother's shoes that had fit so well when Kitty had on her woolen stockings fit not quite as well in her silk ones, and with each grand step she feared one might slip off her foot. She was vaguely aware that some on the floor were gesturing at her, no doubt wondering who her father was and where she fit into society's carefully spun web. As she turned her face to the crowd, she caught the smallest glimpse of the duchess, who was watching her most keenly through a quizzing glass.

The couples moved up and down through the line, until that inevitable moment when her gloved hand touched the tips of Colin's. Her breath caught in her throat as her gaze swept up his body to see his clenched jaw. His eyes, normally a dazzling green, seemed dull somehow. Not that she should have cared.

The agony of their touch lingered even as they parted. Beside her was Lady Mariah, looking radiant, triumphant, with an unusual pendant around her neck. Kitty frowned, a flicker of recognition as she caught a glimpse of it, before the couple breezed past them into their original position, and the dance ended.

Edmund led her off the dance floor, and back to Gwynnie, who was speaking to a small group of ladies and gentleman.

"Here they are!" her friend called out, waving them over.

Gwynnie introduced her to Mr. and Mrs. Kent, who were visitors from the next county.

"You two looked absolutely splendid, Kitty," Gwyneth said. "Indeed, I believe half the floor was wondering who you are."

"And Lord Ellsworth looked to be in absolute misery," said Mr. Kent, standing next to Edmund. "He was positively gray when he put that jewel around Lady Mariah's neck."

"Jewel? What jewel?" Kitty asked, unable to contain her curiosity.

"The Fallen Star—the pendant Lady Mariah is wearing, Miss Boxford. Apparently Lord Ellsworth found the stone years ago, and saved it for this very moment." Mrs. Kent leaned in and lowered her voice. "'Tis a pity he could not have bequeathed it to a woman he actually had some affection for."

"The Fallen Star?" Kitty asked, a queer sensation rippling through her belly. She turned on her heel, scanning the room for Lady

Mariah. It took her but a moment to find her, standing next to Colin, idly toying with a pendant on her neck. "Can you describe it?"

"I did not get a very good look at it, alas," Mrs. Kent said, "but I understand it is a moonstone, with a remarkable flaw that makes it appear as if a star is floating inside it."

For the second time this evening, Kitty felt her stomach lurch. She reached for Gwynnie's arm.

"Kitty?" Gwynnie asked.

"My brooch," was all she managed to say, looking at Gwynnie before turning away from them.

She was vaguely aware of Edmund calling her name, but she ignored it, a new terrible sense of urgency driving her steps. She nearly tumbled as her left shoe almost slipped off her ankle, but she recovered quickly, making a line for Lady Mariah, who stood in a corner with her mother and the duchess. Colin was nowhere to be found, and Kitty found herself quite satisfied if she never saw him again. He hadn't just set Kitty aside. He'd carelessly given away the very jewel she'd lost so many years ago. Her luck.

She would not let it slip through her fingers again.

As expected, Lady Mariah ignored Kitty's approach entirely. But the duchess, who was standing alongside her, did not.

"Miss Boxford, it is a delight to see you again," she said, and for just a moment, Kitty almost believed her. "Thank you again for your assistance this evening. I was just telling Lady Mariah how I wish to procure a small telescope for myself."

Kitty tried to smile, but she found herself utterly fixated on Lady Mariah's neck. Or, more pointedly, the gemstone hanging from it. The gemstone that once belonged in the brooch Kitty had lost so long ago. The Fallen Star.

See what is unseen.

It had been here the entire time. With Colin.

"I would like a word, if possible, with Lady Mariah," she said, her gaze darting from the duchess to Colin's fiancé.

"A word? My heavens," she said, smiling as a cat being presented with a bowl of cream. "I cannot imagine what we might have to discuss that cannot be said in front of her Grace."

"Do not trouble yourself, Lady Mariah. I see Lady Best nearby, eager to pay her respects to me. I shall attend to her and return," she said, her gaze going to Kitty's feet once more. "Your shoes are superb, Miss Boxford."

Kitty curtsied. "Thank you, your Grace. They are my mother's."

"Interesting. You may tell your mother she has exquisite taste." She turned to Mariah and nodded, before leaving the two alone.

"So, do you wish to offer me congratulations? In the end, I have won. But of course, you always knew I would, didn't you?" Lady Mariah said, tilting her chin up, her placid smile laced with vinegar. "He is gone even now, to negotiate the terms of our marriage."

Kitty forced her gaze to stay fixed on Lady Mariah. She would not look down.

"I knew you would have him," she replied. "But that is not why I am here. You have something that belongs to me," Kitty said, her voice clear and steady. "And I thank you to return it."

Lady Mariah laughed. "I can hardly imagine what it is."

Kitty pointed at her neck. "You have my stone. The Fallen Star belongs to me."

Lady Mariah blinked then, clearly taken aback by her demand. "I hardly think so. It was just given to me."

"You may keep the necklace. And the pearls. But the gemstone itself belongs to me. You may ask Lord Ellsworth himself. He found it, long ago, in the grass at Gorland Park." Kitty swallowed, her mind rushing back to that moment as if it was happening in front of her. "Because I dropped it. It fell out of a brooch I wore. He recovered it."

She paused then. "Shall we take a turn on the balcony, Miss Boxford? I find it quite a crush."

She took Kitty by the elbow, and with far too firm a hand, guided her out into the fresh air, then looked to ensure they were alone.

"That's better, don't you think? We don't want to cause a scene," she said, that infuriatingly placid expression falling away, her eyes narrowing and her voice a harsh whisper. "Now, what exactly do you think you are doing?"

"I told you," Kitty said, strangely calm. "You have my gemstone. And I want it back."

She threw her head back and laughed again. "What a fanciful story. What would a strumpet like you be doing with a stone like this?" Her expression hardened. "Unless you stole it. People like you aren't made for nice things."

"People like me?"

"Yes," she said, quite brightly. "There are people like me, born of people of quality. Raised to have refined tastes, manners, and education. And then there are people like you."

"You need not instruct me on breeding, Lady Mariah. My father was a breeder of champion hunting dogs," Kitty replied, straightening. "So you can trust me when I say that I know a proper bitch when I meet one."

Lady Mariah's mouth flew open. A second later, Kitty was stunned by the harsh sting of her palm across her cheek.

"How dare you speak to me this way? You have proven my point exactly, you horrible, horrible person."

Kitty put her hand to her cheek, trying to soothe it, while blinking away the tears that had formed in response to the slap.

"I will have you dragged out of here for attacking me so," Lady Mariah continued, her tone venomous. "And when I am duchess, I will see you evicted from the neighborhood."

Kitty dropped her hand to her side, and stood even straighter.

"You still haven't given me back my gemstone."

"And you shan't have it. It is mine," Mariah said, her voice dripping with condescension. "And your ridiculous story is just a pathetic, grasping excuse to have something that should never belong to you. Like Lord Ellsworth."

Mariah hadn't struck Kitty again, but she might as well have. A fierce anger bubbled up inside her, mixing with sadness and not a little despair.

"You have him. Do you understand? As you've just told me, you won. Lord Ellsworth is yours. Go ahead and gloat. But—" she pointed at the necklace, her voice ragged as she swallowed back the tears she would not let fall, "—the Fallen Star is not yours. You no doubt have hundreds of jewels. You will be duchess and have a thousand more. But that is mine."

"What in the blazes is this?"

It took a moment for her to register the deep tones of Colin's voice. Kitty collected herself and turned to him.

"My lord," she said.

"This horrible woman is trying to steal my jewel. I demand she be removed from the property and locked in irons," Lady Mariah spat. "I had to fight her off with my own bare hands!"

"I am not trying to steal anything." Kitty cleared her throat and tamped down the anger, heartbreak, and desperation that made her want to do nothing more than rip the necklace from Lady Mariah's neck and run. But she would not. "That jewel is mine. It is from the brooch."

"You told me you found the brooch," he replied, "last year. I pulled that out of the ground at Gorland Park—"

"Eleven years ago. When I lost the brooch," she replied. "I did find it—all but a few stones were missing. The largest being this one—the moonstone. Do you recall the Romani woman's words? I let happiness slip through my fingers. It was this stone. I must have it back."

"Well that is a most fanciful story," Lady Mariah said, crossing her arms.

"Here they are, Countess Bedford." The Duke of Weymouth's voice boomed as he stepped out onto the balcony, Lady Mariah's mother in tow. She wore the same pinched look as always, Kitty could not help but notice. "Colin, your mother and your guests are looking for you."

"We shall be but a moment, your Grace," Colin replied, not taking his eyes from Kitty.

"Send her away at once," Lady Mariah snapped. "She practically attacked me, the vixen."

"What on earth is happening here?" Countess Bedford snapped, pushing Kitty away from her daughter. The motion threw Kitty off balance, but the duke reached out for her hand, helping her to recover. "Your Grace, I demand you toss this horrible girl off the property at once."

"She tried to steal my necklace," Lady Mariah protested. "She's too poor and miserable to have anything nice, so she tried to steal this."

"Give it to her, Mariah."

The gravity and direction of Colin's voice took almost everyone by surprise. Including, it would seem, Lady Mariah.

"What did you say?" she asked, her voice squeaking.

"There has been a terrible error," he replied, his voice direct, though softening. "Miss Boxford's recollection of events are correct. The stone belongs to her. Return it, and I shall have a new one fashioned for you. You may choose the stone yourself."

"But—you believe—"

"Of course I do. Miss Boxford cannot lie without turning five shades of pink," he said, his gaze sliding over Kitty, coming to a stop on her cheek. His mouth pressed into a firm line. "What has happened here?"

Before Kitty could stop herself, she put her hand to the place where Mariah had struck her, before pulling it away.

"I told you she attacked me," Mariah protested. "I had to defend myself. It was horrible."

"I see," he said, crossing his arms in front of him. "Mariah, you will return the Fallen Star to Miss Boxford immediately or I shall do it for you."

"I have never—" Lady Mariah's voice crackled as she removed the necklace. "Never been treated so poorly in my entire life. To be so dishonorably treated."

"I did not intend to dishonor you, Lady Mariah," Colin replied, uncrossing his arms, his voice softening. "But this wrong must be righted. There is nothing dishonorable about doing another person a kindness, or undoing a mistake. There is something inherently dishonorable about striking another person over whom you have power."

"She is not a person, Lord Ellsworth," she said, tossing the necklace at Kitty. It came so quickly she was unable to catch it, and it landed at her feet. "She is a servant. A servant in a lady's dress, perhaps, but still nothing more than a servant. And when I am mistress of this estate I will ensure that servants know their place."

Kitty was about to scoop up her necklace when she noticed the duke reaching for his collar, as if he was trying to catch breath.

"Your Grace?"

Kitty rushed to him. His breathing was labored, and she could see him clutching his chest.

He grasped her hand, as Kitty struggled to loosen his cravat.

"Come Mariah…it is clear we are not wanted here," the countess said, her voice loud enough to voice her displeasure to any who wished to hear her. "I wish to retire for the evening. Find your sister."

The sound of skirts rustling and indignant sighs behind her fell away as the two brushed by Lord Ellsworth and disappeared through a nearby door.

"Father!" Colin gasped, then assisted his father to the floor, where he leaned up against a wall. "Shall I call Davis?"

The duke nodded toward his son. "I think—yes."

"I will stay with him." Kitty kept grasping the duke's hand, and called over her shoulder to Colin. "Go."

Colin disappeared, leaving the duke alone with Kitty. He was absolutely stricken with panic—his eyes wide, his face flushed, his breathing quick and shallow.

"Your Grace," she said, desperate to keep her voice steady. "Focus just on the sound of my voice. You need to steady your breath. It will help calm your heart."

She put his hand on her belly, and then hers on his belly, and then took in a deep breath.

"Feel where I am breathing," she said. "Right in my belly. Low and deep." She paused, and breathed deeply by way of example. "Now let's try together."

It took him a few tries, but little by little, his breathing became more measured. Giving him a modicum of encouragement, his panic seemed to lessen. But it was far too optimistic to say he was well.

A moment later, Colin and Davis returned, along with the duchess. Kitty stepped out of the way as the duchess swooped in and administered some medicine.

"Thank you, Miss Boxford, for staying with him," Colin said, his voice strained with worry. He scooped up the jewel Lady Mariah had tossed at her feet, and placed it in her hand, closing her fingers over the moonstone. "I have to see to the duke. To my father."

LESS THAN AN HOUR LATER, Kitty was back at Kennington Grove. The carriage ride from Stormount was silent, the mood similar to that of a funeral. When she arrived home, she'd relayed the entire affair—or almost all of it—to her parents and Mrs. Pembroke, who seemed genuinely dismayed at the events.

Kitty retired to her room, her hair down, a few stray flowers still in her hair, most of the others having fallen in the flight from Stormount. Before long, the silver dress hung in the wardrobe, and her mother's shoes sat beneath it on the floor, the brilliant moonlight causing them to sparkle even through her window. But the princess had become a gamekeeper's daughter once more.

The clock began to strike the hour. Midnight. Not long after she'd started going to the observatory, she'd come to dread that sound. It had been the time the carriage would come to take her away from Lofton Tower. From Colin.

Now he was gone forever.

Restless beyond measure, Kitty pulled on her sturdy walking boots and her dressing gown, and ran out into the night. Most of the stars were dulled by the brilliance of the moon, now high overhead, lighting up the landscape. But they were there, the stars. She'd seen them. They were just waiting to be discovered.

Like her.

It was then the tears came. Hot, angry tears and heavy sobs. Like a hole had opened up inside her. Desperate to escape it, she ran past the gate, across the deserted road and through the woods toward the river. She crouched down beside it, idly running her fingers in the cool water.

She had the stone, at last. The moonlight struck the star inside, and it almost seemed to light up from within. Her luck. Her happiness. This piece of rock that had, over time, become mythical in her mind. She'd found it.

And yet, it meant nothing. Nothing had changed. *Nothing.*

Well, perhaps something had. Her heart was breaking.

Kitty stood, the stone cool in her hands, then threw back her head and called out to the stars.

"What is it you want from me?" she cried out. "I went to Lofton Tower. I found the stone."

She remembered the way he'd looked at her, that moment before the telescope fell and smashed. He'd yearned for her. She knew it. And then...

Nothing.

Worse than nothing, actually.

Because there was something between them. Something that had felt...magical.

"All we wanted was to be happy. Is that too much to ask?"

She bunched up the necklace, and allowing fury to guide her as she threw it as far from her as she could, then ran back to the house. She would no longer be guided by fanciful notions and fortune teller's nonsense.

She would do what she should have done long ago.

Kitty was going to find herself a husband. Her way. It wasn't romantic, which was perfectly fine with her.

She was done with fairy tales.

CHAPTER 22

The sun broke through the velvet darkness of night, the first rays spilling over the green fields and wood of Stormount. Colin stretched as he rose from his favorite chair in Lofton Tower, the hearth in front of him dark, the faint crackling from where the last bit of heat in the embers lingered. He'd escaped there during the night, after his father was resting comfortably and the physician assured both Colin and his mother that he would be well by morning. He needed to be alone, to find comfort, and this place, he thought, would give him that.

What it gave him were constant reminders of Katherine. And maybe in the end, that was what his heart wanted. The echoes of her presence were a sweet torture.

What a cock up this was.

The last vestiges of the brandy he'd taken to help him accomplish the task of securing even a meager amount of sleep lingered in his body. He went to the small kitchen and pumped some water into a nearby basin, then dunked his face in it. He welcomed the shock of the cold fresh water to his blurred senses before drying his face and putting his spectacles back on his face.

It all became clearer then.

When Lady Amelia had left him, he was undeniably heartbroken. She had been a part of his life for so long, and when she left him he could not understand what could draw two people apart who, on paper at least, seemed to be perfect for each other.

He did now. And, perhaps for the first time ever, he could truly say how happy he was for her. She had always been a piece of a puzzle that had fit into his life. And when she'd left him, and followed her heart, it had never been about what she'd gained. And every letter he'd written to her—where he catalogued her beauty, her elegance, her grace—it was always about how she would make the perfect duchess.

But never the perfect wife. The perfect love.

And that was what she'd found, with Lord Grafton. The perfect love for her. She'd broken the rules that had bound her to Colin, that had bound her to what would have been a passionless union for them both, and followed her heart. What a selfish bastard he'd been.

Before he'd dozed off, he'd burned those letters, watching those misguided words curl and blacken, until they had disappeared completely.

A knock at the door interrupted his thoughts. He grabbed a towel, drying his face as he went to the door, his heart in his throat, expecting to see a servant who was coming to relay that his father had taken a turn for the worse. He flung open the door and found a tall woman standing opposite him. Her black hair was shot through with silver, and her olive-toned skin and dark eyes, as well as the bright color of her dress, marked her as one of the Romani, no doubt from the camp that was nearby.

"You have seen what is unseen," she said, her voice measured and calm.

Colin squinted, confused both by her words and her appearance at his door.

"You will excuse me, madam, if I don't—"

She shook her head, shushing him, then ran her fingers through his hair, as if inspecting it, then apparently satisfied, pulled both his hands toward her, examining each one.

"If you have come to read my palm, I do not ascribe to such non—"

She put up her hand then, her fingers wrapped in silver and gold bands, silencing him with nothing more than a gesture.

"Whether you believe or not is not my concern, Lord Ellsworth," she said, continuing her survey of the lines in on his hands. "There are rules that guide the heavens, and you are correct. Your error has been your belief that you know all of them."

He had been mistaken about many things, he'd wanted to say. That he was without passion. That he willed to live a life without it. And, most especially, about how he thought he could live a life without Katherine Boxford.

At last, apparently satisfied, she released his hand, then started digging into her bag.

Colin was about to retreat, and dig out a coin from his pocket, when she produced the Fallen Star.

Wonder mixed with fear. "How did this come to you?"

"Fear took it from her. Despair has led her to cast it aside. Only love can return it to its proper place." She took his hand once more, placed it in his palm, and closed his fingers around it. "You know where this belongs."

"Thank you." He nodded, then bowed deeply to this strange but regal woman who had graced his door. "You shall always be welcome, my lady—you and your people—to my door. Always."

"You are a good man. Now, be a trusting one. Be a determined one."

He watched her disappear down the road, then, not bothering to waste another moment, he returned to Stormount Hall, and went directly to his parent's bedchamber. He knocked softly and poked his head in the door. There was his father, propped up in bed, a book in his hands, his mother alongside him. Though it was early, they were clearly awake and in the middle of a quiet conversation.

"Come in, Colin," his mother called, her voice low and clear, but as always, with the subtle hint of a command.

"Good morning," he said, though he did not especially feel it was. He closed the door behind him and went directly to his father. "How are you this morning, your Grace?"

"I am well," he began, and despite his smile, a line of tension stretched across his brow. "And yet, I am troubled."

Colin sat on the edge his parents' large bed, leaning his back against one of the posts. It struck him that, in this huge home, now still full with dozens of people—including his future wife—that they were quite an island, the three of them.

"I am sorry for all that has transpired," he began. "I should have come to you that very evening Lady Mariah had come to Lofton Tower unannounced. It might have prevented much of this...circus... that you were forced to witness last evening. The moment it happened I should have offered for her and most of this could have been avoided."

"How this could have been avoided is if your mother and I had stayed out of the match making business entirely," his father said, disgust in his voice, shutting his book and tossing it aside. "And I have put you in an uncomfortable position, my boy. A most uncomfortable position."

"You have merely forced on me what I had refused to do for myself —find a bride," Colin said, oddly detached from himself. "If I had been more determined, had not spent so much time wallowing in my own misery, this might have been all for naught."

"I cannot rest knowing what misery lies ahead." His father sat up, and it occurred to Colin that in all the years he'd seen his father with colleagues, even debating in Parliament, there had been few moments where he'd seen the duke acting—well, so much like one—in his entire life. Even if he was lying in his shirt and dressing gown. "I cannot do it, Colin. You must tell me—are you happy?"

Colin swallowed. He stood. He looked out toward Lofton Tower, the very tips of the structure visible through the trees. He knew the rules. He'd always followed them.

He turned back to his father.

"I am not. Before last evening, I might have been indifferent to Lady Mariah. I might have once imagined I could be friends with her." Her treatment of Katherine Boxford last evening was beyond the pale. And it was clear that her treatment of every other soul she would deem beneath her would follow. "But now I can barely stand the idea of being in the same room with her."

The sound of his parent's standing clock filled the silence and stretched over Colin's nerves. At last, his mother sighed.

"Well, that is a relief," she exclaimed, taking a moment to adjust her night cap. "Because I cannot stand being in the same house with the Stapletons. Why, they were quite prepared to leave your father when he was in distress, which is extremely bad form. And since we intend to live here for quite some time yet, we shall have to do something about it."

"Are you prepared for the scandal that will ensue—and the cost—if I break the engagement?" he asked, the weight of the gemstone in his pocket. "Because I know what will make me happy."

His parents exchanged glances, and then his father spoke, his voice steady, but gentle.

"I do not wish to lose you, in body, or soul, to a partnership that services only the family line. I have known too many who have done so, in the drive to make the perfect alliance, that have built fortunes but destroyed lives. Look where trickery and deceit in marriage nearly led you." He paused then, and Colin could see, perhaps for the first time, the fear and sadness that bordered on tears in his father's eyes. All stemming from his deadly encounter this past winter with his long-lost cousin, Hugh Wakefield. A man denied his fortune and title because of an illegitimate marriage. "I nearly lost you, my boy, to that madness."

"But you did not. I am well, you see. Hale and hearty. Just like my parents." Colin took his father's hand. "If, perhaps a little foolish. Or a lot foolish."

"We shall meet with the countess before breakfast and dispense with this unpleasant business." The duke pulled himself up, and with what appeared a new-found energy, pulled his covers off his legs, and stood, then cast a glance at his wife. "So much for a wedding, my dear."

"I want a wedding," Colin said. "More than that, I want a wife. And the only woman I want to be my wife is Katherine Boxford."

His parents exchanged a look.

"On this," Colin said, "I will be firm. I will marry her. If…if she will have me."

"Colin, my dear, what do you know of Miss Boxford? Who are her parents?" his mother asked.

"You know who her parents, are, Mother. Her father is Mr. Harry Boxford. He was gamekeeper at Gorland Park many years ago. Father is having him assist Mr. Campbell with the fish stocks at Long Pond."

"Yes, yes," she said. "But who is her mother? She has two parents, Colin."

"I have met Mrs. Boxford but once. Her name is Sara." He remembered her bearing and her wariness of Colin's motives toward her daughter. "She is a proud but amiable woman."

His mother's eyes narrowed, her lips pursed slightly. Colin knew that look. It was the same look she'd had when she was planning parties or sorting out how to introduce a new gentleman in the neighborhood to the most eligible lady.

"Her shoes were her mother's."

"I have no idea whose shoes she wore." He'd noticed them, of course. They were singular in design. But he'd been distracted by her eyes.

"Of course you did not notice," she clucked. "Men do not notice these things. But I noticed, as did every other woman of a certain age in that room, including, no doubt, the Countess of Bedford. Those shoes belonged to the daughter of Viscount Whitmore."

"Viscount who?"

"Many years ago, there was a great scandal about the daughter of Viscount Whitmore. From Sussex. She wore those shoes the night of her engagement—a gift from her grandmother. They were supposedly handmade by a shoemaker in Venice, who used glass beads fashioned by some of the finest glassmakers in Europe. I remember them perfectly—they were utterly stunning, and there have been none their equal since."

"Are you suggesting Mrs. Boxford is the daughter of a viscount?"

"What I am saying is that those shoes were last on the feet of the daughter of Viscount Whitmore. I was there, Colin. And so was the Countess of Bedford and most of the other ladies above the age of five and forty."

"And what happened to her?"

"The rumor is that she ran off with a groomsman's apprentice after she'd been promised to a rather cruel, if well-connected husband. In the end, she left behind her family, her fortune, and everything for her happiness." She paused, and shook her head. "Her family disowned her. It was a huge scandal, but in the end, as with all things, life went on. I am not certain that her parents ever forgave her. If they did, they took that loss to their graves. And, I believe, the title died with them."

Colin pulled the stone from his pocket. Was this stone another relic from that sad family history? Katherine clearly had no idea of her mother's heritage. Did Mrs. Pembroke?

"Mother, I appreciate you telling me this. If Miss Boxford is nothing more than the daughter of a gamekeeper and gamekeeper's wife, I do not care. She is the only woman I have ever met who cares not that I am a man with a fortune or a title. She is vivacious, caring, and passionate. She has a keen mind and a good heart. She is more than I could have hoped for in a partner. She makes me want to be a better man. And I love her." He let out a low breath in an effort to quell the ache growing in his chest. "And I know you would think well of her."

They were silent for a moment.

"Miss Boxford stayed with your father while that horrendous fiancé of yours was prepared to nearly walk over his ailing body to make her exit," his mother said. She cupped his cheek and smiled. "And if she makes you this happy...well, I am certain I will be pleased with her."

"Ring the bell, Colin," his father ordered. "We have some unpleasant business to deal with first. And then, if you can secure your Miss Boxford, we can have a wedding and then Jane, I wish nothing but peace and quiet for the summer months. I will invite your father-in-law, Colin, to come fishing with me."

❦

THE SINGULAR BLESSING of the morning had come from the most unlikely of places, Evelyn thought. Kennington Grove was full of servants from both her own small staff and that of Silver Cross, packing crates and wrapping the few, most treasured pieces of furniture Evelyn wanted to take with her. The rest would be left for the new tenants.

She'd tasked Miss Boxford with packing her room as well as assisting the staff with Evelyn's. It was hardly required, but she'd been eager to distract the girl after what had turned into a disastrous evening. Evelyn had only herself to blame. She'd taken on Kitty as her personal improvement project, a proxy, perhaps, for her own youth, lost to a cruel husband and society's unwillingness to entertain someone of her limited mobility.

She sat in her parlor, overseeing the packing of the ephemera of her life—small miniatures of her family, mourning lockets and her favorite books, when Edmund strode into the house.

"Good morning, Mother," he said, bending down to give her a kiss on her head. "Have you seen Kitty this morning?"

"She is upstairs, packing. And doing as well as one might expect in these circumstances," she said. "Thank you for dancing with her."

Edmund shrugged. "I was happy to do it. She is very dear to me, as you know. Perhaps after the baby is born, and Gwyneth is recovered, we can venture into London, or to the Lakes. A change of scenery might do us all very well."

"One change of scenery at a time is all I can bear at the moment," Evelyn replied.

"By dinner time you shall be all moved over, and Vincent and I can oversee the last of it." He dug into his pocket, and pulled out a letter. "This arrived late last night. It's from Westemere. Shall I open it for you?"

She nodded, and waited impatiently for Edmund to break the seal, and unfold the note. She scanned the contents, eyes wide, then cleared her throat.

"Would you be a dear, and find Mrs. Boxford? I wish to speak with her."

She looked up at her son, who'd once forsaken his name in a misguided attempt to rid his conscience of an error he'd once made at the hands of his cruel father. A gentleman who'd turned his back on society, and found himself on Harry and Sara Boxford's front step. Irony abounded. Evelyn wondered what Sara would have made of him then. What she thought of them all, now.

"Of course," he said, his brow furrowing in concern. "Is there something amiss?"

"Not at all," she replied. "Any news from Stormount?"

"Not since last evening. I don't think I'd ever seen a man so miserable and heartsick as Colin Middleton last night. When we'd gotten up to dance, he could barely take his eyes off Kitty. Truthfully I don't know whether to feel sorry for him, or to be furious with him. The two have a connection, that is clear. But I don't know that it matters now. He's engaged to someone else."

"Nothing is done until it is done," she said. "For now, we shall keep Miss Boxford busy, before she gets it in her head to do something rash. Send Sara to me. And could you ask Vincent to bring some coffee? And perhaps a spot of brandy."

Edmund checked his watch, then cocked an eyebrow. "It's just past nine, Mother."

"Secrets know no hour, my son," she replied. "Make sure it is the good bottle from your friend Mr. DuMont."

CHAPTER 23

*H*er room was nearly empty—the clothing folded in trunks, her gardening journals and books tucked away in a crate. All that was truly left to do was go back to her garden and arrange for whatever transplants could be dug up and moved by cart to Silver Cross. She would dig them herself in the morning. Her little trunk that held her money box, her favorite hair clips, her current gardening notebook, and the remnants of her mother's old brooch were all that remained.

She slumped on her bed, heartsick and bone weary. Mrs. Pembroke had given Kitty plenty to do to keep her busy, and the work had been something of a distraction. But there was no balm powerful enough to soothe her aching heart. She needed to get far, far away from Cheshire. Maybe back to Sussex, where her father had some family. Or maybe she'd run to Scotland, or to the New World—she just wanted to run.

Of course, she could never run from the sky. And no matter where she was, she knew he'd be here, looking up at those same stars.

"Kitty, may I speak to you?"

"Mother!" Kitty jumped to her feet, and pasted a smile on her face. "Do you need help?"

Her mother came in and Kitty could see at once she was pale and upset. Kitty's thoughts immediately turned to her father. She rushed to her mother.

"Is Father ill?"

Her mother shook her head, sadness and regret weighing down her normally happy demeanor.

"What is it? What is wrong?"

"Let us sit, shall we?" she said, then took Kitty by the hand and sat down on the bed.

Kitty sat next to her, her fatigue leaving her, replaced with dread.

"Mother, if you are concerned about what happened with Lord Ellsworth," Kitty began, "I am quite well. I am. Or, I will be. And I danced in your shoes. They were lovely."

"Katherine, I need to tell you about those shoes."

Her mother began to weave an incredible tale, about a gentleman's daughter who'd once been promised to a very wealthy man. A man of an ancient, important family. And another man—a much simpler one. Who promised her nothing but all that he owned and his love and protection. And she had chosen one life over another, one future at the expense of another. And at the end of it all, her mother, her face red and wet with her tears, took Kitty's hands in hers. "I am sorry, Katherine. So sorry."

Kitty was quiet for some time. Her mother was the daughter of a viscount, just like Mrs. Pembroke. And that made Kitty...what exactly did that make her?

"Mother, you have nothing to apologize for," she said. "I have had nothing but love and affection."

"Oh, but I do." She wiped away her tears with the back of her hand. "My secrets nearly cost you your friendship with Gwyneth, and I fear it has stolen a chance at happiness with Lord Ellsworth."

"I don't understand," Kitty said.

"We left Gorland Park when Countess Snowdon discovered who I was. My parents—and my former fiancé—had spent years looking for me. A substantial reward had been offered for my return, and your father's arrest. She discovered who I was. If we had not left—"

Kitty blinked. "It wasn't my fault?"

"Katherine, my darling, how on earth can you believe it was your fault? You were but a child."

Kitty closed her eyes because she was certain, though she was awake and had not tasted champagne in well over twelve hours, that the room had begun to spin.

"But your brooch," she exclaimed. "I took it. I lost it." Twice, she wanted to say. But she did not have the nerve for that.

"Do you mean the moonstone?" It was her mother's turn to be shocked. "I thought I had lost it long ago. It had been a gift, along with the shoes, from my grandmother. I assumed we'd lost it when we ran from Gorland Park."

"But it was our family's good luck stone. You told me that once," Kitty said.

Her mother smiled a sad smile, and pulled her daughter close. "'Tis but a trinket. And it carried no special luck...not really. My grandmother was a very superstitious woman, Kitty. There was a rumor she was herself part Romani, but no one knows for certain. She believed that the stone would lead someone to their true love. And, I suppose, I'd met your father the first day I wore it, so perhaps there is some truth to it. But if it is gone, then it is gone. I am not angry with you. But you should be very angry with me, I think."

"How could I be?"

"Because..." Her mother's voice broke again. "Because if I had broken my silence a week ago, you could have gone to Stormount as an invited guest, not as a servant. And perhaps today, instead of sitting here in an empty room with an aching heart, you might have been his wife."

"But you had to leave Gorland Park because of your parent's threat. You could not tell me."

"They have passed, Kitty. I do have some family, and one day perhaps, when you are ready, we could try to mend those connections. I do miss some of them. But it was my own selfishness that kept you from Lord Ellsworth. Nothing more."

"I think the chances of me being Lord Ellsworth's wife were never very good." Kitty toyed with the hem on her apron. "If I had come to him as a gentleman's daughter, I would have been one of countless others. In the end, Lady Mariah was intent on being his wife. And now she is. Or will be."

Her mother smiled sadly then, tucking a wayward lock of Kitty's hair behind her ear.

"Once we are in Silver Cross, and this unsettled business is behind us, we can speak about it more. For now, however, if you wish, I can help you finish here."

Kitty shook her head. Her head was full, trying to pull apart the tangled strands of her life—what she'd imagined the truth of her life to be, and what it was. Forces larger than Kitty had always seemed to be at work, pushing her in one direction or another. At one time she'd thought she'd been the cause of it all. Taking her mother's brooch to prove to Gwynnie she had a treasure just as fair as a gentleman's daughter, when her mother had been the very same. Except her mother had chosen her path. Her mother had chosen relative poverty over a life of powerlessness with a cruel man. Even Lady Mariah had decided what she'd wanted in her horrid, roundabout way.

Kitty was alone.

She stood, watching her mother leave, and noticed a rustling in her apron pocket. She dug down into and pulled out a piece of paper. She unfolded it, and read the list.

It was her advert for a husband.

Wanted:

One gamekeeper, currently employed, seeking an active woman to wife.

Aged 20-40.

Applicants with children acceptable.

Gentle nature, not taken to excessive drink.

Humorous disposition.

What else would she ask for?

Ginger hair preferred. Spectacles a must.

She would ask for Lord Ellsworth. But he was already taken.

She quickly added the odd sentence or two about her own abilities, and made mention of a very small dowry she had available to her.

All inquiries were to be made to Silver Cross, care of K. Boxford. Then she untied her apron, folded up her note, and flew down the stairs while she still had her nerve. Maybe Kitty could choose. A pleasant man who might like to garden, and who, one day, might come to look well on her. It was more, she liked to think, than what Lady Mariah might have.

But Lady Mariah also had Colin.

Before the church had rung the hour, Kitty had posted her advertisement on a notice board not far from the very office where she'd first made her application to be Lord Ellsworth's assistant. And, she could not help but remember, Lady Mariah had first made her introductions to him.

Kitty climbed back into the cart and headed back to Kennington Grove. There she would pick up her plants, and move them with her to Silver Cross. And perhaps, just perhaps, she would receive word of a man who might want her. If she wanted him, that was. And then, at last, she might find home.

COLIN RODE his fastest horse to Silver Cross, looking for Katherine. He'd initially headed to Kennington Grove, but caught a wagon loaded with boxes and trunks riding away from the manor house. The driver had informed him that most of the family was now getting settled there, and it was likely that Katherine would be among them.

The morning had been a ghastly but necessary bit of business. His father had issued the invitation to Countess Bedford, and the three landed in his study, ready to start wedding planning and negotiations, when Colin proceeded to inform them that the engagement could not continue. Lady Mariah's conduct toward Miss Boxford had given him serious doubt about whether she would be the right person to be the future Duchess of Stormount.

There were raised voices, and general unpleasantness on behalf of the Stapletons. There were, perhaps surprisingly, perhaps not, a few minor obscenities thrown in his direction. Lady Belinda, the youngest of the two sisters, had an attack of vapors, which was a remarkable event given she was but sixteen. Her recovery—which lasted all of thirty seconds—was even more remarkable.

In the end, it was his mother who challenged the countess's manners, unable to forgive the transgression of ignoring the distress of the man she loved. And she'd been magnificent. The Stapletons left Stormount within the hour, with the promise that the blame for engagement rested solely with Colin.

It was well past noon by the time he'd arrived at Silver Cross. The door was open, and a stream of trunks and crates were being unloaded. There, at the front door, was Lady Gwyneth and Edmund, directing them. Their guarded expressions as he walked in the door pained him, but if this was the first of a hundred trials he needed to pass today, he would do it.

"Lord Ellsworth," Lady Gwyneth said, her gaze darting from Colin to Edmund, her normally welcoming expression restrained. "This is unexpected."

"I have come to throw myself on Katherine's mercy," he said, removing his hat. "And right a horrible wrong."

"Are you coming to seek her hand? I thought you were spoken for," Edmund said.

Colin relayed as much of the details as he dared, preserving as much as possible the reputations of Lady Mariah's name as well as Katherine's.

"I knew it," Lady Gwyneth replied, reaching out for Colin's hand, tears brimming in her eyes. "I knew you could not be so heartbroken for nothing. I knew Kitty could not be so wonderful for nothing. You love her."

"More than I can express," he said. "But I must speak to her at once."

"And your parents," Edmund said. "They will accept this?"

"They will. And they do."

"Kitty is not here," Edmund said. "I assumed she was still at Kennington Grove."

"Perhaps she arrived with her parents," Colin said. "Or Mrs. Pembroke."

"Mother is here, with us," Edmund said. "Let's go find Harry. He might be at the stream."

Colin followed Edmund along a pleasant path that cut through a field, edged in wood. Ahead was the gentle rush of a stream, where two people stood in what appeared to be animated conversation. Colin recognized the pair as Mr. and Mrs. Boxford.

"Ho there!" Edmund cried out, his affection for these two clear. "I bring someone who wishes to speak with you."

The two turned in his direction, and Colin could see at once a tension between them. He paused, and bowed deeply.

"Mr. and Mrs. Boxford," he began. "I am most eager to speak to you about a matter of great importance."

"Is this great importance my daughter, your lordship?" Mr. Boxford said, his manner firm. "Because, as you may be aware, I do not take well to any man toying with my daughter's heart."

"Your daughter's heart is of my utmost concern, Mr. Boxford. Indeed, I would cherish it above any other, including my own." His gaze darted between them. "I have come to beg your permission to allow me to marry her, if she will have me."

"And what of Lady Mariah?"

Mrs. Boxford stood beside her husband, hands clenched firmly at her side.

"Lady Mariah is gone, Mrs. Boxford." He cleared his throat to keep his voice from wavering. "The engagement was of extremely short duration, and indeed, it should have never happened. The fault was mine. I was not bold enough to ask for Miss Boxford's hand when I had the chance. Lady Mariah was never Ka—Miss Boxford's equal in temperament or nature."

"You know of Kitty's parentage then," Mrs. Boxford said. "Is this why you are here now? Because it is easier?"

Colin shook his head.

"I fell in love with Katherine before I knew of her parentage. I told the duke and duchess of my intent before I knew of your connection to society. So it matters not to me. She is dear to me. The dearest another soul can be to another."

"You are a powerful man, Lord Ellsworth. But I have fought powerful people for my family," Mr. Boxford said, turning to his wife, who took his hand. "I will not just allow you to have my daughter simply because you wish it. I know you are also a decent man. Edmund here has spoken well of you. And it is clear you have made my Kitty the happiest I have ever seen her. But also the saddest."

"On my life sir, I pledge my troth to your daughter. On my life, I would give her only the best of me. But only if she wishes it," he said. "I love her too much to trap her in a life she does not want."

Mr. Boxford nodded then turned to his wife. Out of respect, Colin stepped away, leaving them to their privacy. Edmund stood fifty feet away, watching carefully. Colin stood, every second an agony, the gentle rush of the nearby stream and the birdsong above doing nothing to calm his jangled nerves.

"My lord," Mrs. Boxford called out, causing Colin both expectation and dread in a single moment. "If Katherine agrees to this union, Mr. Boxford and I will not stand in your way."

Relief brought a smile to his face. He bowed deeply to them, a sign of his respect, then turned and practically ran back to Silver Cross, Edmund at his heels.

When they arrived, Gwyneth greeted them at the door once more, but Katherine was still nowhere to be found. One by one, Gwyneth asked the servants, the hired movers, and Charlie and Fanny, but no one had seen her since mid-morning. It was now early afternoon, and Colin, normally not one given to flights of fancy or impatience, found himself wanting to crawl the walls. Before long, Mr. and Mrs. Boxford had returned, and they too shared the alarm about their daughter.

"Her things are in her room," Charlie said, bounding down the stairs. "They've not been unpacked yet."

"This is not like Kitty," Gwyneth said, pacing the floor. She turned to a man Colin recognized as Mrs. Pembroke's manservant.

"Are you certain, Vincent, she was not at Kennington Grove when you left?"

"No, my lady. She left on an errand mid-morning. Just after Mrs. Pembroke and Mrs. Boxford spoke. I admit I had been preoccupied with other duties and did not notice her return. She'd taken a cart, I believe, as she seemed to be in a bit of a hurry," he said, worry crinkling the corners of his eyes. "My apologies."

"What on earth would be in Hilsburn that would require her urgent attention?" Mrs. Pembroke asked.

"Oh no. Oh Kitty, you silly girl," Lady Gwyneth said, speaking to no one in particular. "She's gone and done it."

A knock at the door further interrupted Colin's stretched nerves. Done what?

Charlie came to the door. "Excuse me, Mr. and Mrs. Boxford sir, but an older gentleman has come looking to speak with a K. Boxford about this notice."

The boy handed the note to Edmund, whose eyes Colin had never seen as wide.

"Where is he?"

"At the door."

"Come Harry," Edmund said, showing the note to Mr. Boxford. "Your daughter has put up an advertisement for a husband. The first suitor has apparently already arrived."

Colin looked over Mr. Boxford's shoulder, and scanned the note, written in her tidy script. Bloody hell.

"With respect sir," Colin said, heart pounding. "I am the first suitor to have arrived. I would like the opportunity to make the first inquiry."

Mr. Boxford exchanged a look of undisguised incredulity then threw up his hands. "I'll go speak to the gentleman."

Colin sat down at Edmund's writing desk, digging around for a scrap of paper and a quill.

"What are you doing?" his friend demanded.

"What does it look like?" he replied, holding his pen over the paper. "I am making my application."

CHAPTER 24

Kitty was back in her garden at Kennington Grove, surrounded by pots and some old flour bags she'd managed to bargain for at the mill on her trip back from Hilsburn this morning. Along the way back, driving a little one pony cart, she watched several grand carriages heading away from Stormount.

There had been no news regarding the duke's health, which she took to be a positive sign. Good news spread quickly—there had already been talk of Lord Ellsworth's engagement which she'd done her best to ignore. But bad news spread like wildfire, and so she assumed all was well.

There would be talk about her advertisement as well, but she'd decided she would not let it bother her. In the end, it was her life that mattered. Her happiness. And she would take control of it. Not leave it to some fanciful story about stones and shoes. She dug down into the dirt with her shovel, gently loosening the soil around her peas, which were still shoots and easily transplanted. She moved them into the pots, then took a good look at her pumpkins. They were already sprawling, with a few flowers. Was it possible to move them without damaging them beyond repair?

She decided she had to try.

"Miss Boxford!"

Kitty looked up to see Charlie bounding down the road, a letter in his hand. She stood, wiping her hands on her apron.

The boy came to a skittering stop, his arm extended.

"There's a letter here for you, Miss," the boy said. "On account of that list you left in town. The one for a husband."

Kitty's stomach dropped. A reply. Already? It had only been three hours at most.

She took the letter and examined the address, but there was little information to be gained. It merely stated, "K. Boxford, Silver Cross."

"Mr. Boxford and Father have given the gentleman quite the one over, if you must know," the boy said. "But he insisted on being first."

"First? Do you mean there is more than one?"

"Well, there was two. But I don't know if the other gentleman passed the smell test."

"The smell test?"

"I believe that's what Mr. Boxford called it."

Oh dear. Another one of Kitty's brilliant ideas that seemed perfectly fine in her head. Her father, not to mention Edmund, were no doubt going to have a fit.

Kitty opened the letter, which was not sealed. Charlie stood by, studying every possible twitch she made as she began to read. Not wishing to be distracted, she turned her back to him.

Dear Miss Boxford,

Please accept this letter as my application in response to the notice placed this morning in town. I am seven and twenty. I am not a gamekeeper, but under the right tutelage I am certain I could learn the principles of the profession. I have no children at present but if the conditions are right—that is, you might consider me a suitable partner—then producing them would be immensely agreeable. My nature has often been ascribed as serious, but I have been informed by a quite astute woman that I am, in fact, capable of making a joke.

I do not have much experience with dancing, though standing up with you in a ballroom would give me the greatest of pleasures.

I recognize that I do not meet all the conditions on your list. However, I hope you might entertain an interview with me at your convenience.

Kindest regards,

C.M.

P.S. I do have ginger hair if that is in fact a serious requirement. I noted it had been added to the list but scratched out.

By the time Kitty had finished the note, her hands were shaking. What cruel punishment was this?

She turned, ready to ask Charlie the meaning of the letter, but he'd gone. A taller, most decidedly ginger-haired gentleman stood in his place.

Her heart lurched at the sight of him, which was…perplexing. He was, as always, square shouldered, his gold-rimmed spectacles firmly in place. His breeches formed to his legs, met by his polished boots. But in lieu of his expertly tailored wool jacket, a looser frock coat hung from his shoulders, which might have fallen to his knees if he were shorter. His usual fitted waistcoat was absent, replaced by a knitted one that looked uncannily like the one her mother had knitted for her father three winters ago. The cravat was also gone, a simple neckcloth tied in its place. He wore no hat, and a halting, pensive expression.

It was ridiculous and charming all at once. But she could not be charmed by him.

"What are you doing here?"

"I am, as the letter says," he replied, his voice soft, "applying for the position of husband. Though, I admit I really do not know very much at all about gamekeeping. Your father has offered to instruct me, however, if I am the successful candidate."

"My *father* knows about this?" she said, incredulous, unwanted tears pricking at the back of her eyes. "Does he not know that you are already to be someone's husband? It was quite the talk in the town square this morning, I assure you."

He nodded, then raked his fingers through his hair.

"The news in town is sadly mistaken," he replied at last. "I broke my engagement with Mariah before breakfast this morning."

Kitty stilled, holding her breath, uncertain of what she'd heard. She yearned with every inch of her being to reach out to him, to know this was real. Instead, she gripped his note and blinked back tears. "You did what? How?"

"After her treatment of both you and my father last evening, there was no way in good conscience I could be joined to her," he said. "I informed her of that this morning."

"But breaking such a public engagement..." She swallowed deeply, stifling a sob. He had broken the engagement?

"I have let it be made known that it was my doing. My error, and that Mariah was blameless."

He put his hand to her face, his touch a beautiful agony. Gently he brushed her tears away with his fingers. Kitty shook her head as joy and fear warred with each other. She released him and stepped away, pacing, trying to settle the torrent of emotions that threatened to overwhelm her entirely. How could he be here now? How could he have thrown off another woman he so publicly engaged, for her? Unless...

"I told her that my heart had already been taken," he continued, urgency in his voice, "and that my intention was to marry another before her untimely fit of 'memory' about visiting the observatory alone."

Kitty's gaze snapped up then. "Another?"

"I am clumsy in my way, so may not have expressed it as well as I should." He swallowed, looked down at his feet as if he was trying to collect himself, then took her hands in his. "I love you, Katherine Boxford. I am not sure exactly when I started loving you, but it feels like it has been a lifetime. But I think, perhaps, it began that night, when you were in the inn, in your father's trousers. I could not stop thinking of you."

A gentle sob shook her body. Years of disappointment and heartbreak falling away, allowing for a new sensation to take hold.

Joy.

"You have made another joke, I think," she said at last, a gentle laugh piercing through her tears.

"Indeed, I have not." He brushed away her tears and smiled at her with such tenderness and yearning that she didn't know if she could stand it. "Until that day, I had never met anyone with such determination, such surety about what they wanted, and would take such risks as you did that evening. You schooled me that evening, though I was too blind to see it at first, on the value of taking risks to follow one's passion. But more than that..." He paused, swallowing back the emotion that thickened his voice. "You have treated me as a human being, with faults and flaws. You would not let me hide behind my aristocratic bluster, so I could experience that passion for myself, and so I could share it with others.

"You give me such joy, Katherine. And I want to give you joy in return." His smile faltered then, and he straightened, his demeanor becoming more like the Colin she'd first met—stiff and businesslike. "But if not, I leave you to your garden, and will not plague you with platitudes and—"

Kitty, her heart ready to burst out of her chest, put her fingers over his lips, and reached up on her toes.

"I can't believe I am saying this, but you talk too much, Lord Ellsworth."

She reached behind his neck, pulled his mouth down to hers, and kissed him. Not a tender, gentle kiss, but firm and full of need. She parted her lips as his hands wrapped around her waist, pulling her closer. She laced her hands in his hair, reveling in his touch. After a moment, he broke the kiss, his forehead still leaning against hers, quiet.

"I am sorry I failed you," he said, raising his head, his eyes rimmed with tears. It was the first time she'd ever seen a man cry that she could recall, and her heart, if possible, loved him even more for it. "That Fallen Star was meant for you. I should have never allowed it to fall into another person's hands."

Kitty let out a bitter laugh. She'd tossed it last night. In a fit of anger, of fear, of utter despair, she'd thrown it away. By morning, there was some regret. But only for the years she'd spent wondering what her life would have been if she'd still had it.

"I spent a lifetime placing my hopes and dreams in it. But it was just a pretty stone. There was nothing magical about it."

His face fell then, and she realized perhaps, that she'd wounded him. Since when did a man of science who'd dismissed palmistry as superstition take offence at such an observation?

He dug into his pocket and pulled out a small bundle wrapped in a handkerchief.

"So much for romantic gestures then," he said, a sheepish grin on his face that made her want to kiss him all over again. "Still, it is yours. I was there, when you fell into my arms like a falling star all those years ago. And—strange as it may seem, I believe it is my duty to return it to you."

Kitty frowned, confused, then gently pulled back the corners of the linen cloth in her hand. There, to her amazement, was the moonstone.

"I only have the stone…not the setting. I am certain the pearls are being worn by someone else. But it is yours."

Kitty looked up, taken aback by the queer sense of relief she felt at its return. "How did you find it? I tossed it away."

"Would you believe a Traveler came to me this morning?" He shrugged, shaking his head, then chuckled. "It's true. So, it must be magic. Truly, I don't know. But I believe it was not that you were supposed to find it. Rather, I believe I was supposed to give it to you. Like I have given you my heart."

He dropped to his knees then, his beautifully clean, pristine breeches going into the dirt, then took her hand.

"My dearest, Katherine," he said, his voice trembling slightly, "would you do me the honor of becoming my wife?"

She reached out, running her fingers along his hairline, her entire body quaking. She was so happy. And that feeling made her feel… afraid. And he must have sensed it.

"What is it?"

"I'm afraid, Colin. I am so happy, and it makes me a little afraid. Because I didn't think it was safe to feel this way."

"Don't worry, my love," he said, reaching out and taking her hand. "If you fall, I will catch you."

She answered his proposal with a kiss. A kiss, interrupted at length, by the rustling of leaves from beyond her potting shed.

"What on earth was that?" Colin asked, looking to where the noise had come from.

Kitty looked around, and shook her head, seeing a small figure running through the trees.

"Charlie. He must have gotten tired of us kissing. If we stay here very much longer, I suspect Gwynnie will have the entire wedding planned before tea."

He stood, grabbed her bottom, and tilted his head in a fashion that set Kitty's body on fire. "I despise party planning. Let's give them a bit more time, shall we?"

❧

BREAKING a few rules here and there, Colin decided, did wonders for making an enjoyable wedding. The night could not have been more magical if they'd tried.

And his mother certainly had tried.

Breaking absolutely every possible rule about how weddings amongst society were to happen, they'd forsaken the traditional morning breakfast for a stunning, intimate ceremony under the stars.

Katherine, beautiful as always, was stunningly radiant this evening. Gwyneth, with help no doubt from Mrs. Boxford and Mrs. Pembroke, had her bedecked in a stunning silver-white gown, with those remarkable shoes at her feet. Around her neck was the Fallen Star, which his parents had reset in a new pendant that nested the stone in amongst a tasteful rim of diamonds. A great star amongst many.

The gathering itself had been a relatively intimate affair. Of course the entire Pembroke family had attended—Edmund and Gwyneth, along with Mrs. Pembroke and Gwyneth's father, the Earl of Snowdon, who traveled from Bath to see Katherine off. Edmund's cousin, the Marquess of Barronsfield and his wife Rosalind, along with his sister Eleanore, and her husband and Colin's friend, Mr. Bastien DuMont, who themselves were only newly married this past spring. Sir Richard Hamilton, who'd sheltered the Boxfords after their flight from Gorland Park, was also present. The invitation was also extended, at his mother's bewilderment, to the Travelers who were camped nearby, and to the great delight of both he and Katherine, some of them attended, though the woman who'd come to him at Lofton with the stone was not among them.

The episodes that had plagued Colin's father had subsided since the engagement, but Colin took advantage of Bastien's presence to consult with him. The French surgeon had both witnessed and experienced the trauma of war and revolution first hand, and had witnessed many a man with the same malady as the duke. His suggestion had been that the duke may be suffering an illness to the nerves, and not the heart, and while there were few known treatments, it might be handled with understanding as well as ample doses of outdoor walks in peaceful surroundings, good company, and time at Long Pond. It was a medicine that both Edmund and Mr. Boxford were more than pleased to assist Colin in administering.

After the ceremony was concluded, and the vows exchanged, the toasts made and the feast consumed, there had been dancing under the stars. And, with minimal exceptions, he'd broken the rules again by dancing every set with his wife, and found, in fact, that dancing was the most enjoyable of activities. Magical, in fact.

Finally, Colin and Katherine escaped the crowd and jumped into a carriage that took them to Lofton Tower for their wedding night. His mother had forbade him from entering it for two days before the wedding, and it was easy to see why. The place had been transformed by candlelight and garlands of flowers into an enchanting romantic retreat.

"Mrs. Cooper and Mother have outdone themselves," Colin said.

Katherine walked toward the bedroom, beckoning him to follow. He could see the anticipation in her steps. She unlatched the door, allowing it to swing open. He caught a glimpse of more candlelight inside.

"I may have added a few suggestions of my own." Katherine's lips turned up in a sly little smile, her shawl falling off her shoulder. It was a tantalizing invitation. "Would you care to look?"

The double meaning in her words, whether or not they were intended, rippled through his body. The entire bloody evening was an agony, as much as he enjoyed it, because, practically all he'd been able to do all evening—the entire fortnight since their engagement —was look.

"My darling, I want to do far more to you than that."

She smiled, a mischievous, nervous little smile. In two strides he was at the door, scooping her up in his arms and whisking her into the room. The small bed that normally sat in this Spartan room was replaced with something more than twice the size.

"Now, getting that in here must have been a singular feat," he said. "And it would be a terrible pity if we did not make good use of it, would you not agree, my lady?"

"I think we shall," she replied, letting out a nervous laugh as he set her down.

"Now," Colin said, "since we are both, shall we say, novices, I took the liberty of doing a little research on the ways in which we might pleasure each other."

Katherine's eyes widened. "I hope that is a joke, Colin."

He pulled off his jacket. "Not entirely. Firstly, I borrowed one of your father's books on animal husbandry—"

"What?"

"—which was perhaps not as useful as the book that Bastien had brought for me. Though, perhaps that was a joke," he said, thinking back to those rather remarkable illustrations. "Because I am not at all certain I can make my body do those things."

She was laughing now, untying his cravat, her head back, which was, of course, an invitation to kiss her throat. He was rewarded by the delicious little gasps coming from her as he ran his tongue and lips along the base of her neck, up to that little mole just below her ear.

"And then, most shocking of all," he continued, still kissing her and pulling the pins from her hair. "I—"

She giggled again. "Please do not tell me you spoke to Davis on this subject. Or the Royal Society."

"Of course not. Though Adam, my driver, did allude to some terribly naughty book about a woman named Miss Hill that we might have to add to our reading."

She straightened then, playfully pushing him forward, as she unfastened the buttons on his waistcoat, and untucking his shirt. "Heavens, Colin. Who didn't you talk to?"

"Edmund. Because even though we are married he would probably murder me in my bed for asking those questions knowing you were involved, and given his past employment, I am not entirely sure he wouldn't do it."

She raised her eyebrows, then ran her hands under his shirt. She helped pull it over his head, then plucked off his spectacles and set them on a nearby table. And then, the little vixen, she started to run her tongue over his chest, tickling his nipples, which was damn near the finest torture he'd ever been subjected to.

"Well," she began, between breaths as she sucked on his nipples and landed kisses across his chest, "I may have done my own research as well."

"And who did you speak to?"

"Gwynnie of course. And Mrs. Cooper, who has a delightful way about her and quite an intriguing past."

It was Colin's turn to be shocked. "Mrs. Cooper? I never would have guessed."

"That is the most dazzling part of it." She stopped, letting go a small gasp from where he'd been gently teasing her nipple with his hand, before moving to unpin her dress. "And then this evening, Rosalind—the Marchioness of Barronsfield—took me aside and provided me some quite useful insights that we might find—"

The most tremendous sensation rippled through his body then from where her fingers stroked him between his legs. He'd gripped onto her shoulders, and came down with his mouth on the crook of her neck.

"—helpful."

Unable to stand it any longer, his fingers worked at loosening layers of petticoats and stays until there was nothing left on her luscious, perfect body but the jewel around her neck and the shoes on her feet. Kicking off the last of his own clothes, his erection hard and full, he began at the top of her head, honoring every square inch of her body, every curve, every valley, until he'd found her core, hot, wet and ready for him. She parted, and he fell to his knees, and as he'd promised himself that afternoon at the grotto, he worshiped her, tasted her, until she erupted. He laid her back on the bed, his face buried in her hair, her hands firmly on his buttocks as he gently drove into her, his strokes measured at first, and then, her panting driving him on, her legs wrapped about his waist, with more frantic thrusts until that moment of crashing oblivion fell upon him.

After some time, they laid quietly together, entangled in each other's embrace, Colin gently tracing the lines of her body with his fingers. The jewel gleamed in the candlelight, sitting between the most perfect of breasts.

"What shall we do tomorrow, do you think?" he said.

"More of this, I hope," she replied, peppering him with tiny little kisses. "Much more of this."

"Well, then." Colin jumped out of bed and strode out where his clock sat on the mantle. It was twenty minutes past two. He opened the glass and moved the mechanism ahead, then returned to bed. A moment later, the clock struck twelve.

"What is that?" Katherine asked, her pretty brow dipping in confusion as the clock chimed in the distance.

He ran a finger along her hairline, then down her neck. His efforts were rewarded with her lovely little sighs.

"It's midnight, my darling," he replied, nuzzling into her neck.

"It was midnight several hours ago. I believe we were dancing," she replied, her hands exploring his body and driving him positively mad with her touch.

"You wanted to do more of this tomorrow. I found I couldn't wait." He raised himself up on one elbow, so he could gaze down on her glorious curves. She looked up at him, her fingers idly stroking his cheek.

"Tonight was lovely, wasn't it?" she said with a wistful sigh. "It was so beautiful with the stars and the candlelight."

"Magical," Colin agreed, allowing himself to be lost in her eyes. "Just like you."

THE END

A NOTE FROM THE AUTHOR

I hope you enjoyed **Nothing Magical about Midnight**. This is the final instalment in my *Enchanted Tales* Series.

If you're new to the series, introduce yourself to Stephen and Edmund Pembroke in **Not Your Average Beauty**, and follow with **No Prince Charming**, where Colin first makes his appearance, and then tangles with Bastien DuMont in **Never Trust a Rogue in Wolf's Clothing**.

Reviews are welcome - and super important to indie authors, so if can leave a review, I'd be super grateful! Feel free to post one where you purchased the book, or on Goodreads.

My website is www.michellehelliwell.com. Sign for my newsletter and get a heads up on new releases, and special giveaways that are only for my subscribers.

NOT YOUR AVERAGE BEAUTY

When beauty is a curse, only love can break the spell

Stephen Pembroke, the Marquess of Barronsfield, believes that where his love of beauty goes, death follows. Cursed to a loveless existence, and with his legacy at stake, Stephen makes a desperate proposal of marriage to Rosalind Schofield, his steward's new ward - and the plainest girl he has ever met. Rosalind has spent a lifetime being overlooked for prettier faces. When she is singled out for her lack of beauty by the Marquess, she begins to doubt if she is deserving of the love she inwardly craves.

When unusual things start happening around her, Rosalind can't help but wonder if Lord Barronsfield or his curse are who and what they appear to be. When she openly challenges Stephen about the curse, he begins to doubt everything – and comes to realize that this apparently plain, ordinary woman is not as unremarkable as he believed. Strange things *are* happening in Barronsfield. As they move closer to the truth, Rosalind unwittingly finds herself in the sights of the real beast in Barronsfield, and Stephen must decide if his growing love for Rosalind will be his salvation or her doom.

NO PRINCE CHARMING

Love is the fairest of them all

Dashing off in a daring elopement with a prince handpicked by her mother, Lady Gwyneth Snowdon anticipates a lavish future. But when a mysterious stranger kidnaps her, Gwyneth fears her happy ending is doomed.

Used by his maniacal father, Edmund Pembroke turned his back on society.

Seizing the opportunity to say good-bye to his past forever, he makes a deal to separate the pampered countess from a gold-digging imposter. But when Edmund discovers her life is in danger, he is forced to protect the beautiful, well-born Gwyneth Snowdon and to confront his ghosts.

Separated from her plush surroundings, Gwyneth learns she's capable of so much—including love for a man with neither title nor fortune. But she begins to suspects there is more to her rugged, handsome guardian than he's chosen to reveal. After finding herself at the center of a sinister deception, can she dare to trust her heart to a man who's spent years deceiving himself?

NEVER TRUST A ROGUE IN WOLF'S CLOTHING

A heart all the better to love her with...

After three torturous seasons, Lady Eleanore Pembroke is finished with husband hunting and happy ever after. Following the scandal of a broken engagement, eager to bury herself in her work at the local infirmary, she returns home shocked to discover their trusted physician gone, replaced by a dashing scoundrel. Bastien DuMont is a talented doctor, but Eleanore senses his restless heart. She's no longer prepared to risk hers, nor the trust of the people who've come to depend on him.

Caught up in a revolution that dissolved into terror, Bastien learned that devotion is for fools. On the run from a growing list of men who'd love to see him dead, he's forced out of the shadows and into the shoes of a respectable country physician, putting him under the scrutiny of Lady Eleanore, a local do-gooder immune to his roguish charms. When a mysterious figure emerges, threatening his life and the safety of those around him, can Bastien hunt down his opponent before he becomes the prey? Or is exposing his heart the greater danger?

ABOUT THE AUTHOR

Michelle Helliwell started writing her first novel, a time travel fantasy, when she was 15. She moved on to half-hearted attempts at something more literary, then nearly gave up on the writing all together until one fine day in 2005 a co-worker put a romance novel in her hands and told her to "get over yourself".

She did, and the rest, as they say, is history.

Michelle lives with her husband and two sons in Nova Scotia, Canada where moody weather and bagpipes are plentiful, but alas, guys in puffy shirts are too few.

Connect with me online!
www.michellehelliwell.com

9 781999 496500